M000237412

THE WORKS OF

ARETINO

* *

LETTERS AND SONNETS

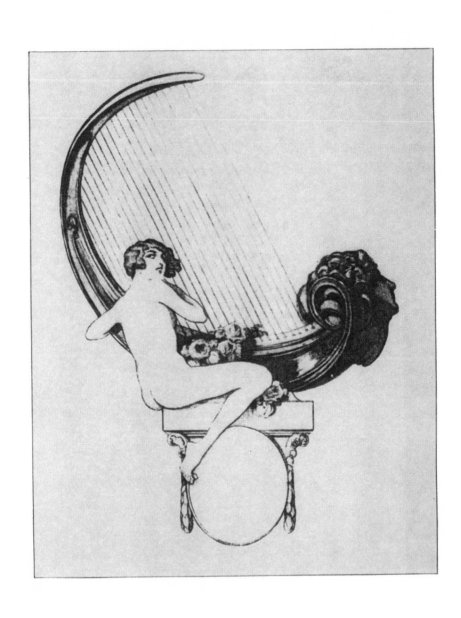

The Works of
ARETINO

Translated into English from the original
Italian, with a critical and
biographical essay

by

SAMUEL PUTNAM

Illustrations by Marquis de Bayros

LETTERS AND SONNETS

WILDSIDE PRESS

Copyright 1926 by
PASCAL COVICI, PUBLISHER

Copyright 1933 by
COVICI, FRIEDE, INC.

This translation of THE DIALOGUES OF ARETINO originally appeared in a limited edition of twelve hundred and fifty numbered copies, issued to subscribers only.

CONTENTS

PIETRO ARETINO

A Biography

Translated from the Italian

of

FRANCESCO DE SANCTIS

by

SAMUEL PUTNAM

PIETRO ARETINO

From the Italian of Francesco De Sanctis[1]

The theological-ethical world of the middle ages touched the extremity of its contradictions in the positive world of Guicciardini, a world purely human and natural, walled in by individual egoism, superior to all the moral chains that bind men together. The living portrait of this world, in its most cynical and most depraved form, is Pietro Aretino. The picture of the century was given in him its last fine pencil strokes.

Pietro was born in 1492, in a hospital of Arezzo, the son of Tita, the beautiful courtezan, the model sculptured and painted by a number of artists. He was without name, without family, without friends and protectors, without education. "I went to school only long enough to learn the *Santa Croce* . . . conniving thievishly, calling for many excuses, not being one of those who pore over the art of the Greeks and Latins." At thirteen years, he robbed his mother and fled to Perugia and took up his lodgings with a bookbinder. At nineteen years, drawn by the fame of the Court of Rome and the report that everybody became rich there, together with the fact that he himself had not a farthing, he went to Rome and was received as a domestic in the house of a rich mer-

---

[1]This vivid essay by the author of the *Storia della Letteratura Italiana*, the leading Italian critic of the Nineteenth century, is printed here for its critical, rather than its biographic interest, but above all, for its qualities as a piece of forceful writing. As to its scholarship, there may be a question, particularly in the light of the latest Aretino researches. For historic accuracy, it cannot compare, for example, with the study by the Englishman, Edward Hutton (*Pietro Aretino, Scourge of Princes*, Constable, London, 1922); There is much of value in De Sanctis' view of Pietro as an embodiment of the riotously chromatic *cinquecento;* his opinions are only marred by a certain moralistic tendency. In my footnotes, I have endeavored to apply an occasional corrective, or at least to note the danger when it occurs.

chant, Agostino Chigi, and, a little later, in the house of the Cardinal of San Giovanni. He sought his fortune with Pope Julius; and, not meeting with success, he became a vagabond and a libertine throughout Lombardy, finally becoming a Capuchin Monk in Ravenna. When Leo the tenth became Pope, and men of letters, buffoons, actors, singers and adventurers of every sort began running to that court, it seemed to him that his place was there; he doffed his habit and went to Rome and, putting on the livery of the Pope, became the latter's valet. High spirited, merry, a libertine, impudent and a go-between, he completed his education and instruction in that school. He learned to put into sonnets his lusts, his adulations and his buffooneries; he began to make a business of it, a business which brought him many fine farthings. But he was always a valet, and he had little to hope in a court in which it was the custom to improvise in Latin. Armed with letters of recommendation, he goes to Milan, to Pisa, to Bologna, to Ferrara, to Mantua and presents himself, brazenly, to the princes and monsignori, with the airs and presumption of a man of letters. He studies, like a woman, the art of pleasing and he lends his aid with complacency to the arts of the charlatan:

"I find myself at Mantua, in the house of the Signor Marchese, in so much grace that he even leaves his bed and board to talk with me and says that he has never had so much pleasure at all, and he has written to the cardinal things of me which have truly been of most honorable assistance, and I have been regaled with three hundred crowns . . . all the court adores me, and he is happy who can come by one of my sets of verses; and as many as I make, the Signor has them copied, and I have made a few in praise of him. So it is with me here, and he gives the whole day to me and does great things, as you shall see at Arezzo . . . at Bologna they commenced to load me with gifts; the Bishop of Pisa made me a present of a great coat of black satin, embroidered in gold, the superbest ever."

They give him the titles of "*messere*" and "*signore*:" the valet is a gentleman, and returns to Rome with a throng of tavern pages, dressed like a Duke, the companion and go-between of gentlemanly pleasures, with, at his side, Estensi and Gonzaga, who sometimes slap him familiarly on the back. He continues the trade in which he has made so good a beginning. One of his "praises" of Clement VII. gains him his first pension; it is the following effusion:

> Or queste si che saran lodi, queste
> lodi chiari saranno, e sole e vere
> appunto come il vero e come il sole.[1]

His spirit, his jovial humor, his libidinous inclinations won him such a reputation that, driven out of Rome on account of his sixteen sonnets, illustrated with obscene designs by Giulio Romano,[2] he was sought as a boon companion by Giovanni de' Medici, the head of the "*bande nere*" called the "*gran diavolo.*" He was little more than thirty years old. Giovanni and Francis I. were disputing his friendship. Giovanni wanted to make the signor of Arezzo the companion of his orgies and lusts, when a German ball cut short, at once, this design and his life. Pietro had now a consciousness of his strength and, leaving the Court, he repaired to Venice, as to a rock of safety, and from there he lorded it over Italy with his pen. Listen to him, as he paints himself in his letters:[3]

[1]"Now this which is to be praise, this praise shall be clear, single and true, exactly like the truth and like the sun."

[2]Engraved by Marcantonio Raimondi, the most famous engraver of his age. Romano, according to the account given by Vasari (Milanesi, Florence, 1906, Vol. V., p. 418), first made the designs and then employed Raimondi to engrave them. Aretino then wrote an indecent sonnet for each—"so that I do not know which was the more revolting, the spectacle presented to the eye by the designs of Giulio or the affront offered to the ear by the words of Aretino." Vasari concludes: "Certain it is that the endowments which God has conferred on men of ability ought not to be abused, as they too frequently are, to the offense of the whole world, and to the promotion of ends which are disapproved by all men."

[3]*Lettere*, I., 2. This letter was written to the Doge of Venice, when the latter intervened between Aretino and the Pope to secure a *privilegio* for the printing of the former's epic poem, Marfisa.

"I, who, in the liberty of many states, have managed to remain a free man, fleeing the court forever, have set up here (at Venice) a perpetual tabernacle against the years which are advancing upon me, for the reason that here treason has no place, here favour can do no wrong to right, here the cruelty of the meretricious does not reign, here the insolence of the effeminate gives no commands, here there is no robbery, here no coercion, here no murder . . . O universal fatherland! O communal liberty! O inn of all the dispersed peoples! . . . She inflames you, others elude; she rules you, others pursue; she gives you pasturage, others starve you; she receives you, others hunt you down; and, as she regales you in your tribulations, she preserves you in charity and in love . . .

"By the Grace of God a free man . .

"I laugh at pedants . . .

"I, in my ignorance, have not followed in the footsteps of Petrarch or Boccaccio, although I know what they are, but I have not wanted to lose time, patience, and reputation in the desire to transform myself into them, since this is not possible. Bread eaten in one's own house does one more good than bread accompanied by fine viands at the table of another. I walk here with leisurely step, in the garden of the Muses, and no word drops from me which I have learned from any stinkpot of old. I wear the face of genius unmasked, and, not knowing an h, I can still teach those who know their l's and their m's; so that now they should hold their peace who think there is no better work under heaven than the "*Dottrinale novellis*" . . .

"As to things in Florence . . . I give myself very little concern for them; the bases of my hope are in God and in Caesar, and, thanks to Their Majesties, I am assured of a hundred crowns pension, which the Marchese del Vasto gives me, and others which the prince of Salerno pays to me, so that I have an income of six hundred, with about a thousand more which I make every year with a folio of paper and a bottle of ink; and this is the manner in which I live in this serenest of cities . . .

"In addition to medallions, coins, carvings in plaster, gold and silver, wood, lead and stucco, I have a reproduction of my effigy on the facade of palaces, and I have had it printed on my comb cases, on the ornaments of my mirrors, on my majolica plates, in the manner of Alexander, of Caesar and of Scipio. And, more, I would have you know that, at Murano, a certain sort of crystal vases are called 'aretini.' And 'aretina' is the name given to a race of ponies, in memory of one which Pope Clement gave to me and which I gave to Duke Frederick. 'Rio dell' Aretino' is the name with which the stream is baptized that bathes one side of the house in which I dwell on the grand canal. And besides the 'Aretino Style,' which comes from the hair-splitting of pedagogues, three of my chamber maids or housekeepers have left me and become ladies, and they are called 'aretine.' Such are the penalties of striving for distinction through a 'Ianua Sum Rudibus.' "[1]

And these were no idle boasts. Ariosto called him "the scourge of princes, the divine Pietro Aretino."[2] A pedant, speaking of the letters of Aretino and those of Bembo, said to Bembo: "I should call you our Cicero and him our Pliny." "But Pietro would not be content with that," replied Bembo.[3] And he was not content with it. To Bernardo Tasso, who praised his letters, he wrote:

"It is certain that the excess of love which you bear your own things and the too little consideration you have for those of others have caused you to compromise your judg-

[1] See Doni's letter, quoted by Camerini, Appendix I.
[2] *Orlando Furioso*, Canto XLVI., 14:
　　　　　　　　　"*ecco il flagello*
De' Principi, il divin Pietro Aretino."
　　Aretino was overcome with delight at this. See also his letter to Ersilia del Monte, quoted by Camerini, and Gaddi's comment, Appendix I.
　　[3] See Aretino's own comment on this, in a letter to Bembo, quoted by Camerini, Appendix I.

ment . . . Beyond confronting you with the opinion of one who knows, additional confirmation is to be found in your mode of procedure in letter writing, in which necessary exercise you display a lack of ability to counterfeit me, either in thought or in comparisons (which with me are born and with you are still born), or in the smoothness and beauty of the fertile correspondences which I ordinarily employ . . . The truth is, in any such contest, you follow me on foot. But you could not do otherwise since your taste is more inclined to the glow of the flowers than to the savour of the fruit; and, so it is, with that angelic grace of style and your celestial harmonies, you show to better advantage in wedding songs and in hymns, the sweetness of which is not in place in letters, which call for the high relief of invention and not an artificial miniature-making . . . Now since it is not an error to praise one's self to a man of some merit in the presence of one who does not know it, I am going to give you here a few maxims in letter writing . . . But since presumption is the smoke of greatness in shadow, which is extinguished in the degree to which it appears to be and is not, in the degree to which it remains satisfied with less instead of striving for more, I, not to be like these, do not say that the virtuosi ought to make a festival of my birthday, although I, without running after posts, without serving courts and without moving a foot, have made a number of dukes, a number of princes and a number of monarchs pay tribute to my virtues, and this for the reason that, throughout the world, fame is sold by me. In Persia and in India,[1] my portrait has its price and my name is esteemed. Finally, I salute you, with the assurance that no one concerned with letter-writing blames you out of envy, but that many who have written letters praise you out of compassion."

So he regarded himself and so the world regarded him. He was believed to be a great man on his own say-so. He did not look for glory; he was not concerned with the

[1]See Aretino's letter to Ersilia del Monte, Appendix I.

future; he wanted the present. And he had it, more than any mortal. Medallions, crowns, titles, pensions, gifts, stuff of gold and silver, chains and rings of gold, statues and paintings, vases and precious gems: he had everything that the cupidity of man could obtain. Julius III. named him a cavalier of St. Peter. And he came near being made cardinal.[1] He had a sole pension of eight hundred twenty crowns. Of gifts, he had, in eighteen years, twenty-five-thousand crowns. He spent, during his life, more than a million francs. Royal gifts came to him from the corsair, Barbarossa,[2] and from the sultan, Solimano. His princely house is thronged with artists, ladies, priests, musicians, monks, valets, pages;[3] and many bring him their presents: this one a vase of gold, this one a picture, this one a purse filled with ducats, and this one clothing and fine stuffs. At the entrance, one sees a bust of white marble, wreathed with laurel; it is Pietro Aretino. Aretino to the right, Aretino to the left: look at those medallions, of all sizes and every metal, suspended from the tapestries of rose-colored velvet: always the image of Pietro Aretino. He died, at seventy-five years, in 1557; and of all his reputation, nothing remained. His works were almost forgotten; his memory was infamous; a well bred man would not pronounce his name in the presence of a lady.

Who was, then, this Pietro, courted by women, feared by his rivals, exalted by writers, the popular idol, kissed by the

---

[1] Aretino at least pretends, rather successfully, not to want a cardinal's hat. Perhaps, he was a little loathe to leave his loved Venice, even for an honor which would have been the supremely ironical crown of an ironical life. (His sense of irony should have told him that.) Nevertheless, we find Titian pleading his cause in the matter with the Emperor Charles V., who, it appears, was inclined to look favorably on the idea. See Hutton, *op. cit.*, pp. 223ff., where Titian's letter to Aretino, describing his interview with Charles, is quoted. The letter is printed in *Lettere all' Aretino*, Bologna, 1874.

[2] A friendship exists between the pirate of the high seas and the buccaneer of the *mondo altero*. Pietro, in one of his letters, exhorts Barbarossa to be kind to Christian captives! Barbarossa had called Aretino "the first of Christian writers." For this fascinating letter, in full, see Appendix I.

[3] See Alessandro Andrea, quoted by Camerini, Appendix I.

Pope, and who rode in cavalcade by the side of Charles V.[1]
He was the consciousness and the image of his century. And
his century made him great.

Machiavelli and Guicciardini said that appetite is the
lever of the world. What they thought, Pietro was.

He had by nature great appetites, and forces which were
proportionate to them. He saw his portrait done by Titian,[2]
the figure of a wolf that seeks its prey. The artist had formed
a background of the hide and claws of a wolf; and the head
of the wolf, like enough in structure, stood above the head
of the man. Scintillating eyes, nostrils far apart, teeth in
evidence through the drooping lower lip, the lower part of
the head, seat of the sensual appetites, very large, toward
which the rest of the head seemed to slope, bald in front . . .
Son of a courtezan, soul of a king . . . he said. Reader of
books, valet of the Pope, Alas! His needs are infinite. It is
not enough for him to eat, he wants to taste; he is not satisfied with pleasure, he wants voluptuousness; he is not satisfied with clothes, he wants pomp; he is not satisfied with
becoming rich himself, he wants to make others rich, to
spend and to expand. And to one who marveled at all this he
replied: . . . "Well, what would you have me do? If I am born
to live this way, what is going to keep me from living this
way?". . . His gilded dreams are: exquisite wines, delicate

[1] The emperor, in his last days, had a strange fondness, not to say a weakness, for the
"screw of princes." The story of this meeting, not without its touching side, will be found
in Hutton, op. cit., where a chapter (Chapter X.) is devoted to the rivalry between Charles
and Francis I. for Aretino's favors. See Camerini's interesting comment, Appendix I.

[2] He served Titian as a model repeatedly.

[3] (De Sanctis' Note:) Here are a few citations:
"And Boccamazza . . . although I always regarded him as a man of abundant wealth,
when I showed him twenty-two women with their babes at their breasts, who had come to
eat the bones of my poor ink—for not a day passes that not more, or at least as many,
hungry ones come to me—was surprised . . . Oh, he said to me, 'and why spend so
unrestrainedly, when you have no more than enough for yourself?' 'Because,' I replied,
'real souls are always unbridled in their expenditures.' "
"Eating . . . the day before yesterday, some hares torn by dogs which the captain
Giovan Tiepoli had sent me, I was so pleased with them that I decided 'Floria prima
lepus' was a saying worthy of being posted up in the hearts of hypocrites on their fast

foods, rich palaces, pretty girls, fine clothes. For all this, he has the appetite, he has the taste. And no one is a more competent judge in the matter of good mouthfuls and of joys, licit and illicit. There is in him not only the sense of pleasure but the sense of art. He seeks, in his joys, the magnificent, the splendid, the beautiful, good taste and elegance.[3]

And he has forces proportionate to his appetites: A body of iron, an energy of will, a knowledge of and a contempt for men, and that marvelous faculty which Guicciardini called "discretion," the instinct to take things as they come. He knows what he wants. His life is not cut up in various directions; it is one in scope, the satisfaction of his appetites, or, as Guicciardini says, his own "particularity." All means are excellent and he adopts them according to occasion. He is now a hypocrite, now impudent, now evasive, now insolent. Now he adulates, now he calumniates. The credulity, fear, vanity and generosity of the man are, in his hands, a ram to batter the breach to victory. He has the keys to all doors. Today, a man like him would be called a "gangster."[4] and many of his letters would be called "blackmail." He is the master of the genre. He speculates, above all, on fear. The language of the century is officious, adulatory; his own tone is disdainful and brazen. Printed calumnies were worse than daggers; a printed thing meant a true thing; and he had his price for slander, silence and eulogy. It made no difference

days, in place of the 'silentium' which a garrulous brother tacks up over the monk's quarters. And while their praises were running to caeli caelorum, I was feasting on the thrushes which had been brought to me by one of your lackeys, and the very taste of them made me hum the 'Inter aves.' They were so fine, indeed, that our messer Tiziano (Titian), upon catching a glimpse of them on a plate and getting a whiff with his nostrils . . deserted a crowd of gentlemen who were giving him a dinner party. And everybody gave great praise to the bird with the long beak which, boiled with a bit of dried beef, two laurel leaves and a pinch of pepper, we ate out of love for you and because it pleased us, even as Fra Mariano, Moro dei Nobili, Porta da Luca, Brandino and the Bishop of Troy were pleased with the ortolans, fig-peckers, pheasants, peacocks and lampreys with which they filled their stomachs, with the consent of their cooks' souls and that of the mad and knavish stars which had given them such big bellies . . . And blessed is he who is mad, and in his madness pleases others and himself."

[4]Camorrista.

to him if he had the reputation of an evil tongue; that was part of his strength. Francis I. sent him a golden chain, made up of linked tongues with vermilion points, as though they had been dipped in poison, and bearing the inscription: "*Lingua eius loquetur mendacium.*"[1] Aretino gave him a thousand thanks. When it was not convenient for him to speak evil of persons, he would speak evil of things, just to keep up his reputation, as in the case of his diatribes against the ecclesiastics, the nobles and the princes. And so, the abject fellow was held an apostle and was called "scourge of princes." Sometimes, he would find a person who was not afraid. Achille della Volta stuck a dagger in his back. Niccolò Franco, his secretary, wrote him messages of vituperation. Pietro Strozzi threatened to kill him if he dared pronounce Strozzi's name. He was beaten, spit upon. And it was he, then, who was afraid, because he was vile and a poltroon. The ambassador from England beat him. And he praised the signor who had given him the opportunity of pardoning the injury. Giovanni, the "*gran diavolo*," on his death bed, said to him: "What makes me suffer most is the sight of a poltroon."[2] . . . But, in general, they preferred to treat him as a Cerberus and to stop his barking by tossing him a cake. His letters are full of malice and effrontery. He takes all forms and all habits, that of the buffoon and that of

[1]Hutton has another interpretation. *Mendacium*, he thinks (*op. cit.*, p. 149), "referred not so much to the lies which Aretino himself owns he told as to the flattering epithets with which he had overwhelmed Francis." It was Aretino's boast (see Hutton, ibid.): "*Per Dio, che la bugia campeggia cosi bene in bocca a me come si faccia la verita in bocca al clero.*—By God, a lie sits in my mouth as well as truth does in the mouth of a cleric." Is it not possible that Francis had the same sense of humor, inverted it may be, or the same sense of irony, that Pietro had? There is also another reading, *judicium*, which, however, appears to have little to support it. (See Hutton's note.) In any event, Aretino always wore this chain, thereafter, and it is to be seen in all his portraits. It was, as Hutton remarks, "the crowning of his reputation," and "Henceforth he was a sort of institution."

[2]This is, it seems to me, a piece of deliberate misrepresentation. See Aretino's own account, *Lettere*, I., 5, quoted at length by Hutton, (*op. cit.*, Chapter VI.) "And he, as soon as he saw me, began to say to me that the thought of the poltroons distressed him more than the pain." Hutton thinks, and I agree with him, that this is "Probably an allusion to the Pope and the politicians, e. g. the Datario"—in other words, to Italy's enemies, the

the braggart, even that of the holy man, slandered and slighted. As a sage, take his letter to the most pious and petrarchian marchesa di Bescara, who had exhorted him to change his life and to write pious works:

" . . . I confess that I am less useful to the world and less acceptable to Christ, spending my efforts in false gossiping, rather than in true works. But the cause of all the evil is the pleasure of others and my own necessity. If princes were as hypocritical as I am needy, I would not draw from my pen anything but misereres. My excellent lady, all do not have the grace of divine inspiration. Some burn with angelic fire, and we have offices and preachings, which are to them music and comedy. You would not turn your eyes to Hercules in the flames nor to Marsia without her hide, and these others would not tarry in the room to see San Lorenzo on the spit nor the apostle flayed alive. Look you: My colleague, Bruci-olo, dedicated his Bible to the king, who is certainly most Christian, and in five years, he has not had an acknowledge-ment. Was it, perhaps, that the book was not well translated and well put together? On the other hand, my *Courtezan*³ drew from him a great chain; he did not so much as smile over the New Testament, for the reason that he is not honest. The excuse for my babblings must be that they were composed by me in order to live, and not out of malice. But, you see, Jesus inspires me to take account of Messer Sebastiano da Pesaro, from whom I have received the thirty crowns I levied on him, and the rest I owe to him, since he

foes of that Italy which Giovanni of the *bande nere* died trying to save, and which speedily went to pieces when he was gone—the sack of Rome, described in the second day of the *Ragionamenti*, followed soon afterward. Aretino and the *gran diavolo* had been too good bosom-cronies, companions in lust and life, to let such a remark as this, with the interpreta-tion De Sanctis gives it, ring true. They were, indeed, two of a kind, in walks of life not so widely separated as they might seem to have been.(For additional data, see Appendix I.)

There is also a misrepresentation of the affair with the British ambassador, if we are to credit Hutton, (*op. cit.*, pp. 219ff.) Aretino was an old man then, and his deportment in the matter appears to have been rather to his credit. The evident animus in such a remark as "it was he, then, who was afraid, because he was vile and a poltroon" rather tends to disqualify the witness, it seems to me.

³His play, *La Cortigiana*.

has been true to his word."

At the end, a thrust,[1] as we would say today. We have here a letter with the breath of an infernal genius. With what bonhomie he makes sport[2] of the pious lady, having all the time the air of praising her! With what cynicism he proclaims his own speculations on lust and on human obscenity, as if they were the most natural things in this world![3] He speculates, also, in devotion and, with an equal indifference, writes obscene books and the lives of saints; his *Ragionamento della Nanna* and his *Vita di santa Caterina da Siena*, the *Cortigiana errante* and the *Vita di Cristo*. And, why not, since he got a reward on this side and on that? He wrote of all matters and in all forms; dialogues, romances, epics, articles, comedies and even a tragedy, the *Orazia*. Imagine what sort of heroes the Orazii could be, what sort of a heroine Orazia, and what sort of Roman populace could issue from the imagination of Pietro. And yet, this is the only work which has artistic intentions, composed after he was already old and satiated and thinking more of glory than he was of money. The result was cold, an abstract and pedestrian world, a world the simplicity and grandeur of which he was incapable of comprehending. In his other works, he felt himself true to his own nature, dedicated to pleasing his public, concerned only with interesting it, getting what he could out of it, making an effect. There is in him a species of mercantile morality;[4] he knows

[1] *Una stoccata*, a fencing term—a "knockout," as *we* would say.

[2] And why, one might ask, should he not? Aretino doubtless knew his correspondent as a pious old meddler, if not a hypocrite.

[3] The capable cynic might put up rather a good argument to prove that they are. It has been done. At any rate, de Sanctis' moralizing, at points, becomes a bit tiresome.

[4] It is interesting to compare De Foe, who came not far from being the British Aretino. See Paul Dottin's *Vie et aventures de Daniel de Foe, auteur de Robinson Crusoe* (Perrin et cie., Paris, 1925.) Reviewing Dottin, the present translator once wrote: "De Foe, who started life as a merchant, who became a scheming politician and who ended as a best-seller, tossing off 'Crusoe' to provide his daughter's dowry, remained, in the end, the merchant, selling his soul to God on the Puritan's hard-driving bargain terms. And 'Robinson' is but the reflection of his creator, keeping always a moralistic profit and loss account, with an ear deaf to the song of birds but keenly attuned to the tinkle of coins in a till."

what are the goods most sought after, the easiest to dispose of and at the dearest price. He created for himself a conscience and an art that were fictitious, and which varied according to the tastes of his patron, the public. For he was the writer the most in the mode, the most popular and the best paid. His obscene books are the model of a literary genre which, under the name of "gallant tales," invaded Europe. Obscenity was a sauce much sought after in Italy, by Boccaccio among others; but here it is dyed in the wool. The lives of the saints are true romances into which all sorts of things are packed, appealing to the fantastic and sentimental nature of hypocrites. Maker of verses sufficiently coarse, Aretino unloaded, in his sonnets and articles, a store of bile and malignity joined with servility. And so, alluding to the munificence of Francis I., he said to "Pier Luigi Farnese:"

> *Impara tu, Pier Luigi ammorbato,*
> *impara, ducarel da tre quattrini,*
> *il costume da un re tanto onorato.*
> *Ogni signor di trenta contadini*
> *e di una bicoccazza usupar vuole*
> *le ceremonie de' culti divini.*[1]

Pietro is not a villain by nature. He is a villain by calculation and from necessity. Reared among unfortunate examples, without religion, without country, without family, deprived of every moral sense, with the most unrestrained appetites and with the intellectual means of satisfying them, he himself is the center of the universe: the world appears made for his service. On this basis, his logic is equal to his temperament. He has a clear perception of means, and no hesitation or scruple in putting them into action. He makes no dissimulation of this; indeed, he glories in it; it is his strength, and he wants everybody to be persuaded of the

[1]Learn you, sickly Pier Luigi, learn, you three-farthings dukelet, the ways of so honored a king. Every signor with thirty peasants and an old wreck of a castle tries to usurp the rites which are paid to the gods."

fact. The world was somewhat after his own imagination. There were many who would have liked to imitate him; but they did not have his genius, his industry, his penetration, his versatility, his spirit. And so, they took it out in admiring him. Among so many adventurers and condottieri, with whom Italy was infected, a vagabond race, without profession and in search of a fortune at any cost, the prince, the model, was he. Titian called him " il condottiero della letteratura."[1] And he was not offended: he strutted over it. Left to his own spontaneity, when he was not oppressed by need and not working by calculation, he displayed good qualities. He was merry, sociable, liberal, as well as magnificent, a tried friend, grateful, and an admirer of great artists like Michelangelo and Titian. He had the logic of evil and the vanity of good.

Pietro, as a man, is an important personage, the study of whom takes us behind the scenes into the mysteries of that Italian society of which he was the image, a mixture of moral depravation, of intellectual force and artistic feeling. But he is not less important as a writer.

Culture at that time was tending to become fixed, and Aretino debated long as to whether he should write in the vulgate or in Latin. The popular idiom already had conquered its rights of citizenship. But the question was as to whether this idiom was to be called "Tuscan" or "Italian." And it was not a matter of words, merely, but of things. For many writers pretended to write as the language was spoken, from one end of Italy to the other, and were not disposed to go to Florence to take lessons. But they preferred Latinizing to Tuscanizing. They recognized as their models Boccaccio and Petrarch, but gave no authority to the living tongue. The living tongue, for them, was that common dialect which resembled Latin, on the one hand, and the common word-of-mouth speech on the other. This mechanism was generally

---

[1] The phrase stuck; it has become famous."Street-car conductor (or **elevatorman**) of literature" might be the equivalent in Americanese.

accepted, with the exception that in Florence the basis of the language was not the common dialect, mixed with local, Lombardian and Venetian elements, but the Tuscan idiom which had been established by writers. Florence, exhausting its intellectual production, had elevated the colonies of Hercules, in the vocabulary of the *Crusca*, by saying: You shall not go beyond this. Bembo and, later, Salviati fixed the grammatical forms. And the rules of writing, in all genres, were laid down in the "rhetorics," which were translations of, or refinements on Aristotle, Cicero and Quintilian. Added to this was the fact that Giulio Camillo pretended to teach all knowledge by a device of his own. This tendency to mechanize is a constant phenomenon in all periods in which production is exhausted; and as a result, culture is arrested, takes refuge in forms and becomes crystallized.

Pietro, of very mediocre culture, looked upon all these rules as pedantry. His own inner life, so spontaneous and so full of productive force, found little point of contact here. Pedantry is his enemy, and he combats it with might and main. And he calls "pedantry" the viewing of things, not in themselves, by direct vision, but through preconceptions, books and rules. Involutions of words and forms are as odious to him as hypocrisy, or the covering of one's self with an affected modesty, or with the skin of the fox while preaching humility and decency, without being any better than the rest.

"How much better is it," he wrote to the cardinal of Ravenna, "for a *gran maestro* to keep in his house a few faith-ful men, free folk and persons of good will, than to attempt to adorn himself with the vulpine modesty of the asinine pedants who write books, who, when they have assassinated and, with their labors, have succeeded in croaking[1] the dead, will not rest until they have crucified the living. I am telling you the truth: it was pedantry that poisoned Medici, it was

[1]The *casa Aretina* was rich in works of Art but contained few books. See Appendix I

pedantry that cut the throat of Duke Alexander, and, what is worse, it has provoked a heresy against our faith through the mouth of Luther, the greatest pedant of them all."

He is not less implacable toward literary pedantry. To Dolce, he wrote:

"Follow the path that nature shows you. Petrarch and Boccaccio are imitated by those who express their conceits with the same sweetness and light[1] with which Petrarch and Boccaccio expressed theirs; you will not find them imitated by the man who would plunder these writers, not of their "wherefores" and their "whences," their tricks and qualifications, but of the poetry that is in them ... The faecal blood of pedants who would poetize feeds on imitation and, while they cackle away in their worthless books, they transform the works they imitate into locutions, which they embroider with phthisical words according to rote. O wandering tribe, I tell you, and I tell you again, that poetry is a caprice of Nature in her lighter moods; it requires nothing but its own madness and, lacking that, it becomes a soundless cymbal, a belfry without a bell; for which reason, he who would compose without taking beauty out of its swaddling clothes is nothing more than a cold potato.[2] ... Take a lesson from what I am going to tell you about that wise painter who, when asked whom he imitated, pointed with his finger to a crowd of men, implying that he drew his models from life and truth, as I do when I speak and write. Nature herself, and Simplicity, her hand-maid,[3] give me what I put into my compositions. And, certainly, I imitate myself, since Nature as a companion is a large order,[4] and art is a clinging beetle; and so, I advise you to strive to become a

[1] The rendering is exact: con la dolcezza e con la leggiadria.
[2] Zugo infreddato. A zugo is a variety of fritter.
[3] Literally, her secretary (secretario).
[4] una compagnone badiale che ci si sbraca. This phrase is only one of many in which Aretino's concentrated vividness is hard to translate. The force of si sbraca is to be noted; sbracarsi is, literally, to take off one's small clothes, or breeches. The phrase is a strong one, and one which painters well might commit to memory.

sculptor of the senses, and not a miniaturist of vocabularies."

Many were trying to write according to nature; above all, one must cite Cellini, whose work is replete with life. But Cellini looked upon himself as an ignorant man, and he wanted Varchi to edit his *Vita* into learned form; while Aretino, on the contrary, looked upon himself as the superior to all these others and was ready to give the name of "pedant" to those who spent their time distilling words. There is in him a critical consciousness so direct and decisive that, in such an age as his, it must strike one as extraordinary. The very freedom and elevation of his judgment took him into the arts, for which he had the proper feeling. To Michelangelo, he wrote: "I sigh to think of your merit so great and my own powers which are so puny." His favorite is his friend and gossip, Titian, whose realism, so complete and so sensual, was attractive to Aretino's nature. Taken with fever, he leans against the window and looks out on the gondolas and the Grand Canal of Venice and falls into a thoughtful and contemplative mood; he, Pietro Aretino! The sight of nature purifies, transforms him. And he writes to Titian:[1]

"Like a man who is weary of himself, I do not know what to do with my mind, my thoughts, and so, I turn my eyes towards the heavens, which, since the day that God created them, never presented so beautiful and elusive a picture of lights and shadows; the atmosphere was the kind those painters strive to express who envy you because they are not you ... The houses ... although made of stone, appeared to be made of some artificial material. And then, you perceived that the air on one side was pure and lively, on another turbid and pale as death. Consider also what marvels I had in the way of clouds which, from the principal point of view, stood half touching the house tops, half melting away in the distance, for a black-gray mist hung over all. I surely was amazed at the varied color they displayed, the

[1]Lettere, III., 48.

nearer ones glowing with the flames of the sun, the more distant flushed with a fainter vermilion. Oh, with what fine drawing the brush of Nature had painted that atmosphere, giving the palaces perspective in the same manner that Vecellio does in his landscapes! On some sides, there appeared an azure-green, on others a greenish-azure, truly composed by the caprice of Nature, who is the mistress of all masters . . . She, with her clear colors and her dark, achieved background and relief in such a manner that I, who know what a spirited brush you wield, three or four times exclaimed: "O Titian, why aren't you here?" . . . through my faith that if you had depicted all I have told you, you would have given men the same confused amazement that I feel."

It is to be noted that this sentiment in the presence of living nature did not produce in him any moral impression or moral elevation,[1] but only an artistic admiration or stupefaction, as in the ordinary Italian of his day. He sees nature through the brush of Titian and the landscapes of Vecellio, but he sees her alive, sees her immediately and with a feeling for art that we seek for in vain in Vasari. Amid so many pedantic works of that time, pertaining to art and the art of writing, his letters on artistic and literary subjects exhibit the first splendors of independent criticism, a criticism that was to outstrip books and traditions and find its base in a love of nature.

Like critic, like writer. Words do not give thought to the world. He takes them all, from wherever they come and whatever they are: Tuscan, local and foreign, noble and plebeian, poetic and prosaic, bitter and sweet, humble and sonorous. And from it issued a written language which is

[1] "It certainly did not," remarks Hutton (*op. cit.*, p. 238), "but why should it? It awoke in him as in any other artist a sheer delight. Surely that was enough? He was not a pantheist to worship Nature, nor, perhaps, would he have cared for the Lesser Celandine. Let us leave the moral elevation to Vasari, and only regret that Vasari was totally lacking in Aretino's critical judgment and artistic appreciation of painting; and let us acknowledge in Aretino the first critic of modern art, in painting and letters, who refers us not to the classics but to nature and to life." See Appendix I.

the dialect commonly spoken today by the cultivated classes in Italy. He abolishes the period, breaks up complexities, dissolves periphrases, does away with pleonasms and ellipses and shatters every artifice of that mechanism known as "literary form," all in his effort to speak naturally. In Lasca, in Cellini, in Cecchi and in Machiavelli, there is the same naturalness; but with them, the Tuscan imprint is every-where to be felt; all is prettiness and grace. Here, on the other hand, we have an uneducated Tuscan, a son of nature, living outside his native province, who speaks all languages and exercises his speculations in them. He flees Tuscanizing as a pedantry, in the quest of expression and relief. A word is good when it renders the thing perceived as it is in his mind, and when he does not have to go looking for it; the thing and the word seem to come to him at once, so great is his facility. The word is not always the proper one and not always adapted to its purpose, because sometimes, abusing his facility, he scribbles and does not write. His motto is: "Come as comes,"[1] and from this spring great inequalities. He wastes no time on Cicero and Boccaccio, but, rather, does just the opposite, seeking not magnificence and grandeur of form, in the search for which an indolent brain squanders time, but the most rapid form and the one most suited to the velocity of his perceptions. He does not even affect brevity, as Davanzati does, a lazy mind, all at grips with words and images; for his attention is not directed outward but in-ward.[2] He abandons mechanical processes and takes no thought of verbal niceties and the lascivious aspects of form. He has so much force and facility in production and so much richness of conceit and imagery, that it all rushes out impetuously and by the most direct route possible. There are

[1]*Come viene viene.*
[2]Cf. the sonnet, *Mentre voi Titian, voi Sansovino* (Lettere, II., 249):

> *Benche il mio stil non puo forma e colore*
> *Al buon di dentro dar; qual puote il vostro*
> *Colorire e formare il bel di fore . . .*

no obstacles, no digressions or distractions; he is immediate and decisive, in style as in life. As his ego is the center of the universe, so is it the center also of his style. The world of representation does not exist by itself, but through him, and he treats it and handles it as a thing of his own, with the same caprice and the same liberty as that with which Folengo treats the world of his imagination. Except that, in the case of Folengo, we have the development of humor, inasmuch as his world is wholly imaginary, and he treats it without any seriousness whatever, for the simple purpose of getting a laugh out of it; whereas the world of Pietro is a real thing, and he has a perfect consciousness of it and treats it for the purpose of exhausting it and carving out of it his style. And for this reason, he does not respect his own argument; he does not hide himself or lose himself in it, but makes of it his instrument, his means, even at the cost of profaning it unworthily. He treats Jesus Christ as a wandering knight. "Poetic lies," he said, speaking of the Virgin, "which become gospels when they come to speak of Him who is the refuge of our hopes." In his *Vita di Santa Caterina*, he wrote that "it practically all rests upon the back of invention ... for, in addition to the fact that in every case whatever results to the glory of God is admitted, the work itself would be nothing without the assistance I have lent it."[1]

Sometimes, he falls by the way, his brain is empty, and he amasses adjectives with a show of oratorical pomp that rivals the charlatan:

"The facile, the religious, the bright, the gracious, the noble, the fervid, the faithful, the veracious, the sweet, the good, the health-bringing, the sacred and the holy sayings of Catherine, virgin, saintly, holy, health-bringing, good, sweet, veracious, faithful, fervid, noble, gracious, bright, religious and facile, had in a manner sequestrated the spirits."

It is like a bell that deafens one's ears. And he was the

[1] An example of daring auctorial frankness, which is punished as the author might have foreseen.

one who talked of a "florid style," a style with which Aretino himself will regale you when he has nothing better to
offer. There are times when he has something to say and is
unable to strike the vein or lacks the feeling, and on such
occasions, he falls into the most confused metaphors and the
most absurd subtleties, especially in his elegies, for which he
was so well paid.

"Since your merits," he wrote to the Duke of Urbino,
"are like the stars in the heaven of glory, they have inclined
the planet of my genius, as it were, to find in my style in
words the image of the mind, so that the true face of those
virtues, desired by the world; may be seen in all parts; but
the power of that genius, notwithstanding it is elevated by
the altitude of the subject, is not able to express the manner
in which goodness, clemency and strength, in equal concord,
have given you, as though by fatal decree, the true name
of prince."

This is a period in the popular word-of-mouth manner,
stretched out in form and conceits. Here there is no "Come
as comes," but won't-come and must-make-come-at-all-costs.
His panegyrics are altogether rhetorical, metaphorical, manu-
factured, falsely pompous and puffed out to the point of
absurdity; they are almost like ironic caricatures under the
guise of praise. Speaking good was not for him so easy a
thing as speaking evil, in which latter pursuit he spent all
the vigor of his cynical and sarcastic nature. He assumes an
emphatic tone and seeks a strangeness of concepts and of
manner, a dialect precious, composed wholly of pearls, but
of false pearls. It is that preciosity which passed into France
with Voiture and Balzac, which was flayed by Moliere,
and which in Italy was to become the physiognomy of our
literature. Here are a few of these false pearls placed in
circulation by Aretino.

"(Your eloquence) moves from the nature of your intellect
with so much fecundity that the language which profits by
it, the conceptions it embodies and the ears which listen to

it remain confused in wonderment . . .

"He took from Solimano in the service of Christianity the mind from the soul, the soul from the body and the body from its arms . . .

"I give myself to you, fathers of your peoples, brothers of your servants, little sons of truth, friends of virtue, companions of strangers, supports of religion, observers of the faith, executors of justice, heirs of charity and subjects of clemency . . .

"To gather up my affection in a hem of your piety . . .

"The face of liberality has for mirror the hearts of those to whom it gives assistance . . .

"Your Excellency seeks of me a few gossipings of which to make a fan against the great heat we are having these days . . .

"To fish with the hook of thought in the depths of the lake of memory . . .

"The honesty of some is adorned with the corroding of others' favor . . .

"The coin of affection stamps in the heart the imperishable name of friends . . .

"To buy hope in the urn of false promises . . . "

This precious and florid style is crossed, from time to time, by flashes of genius: original comparisons, splendid images, new and glowing conceptions, incisive pencil-strokes; and we discover in it, when it is abandoned to itself, and when it does not seek effects, a truth of feeling and of coloring, as in the following letter, so moving in its simplicity:

"The stockings of turquoise and gold, which I have received, caused me as much weeping as pleasure, for the reason that the little girl who should have enjoyed them was receiving extreme unction the morning they arrived; and I cannot write you more on account of the compassion that I feel for her."

The dissolution of the literary mechanism results in a form of writing which is closer to that of conversation, freed from all preconceptions, being the immediate expression of an inner feeling; a style now florid, now precious, is a form of the decline of arts and letters; and here lies the significance of Pietro Aretino as a writer. His influence was not small. He had about him secretaries, pupils and imitators of his manner, like Franco, Dolce, Lando, Doni and other tradesmen. "I live by a Lord-ha'-mercy," wrote Doni. "My books are written before they are composed and read before they are printed." His *Libreria* is still read today for a certain *brio* it possesses and for the curious bits of information to be found in it.

But Pietro has yet a certain other importance, as a writer of comedies. His was a conventional comic world, based on Plautus and Terence, with accessories drawn from the popular and plebeian life of the times. Its bases were equivocations, rewards and the confusion of accidents,[1] all of which kept the interest alive. About this frame-work he set up characters thoroughly conventionalized: the parasite, the gluttonous servant, the courtezan, the thievish servant-maid and go-between, the prodigal son, the avaricious and bantered father, the poltroon who pretends to be brave, the broker, the usurer. A study of our comic figures is interesting to one who would see well into the corruption which characterized the Italy of that day. He will see there family bonds broken and worthless sons deceiving their fathers, while the latter are, themselves, come-ons for usurers, courtezans and pimps, all this accompanied by the laughter of a respectable public. This world was the world of a comedy with its forms patterned after the Latin and sprinkled with jests and obscenities. The most fecund comic writer was Cecchi, who died in 1587, and who, in less than ten days, would improvise comedies, farces, histories and sacred representations. He has the Florentine grace and *brio* in common with Lasca, but he has less spirit and movement, so that sometimes it

[1] Cf. the Shakespearean comedy of errors, which likewise has classical antecedents.

seems, in reading his plays, as though one were standing in a dead sewer. His world and his characters are like a repertory that is known and established, and his haste in composition prevents him from giving them flesh and color. He conveys the impression of being thin, lean and muddy. Pietro sees through all this trickery and does away with it. He recognizes no rules and no traditions and no theatrical usages. "Do not marvel," he says in the prologue to his *Cortigiana*, "if the comic style does not here observe the rules that are laid down, for life is lived in another manner at Rome from that in which it was lived at Athens." Among the rules referred to was this one: that no characters could appear more than five times in a scene. Pietro burlesqued this rule with much spirit: "If you see characters coming out more than five times in a scene, do not laugh, for the chains that bind the mills to the rivers do not confine the follies of today." He looks to the effect; he cuts out delays, removes dramatic obstacles, avoids preparations,[1] episodes, descriptions, long harangues and frequent soliloquies; he seeks, above all, action and movement, and he hurls you, from the very beginning, into that roguish, vividly individualized world of his. He has not Machiavelli's gift of synthesis, the ability to take in, with a firm gaze, a vast ensemble, to bind it together and develop it with a logical fatality, as though it were a piece of argumentation. His is not a speculative genius; he is a man of action, and himself a character in a comedy. For he does not give you action well studied and ordered, as in the *Mandragola*,[2] he flees the ensemble; the world presents itself to him in pieces and in mouthfuls. But, like Machiavelli, he has a profound experience of the human heart and a wide knowledge of character; his characters develop in a related manner, through a variety of accidents, and dominate the scene, generating the invention and the piquancy of situation. How this rogue rejoices us with all

[1] The "exposition" over which our contemporary dramatists dawdle. In this respect, and in his tendency to slay the soliloquy and the aside, Aretino displays marks of modernity.
[2] Machiavelli's play.

the brigandages which he sets upon the stage! It is because
that comic world is his world, the world in which he has
known so much malice and charlatanry. His fundamental
concept is that the world belongs to those who take it,
because there are so many rogues and bold-faced rascals, and
woe to the foolish ones! He deals in jests and injuries, for
the reason that they are so fertile in laughs for the public,
because they are the comic material. His *Ipocrito* is the
apotheosis of a knave who, by the madness of intrigue and
malice, becomes rich, just like Aretino. La Talanta[1] is a
courtezan who deceives all her lovers, and who ends up rich,
esteemed and married to an old and faithful sweetheart under
the beards of her other lovers. His "philosopher," while he
studies Plato and Aristotle, is made a cuckold by his wife,
and then the good man is reconciled with her. In the *Cortigiana*, messer Maco, who wants to be cardinal, and Parabolano, who thinks that, on account of his riches, he has all the
ladies at his feet, are, throughout the comedy, the lure for
courtezans, pimps and knaves. His "big booby of a sailor or
great shield-bearer,"[2] in order not to displease the Duke of
Mantua, his lord, consents to marry a lady whom he has
never seen, though he is himself an enemy of women and of
matrimony. Nor is this a world imaginary and subjective, so
properly pictured is the society of the day, with its customs
egregiously represented in the finest and most minute detail.
Pietro leaped into it, gleefully, as into his element, launching
satires, elegies, epigrams, knaveries and deformities with a
brilliancy and an ardor of movement which were like fire-
works. Some of his characters have remained famous, and
all of them are alive and true. His *marescalco* has inspired
Rabelais and Shakespeare[3] and is a most original scherzo,
while Parabolano has remained the appellation given to vain

[1] Title character in the play of that name.
[2] *marescalco o grande scudiere*. Marescalco is the title character in the comedy, *il
Marescalco*.
[3] Cf. Malvolio. Camerini's "*brio Shakesperiano*."

and fatuous fellows. Messer Maco is the type from which issued Pourceaugnac. His "hypocrite"[1] is a Tartuffe, innocuous and placed in a good light. His "philosopher,"[2] whom he calls Plataristotile, is a caricature of the Platonists of the time. To hear him wax sententious, he is a wise man; but he has no practical experience of the world, and his servant knows it better than he; and Tessa, his wife, knows it better still. This philosopher, whose wife makes sport of him under his nose, pronounces fine sentiments upon women, while the servant, who knows everything, has a good time at his expense.

PLATARISTOTILE. Woman is the guide to evil and the mistress of wickedness.

SERVANT. He who knows that doesn't say it.

PLATARISTOTILE. The breast of woman is strong in deceits.

SERVANT. Which is sad for the one who doesn't perceive . . .

PLATARISTOTILE. He who supports the perfidy of his wife is learning to endure the injuries of his enemies.

SERVANT. That's a fine story [—]

And the servant concludes: "Your Wisdom, you should take what comes in good part and not let yourself go in doctrinal speculations, or if you do, the devil will let you go to grass."[3]

"You speak eloquently," replied the philosopher, "but those things are not to be considered too much by me, on account of the appetite for glory which I have acquired by philosophizing."

His Boccaccio[4] is one of those blackbirds, caught in the claws of a courtezan and flayed alive. The serving maid offers him an ambuscade:

BOCCACCIO. What moves your mistress to wish to speak to me, who am a stranger?

[1]Title character in *Lo Ipocrito*. If we are to credit Horologgi, Aretino was to be found on almost every reading table in France. See Appendix I.

[2]Title character in *il Filosofo*.

[3]*che il diavolo non vi lasciasse poi andare pei canneti.*

[4]In *il Filisofo*.

LISA. Perhaps, the grace that is in you; yes, by my faith, that's it.

BOCCACCIO. You like to say nice things.

LISA. May death take me, if I don't convulse myself in serv- ing you.

BOCCACCIO. Breeding always tells.

LISA. To see her, you would forget all the other beauties . . . Stay where you are, stop and look at the sun, moon and stars coming through that door.

BOCCACCIO. What a fine sight!

LISA. There is grace in your judgment.

BOCCACCIO. If only I'm the man she's looking for . . . Names sometimes get confused.

LISA. Yours is so sweet that it sticks to the lips. See, she's running to you with open arms."

Courtezans are his favorite theme. His Angelica is the type of all the others, and his Nanna[1] is the mistress of the species.

This was the comedy which the century produced, the last act of the *Decamerone*: a world brazen and cynical, the protagonists of which are courtezans, male and female, and the center of which is the court of Rome, a world open to the flagellations of a man who, in his fortress of Venice, was assured of impunity.

According to a popular tradition, and a very expressive one, Pietro died in a fit of laughter, as Margutte and as Italy died.[2]

[1]Of the *Ragionamenti*.

[2]Aretino, whose death was due to apoplexy, died, according to popular account, by falling over backward from his chair in a fit of laughter at an obscene story told him by his sister. This account is repeated in the article on Aretino in the Encyclopedia Britannica. The falling from the chair, at least, is authenticated. This is established by a letter to the Duke of Mantua from his ambassador at Venice, Ludovico Nelli. The letter is printed in A. Luzio's *Giornale Storico della Letterature Italiana*. See Hutton, (*op. cit.*, p. 230). Margutte died watching the antics of a monkey.

THE LETTERS

of

PIETRO ARETINO

"*Scholars and common youths even amongst*
ye lustiest and bravest courtiers
are yet to learn ye lesson
in ye world."

GABRIEL HARVEY: *Marginalia.*

Translators' Note

In his letters, Aretino is to be seen at his worst and at his best. At his worst as an always designing hypocrite, fawning—almost incredibly, at times—on princes, prelates and the powerful ones of the earth, and sniffling the usual religious buncombe and patriotic platitudes. At his best as the good fellow, enjoying the good things of life, a good bottle of wine, a pretty girl, a well-cooked thrush—with a wholesome relish. At his very best, in his letters to Titian and other artists, as a highly sensitized and keenly intelligent art critic. His hypocrisy, as has been said, was part of his game; and it is of interest to note that even in his most servile epistles to kings, popes and emperors, there is to be found, beneath the all too obvious flattery, an undercurrent of threats. See, for example, his letters to the Duke d'Atri and the Duke de Montmorency (XLIV. and XLV.), in which he demands a fixed annual stipend for "praising" Francis I. It is such letters that de Sanctis calls "masterpieces of malice and effrontery."

"He said,"[1] Camerini[2] tells us, "that it was the prick of want and not the spur of fame that led him to soil paper. His letters were mercantile documents, and being honored, with him, consisted in being paid. 'With me', he added, 'there is a necessity of transforming digressions, metaphors, pedagogicalisms into levers that move and pincers that open. It is necessary for me, in my writings, to rouse others from their avaricious sleep, and so I need the baptism of invention and of locutions which will fetch me crowns of gold and not of laurel.' Something, in short, between a 'jimmy' and a lead-pipe.[3] One would not be able to attribute anything more to him, if it were not that a certain irony leaks out, when he abases himself to say:

[1] Writing to Bembo, in a well known letter.

[2] *Prefazione al primo volume delle Lettere dell' Aretino*, Milano, Daelli, 1864, reprinted, *Prefazione alle Commedie*, Casa Editrice Sonzogno, Milano. See also Camerini's article: *I corrispondenti dell' Aretino*, Rivista critica, Milano, 1869. See Appendices I and VI.

[3] il grimaldello e la sveglia.

'No one thinks so ill of me as to believe that I do not know the weak figure I cut and the triviality of my complexion, which is without any point of relief.' Yet . . . Aretino marks a departure from the epistolographers of his century in his presentiments of modernity. He is notable, not so much for those hyperboles, which he himself admitted, and which dovetail with the follies of the seventeenth century, as for the forms and conceits which might be said to be of our time, and which in his day must have made a strange impression. . . . These two masks may be taken as representing the writer (of the day) in his double aspect: the mendicant and literary retainer, like the poets of ancient Rome; and the independent writer, who anticipates modern frankness, but who was slow in developing, even in a free country like England. Aretino sometimes asks charity, some-times demands tribute, and he lacks neither philanthropists nor tributaries. Battista Tornielli wrote him: 'Your pen has made you, as it were, the conqueror of all the princes of the world, who are in the position of being your tributaries and feudal subjects. You ought . . . to be decorated with those titles which were given the old Roman emperors, according to the provinces they had conquered.' "

Not only as a man but as a stylist, Aretino is frequently at his worst in his letters. His style in the state communications is tortuous, ornate and effusive. It reminds one of the oration which a high school junior, who had been a little too attentive to his Cicero,[1] might turn out. It is deadly, the worst of models. This style was severely criticized by French writers, including Bayle, Ménage and Montaigne. Their criticisms will be found in an appendix.[2] But criticism like that of Montaigne, for example, should be taken with such critical correctives as those supplied by Camerini.[3] Even in the murkiest spots, there are astonishing sparks, while there are a number of extended pas-sages of really fine writing—such—to mention but two—as the letter to Titian describing the view from a Venetian win-dow, or the letter describing the death of Giovanni de' Medici.

[1]See Appendix VI.   [2]Ibid.   [3]Ibid.

[[40]]

The letters in which he sets forth his views of writing and his hatred of pedants are almost invariably good reading; it is to be regretted he did not always follow his own precepts.[1]

But it is for the picture they give us of a century and of the Venice of his day that Aretino's letters are preeminently valuable. It is in these letters, remarks Hutton, "that we find perhaps the best picture of the city at this time—in the letters of Aretino, who, vile as he was, was yet a man of genius; scoundrel though he was, was yet full of humanity; brutal though he was, was yet full of pity and love for the miserable, the unfortunate, the poor; ignoble though he was, was yet able to dominate the Italy of his time." The Lettere are, indeed, a piece of valuable historical documentation for the age of Charles V.

However, history is more than likely to be dull reading. The joy lies in the little revelations. Speaking of Casanova, Arthur Machen writes:

" . . . the parts of him which I recall with the greatest pleasure are the small adventures and the back alley business rather than the meetings with kings and popes and philosophers. I like to hear of little things; of the supper of pork chops that the scopatore santissimo provided for his guests; of the ways of Italian strolling players in the eighteenth century 'fitups'; of that magic figure that the witch was to bathe in blood; of the significant salad prepared in the Casino at Venice; of the Italian scholar correcting proofs of the Decameron in a London coffeehouse. There are some people who prefer the small talk in the dressingroom to the larger speech of the stage; and I am one of them."

You will find a number of these "significant salads" in Pietro's letters. They are the spice to a sometimes too heavy pudding. The Letters give us the detail with which to fill in the picture. Outside of eating, drinking, making love, collecting his revenues and running the universe, Aretino had very little to do.

[1]In the present translation, no effort whatever has been made to touch up Aretino's style. It has been left, in the state epistles, in all its labored fulsomeness. The attempt has been, always, to convey the spirit.

THE LETTERS OF PIETRO ARETINO

To The Great Duke of Urbino   I

Dedication of the First Book of Letters[1]

Since your merits are the stars in the heaven of glory, they
have inclined, as it were, the planet of my genius to trace
with my style in words the image of the mind, in order that
the true face of your virtues, desired by all the world, may
be visible in every part. But my powers, advanced as they
are by the altitude of the subject, notwithstanding the fact
that they are moved by so great an influence, are not able to
express the manner in which goodness, clemency and
strength, in equal concord, have conceded to you by fatal
decree the true name of prince. And so I, who am not able
to praise you as I ought, spurred by necessity to do what I
can, am sending you here a few letters, by leave of that fame
of yours, in the attempt to express which words grow cold
and hoarse. And if any reproach me with audacity by saying
that the benignity of my idol is diminished in giving audience to such chatterings as these, I am sure that you will still
be able to pardon the error committed by my presumption
against your nobility. I, who am disenamoured with my condition in the severity of my own judgment, which makes it
clear to me that I am like the noise which two countrymen
make when they call to each other across the market-place,
hasten to dedicate this work to you, hoping that I shall be as
the relics of an antique column, which, covered with mud,
are yet put up on high out of reverence for the subject.
Certainly, vile things become prized when they are placed
in temples. And so, this whole book will be preserved, when

[1]This letter is a splendid example of Aretino's style at its worst, that style which
de Sanctis condemns so severely.

men read in the front the inscription: "Francesco Maria," whose generosity climbs the stairs of the heavens to the stupefaction of the peoples, while the greatness of his fortune even in the ascent, in him alone becomes the will and the power to aid others. As it is, neither my inclination upward nor the election which my temerity makes nor the grace of your gentleness is apt to deter me, not even the dram of fear that is in me, from dedicating such a volume as this to you; for your only goddess is the one called "eloquence," who moves from the nature of your intellect with so much fecundity that the tongue which profits by her, the concepts in which she is embodied and the ears which hear her remain dumfounded with wonder. And so, my writings ought to succeed by passing under the censorship of so great a duke and so great a judge. And yet, I must revere you in your rank and fear you in your judgment. Nor am I alone in this case, but all Italy, because with the one you have enlarged the boundaries of honor, and with the other the confines of genius. Two distinctions has nature placed in the collection of your virtues: leisure and velocity; the former stabilizes the sense, and the latter incites to valor, so that we always know where you are and where, of necessity, you must be. Happy was the gift which Jesus made of you to Mark, his evangelist;[1] beautiful also was the present which he with his arms has made to you, and most beautiful of all, the reward of gratitude shown to you for the inviolability of your faith. Truly, you are the subject of the republic of Venice, and she is the object of those qualities with which you assure her against dangers and resolve her doubts. Does not Charles V., our Caesar, in seeing and hearing you, honor the sight of you and prize the sound of your voice? Since in your countenance one perceives fidelity to the truth and in your words the spirit of deeds. Whoever has viewed the superb works of the temple and the theatre, begun by that greatest of Popes, Julius II., to whose eternal memory

[1] Reference is to St. Mark's, Venice.

you are heir, has seen at the same time the ruins of the Orient
restored to their original form through the providence of
your courageous efforts; and as the church does not give its
solemn sanction to such wrongs, so the leaving of these
works unperfected is an offense against baptism. As God, to
destroy the Amorites, gave to Joshua the privilege of stopping the sun and moon, so ought not the vicar of Christ,
since the Turks have been dispersed, receive into his grace
Urbino, the fame of Italy, the glory of Italians and the hope
of religion? For such divine qualities as these, more than
human demonstrations are required. States, ranks and honors
in any other are like the head of a lion suspended above the
door of a palace, which is looked upon by all as the remains
of a terrible wild beast; but the sources and the fine web and
woof of the boldness of your counsels are the limits of immortality viewed from the sun over the gates of the universe.
And so it is, God and the mind of Your Excellency are outraged when there is any perturbation in that order which
they have established by taking from Solimano,[1] in the
service of Christianity, the mind from the soul, the soul from
the body, the body from his arms, his arms from their
praises, his praises from his name, his name from memory,
and his memory from history's pages.

From Venice, the 10th of December, 1537.

To The King of France   II
　　Concerning the captivity in which Charles V. held him.
　　I do not know, Most Christian Sire, since your loss is an
example of another's gain, who merits the greater praise, the
vanquished or the conqueror: for Francis, in the sport which
fate has made of him, has freed his mind from the doubt that
she could make a prisoner of a king; and Charles, in the gift
which has been conceded to him by chance, has become her
servant by thinking that the same thing could happen to an

[1]Referring to the Duke's part in the Turkish wars.

emperor. Certainly, you are free by seeing how fragile a thing felicity is and how you should contemn her; and he has been put in servitude by learning how variable she is and how much to be feared; and so, His Majesty is robed in cares, of which Yours has been despoiled. Do not grieve for fortune since, having no more to do, she has done all she can to you, by placing you in the state in which you are; for, by her doing this, the virtues which adorn you have become enfranchised, so resplendent are you in the most moderate temperance and the firmest constancy in the world, and by consenting that such virtues as these should administer to your heart and mind, you have made her turn woman who, by the laments of men, is a goddess. For my own part, I believe that Fortune, perceiving that others lose by winning and you win by losing, holds it too cheap to triumph over you, who have triumphed over her, since the necessity which guides you, in the endeavor to cast you down into the abyss, has lifted you up to heaven. All this is evident in the manner in which you support her, as you learn to look upon her and to know that her contrarieties are the lamps of life to him who is not lost so long as he has himself. Look you: victory does not make Caesar happy when it appears, for the reason that its appearance, not having a certain end, is but the shadow of the image of felicity; and not only he, but his stars and those virtues to which he owes so much well-being, are unhappy through having overridden the will of God. Whence, I would propose you as a model to every conqueror, since you cast down with your prudence the one who casts you down by force. The great fact is that Augustus, in whose power you are, has but one life in which to show himself generous to you, while you have so many in which to show yourself magnanimous to him! I speak of clemency, but if it is lacking, he remains subjugated by your wisdom in suffering his lack of clemency, you conquering by patience, which is always victorious; for, among all the virtues, it is the truest and none other can be found more worthy of a man. But when a king like you bedecks himself with it, does it not then become an invention of the gods, not to say of "God"? They merit more praise who know how to suffer misery than those who temper themselves in contentment. A high heart ought to bear calamities and not flee them, since in bearing them appears the grandeur of the mind and in fleeing them the cowardice of the heart. But who ever heard of so great a king, in the sudden fortunes of the day, having to do, by himself alone, the work which his captains, knights and foot-soldiers ought to do? Your title was committed, by your own deliberation, to ensigns and coats of mail, but you kept your dignity when, your sword warm with the enemy's blood, you made Fortune confess that she was facing one who fought, not one who had others do his fighting for him, affirming thereby that human events are not governed without reason, but by a knotty aggregation of causes which are most secret to us, and predestined, before they occur, by immutable laws. Victories are the ruin of the one who wins and the salvation of the one who loses; for the victors, blinded by the insolence of pride, are out of harmony with God and think only of themselves; while the losers, reilluminated with the modesty of humility, forget themselves and think of God. Who does not know that Fortune favors those who sleep in her lap, by taking them to her bosom? Do not be ashamed, then, of the jar she has given you, since you would be deserving of any evil if you blushed for your fate. Collect your mind, which has been dispersed by your annoyances, leaning with all your mind's gifts against the pillar of your strength, keeping always awake that vivacious spirit which burns continually in the heart of valor, virtues which inspire no less fear when they are collected than when they are scattered. And may misfortune, whenever you come upon it, be a bridle which will keep you from running away by thinking of or too much considering your lot; and may it leave upon you the impress of temerity, since you shall surely see the time when the sweet remembrance of present things will be useful to you. For no other reason has it pleased Christ that Your Majesty should be judged by your adversary than that you might be a man, even as He was before you. And if you measure the shadow cast by your body, you will find it neither greater nor less than it was before you became the vanquished and he victorious.

From Rome, the 24th of April, 1525.

To Messer Francesco Degli Albizi   III
   On the Death of Giovanni delle Bande Nere.

As the hour drew near which the fates, with the consent of God, had prescribed as the end for our lord, His Highness moved, with that terrible fierceness of his, against Governo, around which the enemy had fortified themselves, and attacking them in the neighborhood of some furnaces, alas! a musket ball struck him in the leg which had already been wounded by an arquebus. And no sooner had he felt the blow than fear and depression fell upon the army, and ardor and joy died in the hearts of all. And every one, forgetting his own duty, began to weep, reproaching fate for having senselessly slain so noble and, beyond the memory of any century, so altogether excellent a leader, and this at the very beginning of so many superhuman undertakings and in Italy's greatest need. The captains who, out of love and veneration, had followed him blamed Fortune and their commander's own temerity for their loss, speaking, as they lamented him, of his age, which was ripe for enterprise, sufficient in any pinch and capable of overcoming any obstacle. They sighed for the grandeur of his thoughts and the fierceness of his valor. They could not refrain from recalling with what homely comradeship he had shared with them everything, even to his cloak, nor could they keep from mentioning the providential acuteness of his genius nor the astuteness of his mind. With the fiery ardor of their lamentations, they warmed the snows, which lay everywhere as far as the eyes could see. Meanwhile, they had put him on a bed and taken him to Mantua, to the house of the signor Luigi Gonzaga. Here, that very evening, the Duke of Urbino came to visit him, for the duke loved him and adored him to such an extent that he was even afraid to speak in his presence, which was to his credit. And as soon as he saw the duke, he gave signs of being greatly consoled; and the duke, very sincerely, seeing the state he was in, said: "It is not enough for you to be bright and glorious in the trade of arms, if you do not support your name with the observances of the religion under which you were born." And he, understanding that the other had reference to confession, replied: "As in all things I have always done my duty at need, I will do the same now." And as the duke left, he began to talk with me, speaking of Lucantonio with extreme affection; and so, I said: "We will send for him." "Would you have him," he replied, "leave the war to come see a sick man?" He remembered the Count of San Secondo, remarking: "If only he were here, he would be able to take my place." Sometimes, he would scratch his head with his fingers; then he would put his fingers to his mouth and say: "What is going to happen?" —answering the question himself: "I've never done any wrong." But I, on the exhortation of the physicians, came to him and told him: "I should be wronging your mind if, with painted words, I endeavored to persuade you that death is the cure for all evils and more feared than to be feared. But since it is the greatest happiness to do everything freely, let them cut away the effects of this horrible gunshot wound, and in eight days you will make Italy queen who is now a slave; and if you are a bit lame, you can take orders from your limp, instead of from the king whose collar you have never been willing to wear about your neck, since wounds and the loss of limbs are the collars and the medals of the familiars of Mars." "Let it all be done," he replied. At this, the physicians came in and, extolling the bravery of his decision, finished by evening the things they had to do; and then, having made him take a little medicine, they went to put in order the instruments which they needed. It was now the dinner hour, when vomiting assailed him, and he said to me: "The signs of Caesar! It is time now to think of something else besides life." And when he had said this, with joined hands, he made a vow to go to the Apostle of Galizia. But, the time having come, the valorous men returned with instruments suited to their task, and said that if eight or ten persons could be found to hold him, while the agony of the sawing lasted—"Not twenty men," he said with a smile, "would be able to hold me." And recovering possession of himself, with a face as firm as could be, he took the candle in his hands to give light to the doctors. Whereupon, I fled and, stopping my ears, I heard two groans only, and then I heard him calling me. And when I came to him, he said: "I am cured!" and, turning himself this way and that, he made a great rejoicing. And if it had not been that the Duke of Urbino restrained him, he would have made us bring him his foot, with the piece of leg still clinging to it, laughing at us because we were not able to bear the sight of what he had suffered. And his sufferings were worse than those of Alexander or of Trajan, who kept a cheerful face while he pulled out the tiny arrow-head and cut the nerve. The pain, which had left him for a while, two hours before dawn returned upon him with every kind of torment; and hearing him beat upon the wall in a frenzy, I was stabbed to the heart, and dressing in a moment, I ran to him. He, as soon as he saw me, began speaking, saying that the pain he had from thinking about poltroons[1] was worse than his wound. And so, he chatted on with me, in the effort, by not giving any heed to his misfortune, to free his spirit which was already given over to the ambuscade of death. When day dawned, things became so much worse that he made his will, in which he dispensed many thousands of *scudi*, in money

[1] This is the passage which De Sanctis misinterprets

and in goods, among those who had served him, leaving four *giuli* for his sepulture, and of this, the duke was made executor. He came then to confession, most Christianly, and when he saw the friar, said to him: "Father, since I have followed the profession of arms, I have lived according to the custom of soldiers, even as I should have lived according to religion, if I had put on the habit that you wear; and if it were not forbidden, I would confess myself in the presence of everybody, for I have not done anything unworthy of myself." The evening passed, when the marquis, moved by his own innate benignity and my prayers, came to him, kissed him tenderly on the head and spoke words which I never would have believed any prince, except Francesco Maria, could utter. And with these proper sayings, His Excellency concluded: "Since your fierce nature has never deigned to make use of anything that belonged to me, ask me one favor that is suited to your quality and to mine." "Love me when I am dead," he replied. "The virtues by which you have acquired so much glory," said the Marquis, "will make you not loved, but adored by me and others." At the end, he turned to me and asked me to have madonna Maria bring Cosimo.[1] At this, death, which was already summoning him below, renewed its agonies. And now, the whole household, without observing longer the modesty of respect, surged about him, the servants mingling with their betters about the bed and, overshadowed by a great depression, weeping for the bread, the hopes and the service which they were losing with their master, each striving to catch the dying man's eyes with his own, in order to show the depth of his affliction. In such surroundings as these, he took the hand of His Excellency, saying: "You are losing today the greatest friend and best servant that you ever had." And His Most Illustrious Highness, putting on a false tongue and face, on which he had feigned the semblance of joy, tried to make him believe that he would be cured; and he,

[1]Giovanni's son.

whom the thought of death did not frighten, although he was sure he was going to die, began to speak of the successful conduct of the war: things which would have been stupen-dous, had we felt that he was now alive, and not half-dead already. And so, he continued fighting till the ninth hour of the night, which was the vigil of St. Andrew. And because his torments had become unbearable, he begged me to put him to sleep by reading to him; and as I did so, he seemed to go from sleep to sleep. Finally, having slept, it may have been, a quarter of an hour, he awoke and said: "I thought that I was making my will, and here I am cured and did not know it. If I keep on getting better like this, I'll show the Germans how to fight and how I revenge myself." When he had said this, the light failed, and he yielded to the perpetual darkness. Then, having himself asked for extreme unction, he received the sacrament by saying: "I don't want to die among all these bandages." And so, they brought a camp bed and placed him on it, and while his mind slept, he was taken by death.[1]

Such was the end of the great Giovanni de' Medici, who was gifted from his cradle with as much generosity as ever was. The vigor of his mind was incredible. Liberality in him was a greater force than power, and he gave more to his soldiers than he left for himself, a soldier also. He always endured labor with the grace of patience, and anger never dominated him for long; he had transformed his actions before he was through speaking. He prized brave men more than riches, which he only desired as a reward for his fol-lowers. He was difficult to know, by one who did not know him, either in the skirmish or the camp. When he fought, he always appeared in the character of a private in the ranks, and in times of peace, he made no difference between himself and others; the cheapness of the clothes with which he disordered his person was a testimony of the love he bore the army, only decorating his legs, arms and chest with the

[1] e . . . mentre il suo animo dormiva, fu occupato da la morte.

insignia that he bore on his shoulders. He was very eager for praise and glory and, while pretending to despise it, longed for it. But the thing which, above all, won the hearts of his men was his habit of saying: "Follow me, don't precede me." There is no doubt that his virtues were a part of his nature and his vices the faults of youth. And would to God we could see his like today! and that every one might have known the goodness of the man as I knew it. He excelled, in affability, the most affable. His aim was fame and not profit; and his possessions, sold to his son in order to supply him with means to pay his men, are a sign that my boasts of him are due to his merits and not to my own adulations. He was always the first to mount his horse and the last to dismount, and in fighting, he rejoiced in the ardor of his own audacity. He proposed and executed plans, and in council, he did not put on a high and lofty air, as though to say: "Enterprises are governed by reputations." But he always saw to it that the plans of those who had made a trade of the sword were followed. He was so expert in the art of war that, at night, he would place the escorts back upon the right road when they had lost their way. He was marvelous in preserving peace among his soldiers, overcoming everything with love, with fear, with punishment or with rewards. Never was there a man who knew better how to employ cunning and force in an asault on the enemy; nor did he arm his heart with a false bravery, but rather thundered with a natural ardor against the fear-stricken. Idleness was his capital enemy. No one before him employed Turkish horses. He introduced a comfortable attire into military fashions. He delighted in an abundance of good food, but not for himself; he satisfied his own thirst with a little water, tinged with wine. In short, every one might envy him; no one could imitate him. And Florence and Rome (would to God I were lying!) upon hearing all this will hold that it is none of their affair. I can hear already the growls of the Pope, who will believe that he is better off in having lost such a man.

From Mantua, the 10th of December, 1526.

To Madonna Maria de' Medici   IV
  Condoling Her for the Death of Giovanni delle Bande Nere, Her Husband.

I have no desire, Signora, to contend with you in your grief. Not that I might not be successful, for I mourned the death of your husband more than any person living; but my efforts in overcoming your sorrow would be lost, for you are his wife, and all griefs in want of comfort are added to yours. And it is not to be assumed, therefore, that my passion does not precede yours, since having accustomed himself here to do without caresses, he had grown hard toward love, which was so much more tender in me that not an hour, not a moment, not an instant could I stand its absence, and his affection for me is better known than that which he bore you. And I must be believed, since I have always seen and you always have merely heard; and others take more pleasure in the virtue of their own eyes than they do in the reports of fame. And, in the event that I yield my passion to your suffering, it is because I give so much pre-eminence to the valor and the wisdom I know are yours, realizing that there is more capacity for things in you, a woman, than in me, a man; and yet, even so, grief is greater on the side where more, not less, is known. But give me, if you will, the second place in your affliction, which is so supreme in my own heart that there is no room for any greater grief. And though he was dead, I have viewed the exhalations of his illustrious spirit, both in the formation of the face, which Giulio di Rafaello made, and in the act of closing him in his sepulchre, which I did with my own hands. But the comfort which the eternity of his memory has given me has sustained me in life. The public voice, proclaiming his virtues, which were the joys and the ornaments of your own widowhood, has dried my tears. The stories of his deeds do not bring me depression, but make me glad. And I feed on such remarks from great persons as: "He is dead and with him the work of nature. He is gone, the exemplar of the ancient faith. He has departed, the true and mighty arm of battle." And of a very certainty, there was never any other who so raised the hopes of the Italian arms. What finer tribute could one have who has been taken out of this world than that which was paid to him by King Francis, who many times was heard to say: "If Signor Giovanni had not been wounded, fortune would not have made me a prisoner." Behold, he is scarcely underground before the pride-filled barbarians, rising up to heaven, strike fear into the hearts of the most courageous; and already fear rules Clement, who has learned to approve the death of him who, while alive, was his able supporter. But the wrath of God, whose will it is to proceed over the failings of others, has taken him away. His Majesty has taken him to Himself in order to chastise the errant ones. And so, we consent to the divine will, without our hearts being stabbed any more, giving ear to the harmony of his praise. It restrains our heart in the delight which it takes in his honors; and speaking of his victories, we bring him light with the rays of his own glory, which has gone on before his bier, even while the funeral pomps were pausing in astonishment at the splendid sight, among the famous captains, of him whom they had brought to bury, on their own honored shoulders. And the marchese, with all the nobility of the house of Gonzaga and of his court, with a crowd of people behind and a throng of women, their interest turned to amazement, at the windows above, went to pay reverence to the body of him who was your spouse and my lord, affirming that he had never beheld the obsequies of a greater warrior. Let your mind repose in the lap of his memory, and send Cosimo to His Excellency, who has commanded me to write to you, on account of that desire to follow in the steps of his father which the latter has bequeathed to his young son. And if I did not believe that God would render to you with twofold interest the dignities which have been stolen from my idol by death and an invidious destiny, I should throw myself into the arms of despair. But let us live, for so it shall be, because it cannot be otherwise.

From Mantua, the 10th of December, 1526.

To The Emperor   v
  In Which He Exhorts Him to Liberate Pope Clement VII
It is quite true that felicity grows with a greater vehemence than that with which it is born; and this is to be seen in the person of Your Majesty, under whose judgment fortune and your own virtue have placed the liberty of the pontiff, even before the door has scarcely closed on that prison from which you lately drew the king, to overcome him with your pity as you had conquered him with your arms. Truly, every one confesses that there is in you something of God, whose goodness causes you to exercise that clemency of yours; for no other would have been able to endure such a trade, and only you have a mind capable of taking in the grandeur of those compassions which are the scourges of the humiliated pride of the perverse, who are punished by your kindness. What mind, what heart, what intellect, except your mind, your heart, your intellect would have conceived the desire to free an enemy? Who except you would have rested his fate in the promises, the instability and the nobility of a vanquished prince, since it is characteristic of those who have lost to give over soul and body, as well as their treasuries and their peoples to revenge? You have had ample opportunity to view the world in the light in which it must appear to the breast of a Caesar; you have known the generosity of mercy and the security that lies in valor. You have understood that in the former lies hope and

in the latter cause to fear, and that it is given to us to flee neither the one nor the other. Beyond this, who ever heard of any man, save Charles, who, in the summit of victory, thought of God and of his own better nature? How you have thought of God is shown by the grace which, in this matter, you have rendered Him; and how you have thought of yourself is shown in the fact that you look upon yourself as a mere mortal. What lamps shall be burned in front of the image of the name of so much self-knowledge! Since to know God in felicity is to stabilize one's self in perpetual beatitude; and he who knows himself in the prosperity of his desires, makes himself, thereby, known to God, and who is known of God takes on some of His qualities. And so, put into operation the benignity of that clemency of which I have spoken, without which fame is plucked and glory extinguished. And since this is the triumphal crown for the one who has triumphed, the reasons which lead him to grant pardon are of greater dignity than the virtues to which he owes his conquest, and that victory may be said to have been lost which is not accompanied by such clemency. But if this clemency, the shadow of the arm of God, rains down into your heart, who can doubt that the pastor of the church shall be freed from the position into which he has been placed—placed there, not because he has abrogated to himself the license of war, but, rather, by the will of heaven, which has breathed over the head of the court a wind of adversity, in which all Rome has suffered? But since the justice of your mercy does not exact payment in cruelty, may it please you that the ruin go no further. In your judgment rests piety and the welfare of the Pope; release him, and let him go free, yielding, to that favor which has been conceded by Christ to your victories, His vicar, being loath to consent that the joy of victory should interfere with the offices of your own divine custom. This being the case, most certainly, among all the crowns which you have acquired, and which God and the fates owe you for the remainder of your illustrious life,

[57]

none other will be seen more worthy of admiration. But who would not place his hope in the best, the religious and courteous Majesty of Charles V., who is always our own august Caesar?

From Venice, the 20th of May, 1527.

To CLEMENT VII   VI
In Which He Exhorts Him to Pardon The Emperor Charles V.

While fortune, my lord, does, indeed, rule the affairs of men in a manner which no foresight on their part can resist; nevertheless, where God has placed His hand, His jurisdiction must prevail. For which reason, one who has fallen, as has Your Holiness, into her bad graces should turn to Jesus with his prayers, and not to Fate with his laments. It was a necessity that the vicar of Christ, by suffering the miseries of chance, should pay the debts due for the short-comings of others; nor would that justice with which heaven corrects our errors be clear to all the world, if your prison were not a witness. So console yourself in your anxieties, since it is His will that has placed you in the judgment of Caesar, a situation in which you may experience, at once, divine mercy and human clemency. But if it is an honor for a prince, who has been always brave, always cautious and always provident against the insults of fate—if it is an honor for him, after he has known those insults, to bear in peace whatever misfortune the malignity of destiny would have him bear, how great shall be your glory if, cinctured with patience, after having come to the end of your industry, your strength and your prudence, you choose to suffer all that the will of God may place before you? Collect that supreme mind of yours and, examining each virtue that is in you, tell me if it is worthy of you not to hope to surmount more stairs than those you have already climbed. Nor is there any doubt that God will sustain the religion of His church, or that, sustaining it, he will fail to guide you; and with His guidance, your downfall lies merely in the appearance, not in the fact. It is, however, in fact and not in appearance that your pontifical mind must act, by thinking of pardon rather than of vengeance; for by resolving to pardon and not to take revenge you prepare for yourself an end befitting your own high dignity and the office that you hold. What work is better fitted to enlarge the limits of the name of "most holy" and that of "most blessed" than the one of overcoming hatred with piety and perfidy with liberality? The wheel sharpens steel and renders it apt to cut the hardness of things: and in the same manner do adversities serve as a whet to generous minds, by teaching them to make sport of fortune, which, on the other hand, is to be vituperated, if you do not place to her account the grandeur of the accident which has deprived you of your liberty. It cannot be denied that you have been assailed with every species of cruel occurrence, and your misfortunes have brought perversity to the fatherland, timidity to our arms, ingratitude to those who have profited by your benevolence, a wavering to the faith and envy to potentates. But if God had had nothing to do with it, your own prudence would yet teach men how to serve, as well as how to rule. Yield, then, all things to Him who can do all things, and when you fall into mischance, thank Him for it; and since the emperor is the firmament of that faith of which you are the father, God has given you into his power in order that you might graft the papal will to that of Caesar, to the end that the great accretion of your honors may be resplendent in all parts of the universe. The good Charles, I assure you, is all kindness and will soon restore you to your primal state; I can see him even now on his knees before you with that humility which is due to him who holds the place of Christ, and due also to his own rank of Caesar. In His Majesty, there is no pride. Give your-self, then, to the arms of that power which has been con-ceded from above: and drawing once more the Catholic sword against the proud bosom of the Orient, transform the latter into the object of your disdain. Thus out of this sorry pass to which the licentious sins of the clergy have brought you, shall issue, with praise and glory, the reward of that patience in suffering which has been displayed by Your Holiness, whose feet I most devotedly kiss.

From Venice, the last day of May, 1527.

To Messer Girolamo Agnelli   VII
In Which the Author Thanks Him for a Gift of Wine.[1]

I do not wish to speak, dear brother, of the sixty *scudi* which you have sent me on the account of the horse. I shall merely remark that, if I had the name of a saint, instead of that of a demon, or if I were the friend of the Pope in place of being his enemy, folks surely would say, on seeing the crowd about my door, either that I was working miracles or that it must be the day of jubilee. And all this comes from the fine gift of wine you sent me. I do not believe there are such servants anywhere as mine. As soon as it is daylight, they begin to fill the flasks of the retainers to all the ambassadors there are—save his grace, the ambassador of France, to give him all the credit that his king deserves. And I, for my part, do not put on airs, as those bald-headed courtiers do, when their lord claps them on the back or gives them some of his cast-off things. Though I have reason enough to play the great man, seeing that every good companion in town gets up a thirst to come and swill down two or three beakers with me. Nor when I eat, sit or walk is there any other conversation except about what perfect wine I have; so you see, I am better known on my own account than I am on yours, and it would be a disgrace, indeed, if anything happened to interrupt such solemn-fine drinking. The finest thing about it, it seems to me, is the fact that it ends up in the mouths of the wenches and tavern lads, who love its kissing, biting taste. And the tears that come to one's eyes

[1]Here, we have the other note. Aretino is himself.

when he drinks it make me weep even now, as I write this. It makes me forget all the other wines you've sent me. And I am only sorry your brother, Benedetto, sent me those two coifs of gold and turquoise silk, since I should like to exchange them for more wine like this. If it were not that I fear Bacchus and Apollo do not get on well together, I should dedicate an opus to the cask in which it stood, which calls for other devotions than those paid to the blessed Lena of the oil. There is nothing more for me to say, except that, in despite of immortality, I shall become divine, if only once a year I get such a taste of the grape as this.

From Venice, the 11th of November, 1520.

To The Bishop of Vasone   VIII

In Which He Accepts a Collar and Refuses the Title of Cavaliere.

The collar which you sent me is the most pleasing and lovely one that was ever seen. It is so lovely, indeed, that I either must not wear it or, if I do wear it, I must conceal both from whom it comes and who the wearer is. I certainly shall never part with it, both because it comes from one whom I respect and love above all other men, and because of its own novel charm. In short, I accept the chain, but not your proposal to make me a *cavaliere* through an imperial *privilegio;* for, as I have said in my *Marescalco,* a *cavaliere* without entree is a wall without crosses, that everybody wets against. Leave such dignities to those citizens who swell up over them, and who, at every opportunity, put in with "we cavalieri." As for myself, I am content with what I am, since to my honors are added the ability to support myself. But let us speak of something else. The valorous joy that came to me with your chain I shall keep as long as I am able. And as to my keeping it invisible, the remedy for that lies in the additional favor which you are in a position to render me in my needs, which I would remind you to remember to the Pope.

From Venice, the 17th of September, 1530.

To The Most Serene Andrea Gritti, Doge of Venice   IX
In Which He Thanks His Highness for Having Reconciled Him with the Pope.

I, sublime prince, have two obligations toward Christ, according to the station in which God preserves me. One is to adjust myself, whatever He may do, to His will; the other is to show my gratitude to you for my present condition; for it is through you, I confess, that my honor and my life have been saved. The credence which I always had given to the reports of this land, and to the fame of its worthy Doge, has now tasted the fruits of its own just hope. And so, I ought to celebrate the city and revere you: the former for having taken me in; you for having defended me against the persecutions of others, leading me back into the grace of Clement by appeasing the wrath of His Holiness, to the satisfaction of my own reason, which is very good and which, in the failure of the papal promises, observes that silence which Your Serene Highness has imposed on me. Here may be seen the difference between the faith of a virtuous man and that of a great man. But I who, in the liberty of many states, have contrived to remain a free man, fleeing courts forever, have set up here a perpetual tabernacle against the years which are advancing upon me; because here, treason has no place; here, favor does no wrong to right; here, the cruelty of the meretricious does not reign; here, the insolence of ganymedes gives no commands; here, there is no robbery; here, there is no coercion; and here, there is no murder. And for this reason I, who have made kings tremble and who have assured them of prosperity, give myself to you, the fathers of your people, the brothers of your servants, the little sons of truth, the friends of virtue, the companions of strangers, the supports of religion, the observers of the faith, the executors of justice, the heirs of charity and the subjects of clemency. For the same reason, illustrious prince, receive my affection into a hem of your piety, so that I may go on praising the nurse of cities and the mother elect of God. Make her the most famous of any in the world, by moderating her customs, by giving humanity to men, by humiliating the proud and by pardoning the erring. Such an exercise is, indeed, your proper task, as is the giving of a beginning to peace and an end to wars. It is for this reason that the angels guide their celestial balls, strengthening their hearts and rolling their splendors over the field of the air above, exceeding, under the ordering of their own laws, that span of life which has been prescribed by nature. O universal fatherland! O communal liberty! O inn of all the dispersed peoples! How great would be the woes of Italy if your bounty were any the less! Here, there is refuge for the nations; here, there is security for richness; and here, there is safety for honors. She receives you with open arms; others shun you. She rules you; others abase you. She pastures you; others starve you. She takes you in; others hunt you down. And while she regales you in your tribulations, she preserves you in charity and in love. And so, I rightly bow to her, and through her offer my prayers to God, whose Majesty by means of altars and sacrifices has willed that Venice should be the rival of eternity in this world, that world which is astonished at Nature's having, miraculously, set her down in so impossible a place; the heavens are richer with her gifts, and she shines there, in her nobility, in her magnificence, in her dominion, in her edifices, in her temples, in her pious houses, in her counsels, in her fame and in her glory, more than any other ever did. She is Rome's reproach, since here there are no minds which could or would tyrannize over liberty and make a slave of the minds of their people. Wherefore, I, with the greatest of reverence, salute and respect your Most Sincere and Serene Highness, who has been placed in the seat of public power, as I would not salute or respect any king or emperor of ancient times. And no less do I wish that your generous life may, with the privilege of God, enter into eternity long after mine. For there is no other payment I can render for the benefits with which you have sustained me; and so, may your Sublimity be paid in the prophecy, by means of which I have endeavored to lengthen your days, which shall, surely, be very long, because Your Highness knows how to employ them.

From Venice (1530).

To Pope Clement x
In Which He Repents of Having Written Against His Holiness.

The cruelty of stubborness is not conformable to either Your Holiness' rank or temper; for you have shown yourself more facile in results than in intercessions. Monsignor Girolamo da Vicenza, bishop of Vasone, your major-domo, here in the house of the queen of Cyprus, the sister of Cornaro, has placed in my hands your brief. And since it was given to him with certain commandments, he has told me all that you told him to tell me: how even the event of a quartermaster of Rhodes becoming Pope and the Pope a prisoner did not so amaze you as the fact that I had lacerated your name in my writings, especially since I knew why it was you did not punish those others for their attempted assassination of me.[1] Holy Father, in all things, my heart has always been in agreement with my tongue; but in touching your honor, its fidelity always has protested that there was no blame in its reproof of you. But if those who have gained the heights of greatness by your aid have outraged you with their deeds, is it any marvel if I have injured you with my idle words? I feel repentance and shame for two things. I repent the fact that I have blamed that Pope whose glory

[1]Hutton, pp. 73 ff.

I always held dearer than my life; and I am ashamed that, if I had to blame you, it should have happened in the heat of your misfortunes. But that fate which locked you in the *Castello* would not have been the worst, if it had not made you my enemy once more. As it is, I thank God who has taken from your mind the harshness of contempt and from my pen the sweetness of revenge. For the future, I shall be the good servant I was when my virtue, feeding on your praise, armed itself against Rome in the vacancy of the seat of Leo,[1] and my conduct shall be such that the Most Serene Gritti, whose modesty has interposed between your patience and my fury, shall have cause to reward, rather than to punish me. In the meanwhile, with the very best wishes, I kiss Your Holiness' sacred feet with the same tenderness of heart with which I have kissed them in the past.

From Venice, the 20th of September, 1530.

To COUNT MANFREDO DI COLLALTO   XI
    Thanking Him for a Gift of Thrushes.

Dining, signor, the other day with some friends on a mess of hares that had been torn by dogs, and which the Captain Giovan Tiepoli had sent me, I was so pleased that I decided "*Gloria prima lepus*" was a saying worthy of being posted up in the hypocrites' choir on feast days, in place of the "*Silentium*" which a garrulous friar tacks up over the monks' quarters. And while their praises were going "*caeli caelorum*," one of your lackeys came along and brought me your thrushes; and as I tasted them, I found myself humming the "*Inter aves turdus*." They were so good, indeed, that our master Titian, upon seeing them on a platter and getting a whiff of them with his nostrils, gave one look at the snow which, while the table was being laid, was falling outside and decided to disappoint a group of gentlemen who were giving him a dinner party. And they all gave great praise to the

[1]See Hutton, Chapter III.

〔65〕

bird with the long beak which, boiled with a bit of dried beef, two leaves of laurel and a pinch of pepper, we ate from love of you and because we liked it. We liked it as well as Fra Mariano, Moro dei Nobili, Proto da Luca, Brandino and the Bishop of Troy liked the ortalans, fig-peckers, pheasants, peacocks and lampreys with which they filled their stomachs, with the consent of their cooks' souls and that of the mad and knavish stars which had given them such big bellies—bellies that were gourmands' treasuries and paradises of fine viands; which was the idea of high life that such asses had. But woe to the fine art of poltroonery, if all of us had been born sage and sober! For doctrine, sobriety, and wisdom are a cloak in the wind of princes. Happy is he who is a bit mad, and who, in his madness, pleases himself and others! Certainly, Leo had a nature that ran from extreme to extreme, and it would not be for every one to judge which delighted him most, gifts or the chatter of his buffoons; and this is proved by the fact that he gave as much heed to one as the other, exalting one as well as the other. And when he would say to me: "Whose servant would you rather have been" (you know that I was his servant) "Virgil's or the poet-laureate's?" I would reply: "The laureate's, master; for he, drinking by himself in the *Castello* in July, had more good hot toddies[1] than Sire Maro could have gotten if he had written two thousand fawning *Aeneids* and a million *Georgics*. For there is no doubt that the great masters love strong-drinkers better than good-versifiers. I commend myself to Your Lordship.

From Venice, the 10th of October, 1532.

To THE KING OF FRANCE   XII
    In Which He Thanks Him for the Gift of a Chain of Gold[2]
    SIRE, your gift is so in keeping with the most Christian Francis, and so of the very essence of liberality, that, as to

[1] *il vin temperato con l'acqua calda.*
[2] The famous one. See *Introduction.*

[66]

earthly things, you would almost rival God in my thanks, if I thanked you with haste; for true courtesy walks with its own feet, while a limping pretence goes with those of ambition. Men who are tossed on the sea or struck down on land are accustomed to turn to Christ, and when his goodness, in response to their zealously ardent hearts and faithful feet, suddenly frees them from peril, they are wont to hang up their votive offerings in his temples. And so, the virtuous, devoured by their necessities, turn to you, and Your Highness thus becomes the second God of the peoples. But gifts are so slow in coming to those who receive them that they are like placing food before a man who has gone without eating for three days; when he goes to break his fast, he finds that he cannot touch what is set before him, and so either dies or is in danger of it. Behold, it is three years now since you promised me a five-pound gold chain, and I could not have been more doubtful of the coming of the Messiah of the Jews, when along it came, with its vermilion-tinted tongues and with the inscription:

LINGUA EIUS LOQUETUR MEDACIUM[1]

By God! if a lie does not sit better in my mouth than the truth in the mouth of a cleric. I suppose, if I were to tell you that you are to your people what God is to the world, and that you are a father to your little sons, I should be telling a lie? If I told you that you have all the rare virtues, bravery and justice and clemency and gravity and magnanimity and a knowledge of things, I should be a liar? If I told you that you know how to rule yourself to the amazement of all, should I not be speaking the truth? If I told you that your subjects feel your power more in the benefits they receive than in the injuries they suffer, should I be speaking evil? If I cry out that you are the father of virtue, the brother of your servants, the little son of religion, the companion of the faith and the support of charity, shall I not be speaking

[1]See my note on the De Sanctis passage regarding this inscription.

well? If I proclaim that the great merit of your valor moves others in their love to make you the heir of the kingdom, shall you oppose me? It is true, that if I cared to brag of this present of the collar as a present, I should be lying, because that cannot be called a "gift" which, devoured by hope in the expectation, is no sooner seen than sold. And so, if I did not know that your kindness is without measure and innocent in intent, if I were not resolved to believe that I have always enjoyed it, I should tear out all these linked tongues and make them ring so that the ministers of the royal treasuries would hear them for days to come, in order that they might learn to send in haste what their king gives quickly.[1] But as I know there is no deceit in your loyalty, I ought not to be contemptuous in my own virtue, which shall always be the humble prattler of the ineffable benignity of Your Majesty, in whose grace Christ keep me.

From Venice, the 10th of November, 1533.

To THE GREAT CARDINAL IPPOLITO de' MEDICI   XIII
   He Wishes to Go to Constantinople.

Since I am under obligations, my lord, to the courtesy of the king of France and to that of the Cardinal Ippolito, who have relieved me somewhat of the necessities I experience, on account of the envy with which my enemies have con-quered the kindness of His Holiness—since I am under such obligations as these, I should not think of going to Con-stantinople, whither the liberality of Gritti[2] draws me and my own poverty drags me, if it were not that you already have done what you could in my behalf, as I have asked you, with His Majesty; but since he disdains to do anything for me in that direction, I shall go on serving you with the same heart with which a just man serves his God. And so, Are-

---

[1]Aretino was under the impression that Francis' agents had held up the gift.

[2]The natural son of Lorenzo de' Medici, who was his father's representative at Constantinople, and who wrote urging Pietro to come to him that he might enjoy "that charming conversation of yours." See *Introduction.*

tino, a veracious man, except in the reproofs which reasons all too bitter have caused him to make our lord,[1] an old man and a wretched one, must needs go to seek his bread in Turkey, leaving to the happy Christians the pimps, flatterers and hermaphrodites, tools of princes, who, closing their eyes to the example which your own royal nature gives them, live only by begging the goods which you scatter with so lavish a hand, at all times and in all places. With your permission, then, I, who have redeemed the truth with my own blood, will go there and, while others show the ranks, entree and favors they have acquired through their vices at the court of Rome, I will show the wounds which I have received for my virtues, the sight of which, though it never has moved these lords to pity, will move those savages to compassion. And Christ, who to some great end has saved me so many times from death, shall be with me always, because I have held to his truth; and moreover, I am not Pietro, but a miraculous monster among men.[2] In this faith, I alone wear my heart on my forehead,[3] where all the world may see the respect I bear you. I know that, by leaving, I am wronging your own greatness of heart, despairing of that grace of yours with which you console the afflicted. But the reason lies in the fear which the years bring to me, and the suspicion that I have the ill will of some who, being unable to forgive me for the wounds they have made me suffer, may, it is possible, cause your warm will towards me to grow cold. Besides, I plan to go on preaching in the Orient, as I have preached here, until the peoples that do not know reverence shall revere you. In divorcing myself from Italy, perhaps forever, I do not lament the reasons which have led to my exile, but, rather, the fact that I have been able to leave behind me no testimonial of the love I bear you, as I do leave behind me the hatred I

[1]The Pope.
[2]*per esser io non pur Pietro, ma un miraculoso mostro degli uomini.*
[3]Cf. Cicero's Catalinarian: *Sit inscriptum in fronte unius cuiusque quid de republica sentiat.*

bear to others; although I am comforted by the hope that I shall be able, in my new lot, to supply the old lack of fortune. May God consent, before I die, that I may be able to repay that courtesy of yours which has come voluntarily to aid me in my needs. I speak with a sincere soul, stripped of all fraud and adulation—which only make me miserable, so great is my abhorrence for them, though others are happy in practicing them.

From Venice, the 19th of December, 1533.

To VERGERIO   XIV
In Which He Speaks of the Avarice of Clement VII.
and of the Liberality of Francis I.

It was with great consolation that I received Your Lord-ship's two letters, and they were all the more gratifying because unexpected; for when one begins mingling with prelates, he becomes like them, and it is all the greater miracle to find that Vergerio is the same Vergerio I used to know, and to perceive that he has not become, as I should have done, the apprentice[1] and good fellow of the priests. On the contrary, I discover the same gentle and lovable Pietro Paolo that you have always been, with me and with all; and so, I am glad, rather than sorry, for the transforma-tion from the first profession to the second, since if self-preservation were the essence of good, I should have said you were better off at the Venetian than at the Roman court. But if you persevere, as I see you are doing, in the ways of a righteous man, I judge your choice most wise, for, of a truth, you are playing time against a larger hope. But to return to your letters, in which you speak to me of the worthy merits of the best king of the Romans, I may say that I have already been informed of them by my friend, the Duke d'Atri. His Excellency has given me a long story of

---

[1]We have here almost our modern slang phrase, "be the goat": *che io sia alievo dei preti. Alievo* is also a foal or calf.

His Highness' kindness, his religion and his liberality, and how he brings to the office of prince more kindness, more religion and more faith than are to be found anywhere else in the world. And it is by just such a path as this that King Francis ascends, without whose courtesy every species of virtue would be a species of divine progeny abandoned by heaven. Lest it may appear that I am praising His Majesty for his gift of a collar, I would have you see what he has done for the divine Luigi Alamanni, for Giulio Camillo, for my friend, Alberto, and for so many other fine spirits. He entertains painters, rewards sculptors and contents musicians. And in case your lordship should ever go to Nizza for an interview, you will see there the strangest miracle that was ever heard of. As Gaurico, a prophet after the fact, speaking of my chain of tongues, says: the liberality of Francis is such that if only the pontiff could see it, it would convert even his innate misery and incomprehensible avarice into prodigality. Oh! would not that be a greater miracle than any Gilberto ever wrought? By God, if his immense and royal courtesy could only turn Clement into a Leo! O God, what a fine life it would be, if the Holy Father, like a chameleon, were to put on the colors of a truly Christian mind! But have I nothing to say to you? The herd of Pasquins is afraid that the king, by dealing with the Pope, may transform himself into one, from which God save us! And, while I have succeeded in getting out of him this fantasy, he was more stubborn about it than is the Cardinal de' Medici in giving to the well-deserving all that he has, all that he hopes to have or ever had; and all these follies, I may tell you, he commits in order that he may be imitated by other princes. But I hope to Christ he does not thereby acquire for himself an envy that will rob him of his life and rob the virtuous of their support.

From Venice, the 20th of January, 1534.

He Would Not Serve in the Papal Court

I, Elegant Spirit, wondered more, when I read a letter of
Bernardi's about my coming to take service in the papal
court, than the good folks would have wondered, if Farnese
had not risen to that rank which the deceits of simony and of
men had forbidden him for so many years. And I may tell
your Most Celebrated Lordship that, being prey to a most
malignant fever and being wholly occupied in my bed, I was
shown an article in which Monsignor Giovanbattista exhorted me to proclaim the merits of His Holiness, who had
been made pontiff by divine will and not by human favor.
At that time, quite appropriately, they brought me my
Salmi from the press; whereupon I, to show that I had no
need to be exhorted to praise so just an old man, directed
Ricchi to send you one of these books. Then, moved by I do
not know what impulse, I commissioned him to ask you, in
my name, to obtain from his Holiness a letter of friendship,
and I told him twice to make clear to you that I was not
seeking this in order to come out scot-free, nor because I
wished to come to Rome nor for any reason at all, except to
have the means of enjoying a little pleasure once a month.
And as it seemed to me that what I asked should not be
denied to the Rector Arlotto, I waited. As to the fact that
Messer Agostino, who has gone to Lucca, had published a
work in his usual manner, I was in no wise to blame. From
this error, I have drawn both pleasure and displeasure. It
pleased me because it brought me a letter from you, dearer
to me than those of kings; and it displeased me because I
knew you had been pained not by the thought of how you
were going to satisfy the desire you thought was mine, but
by the reflection that you had not yet been able to accomplish it. And for all of this, I thank you, with my heart and
with my soul. I am writing to His Excellency, the Signor
Pier Luigi. God knows, I have always been his servant, and

when the devil takes me and makes a servant out of a free man, I would sooner serve him than the Father, because I am used to camps; from soldiers I have had honors and money, and from priests insults and robberies. And I would sooner be confined in a prison for ten years than in a palace with Accursio, Sarapica and Troiano.[1] What my friends eat in my house is worth more than what I hoped to get at court, and the clothes I wear on my back are better than those Ganymedes ever saw. To conclude, please put a stop to any movement that may have been started to bring me back to Rome, for I would not live there with St. Peter, himself, much less with his successor. I am, indeed, grateful for being remembered by so great a pastor, whose Holiness, I know, will deign to read two or three pages of my *Vita di Cristo*, which will be out soon. I implore you, in case you happen to speak with the innately good and virtuous del Molza, to remember me to him.

From Venice, the 15th day of January, 1535.

To SIGNOR BINO SIGNORELLI   XVI

Of Giovanni delle Bande Nere.

I, Captain, in the news of the two victories which, in open stockade, having taken one of his adversaries and slain the other, Messer Antonnino has obtained, have taken, as I believe, not only as much pleasure as all the numerous friends and relatives he has, but, it seems to me, even more, since my pleasure is increased by the fact that he has proved his own valor to himself. But why is not Giovanni de' Medici living yet? Why is he not here to complete our consolation by letting us see him reap the rewards of his own glorious virtues and his glorious deeds? It is a great thing that we now see not only his nobles, but even the stewards and butlers who once served him, become illustrious captains! Everybody knows his grooms, his light horse and his men of

[1]Papal favorites.

arms, and the latter, in whatever position they are placed, shine like the most resplendent *cavalieri*. Nevertheless, it is a fine boast which Francesco Maria, among so many others, may make, that, fierce lord that he was, by reason of his kindness as well as because of his merits as a grand duke, the riders of His Excellency were reverenced, not merely obeyed. Tell me, you who, since death separated you from his regal conversation and the schooling of his invincible actions, have sought out and conversed with an infinite variety of soldier—tell me if you have found a complexion so generous, so affable and so regardful of honor, necessity and the blood of his followers? Do you not weep when you chance to remember how you felt when he used to share with us his horses, his money and even his garments? Do you not fall to weeping when you think how you were always his friend and companion? For my part, I always looked upon his outbursts of anger as a manifestation of the greatness of his nature, and nothing more; and the world knows that whoever was not a coward could look into his heart and share with him his rule. How many have wanted to usurp his name through the *bravura* of their slaughterings? Every occurrence that moved him to speak came from his nature and his custom; and he alone it was who looked upon brave men as riches. How often have I seen them at his feet, wounded, famished and alone, and then, in three hours' time, lodged, provided with horses and servants, clothed and well fed! He was the true interpreter of the military physiog-nomy, and in the lines of his face and forehead could be read a comprehension of the animosities and the vileness of others. For this reason, being our brother and accepted by the grace of his friendship as a gentleman, he could not but conquer whomsoever he fought with; and always, when I hear the fame of his deeds, I feel that they are dear to me but not new. And now, may Your Highness be moved to command me in any way in which I may delight or serve you.

From Venice, the 28th of April, 1535.

On the Death of the Cardinal Ippolito de' Medici.

Who ever would have believed, brother, that I would
have to praise the fate which drove me from Rome; and yet,
if it had not been for that, would the kindness of my faith and
the tenderness of my nature ever have been made at home
with the ineffable affability of him who, betrayed by the
invincible courtesies of his own royal nature, is now dead?
My sorrow at having known him and having taken his gifts
is even greater than my joy in having known him and having received them. For if I had not known him, or the taste
of his liberality, his countenance, which shall always remain
fixed in my mind, would not afflict me as it now does; nor
would the obligation I feel for the good he has done me be
now moving me, as it does move me, to render suitable
gratitude to his memory. But if I, who barely saw him and
rarely enjoyed his presents, thinking of the misery of chance,
suffered an insufferable grief, how much greater should be
that which consumes you, who, with the keys of your
dignities opening to you at every hour the doors of that
magnanimous breast, ministered to his soul? It seems to me
impossible—it seems to me you would have to be more
than a man, if you bore without grief the absence of that
celestial face, in which health-bringing atmosphere the hopes
of all were nourished—of all who knew how to hope in the
benignity of his works. I am amazed at the method of Death
in outraging an immortal personality. Surely, when she saw
in his mind the preparations of his fine virtues, she ought to
have drawn back her weapons against the one who provoked
her to so inhuman an office. Alas! tell me, out of the divinity
of your spirit, to which it was permitted to penetrate all the
profundities of his heart: what were the splendors of those
places in which he lodged the excellences of his generosity?
Tell me: how was the room of the love he bore his friends
furnished? Tell me: how was that nest built in which he

received the miseries of the virtuous? Tell me: how did he dwell in his own ardent valor? Describe to me the inns in which sojourned his charity, his benignity and his religion. Point out to me the footprints which his graces, promenading always about the world, have left. Ah, unheard of wickedness! Ah, mad Tuscan![1] Ah, unjust mind! Why did you offend one who not only had not offended you, but who, with his own splendors, had made your life resplendent? But what influences are those of the heavens? Those influences struggle because they comprehend the power of the fatal effects of such a deed; and as though they envied him, they consent that fortune, in the flowering of the years, shall make us cruelly lack, as we have lacked, this refuge of the rare virtues. But you who, thanks to the charity with which the stars have used you, are in a position to give life to others, do you avenge the outrages which have been done to us by death and destiny, and, feeding with the food of eternity the name of the one who was the nourishment to all the necessities of you and others, give cause to every prince to receive under his roof the familiars of the muse; for it is clear that the memory of such a lord commends itself to their pages. But as those lords who rejoice in the riches of Christ imitate the footsteps of the eternal Cardinal de' Medici, so by your own and other intellects shall be satisfied the excessive debt which every generation owes itself. And this and no other is the light in which the matter is viewed by Rome, which from century to century shames the courts by reproving their supreme magnificences.

From Venice, the 20th of August, 1535.

To The Count Massimiliano Stampa   XVIII
    On the Death of Francesco Il Sforza.
    The duke is dead, and one must believe that such an event has taken with it, not only your happiness, but also a part of

[1]Referring to the Cardinal's slayer.

your soul, since you were nourished by the same milk and so were, in a manner, joined in one flesh, even as you always were one in will. But you should find peace in the thought that human privileges are those sorrows which afflict every one living, and which God permits so that we may trust solely in Him. And upon thinking well of your adversity, you should thank fate which has taught you to know heaven and to make sport of the world. Furthermore, if I, who am so weak in spirit, have suffered, at one stroke, three blows of fate, what reason is there that you, who are so strong, should not be able to make your peace with grief, since you have suffered but one? Fell first, struck down by a bullet, the great Luigi Gritti; following him, laid low by poison, our only Cardinal de' Medici; and now, as though to ruin me under the weight of misfortunes, comes the end of His Excellency. He, after all, should be happy, who, a wanderer from the age of six, and knowing exile before he knew his native land, after so many confusions, so many accidents of war, disease and famine, after so many travails on the part of his followers and all the afflictions which the necessity of the times has imposed on his people, was able, in the quietest State that could be desired, in the warmest love that Milan could bear him, in all security and with the friendship of Caesar, as well as the grace of all Italy, to render up his spirit to Him who gave it; and so, without noise, without fear and without hatred, he has left to the succession the most just, the loftiest and the most fortunate emperor that ever was. All praise and all glory be given to Francesco Sforza, who, in the virtue of his own bosom, kicking fortune under heel, had the happiness both to die in his native land and to die a prince. Therefore, *signor mio*, cheer with that accustomed serenity of yours the hearts of those who revere you even as I revere you; and may your comfort be the felicity in which so great a one has left you. Show to His Majesty that you are as much pleased with the State you have come into as you are grieved at the loss of him; and rejoice in the in-

[77]

violable faith which he always reposed in you, when he was emboldened to receive you into the lap of his divine favor. May your consolation be the report which comes, from the tongues of the soldiery, the learned and the nobility, of your courtesy, which is your trumpet everywhere; and giving no heed to the devastations of time, rout fate and bury death, permitting your thoughts to return to their original state. And do not any longer mingle the bitter with the sweet of life, since you are naturally the friend of gladness. There lies the sacred body of the best of dukes; give him an honored sepulchre and see that his spirit is paid the rites that are its due, recalling that, since he made you in his image, it is not fitting that his name should go unremembered. Look at me, I do not vary with the variations of fortune; and even if the rank which your liberality has made me hope for should fail me, I shall not fail ever to celebrate him dead, as you living, since the object of the devotion that I feel for Massimiliano is not reward. I am what I always was, and the stars may make me miserable, but they shall not make me a liar. I, in my last letter, which was filled with sorrowful forebodings, wrote you of the variable end of things, and how the finest of pomps fade into mist. I concluded by promising such stability as ink can give, and you shall have the work I promised. Be at peace and, being at peace, thank Christ who has made you what you are.

From Venice, the 25th of November, 1535.

To The Great Antonio da Leva   XIX
*In Which He Comforts Him for the Death of His Little
Daughter, Giovanna.*

Your Excellency ought not to marvel at the theft of your little daughter, which heaven has committed by the hand of death, nor should you raise an eyelash at what the continuous accidents of evil bring. You should rather be astonished if adversity does not assail you, since every grave occurrence of that sort comes from God, who does not consent that men shall be his companions, as you, whose glory illuminated the world, were, unless they are oppressed by those sufferings to which the title of "most blessed" might be given—not merely "blessed." Alas! Your honored daughter is dead; but is that any miracle? Did she not have to die? Was she not born for that purpose? Must we not make way for those who come? Has not Christ shared this lot with us? And if she had not died, by what way would she have gone to paradise? And if all this is so, is weeping worthy of your soul? A little earth, which resolves itself into earth again, does not merit tears. And if that flesh which you loved so tenderly brings you affliction, comfort yourself with the thought that she is now in the lap of her Maker. And while the captains of the eternal militia rejoice as they hear sung the deeds of their great father, the angels also are glad at seeing her come back to them, as beautiful, as pure and as gleaming as she left. But what am I saying? Neither son nor daughter of yours has died, for your true sons cannot die, since fame, the soul of noble names, is the consort of your valor, and Giovanna and the others cannot take away your victories and your triumphs. Let, then, your grandsons be praises and honors, and, after them, armies and the peoples whom you rule and conquer. Your blood-children are merely yours by nature and have nothing to do with your immortality. Look to that which lasts forever, and not to that which lasts but an hour. And when pain perturbs your breast, turn your thoughts to yourself; console yourself by thinking of yourself alone, and say: "I am." And saying that, you shall shine once more in your own proper spirit as a divine being. There is little doubt that Antonio is more God than man, since if he were more man than God, he would not, from a private citizen, have become a prince, and from a mortal an immortal. His dignity takes from Alexander the glory of being born a king and is like Caesar's in that he is not called emperor; for it was virtue and not

fortune that crowned Caesar in the same world that shall crown you. And that will not be long, so soon as you shall have looked into yourself and seen there all that is to be seen. The fortunate Augustus should regard it as a felicity to have as his devoted servant the good Leva, without whose counsels and without whose arms His Majesty would not make any impression. But he has done much without His Majesty, and has been so fortunate that history, which commemorates him, shall be no less astonished than Milan is astonished now—astonished to see itself come back under the sway of your calm prudence, which shall acquit it for whatever misfortunes it may have suffered in the past through the iniquity of the times, misfortunes which, with his universal peace, Charles V shall set right again, to whose empire no limits can be fixed. Since he alone knows how to fight and how to conquer, there is no reason why you should not return laden with all the spoils of the Orient. Do this, and your season of grief shall end, wars shall be disposed of, faith shall appear again and justice shall take up her abode with us once more. And religion, by the aid of Caesar, being more revered than ever, the universe shall give itself to building temples to him, consecrating statues and erecting votive shrines. And since His Highness never has been able, never has desired, to act without your mind, you shall partic-ipate in those celestial pre-eminences which the peoples shall give him, placing him among the number of the gods, along with your own divine Excellency, whose kindness is consolation to the hopes of all who deserve to hope in you.

From Venice, the last day of November, 1535.

To The Emperor   XX

   Concerning the New War between Francis I and Charles V.

   Having always looked upon Your Majesty as nearer to God than any man that ever was, it being a property of God to give ear to the prayers of servants, as much as to the vows of princes, I hasten to salute the faith, the religion, the piety, the fortune, the mercy, the kindness, the prudence and the valor of Your Highness with this, my own. And if this paper had a soul, I should prefer it to all the glorious ones of antiquity, since it is to be not only read but touched by the true friend of Christ, Charles the august, to whose merits all the universe must bow. And if it is true that God, to make room for his own merits, enlarged the world, then he ought also to raise the heavens, since there is not room enough in all the air for the flight of your fame. Who can but believe that the divine graces, reposed in Moses, in Joshua and in David (who conquered with their prayers and with their arms) are infused in your own most lofty breast, as well as lodged in that blind fury which overwhelms the armies that move against you. I, O Caesar, should liken you to a torrent, swollen with rains, snows and sun-melted ice, swallowed by the fields that think they are drinking, while your own superb course is making a bed of them. I tell you that this new onslaught shall disappear, as every one that is made upon you always does disappear, and as every race, every banner and every name that con-tends with you shall disappear, for who fights with Caesar fights with God, and who fights with God confounds him-self, and he who annuls his own being remains nothing. Since every one who persecutes you falls into the river, why doubt of the happy outcome of your fortunes? I kiss that sacred hand of yours, adored by all who know it through faith, through liberality and through the power of arms.

From Venice, the 10th day of March, 1536.

To The Great Antonio Da Leva   XXI
    On The Same Subject.
    This is the last step, O ardent soul, by which that name of yours shall attain the end of human honors. The hour has

now come in which that clear mind of yours, armed with its own proper counsels, shall teach the army how to fight, in fighting how to conquer, and in conquering how to triumph. You are now at the point where glory may be laid hold of, if you must be immortal. It is a great thing to say, and one almost impossible to believe, that leisure is pain to you and labor is repose! Whose body, except yours, ever languished in peace and grew well in war? God does all things well, and so, he restrains you better than with an indisposition; and if he did not do this, you would be lording it over the kingdom of Mars, whose executor you are. And if any one doubts that there is a man born with such qualities, he has but to regard the results which always issue from your spirited genius. You make the banners of pertinacity and terror tremble, you move peoples with your prudence and your valor, and you open a path through difficulties by the virtue of your arms. It is certain that every victory brings its doubts, but in an imperial victory there is none; and even if there were, they would be reassured by the wise foresight of Your Excellency, who should be greatly rejoiced at the fact that His Majesty, having merely heard of the things you have done in his service, has taken you into the heart of his grace, and so, what reward will he bestow for the works which you shall do in his own high presence? Your good sense will produce the greatest effect in his eyes; that effect, indeed, will appear superhuman, inasmuch as it will be wrought in the face of the strongest obstacles. The fact that you are never relied upon in vain is what feeds the fame of your honors. You are like the lion, which sometimes takes its prey among the smaller animals. This war should be to you as, in ancient times, was the Piazza di Navona, in the middle of which was erected a stake which the Roman youth assailed every day with a stick, for no other purpose than to exercise their robust arms, that they might be able to put a yoke on the world's neck. One lives, so long as he has a sword in his hand, on the point of which rests pro-

[83]

motion, fame and the praises of those who are wise enough to follow in your footsteps—steps which lead to the heavens.

From Venice, the 4th day of June, 1536.

To CAESAR[1]

Praises.

Those warm thanks, sovereign emperor, which one who has attained his desires renders to Christ, I render to the celestial benignity of Your Majesty, who not only have deigned to receive my unworthy letters, but who have, by the integrity of your promises, snatched away the poverty of my hopes. O greatest ruler of the peoples and of king-doms, truly, you are the only monarch who show that you are made in the image of God; for you are the only one who transcends the stars with the feathers of humility; you alone of kings make inviolable the laws of religion; you alone of princes arm yourself for the honor of Jesus; you alone of lords do not despise human generosity, but, as though each were the nearest of kin, you embrace us and, in doing so, relieve us of that fear in which the most just dagger of your eternal power holds the depravity of the erring. And so it was, Rome, trembling, feared the face of her conqueror; but soon, perceiving that her own virtue and fate lay in a valorous prudence, better armed with simplicity than with steel, she began to adore you, giving, after Jesus, praises and glory to you alone, as did the other cities through which you passed, which you, in grace and in love, made the com-panions of your mercy, so that they took the palm of affability from all others and gave it to you. It is a great thing that, while the Caesars of old, with all their counsels and arms, sweated five centuries and a half in the pacification of the state of Italy, you have taken possession in a day; and where your strength ends, your kindness begins, by means of which you dominate minds no less than nations. I, O

[1]Charles V. This, or Augustus, is Aretino's usual adulatory term.

Caesar, who soil your high deeds with my low words, do so that I may boast of having written to one who is elected to immortality; for when you are enshrined among the deities, it will be permitted me to do so no longer, and I shall then have to bring votive offerings, rather than send letters. For, in short, it cannot be denied that Your Majesty merits altars and sacrifices, and that you have your place in the sky with the other gods. Nevertheless, it would seem to writers that your rare deeds cannot last throughout the world unless record is made of them, and they say that pens and tongues, armed with a steel and a fire that always cuts and always burns, are adapted, fighting for your honors, to enlarge the confines of your name as much as your captains do the bounds of your empire. Sane and highest, on every occasion, is the judgment of Caesar, but not to bait ink with gifts defeats itself, leaving the duty to those who have need of the preachings of others. Alexander the Great, on viewing the tomb of Achilles, sighed with envy for the hero of song, desiring such an honor for himself and feeling that his own deeds had more fame than glory. And so that first Caesar, who wrote commentaries in his own praise, hiding behind the grandeur of his style many things, may have stolen some of his splendor from those who did not write. But since your Divine Majesty knows that falsehood is the mother of history, which, by its nature, adds to that which was and is, having honors which are enough for all future ages, you should see to it that your miracles, handed down from generation to generation as the legitimate heritage of men, go on living by their own virtues, and not by the say-so of others. And so I look forward to consoling myself with your august courtesy, without which my writings would be obliged to pay you usury. And I here kiss those unconquered hands, destined to place the chains of servitude on the arms of all the Orient.

From Venice, the 4th day of June, 1536.

Descriptions of the Preparations for the Coming Of Charles V to Florence.

If, after Xerxes the king had been conquered, you had been there when Paul sent to the Athenians for a philoso-pher to teach his sons and a painter to decorate his chariot, he would have invited you and not Metrodorus, for you are historian, poet, philosopher and painter. I am one of those who would not be able to describe to you in a thousand years the order of Caesar's triumph, nor the pomp of the peoples and the arches, even if I had that dexterity of ornate words with which you have written me. I, for my part, see in your letter the two great colonnades with the "*Plus ultra*" across them; I see the monsters painted on the bases; I see the epigram, with the eagle above it and that falsehood which bites the tongue while it sustains the arms of His Majesty. I see the edifice of the great gate and the *diligenzia* of Barticino; I see the tumult which the innumerable princes make as they follow the august Charles. I see the pontifi-cally most reverend ones with our Lord Alexander who go to meet him. I see, also, with what dexterity he dismounts from his horse, presenting the hearts and the keys of Florence. I hear him saying to His Highness: "And this, and this, which I hold, is yours." I see the throng of pages on the imperial horses, and my sight is dazzled by the tremu-lous gleam of golden aglets with which the drapes of the Florentine youth are bristling. I see the two beadles whose custom it is to remain in front of the Emperor, and the *cavalierizzo* with the sword of his justice; and I bow to His Excellency as, in my mind's eye, I see him between the Duke d'Alba and the count di Benevento. I do not see the prelates who are with Caesar, because I do not have an eye that can see priests, saving the grace of my friend, Marzi. I see the *arco del Canto* at the Cuculia. I see the august hilarity and read the titles on all the equipages. I see all the devices of the mother-in-law of our Lord. I see the figure of Piety with the two fat cherubs upon it. I see the figure of Strength and about it the cuirasses and the helmets; and of all the inventions, I am pleased with the liberality of the horn, from which flows crowns, among them that of the king of the Romans and that of the king of Tunis, but the other, which appears half out, belongs rather to our day. I see Faith with cross in hand and the vase at her feet, and the words are divine; and the arch with the eagle and the inscription appears to me tremendous. I find unique the story in which is figured the flight of the Turks, and the coronation of Ferdinand is very fine, and even more beautiful from the fact that Caesar is present. I see, on the other side, the bound prisoners with their barbarous faces, the strange habits on their heads and their varied gestures; and I give great thanks to the father and to the son who so graciously have brought together this great mass. But that flight of horses on the facade of San Felice is marvelous. I see Faith and Justice, bare swords in hand, hunting down Barbarossa. I see the dead under the terrible horses. I see the painting which is a design of Asia and the sculpture which is a sketch of Africa. I see on the base the car filled with spoils and trophies. I see the sweating of the lads who, in accordance with ancient usage, bear the litter. I see the king of Tunis in a coronation history. I see victories with their most gracious epigrams, with all the beauty that there is above and below, and it seems to me that I am one of those who have stopped with upturned face to admire the miraculous work. I see the *via Maggia*, the *ponte a Santa Trinita* and the *strada del Canto* and the Cuculia, all filled with crowds in bizarre attitudes. Beyond this, I see being brought to perfection the new *fabrica*. I see the wood, thanks to your brush, not different from variegated stones. I see Hercules strangling the hydra, and I feel sure that the living one was not so robust, nor so short-necked, nor so full of nerves, nor so thick with muscles as that which has issued from the gifted hands of my friend,

[87]

Tribolo. I see, near the *ponte Santa Trinita*, the river d'Arno, like bronze, and I perceive that it is raining the same waters. I see the other rivers, and Bagradas of Africa, and the Iber of Spain. The spoil of the serpent brought to Rome is natural, as are the horns of plenty and the letters; but one should know that they are from the hands of Tribolo. I should like the second palm to be given to Friar de' Servi, since he is a disciple of the master, and since it is characteristic of most friars to be able to do nothing but kill their soup. Now the Wolf mountain in the river of Germany and of Pannonia is borne by no other than a man of merit, and the bases of this work which are wrought in so delicate a manner, are not new to me. I am sorry the aforesaid exquisite Tribolo did not have time, or he surely would have done such a horse of fate that the one by Leonardo at Milan would be forgotten. I see the Victory, palm in hand and with the bats' wings, at the corner of the Strozzi; and if I did not have a good stomach, I should vomit at seeing that bean-faced Victory with the swollen arm. And yet, I tell you, the one who did it is prouder of it than the emperor, in whose honor such marvels are made. But it's the truth that the most stupid always get ahead by having more money than reputation. I see the colossus clad in the golden fleece, and his gleaming sword strikes me with fear. I see the trophies and I read the histories painted on the base with the Jason, an impression of His Majesty, but the big fat friar would burst if he did not make it clear to others that he is the friar in this *Morgantaccio* of his. I see above the portal of Santa Maria del fiore the inscription between the two great eagles with the grotesques; and I know how much praise they merit for having come from Giorgio, the pilgrim intellect. I lose myself, upon entering the church, in the splendor of the lights reverberating in the gold of the draperies. I see the Justice and the Prudence in the *via dei Martelli*, much maltreated by the one who made them; as is the *mondaccio*, although it is the best of them. Meanwhile I re-create for myself the view in the *Pace* in the rear of the palace of the Medici, the arms lighted by the torch; and it was with good reason that in the most worthy place of the city this was the work the most praised. It was a happy thought to adorn with verdure the ornate *casa*, to make it look like a room of the woodland gods; and the parted foliage has I cannot tell you what appearance of sacredness and religion, which is well suited to the ardor of the heat. And, to conclude, I have seen all this in the sample of your work. To get an idea of the greatness of our leader, one must see such preparations as these. In short, it would not be possible to find more beautiful things nor ones more appropriate to the titles and the distichs in praise of the emperor.

From Venice, the 7th of June, 1536.

To THE CAVALIER MALVEZZI   XXIV
    In Praise of Friendship and Sincerity.

It has been many a day since I had a letter that moved me more than yours. And the gentle affection which issues from the kindness of your heart is evident to me in the words you write: it is a gift which your gentle blood has conferred upon you. It is a noble thing to love a woman, and it is divine to wish a virtuous man well, for love, directed to virtue, has in it something of the quality of God; it, more-over, endures forever and cannot be diminished by envy or jealousy. It is for this reason that I esteem great the love you bear me, not because my own merit is great, but be-cause you make me worthy of it, since you appear to see in me the qualities of which I have spoken. But with what service, with what labor can I ever repay that cordial benevo-lence of yours? If I shall be able to repay it otherwise, I shall do so, but if not, good will will have to be paid in good will, and I shall endeavor to feel for you the affection you feel towards me. I thank you for having remembered me to Colonna; you really ought to call him Pompey the Great and to pride yourself also on having been his patron, since in all his deeds your own miraculous greatness shines with the most real splendor; just as I do not doubt will shine one day that bitter honesty with which I have followed the path of truth. . . I can only hope that the goodness of my nature will be confessed, from year to year, in the same manner in which you confess it, although, so far as the world is concerned, I might call myself happy if I could only be satisfied with a lie as I am with the truth. And yet the name which, with the just, I have acquired by being what I am, to me is infinite riches. I am one who will bear poverty sooner than he will a lie. But let him go. He will not find a pretext in the Marchesa di Pescara letter; nor, by rendering me incapable of sending him one with all my accustomed diligence, will he convince me that he is a veracious person. Who will ever believe that I am in the habit of begging? Such a mistake comes from my having judged that they were not worthy of true fame, having written them only upon occasion and familiarly. It is certain that they are deserving of little praise, and if they have any, they should attribute it to the courtesy of others. And I am not proud merely because I do not go to excess when I speak of them. And so, I await your wishes.

From Venice, the 20th of June, 1536.

To SIGNOR DON LUIGI DA LEVA   XXV
In Which He Celebrates Antonio da Leva, Dead at Marseilles.

Since your great father has known so well how to live and how to die, put from you all overplus of grief, which merely places upon the shoulders of the heart the compassion of the flesh. And since his end has made room for your principality, commence, then, to exercise in the field of his merits the thoughts which he exercised in the pursuit of fame, with whose wings he has taken flight for all time over all the world. Bringing on his own death by going to France, he has willed to die at the peak of glory, as a thing that is blessed. Though God many years before had taken him from the commonalty of men, while consenting that his wonder-ful spirit should lodge in his members; for he, abandoning his body in the presence of his most lofty emperor, gave completely the last happy touch of his measureless virtues—those virtues which, with invincible hands, have wreathed laurel crowns for all the victories of Caesar. What life was ever more deserving of the death that the great Antonio met, who spent himself in the sight of Augustus and in the bosom of the most famous and most glorious of armies that the sun of our day ever saw? And that nothing might be lacking, his praises, his honors, his fame and his glory have drawn tears from the eyes of Charles' great Majesty. And his bones, surrounded by friendly armies, disdaining enemy soil, with terrible pomp, as though in the triumph that was his due, have been brought back to Italy as true relics by an ardent soldiery, all of which was a miracle to those gener-ous souls who, with sane mind, recalled how even in the loss of his natural forces he had been able to win so many hopeless wars. Surely, future centuries will have cause for astonishment, when they hear from history how every prince who was revered and feared, revered and feared him. And I do not know if Alexander, raising himself from a base so low, attained a greater height. There is no confine in the summit of the heavens which has not heard his name. His effigy remains in the hearts of his soldiers who, laden with spoils and adorned with prayers, have borne his death with the same patience with which he supported his labors. Death could bring no fear to the intrepid heart of so great a captain, because he, used to meeting death in battle and at every hour, did not dread the latter's terrors.

And now, let us speak of myself who, losing my genius in the infinity of his praise, am still unable to praise him; and hence, although I have been elevated by his beneficences,

I am unable to get up the heat to speak of them, and I am ashamed not to speak of them. Surely, I should like to sculpt with my pen those virtues of his which never sighted anything so terrifying of aspect that they recoiled from doing what he thought to be useful and honorable. I should like also to paint a picture showing how the insolence of unexpected circumstance was never able to oppress him, circumstance being rather itself perturbed. He not only saw what was to come and what was to be fled, but perceiving it, he could not be deterred by any labor or peril from carrying out the work he had begun. It is well known that, in the course of military discipline, there was no task looked upon as difficult or impossible which he did not overcome; but always, with an invincible superiority, he removed enemies and fears from his path. His foresight, wrapped in its own proper spirit, took the palm from the readiest hands, the most audacious minds and the most robust beings that ever were.

From Venice, the 15th of November, 1536.

To Signor Ercole, Duke of Ferrara   XXVI
*In Which He Describes the Delusion of the Venetians
over the Delayed Arrival of the Duke.*

If, the minds of men being like the wind, the wind had a form like men, I, Signor, would teach it to crucify those good folks who are awaiting your coming with the same bounding heart with which cardinals draw on the stockings of the Pope. How cruel it was on Sunday to see, on all the balconies of the Grand Canal, angels and archangels consuming themselves over the arrival of Your Excellency! And what compassion I felt at seeing myself there with all the tribes of Israel at table! My own fate was enough, which had kept me for a year and a half fixed in the hope of Your Highness' coming; this was enough without any more. I survived the crush at the appearance of the queen and her consort, the duchess; but I was not able to do so at your entrance, for the uncomfortable and cursing crowd kept crying, "He's coming!" and "He won't come" and "There he is! There he is!" like loafers at a race track. But, above all, you brought anger to the legion of lads who were turning the synagogues upside-down, not to speak of the Jews who were trying to put them in order, the expense of which left wounds in their purses like those a friend leaves in the flesh. But if Aeolus, the cheat, who was the cause of all this, had not been possessed of the discretion of a priest, he would have had the good sense to quiet down and let you reach this paradise. I say paradise, for here you will not encounter any of those looks with which avaricious and insatiable Rome eats you alive; here, they will, rather, look at you with the light of kindness as they reverently place you in the seat of honor. You will see here not the bucentaur, but a theatre encircled, in the form of firm and lofty columns, by most just Brutuses and Catos; they court the serenity of their prince who, placed in the middle, appears to be the architect of feeling, and with the altitude of their countenances, they give laws and liberty to the world. You will see all this of which I am telling you, and we shall see, for once, a lord and not a mere executor of exequies, as a great master appears to me to be, who, with his balanced pomps, enters a city not to rejoice it but to render it disconsolate with his funereal shows. And perhaps you have found it necessary to draw the rapier or to lay a price on the heads of subjects in order to re-embellish your court, as kings have to do? Certainly, Your Most Excellent Lordship has the favor of God, of fortune and of nature, which has lost no time in making you happy, before cold blood turns the generous mind of youth into a mercenary. Ah, well! come and, coming, accompany the superb pomp of your arrival with the splendor of liberality, for it is the breath of that voice which announces to all the world that you are here. Have no doubt of it, a triumph without the adornment of courtesy is not

[93]

worth as much as one of those fine fellows in the *piazza* with a velvet coat on his back, a ragged jerkin and a rag-tag-and-bobtail of a family at his heels. For my part, I am more inclined to praise the brocade and fine cloth which with you appear to be the rooms and chambers of the mind, than those who in the ducal palace cause wonderment to be astonished. And so, come, whether the wind wills it or not.

From Venice, the 24th of January, 1537.

To THE SIGNOR ERCOLE, DUKE OF FERRARA   XXVII
In Which He Thanks Him for a Distinguished Gift.

Your Highness, my lord, who excels every other prince in intellect and humanity, must for that very reason excuse me for not having come to make my reverence in your palace; since this has not been due to pride nor ingratitude nor ignorance, but purely to modesty and a knowledge of my own lowliness, which, while you were here, always suc-ceeded in cooling the heat of my ardor, inspired by the obli-gations I feel toward you and the affection that I have for you, though my impulse was to run to your feet. And in any case, without merit as I am, I should have broken the bonds of respect if I had not restrained myself and been restrained by the multitude of your occupations, as well as by the fact that there was no one at hand properly to introduce me into your sight. Messer Nicolo Buonleo and Messer Agostin da Mosto will tell you faithfully with what submission I besought them that, when the proper time for kissing your hand had come, they would let me know; and when this was not done, I was convinced that my virtue was not dear to you. But the hundred gold ducats brought me by your ambassador here have fastened on me the snare of servitude, and I shall ever after be faithful to you. And my faith has grown since it has been made clear to me that only the duke of Ferrara can equal the signor Ercole. For with all the glories which he may have acquired, a true prince ought to be master of himself and ought to propose and carry out those intentions which are in accord with his own will; he ought to receive into his grace those whom his own judgment selects, and with the gift of his own fantasy, he ought to do that which receives his own approbation, not that which is approved by his favorites. But to do tacit benefits to men is a pure act of God. Behold, his Caesarean Majesty made me a present six months before we were acquainted, and now Your Excellency has three times rewarded me, without knowing me at all. For my part, I esteem it a disgrace for one who knows to trumpet a century in the face of a villainous courtesy which slays the hope that expects but never receives it; and so, all too sweet is the pleasure which presents not hoped for give one. I have experienced this through your own tempered liberality, which I shall compensate with memories that may be eternal. As to the medallion, I am not sending it because a lord like you would deign to honor it with his eyes, but because it is a marvel of the miraculous workmanship of Lione, your lordship's servant, and this should make the gift more innocently valuable, as well as the fact that he is a countryman of mine. The crowd cries you wrong to your back, but such calumny is the privilege of virtue, which is always trampled on by ignorance. Should, then, a spirit that is comparable to the ancients be hunted out of the place where he is more than necessary and which he adorns with his presence? He fled, but who would not have fled, having good comfort? For it is wise foresight to flee the plenitude of fury, since the envy of enemies, most of the time, overcomes the goodness of justice, for justice, altered by the indictments of the calumniator, in the first severe and rigid moves it makes, so terrifies the slandered one that, confounding the pretext in the quarrel, he comes to lose all reason and the one who has committed no sin at all appears a criminal. And then pardon comes, when the virtue of the accused is greater than vice and able to punish the latter with its own ammunition. Without saying any more of this, I kiss the hand of Your Excellency.

From Venice, the 5th of February, 1537.

To Chieti, in Rome   XXVIII
  (*Gian Pietro Carafa, Bishop of Chieti*).
    He Promises Him Public Praises.

Most just man, in you I do not enjoy the kindness of the cardinalate, for the reason that where the thought never was, the rank is not; but, being a Christian, I join with you in thanking God who has clothed your will in such a habit for the interest of the Church, that Church which Paul III. sustains, whose merits in the presence of his modest life will win for him all the days which Peter's gained for him. And whoever doubts that the choice of so many servants of Jesus is preceded by divine inspirations has but to observe the virtue which his judgment has displayed in the selection of these. O saint of old, if glory were to be acquired by adding ornaments to the sacredness of the Vatican, what would Your Holiness merit who, besides surrounding yourself with such worthy cardinals, and overcoming invincible avarice with your generous mind, have filled that same mind with the treasures which those interpreters of the word have preserved who, in the profundity of their senses, keep the secrets of God; whence it is the false doctrines of Luther shall be drowned in the froth of their own foam, for even while they bark, the fire of malignity boils up in their mouths. Let us, then, exult in Christ because our religion, thanks to His true vicar and your own kind and true example, continues to reprove his venerable princes. Your example restores its chastity, its simplicity and its humility. Your example clothes it with your own charity, your own justice and your own mercy. Your example teaches it your own truth, your own zeal and your own sincerity. She finds in you that order, those offices and those prayers which used to be her weapons when her servants found their riches in her poverty and, like all good pastors, guarded their flocks from the itch and from the bewitchment of heresies which, breath-ing poison and spitting madness, would have caused them to perish. They correct their flocks with the rod of faith delighting them with the sound of the gospel and covering them with the shadow of the name of Christ, taking away their thirst and their hunger at the fountain of his grace and in the meadows of his precepts; and as they do this, their faith throughout the entire world raises altars and offers sacrifices in accordance with the example which you have set the followers of that religion of which I speak. You teach them to purify their minds and to temper their wills and to quiet their spirits: so that the divine will, trans-formed in you, appears that of a cardinal. It works and exe-cutes in your stead all the things pertaining to one who, by such a path, has reached such a position. And since things are thus, the virtuously wretched, who on all sides have fallen a prey to their necessities, now look for relief and they hope, by means of your piety, to obtain sustenance from the best of pontiffs. And when they do obtain it, they will have reason to give breath to the trumpets of the Holy Scriptures, no longer, with the voice of despair, having to sound the horn to the defects of others. What miracles may we not hope for from that genius and that intellect, manifesting itself not in episcopacies, which others have given to persons deprived of good custom, of nobility and of doctrine, but providing an honest asylum and a sober convenience, by means of which God may be studied, and adored with studied labors. And what more pious office could you per-form than that of moving His Holiness to offer his hand to the best and wisest, who are trampled under foot by malice and by ignorance? In the field, in the hospital, in the stalls, at the stirrup and at the shrine they are outdistanced by the debauchery of the unjust. And why not take the crosses and seals from the barbers and tailors and adorn the lettered ones? Why not give them to these? And yet, we wonder that others bite back. Whoever does so, do you cut out his tongue with courtesy and stop his mouth with charity, by taking from the infamous and giving to the famous. Take the example of Caesar, who saw the gifts that heaven had given me and, seeing at the same time that those gifts were going begging, consoled me. And His Majesty, who is, without any deception, a celestial man, a column of the holy laws, a paragon of clemency, the hero of Christ and the enemy of demerit, has done all this as an honor to my own free virtue, giving me good cause to write and speak well of him. What more? Our Redeemer entered into the heart of Saul in such a manner that Saul became the trumpet of His name; even as I shall become a trumpet to the ministers of his temple, being an imitator of august charity. All of which I do not believe and do not hope, because there is nothing to hope and nothing to believe.

From Venice, the 7th of February, 1537.

To Signor Valerio Ursino   XXIX
    He Blames Lorenzino for the Assassination of Ales-
    sandro de' Medici.

Of what nature is that enmity which fortune bears the felicity of men, Your Lordship has had a chance to judge in the case of our duke, and you have also seen what happens to a man who is subjected to her caprices. There are two ends which a ruler may expect of her instability: high station and a precipitous fall, although, as the fall is greater than the climb, so the number of those who fall is greater than those who mount. And all this comes about because she, who is neither constant nor reasonable, is in continual conflict with constancy and reason; and so, any one who leans on her is ruined. What happiness would be his who rules, did not this fate always hold him by the hair? As to her origin, the Platonists and Aristotelians babble their own opinions, but I,

in the science of my ignorance, am convinced that this fate
is a humor of the stars, combined with the caprices of the
heavens, and it seems to me that this wicked world is merely
a ball with which they play, bouncing now up, now down,
in accordance with their suggestions. I confess that more
evils come from our own faults than by reason of her, and
I am certain that His Excellency might have been able to
guard himself against her. He had too limitless a faith in
himself, in his parentage and in the great wife whom he had
secured. But what sort of humanity is this to which we
belong which will permit one who strikes his own prince
down to be praised? Is it possible that the words of Cicero
have supplanted the example of God, who always sees to it
that such a one imitates the end of Brutus and of Cassius?
Oh! if only minds could be seen as plainly as works, how
many judges would change their opinions, calling that
"infamy" which now appears to every one to be glory; for
ambition and the worst heat of envy soil their sword in the
generosity of others' blood, and these are the more audacious
in their attempts, the more eager they are for position. But
since others are not ashamed to follow ambitious and envious
counsels, vileness has given the name of "glorious" to disgrace. Read well and see with what fine proems Cicero
exalted Caesar as soon as he saw him at the summit of his
greatness. I am sure he knew how to convert eloquence into
adulation; and the discourses which he formerly had pronounced on tyranny were but snares which, even as he
breathed those speeches, he was holding over the heads of
those who were to cut off his head for this. There is no
doubt that one who became a Tiberius or a Caligula carved
a statue to the one he had put under the ground. But for
one who rules the people with an unheard of justice, his
days should grow with his days. I speak the truth, and not
out of the hatred I bear the one who has taken away my
benefactor. Certain it is one who was not ashamed to accept
benefits from such a man, ought not to be ashamed to render

him obedience, and if he is ashamed, let him eat his own bread or another's and then kill him, for that would be a more praiseworthy thing. Fine honor those persons acquire who attempt to cast down those who have raised them up! But since it is a custom common to the seed of the Medici to do good to those who do them evil, I, saying no more, kiss the hand of Your Most Illustrious Lordship.

From Venice, the 10th of February, 1537.

To Cardinal Caracciolo   XXX
In Which He Defends Himself against the Charge of Having Written against Charles V.

Justice, Monsignore, which does not wish to be held injustice, concedes to every malefactor the right to defend himself against the accusations which are heaped on his head, nor would he even then be sentenced by you if you had not first verified the crimes to which he had confessed; this procedure is observed by the authorities and the constables in every bailiwick. But my innocence, on the other hand, is condemned by the great majority of persons in very respectable places, even before I myself know what the thing is for which I am blamed. As witness to this, take the volume, not a mere letter, which others would like to make appear was written by me to the most illustrious Count Guido Rangone in prejudice to Caesar, whose praise can neither be increased nor diminished. And inasmuch as the author of that ribaldry has endeavored to color the face of his lies with the brush of my truths, without any further certification, it is sent to Don Lope, as a reproof to him for the offices which his Mercy has done me, just as though it were not the honest thing for one who pretends to have the honor of His Majesty at heart to do what he can to aid him. Patron of mine, if calumny did not find the ears of princes open to its feigned exclamations, the suspicion and ignorance which follow it would not be able to make you believe what is not so and what could not be so. I am convinced that at least the Cardinal Caracciolo, with his long experience, would have recognized the fact that it is envy that brings libel, if it had not been that fraud and intrigue kept him absorbed, and that as soon as he read the poisonous slanders he would have experienced from the hand of truth the lash of penitence. However, I have been more offended by the credence which the slender judgment of others has given him than by the attempt to break the bonds of that good will conceded to me by august kindness. A certain Fragnano relates to me that, although many foolish things come out in Milan under my name, practically every one knows that they are not mine; which goes to show that the people are better judges than the senators. I, when I launch this or that thunderbolt, go ahead and do it, without reflecting that, after the deed, the humility of penitence may absolve me from indignation or from peril. My nature demands the privilege of speaking fully and freely, nor is my mouth ever to be sewed up; and heaven, which made me like this, assures me at the same time of the fear of men. But let us turn to the count, who is not so far removed from the world that we may not enlighten him. If he should affirm that I have written him that which Christ himself cannot say I have written, but which it may be believed I have written, then who carried the letter? Who copied it? From where did it come? And where is it now? If he says no, you will be satisfied. I speak of this to you for the reason that you take precedence over all the rest, not because I think you believe that I am in the wrong. In which case, quiet yourself, for Your Lordship is not the person to accept vituperations composed in so vile a manner, nor did you ever see a letter from me which exceeded a folio in size. But suppose we let that go. If money well falsified and diamonds well counterfeited are discovered by the keeper of the mint and the jeweler, who can doubt that those who know will be able to say whether malignity has succeeded in imitating the pith of my pen or not? And,

I may tell you, the count told his consort there was one in Carmigliola who had defamed Fregoso under my name; and in witness of this, there is a note from the hand of the countess to the ambassador Soria. And when the signor Luigi Gonzaga was asked about it, he, upon hearing of the affair, wrote to me: "I cannot believe that you would have used such terms toward my kinsman; and besides, it is not merely difficult, but next to impossible to imitate you." So you see, the prudence of his accurate foresight did not flame up in anger against me, for where gratitude is concerned, I do not yield first place to any one; and if the glory of the great Charles could be made greater, I should be the one to increase it. Even the stars do not see the devotion I have to the merits of the divine emperor. And the memory of the eternal Antonio da Leva has left such roots in my heart that I hope I shall not die without having paid the debt I owe him. Read what I wrote to the two of them in Sivigliano, and then you may talk. Read my letter thanking His Majesty for the pension, and see in what honor I hold His Highness. But since reason sometimes does not understand, where the pertinacity of incredulity is minister to minds bearing the stamp of first impressions, the good Castaldo, cavalier without flaw, shall plead my cause. O Christ! I who, not to cast any shadow upon my service to His Highness, have not consented, either for promises or for gifts, to salute with the winds that blow toward France, must I be sworn on a Bible for a trifle with the others? But without further argument, upon seeing that their most serene lordships are touched in the matter, whoever affirms such a thing ought to be ashamed; for since they, by the unmeasured greatness of their free laws, have let me make a place for myself in life in this unique and nourishing city, I am thereby dedicated to the service of them all. And as the good folk know, I, for ten years, have always celebrated the day on which I was taken under the hem of Venetian clemency. But I have no desire, in justifying myself, to make such liberty my shield. I will come to you, if you wish me to do so; I will enter into prison and make my deposition to the Caesarean pleader, who shall have no cause to repent the fact that he has been my benefactor; and these tests to which I am willing to put myself shall drive away the clouds of malignity from the sun of my faith. And so, may you forget my contumacy, which I hope has been purged in the sincerity of my excuses. Sift the truth, the simple and inno-cent truth, and it will verify all that I say, and change your ill will to good, for it would be too insolent a temerity, if I were to be punished for the defects of others. I have not the type of mind which pays attention to whatever others may say or write, who do not perceive that I always proceed against the vicious with a sharp reprehension and not in cold malice; for a pure malice is the sustenance of those who, very wrongly, would load me with blame. Nor will it be too much for you to believe things to be as I swear to you they are.

From Venice, the 25th of March, 1537.

To SIGNOR GIAMBATTISTA CASTALDO   XXXI
  On The Same Subject.

Putting together, my brother, all the pains I have ever endured, I could not make them equal what I have suffered at Don Lope's not being able to understand that the letters handed to him by the cardinal and written against the emper-or and Antonio da Leva, whose great kindness to me has so usurped the affection of my soul, did not come from me; so that I actually appear ungrateful to you, my other bene-factors. The one who gave credence to this, with two blows, has attempted to mar the face of my honor: one, by attempt-ing to make me appear ungrateful for the gifts of His Majesty and Your Highness; the other, by conveying the impression that I am not what I am, but some sort of dullard, for that is what the composition of the letter which I have spoken of would indicate. Look at the copy written to his eminence, which I am sending you with this letter, and then compare the intellect of the one who, out of envy, has tried to counterfeit me. May God never come to my aid, if a stripling of fifteen, who had asked me for an amorous letter, which I caused to be composed by a youth who was rarely versed in doctrine and poetry, did not recognize the thing as not being mine. It is the truth that courtezans have better insight than great lords. It will soon be known who is the author of such outrages, for treason and conspiracy cannot remain underground. And when the villain has been found who, by falsifying virtue, deserves a punishment other than does he who falsifies the coin of the mint, I only ask that he be left to my anger. For where my fame is concerned, I will not bear it, since a man who permits his honor to be taken, permits his life to be taken,[1] and who does not resent such an affront as this is a beast in the form of a man. Nor have I anything else to say to Your Lordship.

From Venice, the 25th of March, 1537.

To MESSER GIANNANTONIO DA FOLIGNO   XXXII
    In Praise of Himself.

My happiness, virtuous man, would be too great, if only every one who doubts that golden virtue which I have of God would but put it to the test; for I am certain that all then would employ the same office which you have employed in the letter which you have been pleased to send me. Hence, I bless the reason that led you in the past to deign to read my writings, since by that means I have acquired such a friend as you. Certainly, my compositions deserve not to be read on account of their low and little spirit, and not because they contain no malice. I laugh at the public which finds fault with them, because it is its custom to blame laudable things while praising the disgraceful ones, and it is also its

---

[1]Cf. Shakespeare's "Who steals my purse," etc.

[104]

nature to seek to make a hue and cry by every means in its power. You see, it is like this, I happen to touch one of the great ones and as I do so, this and that ruffianly courtier begins to whisper and, with his studied insults, baptizes me in his own manner, thinking that he is robbing me of favor. Some one else does it in order to appear to be one of us, and not because there is in him either goodness or good judgment; and so it is, the innumerable disciples of ignorance with sinister intent kick under heel the honors of others. I have written what I have written for the sake of virtue, whose glory had been captured by the darkness of the avarice of lords. And before I commenced to lacerate those lords, the virtuous were begging the honest commodities of life, and if any one retrieved himself from the vexations of necessity, he achieved it as a buffoon and not as a person of merit, whence it is, my pen, armed with its own terrors, has so affected the great ones that they, coming to their senses, have taken in the fine intellects with a forced courtesy more hateful than want. The good, then, ought to hold me dear, since with my blood I have always fought for virtue, and it is by me alone, in this our day, that virtue wears a brocaded vest, drinks from golden cups, is adorned with gems, has collars and money, rides in cavalcade with the queen and is served by the empress and revered as a goddess; and it would be impious not to say that I have restored it to its antique state. And since I am its redeemer, what are envy and the mob babbling about? My brother, I do not make this boast out of pride, but merely to reply to the one who may affirm that my gospels are no more than slander. My gifts come to me by the streets which my own safe arms have made, making sport of intrigues and lordly ambuscades; and then they turn to the praise of God, as I turn myself, since it all has been wrought by His grace and not through my own genius. And this shall be my effort for the future, so to live that when I die, even those who in the past would have laughed at my death will weep for me. Let there be between us a contract of perpetual friendship, and let the punishment, which, with so many warm words, you say you wish me to give you for your past incredulity—let that punishment be the bond of brotherhood which I here pledge you.

From Venice, the 3rd of April, 1537.

To The Count Manfredo di Collalto   XXXIII

In Which He Reminds Him of the Promise of the Gift of a Kid.

Your promising me a kid, my good fellow, was the act of a lord, and your not having kept that promise is characteristic of a priest. I hope you will decide, having been a priest, to be a lord, the title which I must in any event give you when I write to you, whether the kid comes or not. As the morality of the philosophers continues to wash our lives with the waters of truth, it is always wiping out the stains stamped on our members by vice; and our infected clothes, locked in their trunks, always keep the disease of the one who wore them. And it is the very devil to touch so cursed a habit. I do not deny that you are good; but you would have been perfect, if you had not put on your back the domestic habit of Leo. Certainly, you might do worse than, not keeping your word with me, to give as an excuse, "I am a priest"; this, if one admitted it, would be excuse enough, for their truth is lies, their faith deceit and their friendship hatred. And blessed are you who stopped being a priest in time! And if the nobility of your blood and the magnanimity of your nature were any the less in you, woe to Your Lordship! for the lineage of Collalto, both by its antiquity and its virtue, is such that it would be able to make the best of a worse generation than the one I speak of, if a worse could be found. But begging you to take all I have said in good sport, I, with this, salute you.

From Venice, the 6th of April, 1537.

Counsels on the Mode of Governing.

The wretched end, my lord, of His Excellency, and the happy beginning which Your Highness has made have been to me like two thunderbolts which fall upon the shepherd at one time, one of which deprives him of his senses, while the other restores his senses to him. Hearing of his fate tore my heart, and learning of your success has ravished me; whence it is, I have discovered at one stroke the nature of grief and gladness. Surely, the death of no duke could have caused me more sorrow than did that of Alessandro, nor is there any duke living who could possibly have pleased me more than does Cosimo. For I am he who served that great father of yours living and buried him when he was dead. I am he who in Mantua caused him to be honored and wept by those who perhaps would not have honored or wept for him. I am he who took his praises out of the mouths of those who blamed him from envy. I am he who has placed in the hands of the incredulous the torches of his glory. I am he who loved and celebrated him more than all others in the degree to which I, better than others, knew him worthy of love and memory. I amused his labors, comforted his pains and tempered his anger. I to him was father, brother, friend and servant. And when God, to punish the errors of Italy with the scourge of the barbarians, took him away, my virtue kept his name company as my person had kept him company in life, and in my adoration, I have always said that the true honor of the most lofty house of Medici came from his arms and not from the mitres of the Popes. The fruit of his merits is that high station in which heaven perpetuated you on that day on which you were chosen, thanks to the providence of the stars and the good faith of friends. Only a few here and there did injury to their own power and their own will by not voting for you, for you have adorned pres-ence and mind with such graces and virtues that, I hasten to tell you, they have few if any gifts to bring you. But as to your own future, you should endeavor to enlarge the confines of your State, and since you have learned neither to rule nor to live by chance, one may say that you have learned how to rule and how to live. By God, the name and soul of a man deserve to die who holds his appetites dearer than himself and for this cause puts his city and his people to great risk. But his death is the example which shall always be your life, because, under the fear of God and the shadow of Caesar, I am sure you will always guard that continence in which lies more faith and security than there is in armies; for she sleeps in her own bed, eats at her own table, walks in her own halls and, standing on her own honesty, does not betray secrets or favor or money or person to the poisonous darts of others, nor, as she lies alone at night in her bedroom, is her throat cut by that sword which the worst will of envy and ambition lend to the hand of deceit, bringing ruin on the one who was well seated.[1] Make your home with those who wear their hearts on their foreheads,[2] and let the valorous Signoia Maria, your mother, stand near by to give you support and repose. Eat and drink in accordance with your own taste, and not that of buffoons and adulators. May the honor of the Vitellescan seed, valorous and sincere, always stand by your side. Put on the eyes of the good Ottaviano, and be always awake to all who would take your foot to snare it. Let the counsels of Cardinal Cibo be especially grateful to you, for there is in his clarity none of the designs of those who would counsel you to leave the city, for these are merely working for whatever their own liberty desires, and hope and fate open to them whatever paths promise to lead to ascendancy. For who does not want to be a lord deserves to be a slave, and it is better to be patron of Florence than to be good fellow to the world. It was cheapness and not sanity of mind that led Celestino to refuse the

[1]*Che ben siede*: cf. our "sitting pretty."
[2]Cicero again.

papacy. Since you have come to power without violence of any sort, you ought all the more to endeavor to strengthen yourself in your dominion. Who is offended, who is robbed, who is hunted down, who is vituperated, and who is threatened by you? It is the evil-minded who will not confess that God has placed you on high as the legitimate heir to that grandeur in which the son-in-law of Augustus lived and reigned. That ferocity with which your tremendous sire fought for you should make you feared, even as you are loved. And as your own great qualities grow with the years, you will be sought out by all who flee you; and then that clemency, which is your ornament, will have a chance to make itself known to those who have not willed to know it. In the meanwhile, I commend myself to you as your humble servant.

From Venice, the 5th of May, 1537.

To MESSER PAOLO PIETRASANTA   XXXV
He Philosophizes on the Desire to Learn.

My ignorance, wise man, vaunted by your learning, is like a vile man praised by a courageous one, who remains an object of scorn despite all the noise he makes to give the impression that he is what a lie has made him out to be. Your asking me whence comes the desire to learn, which leads the wise over all the seas and lands of the world, implies that I am able to give you the reason; and since I am not what I seem to be in this case, in attempting to give you the reason, I remain as foolish as the coward of whom I have spoken. Our souls, created among the intelligences of heaven, upon being infused into those bodies which their stars, by God's power, have chosen, are no sooner locked in their prison of flesh than, through the life which lodges them, they give birth to spirits, and these spirits, on account of their origin, burn continually with a desire to understand those things which their Master, who endows the angels, has to teach them; and then, these spirits of which I have told you, enamored of their own desire, find their greatest pleasure in attempting to discover the secrets of God and of nature. It was, I believe, just such a passion as this that moved Daedalus, Melampus, Pythagoras, Homer, Museus, Plato, Democritus, Apollo, Dionysus, Hercules and the other god-like ones. But it is to be noted that this tempered will to know is not to be perceived in all, although the soul may be of equal virtue in them all, and this comes from the mortal wall, which is more or less rugged. When souls (which are a spark of divine simplicity and pure goodness) enter the vases prescribed by their Creator, the spirits foretold discover outside a great desire to learn, and this desire is greater or less as the mansion which houses them is more or less transparent; and for this reason, the soul showed in Demosthenes effects other than in Thersites. You may laugh, if you like, at my rustic philosophy, and, indeed, I have written it to make you laugh, but it was the profound letter which, with your accustomed courtesy, you directed to me that started me off on these ravings, which are but the shadow of shadows. If my fate had willed that you should know me in person, as you display a desire to do, you would have learned to speak only the truth; and I should have been pleased, for you would not then have been praising me with fictions. I am not worthy enough for a man like you to put himself out to know me, but perhaps such a one may be permitted to entertain the remote thought. But all my concern is for Messer Giulio Cesare, my son no less than yours, who is all too dear to us. And he, in his affection, only spoke the truth when he told you how I had praised your compositions and in what reverence I held you; the rest are but flowers to adorn the conversational garland which you are pleased to pluck for me. But I am grateful to him above all for the fact that my name has been honored by the tongue and the pen of a Pietrasanta, the happy interpreter of sacred writings. And hereafter, may Your Lordship make such disposition of me as of your-

self, for I am become yours; and write to me, as I shall write
to you, with the same affection with which I write to the
emperor.

From Venice, the 11th of May, 1537.

To MESSER GIANNANTONIO SERENA   XXXVI
    Virtuous Counsels
    The rich and brazen audacity of the evil ones is the cause
of that buzzing of tongues which others raise against you;
fame also is the cause of that error into which those fall who,
proud in their own faculties, hold that all they do and say is
well done and well said. Is it possible that you would not
want to know at least a particle of yourself, giving material
to envy to proceed against you with calumny and with
malediction? Regard a little the peril of honor and the dam-
age of the soul. Look at God, who has established the institution of matrimony in order that the human species might
multiply and one take another's place, so that each generation, being conscious of the gift of life from His goodness,
may keep the seats of paradise filled with spirits. And
nature has placed the desire of coitus in different sexes in
order that, the limits of life being brief, we may be renewed
in our sons; for this reason, the joining of the male and the
female has been found to be nature, a providence which, by
its unbroken succession, has preserved the race to our times.
What injury could be worse and one bringing with it more
cruelty than that which would take from one's self and one's
wife the titles of father and mother; for these names are
worthy of all veneration, and all honors are their due.
It is a fine thing to follow the good way of life, adorning
with one's own modesty that virtue which is neighbor to
God, observing natural decrees, copulating at the proper
times, becoming fathers of a noble seed and confirming them
in the orderings of that prudence which he who first created
us gave, to the end that the consciousness of having done

[111]

otherwise may have no cause to heap reproach upon us for our own sin.. Turn, then, to the love of your companion, in whom shines the grace of color. Her tresses, falling over her shoulders, her temples and her neck, are as brilliant as hyacinths entwined with the subtlety of art, the skill of which, on the side, by her ears, and at the summit of her forehead, makes her as rich as are the bees of the meadow. And crystal is not so clear as is her inviolable chastity, a miraculous treasure in these shameless times. And so, you should lead a life full of rejoicing and in it bring up the heir to your patrimony. You are healthy, young, rich and most prudent; whence, if you but hold in rein your precipitous inclinations, life will be a great happiness for you. Free yourself of false friends and consort with the true, seek the intimacy of honorable persons and not of infamous ones, for the former give reputation and the latter take it away. Otherwise, your wealth, your reputation and your life will always be in great risk. I look upon you as a companion and a son, and age and duty inspire the affection with which I write to you. And I would rather have you goaded with reproofs than greased with adulations.

From Venice, the 12th of May, 1537.

To MESSER FRANCESCO DA L'ARME   XXXVII
    Of Things Properly Literary

   I, courteous friend, who held that I had been excluded from your memory, was greatly rejoiced to hear that I am still alive to you and, thanks to you, still have a part in the life of others. You are, indeed, honored, since, while remembering old friends, you are constantly acquiring new ones, and in acquiring them you observe the conduct of a gentleman and satisfy the behests of your nature, which always finds pleasure in friendship. It is certain that no one can know what is gentleness or true familiarity who has not practiced it with you; and the most grateful amusement which eligible foreigners find in that city is the entertainment afforded by your pleasant manners. Since this is so, do not wonder if I am constantly jealous of losing you; I would rather be forgotten by a prince than by such a person as you. And in this, our Don Antonio concurs with me, in whose *Croniche* my name stands at the head of the table of contents, smiling out from that sonnet that killed Broccardo. But what would I have done to him with deeds, if I killed him with words? My cavalier Bucchi ought to make mention of this in his *Annali*, which you say he is doing, di *Bologna*. Your Lordship has taken a load off your own back, since no other than a Bolognese would be suited to write the deeds of this and that count. I am grieved, as I am at the life of one who does not deserve to live, by the fact that, having no new compositions, I am not able to appease the desire of prelates and nobles who would like them. Old age makes my genius grow lazy, and Love, which ought to keep it awake, puts it to sleep in my case. I used to turn out forty stanzas every morning; now I scarcely produce one. In seven mornings I composed the *Psalms*, in ten the *Courtezan* and the *Marescalco*, in forty-eight the two *Dialogues*, in thirty the *Life of Christ*. I suffered six months in the production of the *Sirena*. I swear to you, by that truth which is my guide, that, beyond a few letters, I write nothing. For this may Monsignor di Parenza, to whom I owe much for the pleasure he takes in my stories, di Mairoica, di Santa Severina and their nephews pardon me; as soon as I produce something worthy of them, they shall have it. In the meanwhile, I kiss the hands of their most reverent lordships. Nor is it news to me that the archbishop Cornaro and the bishop of Vercelli hold the court which cardinals ought to keep, giving shelter to all sorts of virtuosi, because they are real persons and of illustrious origin. Commend me to the good count Cornelio Lambertini, whose peace has been perturbed by the sweet and puissant desire for glory of his young son, who is not suspicious enough of the faith which war keeps with the most valorous. Salute for me Messer Oppici Guidotti, from whose house poets go as sinners do from a church. Say to my good friend, Girolamo da Travigi, the painter, and to Giovanni, the sculptor, that I am utterly theirs. Finally, I beseech you, if my prayers are as powerful with you as your commandments are with me, offer my services to the signor Mario Bandini, who is elegance, courtesy and gentleness itself.

From Venice, the 15th of May, 1537.

To Messer Agostino Ricchi   XXXVIII
Striking a Balance.

I am glad, most learned son, that wretches blame me; for if they praised me, it would seem that I was like them. The envious, when they offend my virtue, think they are making me sad, when as a matter of fact, they delight me, because I know that I am beginning to become glorious when I am envied. I implore God that he who envies me may have eyes in all the places from which my happiness comes, so that he may see it bursting forth by a thousand paths. The ribald hold me a villain, because I am not a flatterer, and they call me a pauper to injure me, but they honor me by doing so, for he who is poor is good. I only desire what I need to keep from being odious, and not so little as to move others to have compassion on me; and I shall have it, in any manner. My hope promises me this, which is just, because it springs from some merit. But if the greatest faculty in the world is the ability to give to friends, who has more than I, who have given everything in order that I might not be like the princes, who are avaricious of gold and liberal with glory? I, to the shame of those who say I have nothing, may tell you that I have had ten thousand *scudi* from 1527 to the present day, not counting the cloth of gold and silk which has been worn on my own back and those of others; a pen and a little paper have drawn these out of the heart of avarice. I am, indeed, a king, because I know how to rule myself. In short, let others say of me what they will, I know how to conquer perversity with patience and with kindness, qualities which I employ in making myself praised. As you know, Ambrogio[1] up to now has done marvels; indeed, for a mere lad, he is doing miraculously well, and there is an excess of judgment and of style in those verses of his, which he always has in his bosom or up his sleeve, as if he were the ass of his own muses. Pretty soon, since hope is a habit that sits well on the back of everybody, he will be hoping to satisfy his desires with a woman so that he can make sport of Narcissus.

From Venice, the 10th of May, 1537.

To CAESAR   XXXIX
    Praises.

Your Majesty, sovereign emperor, has such a destiny that, if the greatness of the heavens were only a little less, you would equal or come near equalling it; and the world which takes your measure regards as immeasurable the power of Charles. And yet, combining all that you have ever been and all that you have ever done, one does not arrive at what you are or what you do, when the mob reflects that you have taken the king[2] and made the pope[3] prisoner and hunted down the infidels of Hungary and, in conquering Africa, have liberated eighteen thousand Christians from their chains and have entered the heart of France with your army. The miracle with which you astonish and terrify the peoples is the universe itself, which bends itself almost wholly to rendering you impotent, and which only succeeds in making you omnipotent, as, in the preparations which you make, your tremendous power becomes apparent. Behold the millions in gold which you have taken from the viscera of Gaul, behold the throngs of asses and the infinite number of

[1] Ambrogio degli Eusebii, his secretary.
[2] Francis I.
[3] Clement VII.

horses, behold the innumerable ships, and behold the Turk. But what is, and what is to be, the state of affairs? What are others doing and what are they going to do? But those who threaten the emperor, who all the while keeps his immobile back to them, are like the gigantic fools who pile mountains on mountains; they are like Nimrod who built the tower, presuming to think he could lift God from his throne, whose power, silent and self-keeping, looks down upon the temerity of pride and disperses it with those thunderbolts in which are concealed the claws of the eagle that Jove gave to Caesar. But the monsters who dared make war on God are less insolent than those chimaera-ridden ones who would combat Caesar; for the former, in what they do are repugnant merely to nature; while the latter are repugnant both to nature and to God. To nature, in that they would force her to do what she is not able; to God, by believing that, in doing wrong, they are circumventing the watch which His goodness keeps over your goodness. I speak with the tongue of the just, who look to Christ as the one who arms the legions of angels; for you, who are the support of your faith, overcome all who, out of envy of your glory, would conquer you. In the meanwhile, the report which was given you of many things in Italy, upon your departure from Genoa, has proved false, and none have turned their backs on Your Majesty, while Florence, in hand with Fortune, does not repent having loved you. But if God and Fate are with Your Highness, who is not with you?

From Venice, the 20th of May, 1537

To THE COUNTESS ARGENTINA RANGONA PALAVICINA   XL
In Which He Thanks Her for Her Continuous Gifts

I, Signora Contessa, happening last night to lift my eyes to the stars, found myself trying to count them, and I had to laugh at myself, because it seemed to me that I was trying to count, one by one, the presents which Your Most Illustrious Ladyship has made me since you were here with us. And as I was telling the joke to some gentlemen, along came your servant who brought me the snuff box with a medallion of gold and twenty-four tags, like those which His Excellency, the count, your husband, brought me the last time he came back from France. And I, ogling it, said: "So this was lacking from all that infinite number!" So you see what a great thing it is you have done by making me this gift. How long is it since I had the two robes of silk of which you despoiled yourself the day you sent them to me? How long is it since I had the veils of gold and the rich sleeves and the most beautiful of bonnets? How long is it since you sent me the ten and ten and eight *scudi*? How long is it since you had the cask placed in my cellar? How long is it since you presented me with the handworked handkerchiefs? How long is it since you placed the turquoise on my finger? It is six months, rather not four. Surely, I shall drown in the deluge of your courtesy. But since I know that you would not change your consort for the emperor, I will not say it is a sin that you are not the wife of His Majesty. I believe that both you and he, in accumulating nothing, accumulate enough for yourselves; and so, you rival yourselves in giving even to him who does not ask of you. But all the lords and ladies would like to be like this and show to all fortunes the same indifference. For nearly ten years, you resided here with a throng of men and women living at your expense, and at Mestre, you had the upkeep of enough people and horses to have drained the sea of water, and not merely your purse of money. But it is true that God is the treasurer to large spenders, and it is even more clear that virtue and faith have gladly pushed the great Guido up to the heavens.

From Venice, the 22nd of May, 1537

To MESSER AMBROGIO DEGLI EUSEBII   XLI

In Which He Dissuades Him from Taking a Wife

I had thought, my son, that I was bringing you up in

poetical studies, and I find that I was supporting you in amorous employments, and when I thought I was listening to your verses I was hearing your sobs. But you would have made less of a mistake in acquiring a friend than in picking a wife. To tell you the truth, I have great compassion for you, because the man who is in love is a wretch, tormented by miserable calamities. But this comes from your not having resisted the first assaults of Love, as I warned you to do; if you had done so, you might have conquered that passion which, when its lustful desires have been satisfied, repents the pleasure it has received. When it comes to marrying, blessed are they who marry by word and refrain from marrying in fact! Do you know whom wives are good for? For those who want to become like Job, for by suffering their perfidy at home, a man is bound to suffer away from home and so become the monarch of patience. Granted that she is as beautiful as you say, you are assuring yourself of her at great peril; if she is ugly, you will become the slave of penitence. And the more you praise the sufficiency of her virtue, the more you will blame your own small judgment, for songs and letters are the keys that open the doors of their chastity. They do not regard matrimony as necessary and sacred, for the reason that their blessings are offspring, the sacraments and faith; but you will be offending the revered name of father, if you desire, by usurping it to become an irreverent son. But the worst of it is the inconvenience which she will give you and you her; for which reason, your free couch will become the servant of strife and the hospital of quarrels. The fact is, you show you are becoming an old man, since you do not always wish to appear a youth; so you had best leave the weight of a wife to Atlas' shoulders. Leave their laments for the ears of tradesmen. Leave their caprices to the man who knows how to beat them and who can put up with them. Cling to the bough of honor, from which the man who gets into trouble over women hangs himself. Come and go from your house

{ 118 }

without saying "whom am I leaving her to and with whom shall I find her," nor let jealousy make a meal of your teeth. Be able to appear in church or in the *piazzo* without fear of that whispering which always goes on behind the back of the husband of any woman. And if you wish an heir, get one with other women; and if the consciousness of adultery gives you remorse, do better still and legitimatize your offspring with your own kindness and their virtue, for every good and virtuous man ennobles his own birth and puts a stop to all talk about the infamy of his mother. And if continence rules your desires, I would laud your prudence and comfort you with Poetry, to whom you are under obligations since she it was who gave you a name before you were likely to be known. Love her and devote yourself to her; if you do not, your fame, which is beginning to spread its wings, will be betrayed by yourself, if you are not ashamed even to think of leaving eternal glory for a lascivious pleasure which lasts but a day.

From Venice, the first of June, 1537.

To Signor Giambattista Castaldo   XLII
   In Which He Urges Him to Restore Her Son to Signora
      Flaminia.

The signora Flaminia, courteous cavalier, has sent me from Rome a second present, pleasing as the first; and he who accepts a gift from another is under obligations to that other, for gifts are the ambassadors of those who hope by means of them to gratify their desires. The short of what I have to tell you is that she, who knows by rumor how dear I am to you, has selected me to obtain from your hands her little son; and so you will pardon me if I, who do not know the causes of your separation, presume with temerity to intercede for her, for it is not right to ask friends for unjust things. Reason, I know, would dictate that, since you are possessed of every rare custom and virtue, I should urge you to keep the child rather than to give him up, for he can be as much better off with you as he is sure to be worse off with her. I am quite susceptible to the supplications of mothers and the sound of the word, because they live and die in the life and death of their children and suffer in their souls when the latter are far away: and so, I beseech you, whatever you would do in this case for any one who asks you, do for me, who in this am entreated by many whom I am glad to have command me. The poor mother would like with the bridle of matrimony to rein the license of an honesty that takes no more pleasure in the delights of the world, and it seems to me that her not having him near her forbids this. But if those voices which are the affections of the soul may pene-trate to the ears of God, may mine, which are formed of affection itself, reach your ears; and then they who are press-ing me in this matter will have to confess that I have done what I could to console her.

From Venice, the 2nd of June, 1537.

To MESSER FRANCESCO MARCOLINI   XLIII
   Of Certain First Fruits.

Surely, my good fellow, if I were in the habit of pecking at my brains as every pedant does, since the cognomen of "divine" has been tacked on the back of my name, I should believe, without doubt, that, as it was the ancient custom to offer to the gods the first fruits of earth and flock, I am, if not a half, at least a third god, in so constant a stream do your presents come, the first fruits of your hand in nature and in art. But knowing as I do that what little virtue I have merely irrigates your own divinity, in order not to become drunk with the latter, I place your gifts to the account of your being too human. You began with orange flowers to sharpen my appetite, pickling them as my maids do the *caccialepri*, pimpernels, dragons and a hundred other kinds of herbs, and these are offered to me in panniers and rush baskets so well woven that, in accepting the salad, it is difficult to return the baskets; and your lady, I am sure, would not make so much fuss about this, if she saw what a good time my women have in taking them. I am sure I do not know where you collect all the varieties of flowers, of violets and pears which, when they do not come bursting out of the bottle, you send to me full-flowered and odorous. Here I have bunches of sweet violets before it is yet April; and here, my lap is full of roses when there is not one to be seen, by a miracle, anywhere. Scarcely do the cherries begin to put on red cheeks before you send me my fill of ripe ones. But where did I leave those strawberries, covered with their native odor of musk? And the cucumbers, which had barely begun to bud and which my Perina and my Caterina leaped to see? Who would not drink from the brilliant new beakers? And who would not annoint his beard and wash his hands with the oil and soap which you so often give me? And who would not clean his teeth with those toothpicks of yours? I am willing to lay a wager with any one who says I was not the one to see the first figs this season, raised in your delight-ful garden. And so I was first with the musk-pears, melons, plums, grapes and fish. But where are the artichokes which you for so long have sent to my table? And where the gourds which I have eaten, fried in the platter, before I would have sworn they were in bloom? Of beans I do not speak, except to remind you in case you have forgotten. And because in all the things you have given me I have glimpsed your heart, I keep those same gifts in my own heart. And it will not be long before I shall pay you as I am able for every tuft of violets, white, vermilion or yellow, with which you have delighted me.

From Venice, the 3rd of June, 1537.

To The Duke d'Atri XLIV

For Praising Frances I, He Wants a Fixed Stipend.

Il Comitolo, the Perugian, most illustrious prince, acting

for his lordship, the most illustrious Count Guido, who is with His Majesty, King Francis, has consoled me by advising me of the words which, in my behalf, your Excellency has had with Monsignor Montmorency, the great *maestro* of France, in the presence of Luigi Alamanni, who is honored by the world and respected by me. All of which I knew before I was told, and I was certain of it before it even occurred to me to doubt it, for your kindness is sincere, and the love you bear me a candid one. Hence, the new hope I have, thanks to your benignity, goes on its own feet, for you have made His Majesty understand that I have been, and forever shall be, his servant, since he is the subject of all the homilies and histories that constitute my work. But the fact that I am not used to living on dreams and have always looked out for myself, together with the glory he has conferred on me, has made me esteemed and well taken care of. For three years I postponed putting on the chain that was to come, and now four years have passed in which there has not come to me so much as a greeting; and so, I have given my allegiance to one who gives without promising. I speak of the emperor, the servant of Christ and lord of fate. Take the case of the Cardinal di Lorena. Seeing in my heart the image of his king, he made me presents, and because the gifts he made me were not enough, he reassured me with hopes which, dissolving into French smoke, made me despair of French affection. But whenever he gives me an honest opportunity, I shall recognize the benefit; and if the great *maestro* will only do what he said he would, I shall exalt him with real honors. And to what person could Alamanno be of assistance, the assisting of whom would be of more assistance to him than would the assistance which he might give to me?[1] But without further assistance, I am the humble servant of His Excellency, the lieutenant-general of His Majesty, and Your Lordship's.

From Venice, the 8th of June, 1537.

[1] A good example of Aretino's word play.

The Duke of Montmorency

On the Same Subject; Four Hundred Scudi a Year

Your Excellency probably has forgotten the affection you showed to me in the promise which you gave me of the neck-lace and in the letter which you addressed to me with the necklace itself; but I have never ceased to remember the favor which you did by promising it to me nor the consola-tion you gave me in sending it. But if God had only granted that you should remember I am your servant, even as I am always mindful that you are my lord, many things that have been said would not have been said, and many that have not been said would have been said. But the motive of the chain, I know, was that I might be quiet forever, since as he saw it, by praising His Majesty,[1] I was telling a lie. But, having no respect for short measure, I have adorned all my letters with His Majesty's name. And when the four hundred crowns a year have been given me for my living, with the truth for which I am known I will speak of the fame of your king; for I am a captain myself, and my malice does not steal soldiers' pay, cause peoples to revolt or betray forts; but with my inky cohorts, and with the truth painted on my banners, I acquire more glory for a prince I serve than armed men do. My pen pays its honors and blame in cash. I, in a morning, without other literary employment, indulge in the praise and the vituperation of those, not whom I adore and hate, but who deserve to be adored and hated. And so, keep the word which you gave in the presence of many, who are now scattered all over Italy; and I shall be all that duty may desire. This comes from the grace which the heavens have given to one most Christian, to whom all show affection and whom all call upon and desire. But if he who, not to fall away from the French nature, never remembers his friends if not in their needs—if he is desired by all, what

---

[1]Charles V.

would he be if he were remembered for all time? In conclusion, I bow to Your Most Illustrious Excellency, in
reminding you how Darius used to say that he would rather
have one Zopyrus for an advocate than possess a thousand
Babylons.

From Venice, the 8th of June, 1537.

To Sebastiano, The Painter, Brother of Piombo XLVI
Of the Baptism of His Own Little Daughter, Adria

Although, father, our fraternal affection needs no other
chains to bind it, I have wished also to cincture it with
those of a godfather, in order that your own benign and
holy way of life might become the ornament of that friendship which virtue itself has established between us eternally.
It has pleased God that the child should be a woman,
although I, no different from the rest of fathers, had wished
it might be a man child, as if it were not the truth that
daughters, all suspicion of honor aside, which must be well
looked to, were not the greater consolation. Look you: the
boy, at twelve or thirteen years, commences to strain at the
paternal bit and, bursting out of school and the bonds of
obedience, makes those who conceived and bore him sorry

for it. But of more importance are the mischief and threats
of mischief with which every night and day they assail their
fathers and mothers, whence come maledictions and the
chastisements of the justice of God. But a daughter is the
couch on which, in his graying years, the one who created
her takes his repose; nor does an hour pass in which her
parents do not rejoice in her lovableness, who solicitously
cares for them in their needs. And so, I no sooner saw a
child in my own image than, putting aside all displeasure
that she was not something else, I was so overcome by the
tenderness of nature that at the moment I experienced all the
sweetness which comes of blood ties. The fear that she might
die before many more days of life caused me to have her

baptized at home; for which purpose, a gentleman in your stead held her in accordance with the Christian custom. I should not have acted so hastily, had I not feared from hour to hour that she would fly away to paradise. But Christ has preserved her to be the amusement of my last years and for a witness to that life which others gave to me and I to her; for all of which I give Him thanks, praying Him that I may live to see her married. In the meanwhile, I must consent to be her plaything, for we are the buffoons of our children. Their simplicity always tramples us under foot, pulls our beard, strikes us in the face, rumples our hair; for it is in such coin as this they sell the kisses and the embraces which bind us. There is no delight which could equal such a pleasure, if the fear of some misfortune to them did not constantly keep our minds perturbed. Every tear they shed, every cry they give, every sigh that comes from their mouths or their bosoms disturbs our very souls. There is not a leaf falls or a hair floats on the air that it does not seem to us a leaden weight which must fall on their heads to kill them; nor does nature break their slumber or dull their hunger without our trembling for their well-being. Yes, the sweet is strangely mixed with the bitter; and the more pleasing they are, the more acute is the jealous fear of losing them. God keep my little daughter, for she is of so gracious a disposition that, if I should lose her, I am sure I should die. Adria is her name, and she is well called that, since in the bosom of the waves by divine will she was born. And I glory in this, for this site is the garden of nature; and I, in the ten years I have lived here, have experienced more contentment than I ever should have known had I lived, despairingly, in Rome. And when fate permitted me to be in your company, I have been happy; for even though we are absent, I esteem it a great privilege to be your friend, fellow and brother.

From Venice, the 15th of June, 1537.

In Which He Promises Not to Speak Ill of the Ladies.

In order that Your Highness may not believe that I am one of those *maestri* of whom it is fitting never to speak the truth, I am writing to you, as I promised you when you were here, to assure you that I regarded it as a happiness to know you, both because of your greatness and because of the opinion which you had of me in the matter of the ladies. I, who am more theirs than are the priests or the devil's friars, have always held them in reverence, but I have kept the thing to myself, for the reason that they have been courtesy itself in their restraint. And I deliberately refrained from praising them until one should have shown herself liberal toward me. But the divinity of the Siren was too much for my deliberation; and so, I was constrained to hymn them in the manner you know and, hymning them, to confess their merits and my own virtue, which attained the fruit it desired in drawing such stanzas from the chaste and pure love which I, paternally, bore them. But I am willing to pledge myself not to speak in the opposite manner, for you seem to be under the impression that I mishandle the ladies as I do the gentlemen, whom I mistreat whenever, through the avarice of others, cricket-whims make a cage of my head, whereupon people begin to crush me with tribute. Surely, the vileness which would have lain in touching them has restrained my tongue and pen, for if this were not so, they would even now be paying me tribute as the princes do, for I would have uncovered all the altars of Naples and Milan and Mantua and Ferrara and of all Italy to find the foolish, the wise, the tradeswomen, the sibyls, the learned, those who work miracles, the ugly and some of the prodigies for the honor of the world. Oh, what a triumph would have been there! Oh, what a fine story could be made out of that! It is no little thing that I know their secrets as well as if I were their confessor. For some thought must be given to the subtlety of the devil and the instability of poets; because, whenever a fit of fury assails me, behold, Rome, Bologna and everything in ruins. But there is no danger for us, since God wills that whoever has any stain in himself should fight with his chameleon nature; and indeed, looking upon your face and hearing the name which the limpid Latin pen of Nicolò Franco had given to your marvelous beauty, the sight and sound made your beauty chaste, glorious and perfect, even as you yourself are, who, by the grace of heaven and through no human favor, have been joined in matrimony to that Ferrante whose virtue harbors the mind of a Caesar. I am sure he could not be the husband of a better wife, nor you the wife of a better husband. For which reason your own Highness and his are looked upon by me with the astonishment of those who made you what you are.

From Venice, the 17th of June, 1537.

To MESSER FRANCESCO MARCOLINI   XLVIII
    Concerning a Volume of Letters.

With the same good will, my good fellow, with which I have given you my other works, I give you these few letters, which have been collected through the love that my young men have for the things I do. Let my reward be your appreciation of the gift, for I esteem it a greater glory to present them to others than to have composed them—fortuitously, as you know, and as for having them printed at one's own cost and selling by one's own solicitation the books drawn from one's fancy, that appears to me to be a feeding upon one's own members. And he who every evening goes to the shop to collect the sales of the day partakes of the nature of the pimp who, before he goes to bed, empties the purse of his woman. I hope, with the favor of God, that the courtesy of princes may pay me for the labor of writing and not a wretched purchaser, for I would rather endure discomfort than do wrong to virtue by reducing the liberal arts to

mechanics. It is obvious that those who sell their manu-
scripts become the porters of their own infamy. Learn to be
a merchant of the useful by following the trade of a book-
seller and you renounce the name of poet. It is not pleasing to
Christ that that which is the function of certain beasts should
be the trade of my own generous nature. A fine thing it
would be if I, who spend a small treasury every year, were to
imitate the gambler who places a hundred ducats on a bet
and then goes home and beats his wife for not filling the
lamps with cheap oil. Let them be well printed and in genteel
folios; I care for no other price. And so, from hand to hand,
you others shall be the heirs to that which has issued from
my genius.

From Venice, the 22nd of June, 1537.

To MESSER PAOLO PIETRASANTA   XLIX

    Of His Own Ignorance.

If it would not be merely cutting off the heads of the
hydra, I, brother, should be tempted to burn everything I
have written, seeking to make myself remembered only in
your letters, which I should keep, for whoever was to read
those divinely intelligent words with which you are in the
habit of addressing me and praising me, without reading
any of my own works, would be convinced that I was
another Plato. You are, surely, out of the ordinary run of
lying philosophers, and you do not find it necessary to go
around with elevated eyebrows and contemplative gestures.
You do not babble of the grandeur of the stars nor seek to
take the measure of the sun, nor do you swear that the
aspects of the moon in its various phases are just what you
say they are, and you do not obstinately affirm that the
thunder, lightning, rain and winds, which are but the little
differences which Mother Nature has with herself, must
come from the causes you perceive. The reasons which you
assign are not monstrous and confused. The altitude of the
air and the profundity of the sea are not determined by

Pietrasanta. He does not square the orbit of the earth with circles or with spheres; but, on the other hand, the intellect which God has given you penetrates the nature of that same deity, until you come to understand the essential unity of the individual Trinity; and as you consider and solve the reasons of souls and bodies, you make us understand the immortality of the former and the fragility of the latter. And the sun is not so clear to us as the Sacred Scriptures are to you; the spirit of the Hebraic meànings is so well understood by you, in the acuteness of your science, that we need no other interpreter to open for us the secret truths of eternal life. The practical quality of your virtue looks to effects and deeds, and in this you observe that golden mean which is the seat of the blessed. That virtue explains to us the difficulties which we encounter in our efforts to know the Supreme Force; and so near is the doctrine of your tongue to the truth that you seem to be showing us the truth even while you are seeking to find a means of making it clear to us; whence, I may say to you that, in considering the essence of the true God, you are tasting the fruit of the tree of perfect knowledge. But how much greater an obligation do you have toward heaven than do I! for I can only open my mouth and let fall, quite by chance, weak sayings and futile words, doing with my ink on paper what those persons do with chalk who take pleasure in defacing the white walls of hostelries.[1] And here, I must confess that I have, in this, some little knowledge of myself. The truth is, I have repudiated all my past compositions, and I am just beginning to learn and to write, although I am not able to do this as I ought. But my excuse must be the unfriendly fortune which has forced me to gain my bread through the industry of my pen, since I am by nature not one who would deign to procure it in any other fashion. I conclude by acknowledging all that your own graces and those of every learned man

---

[1]This is a rather startling bit of self-insight. There is in Aretino, as in George Grosz, no little of the street urchin, scrawling obscenities on a wall.

deserve, for the knowledge of knowing nothing, which is in me, comes from the modesty of an occult virtue. And so, love me.

From Venice, the 23rd of June, 1537.

To The Count di San Secondo L

The Torments of Love.

Go easy, signor, with your attempts to please me, for I would not have you so hound me with your abundance that, wishing to be a man and repay you and not being able to do so, I shall appear to you a beast. To me it is more than enough that, in writing to Signor Cosimo de' Medici, among all the other things you had to do, you took care to remember me to him. But all else is idle talk, when one has on his back the devil of love, who, I may believe, since she does not spare my old age, does not spare your youth. What cruel nights, what fiery days, thanks to her ribaldries! I had cut down my diet in order to get thin (though I am sure it is not the food but the leisure of this city which has given me such a paunch and such an appetite); but it did not help any. I lost first one of my women and then another, until I became like a victim of plague or famine who is but the shadow of his former self. Truly, I have more pity for those who suffer from love than for those who die of hunger or who go to justice wrongly; for dying of hunger comes from idleness, and being unjustly punished is the result of an evil fate; but the cruelty which falls on the head of an *innamorato* is an assassination, slaying his faith, his solicitude and the service he should render himself. I have always found myself, and find myself still, and always shall find myself, thanks to God's grace and my own, without money, on the verge of losing patrons, friends and relatives, in imminent danger of death, burdened with debt or facing a thousand other catastrophes; and my conclusion is that all these other pains are as sweet as sugar in comparison with the hammerings of jealousy, expectation, lies and deceits, which crucify the days and nights of one in love. Desire is poison at lunch and wormwood at dinner; your bed is a stone, friendship is hateful and your fancy is always fixed on one thing; until I am astonished that it is possible for the mind to be in so continuous a tempest without losing itself in the eternal battle of its thoughts, which make it pursue the loved object while it tears out its own heart. All this would be amusing enough, if there were in women some little recompense. But they, playing an amorous game of cards, discard, every time, their aces and their kings. But a certain thing which a Perugian said ought to be carved in letters of gold. He had come out of a love affair with a lady-friend with so bad a case of syphilis that he would have been the despair of the wood of India; he was covered with it, from head to foot, very bestially. It had embroidered his hands, enameled his face, bejeweled his neck and strung his throat with coins, so that he looked as though he were made of mosaic. And being in this sorry plight, he was seen by one of those . . . you understand; and after the usual marvelment and consolations, the fellow said: "Brother, it would have been a good thing for you, if you had learned my art!" "I wish to Christ I had!" replied the other, "since it was for this hide that I have sacrificed a hundred times to our Saint Arcolano; but because God was not pleased with my pledge, you see what happened to me." And ending on this parable, I will commend myself to Your Lordship.

From Venice, the 24th of June, 1537.

To MESSER NICOLÒ FRANCO   LI

Against Rhetoric.

Follow the path that nature shows you, if you wish your writings to stand out from the page on which they are written, and laugh at those who steal famished words, because there is a great difference between imitators and thieves, and it is the latter whom I damn. Gardeners scold those who trample the herbs to gather their condiments and not those who pluck them gracefully, and they make a sour face at those who, to get the fruit they want, break the branches and not at those who pick two or three plums, scarcely moving the boughs. I tell you most assuredly that, with the exception of a few, all the others are bent on stealing and not on imitating. Tell me: is not the thief, who transforms the habit he has stolen so he can wear it without its being recognized by its owner, a man of more genius than the one who, being unable to conceal his theft, gets caught at it? You heard the other day, when Grazia read us the divine Sperone's great dialogue, a remark from the eloquent mouth of my Fortunio to the effect that it sounded as though Plato, in certain places, had been the imitator; and he said this because the author had made his own the passages he had made use of. Look you: the nurse instructs the infant she nourishes, taking his feet and teaching him to walk, putting her own smile into his eyes, her own words upon his tongue, her own manners into his gestures until Nature, as he grows older, teaches him attitudes of his own. And he, little by little, having learned to eat, to walk and to talk, forms a series of new customs; and leaving the embrace of his nurse, he puts into operation his own native habits; and so it is with all of us; we retain only so much of our early instruction as birds do a knowledge of the mother and father from whom they fly away. This he must do who would amount to anything as a poet and, taking only a spiritual inspiration, he should emerge with a harmony formed by his own proper organs. For the ears of others are now satiated with "needs-be's" and "otherwise's," and the sight of them in a book moves us to laughter in the same manner as would a cavalier who was to appear in the *piazza* all decked out in armor, with golden egrets and a trencher cap; we would say that such a man was mad or masquerading. And yet, in another age, this was the apparel of Duke Borso and of Bartolomeo

Coglioni. Of what use are those pleasing colors which are employed to paint designless clusters of little boughs? Their glory lies in the enlarged use which Michelangelo makes of them, who so employs nature and art that it is hard to say who is the master and who is the disciple. Another would have him, since he is a good painter, counterfeit a piece of velvet or a belt-buckle! "The truth is in fools," said Giovanni da Udine[1] to some persons who were amazed at his miraculous grotesques in the *loggia* of Leo and the vineyard of Clement. And to tell you the truth, Petrarch and Boccaccio are imitated by those who would express their conceits with the same sweetness and light[2] with which Petrarch and Boccaccio expressed theirs; you will not find the latter imitated by the man who would plunder them, not of their "wherefore's" and their "whence's," their tricks and qualifications, but of the poetry that is in them. And when the devil blinds us to the point where we run away bodily with some one, forcing us to imitate Virgil, who stole from Homer, or Sanazaro, who cheated on Virgil, the sin is pardoned us. But the faecal blood of pedants who would poetize feeds on imitation, and while they cackle away in their worthless books, they transfigure the works they imitate into locutions, which they embroider with phthisical words, according to rote. O wandering tribe, I tell you, and I tell you again, that poetry is a whim of Nature in her lighter moods; it requires nothing but its own madness and, lacking that, it becomes a soundless cymbal, a belfry without a bell. For which reason, he who would compose without taking beauty out of its swaddling clothes is nothing more than a cold potato. Any one who doubts may make the matter clearer to himself by means of the following analogy: the alchemists, who, with all imaginable industry, employ the imagination of art for the satisfaction of their own patient avarice, never succeed in producing gold, but merely

[1]The painter.
[2]*con la dolcezza e con la leggiadria.*

[134]

a good imitation; whereas nature, giving herself not the least trouble in the world, brings it forth fine and pure. Take a lesson from what I am going to tell you of that wise painter who, when asked whom he imitated, pointed with his finger to a crowd of men, inferring that he drew his models from life and truth, as I do when I speak and write. Nature herself, and Simplicity, her handmaid, give me what I put into my compositions, and my own fatherland un-loosens the knots in my tongue when it tries, superstitiously, to twist itself into foreign chatterings. In short, any one who soils paper can use "*chente*" and "*scaltro*" for "*agente*" and "*paziente*". But do you look to the nerves and leave the skin to the tanners of literature, who stand there begging a penny's worth of fame with the genius of a highwayman—not that of a learned man, such as you are. It is true that I imitate myself, since Nature as a companion is a large order and art is, of necessity, a clinging beetle. But I advise you to strive to become a sculptor of the senses, and not a minia-turist of vocabularies.

From Venice, the 25th of June, 1537.

To SIGNOR GIROLAMO DA CORREGGIO   LII
    Fishes and Wine.
    I have tried out the fish you sent me, along with those which I received from the Count Lodovico Rangone da Roccabianca, and both have the same delicate, juicy flavor. And you may believe me that, even if they were half spoiled and had lost their freshness, they were dearer to me than the presents of cash and goods which the princes give me. And as I shared with others the bergamot pears which the signora Veronica sent me, I have done the same with the fishes. It seemed to me, as I made a meal of them, that I was eating the apples which caused Adam, of blessed memory, to fall, and Adam would have been astonished to find himself in such a terrestrial paradise as this; for Correg-

gio is the inn to all who would hoist a flank without paying the hostler. Surely, whoever did him wrong would be committing a sin, for he is the vagabonds' garden of refuge; and if the world liked to wear bouquets, it would carry him in its hand as the prize gilly-flower. You well know our Messer Giambattista Strozzo, *pater patriae*, who would make a man with his belly full die of hunger, by sharpening the appetite with the praises which he gives to his own wines, breads, roasts, melons and all the luxuries of the palate. And he is so obstinate in his contentions, that if your mother had not sent me those casks of white and red wine, the impression would have gone abroad that I did not believe in the perfection of such a country as yours. The Count Claudio Rangone sent me some of his wine from Modena, and it was very gentle; but it did not have so clear a color or so biting a taste as yours. I am sure that, in Your Lordship's land, Bacchus must long since have been canonized; and the aforesaid Strozzo still goes on trying to convince me that he is the lieutenant of Parnassus, but meanwhile, I am plucking the flowers of your own poetic divinities.

From Venice, the 29th of June, 1537.

To THE MAGNIFICENT OTTAVIANO DE' MEDICI   LIII
    On the League Against the Turks.

Upon seeing, my lord, and having counted out to me by the gentle Messer Francesco Lione the fifty *scudi* which Duke Cosimo, by your leave, has been generous enough to present me, my conscience itself was ashamed, and that is the reason why I have been so restrained, though I ought not to have doubted the liberality and the love of the son of such a father. It was the office of a prudently discreet man to wait his time to remind you of the old and new bonds of service; but since it is a common though vicious error, the adulations of hope and the stimulus of need call for pardon, and I am sure these spurs will win a pardon for me in this case. On the other hand, the courtesy which His Excellency has shown me is a good augury for the beginning of his rule, for none but the best princes and those who reign by the election of God and the counsels of the best men, pay tribute to me, overcoming, thus, hatred and pertinacity with clemency and kindness, like those of that great youth whose praise will always be the food of my labor. You may be assured that my work will have a bearing upon the name and rank of His Most Illustrious Lordship, as will be seen in the copious letters I have written to Caesar, a collection of which I propose to send to the magnanimous Signora Maria, who is, perhaps, a bit thoughtful in all these tumults provoked by the Turks and the French, tumults which shatter the ears of the world, and which are like the winds and the waves, which, raging about the reefs, drive all ships to port. For my part, I believe that God consents to this in order to glorify the power of the religious Venetians, for whose incredible preparations the bosom of all the seas is not large enough; and it is nothing short of a miracle, the way in which this city of Christ provides itself with money, not for war (for she is at war with none), but in order to guard herself against those who would declare war upon her,[1] and this it is which accounts for her streets being filled with pomp and joy and senators. The other states raise their funds by impost, amid great confusion and the laments of their people; but here, there is as much rivalry in finding gold as there is in bartering dignities. For the prudence of the Emperor Charles may boast that it has been wise in knowing and cherishing this city. And it is generally conceded that St. Marks' is the fatal comb which Fortune wears on her forehead, and from it hang victories and defeats.

From Venice, the first day of July, 1537.

[1]From which, it may be seen, the doctrine of "preparedness" is at least as old as the sixteenth century.

Exhortations and Counsels

There is no doubt that emperors and kings are elected of God[1]; and for this reason, they are sacred and adored, as figures drawn of that Image of which we are able to make only a conjecture; and from this source comes their faculty of listening to and consoling their subjects, with their royal grace and their benefits. He who ascends the throne violently through the force or the favor of others, either reigns with infamy or brings ruin and vituperation on himself; but those who receive their sceptre from the supernal will shall rule for all eternity. Did not your power, achieving the impossible, seat Alessandro against the will of fate? And he rules only so long as your fortune sustains him, and lacking your aid, he must fall. But even if the shadow of fate is against us, will it be easy to stop Duke Cosimo, when we have the consent of Christ and of Caesar? Who can deny that divine choice has placed him where his thoughts are fixed? For which reason, we may liken him to David, called from his flocks to a kingdom by the signs of God's will. He, being a lamp of virtue and of goodness, sustained by a pilgrim spirit, will find his whole mind inflamed, his will warm, his heart ardent and his mind fervent in your service. You do not raise to greatness a corrupt person, who has need of a lordship and the high regard of others, but one from whom something may always be hoped, not feared, one who shall be a prince and not a tyrant, one who will know how to give to his subjects and not steal from them, one who will know how to confer honor upon them and not shame, one, in short, who will know how to caress and how to correct. For this the peoples, who by nature love quiet, will adore your modesty alone; and that force, which sometimes forces a prince to be other than good, will be so tempered with good sense that it will be held perfect in the execution of

[1]And the "divine right of kings" is somewhat older than James I.

your procedures, and you shall surely be better known for the goodness of your mind than for the pomp of your dominion. Do not delay, then, in giving to one who has not delayed his gifts even to the barbarians, so that all the nations may be astonished by the magnificence of the holy emperor who, in making largess of what he received from the crown of Tunis, comes near clinging to God by the skirts since he who gives largely is very near to God.

But this would be all too little reward for the immense affection and the firm faith which have saved Florence for you, giving to you alone the State. It is a thing worthy of your mind, of your greatness, and of the merits of those who hold it a liberty to serve you to join him in matrimony with your own glorious daughter, who, by taking any other title, would be, perhaps, untrue to her fate, which has destined her to be the queen of our hearts and hopes, and whom we should very much like to have live under the just laws of the House of Medici, that house whose power is already known to Austria, which has been cast down by the arm of Augustus in his own blood. For no other reason did heaven permit the death of the former duke, than to make clear how you should be incarnated in Tuscan flesh, for otherwise, you would never believe, and others would never be able to show you, how dear you were and are to us. And so, with swift deliberation, give to your daughter a consort, to the city a patron and to your friends contentment. See the good Cosimo who, silent in his uprightness, is waiting expectantly to be consoled by that grace which you should scatter over him; for the good wish for it, the times demand it, and so it ought to be. Furthermore, if no one else merited so great a gift as this from so great a monarch, he would merit it from the fact that he does not come of an adulterous parentage, but one illustrious by the virtues of the father and the mother. His father, surely, was the terror of men, and his mother the astonishment of the ladies. Thus, in doing this, you accomplish many laudible effects. By doing so, you reward the efforts of his parents, elevate the purity of their offspring and avenge yourself and us against fate and envy; you avenge yourself by making him your son-in-law, in place of the one whom fate and envy have taken from you; and you avenge us by giving us a lord in place of the one whom they stole from us. You should take into consideration, above all, the fact that such a betrothal would restore the heart, refresh the mind and revive the voice of those who adore you, and, at the same time, would cut out the eyes, tear out the tongue and bind the arms of those who hate you; the nights do not flee so quickly as hope dries in the hand, and so, we have no recourse but your mercy; none in our armies. Any delay in this matter is a torment to Caesar's servants and a joy to his adversaries. Bending, then, on my knees in reverence to that Majesty, I ask your Majesty if it is honest that the most just Charles, by delaying, should make a feast for his enemies and bring woe to his friends.

From Venice, the 6th of July, 1537.

To Messer Giovanni Pollastra   LV
  In Which He Refuses a Dedication.

The great good will which you have for me, my good fellow, sometimes causes the great love I bear you to be too sure of itself; and so, I become lazy, where I ought to be solicitous by visiting you with my letters at least twice a month. And I do this because the security which, for so many years, I have felt with regard to you promises me that, whether I write to you or not, I am always in your heart, neither more nor less than if I wrote every day; and so, from being your loving brother, by this I ought to become a hateful villain. But that such is not the case, I am assured by my friend, Messer Tarlato Vitali, whom, upon his leaving here, I commissioned to take to you my fraternal kisses; and since I know him to be a very courteous gentleman, I am sure he has already done so. But do you really believe that I am as lacking in affection as I am in words? I swear to you, by that fervent and most tender love which I bear my little daughter, whom God has given me for a solace to my old age, that where your interest is concerned, spilling water is to me like spilling blood, and I hold you in my heart in the same place of pre-eminence which I reserve for my service to Caesar. I keep my friends as misers do their treasure, because, of all the things granted us by wisdom, none is greater or better than friendship. It is an honest union of eternal wills, and in virtuous and just men it has no end, even as it shall have no end with us, for as we go on loving each other, we keep it always laden with its own fruits. I am admonished, in every manner possible, by the reproof I feel in not having written you twice since I have been here; but something, I do not know what, in the memory I hold of you, even as I read your words, has refused to unloose my tongue, and only with labor has consented that I take my pen and tell you how in the work you have addressed to me appears the love you bear your country, the charity which you show a friend and your own innate greatness of soul. But it would be a great temerity in me to accept your dedication, sensing myself to be a person of no rank and a man of small merit. And so, I advise you to turn to the Marchese del Vasto,[1] or to whomsoever may appear to you better fitted to receive the fruit of your labors; to me, it is enough to have the certainty of your good opinion, which, in the benignity of your judgment, has adjudged me worthy of being honored by the writings which come from your fertile genius. In place of this, do me the favor before you die of letting me see some of your verses. If you can do so without the inconvenience of coming here and returning to your home again, you ought to have some of your verse and prose printed. I tell you, this is an age in which the work of any one, no matter who

[1] The pompous old marquis, to whom Aretino ended by dedicating his own *Marfisa*. See *Introduction*. •

he is, is not taken by the printers as a gift, and if you do not pay their terms, you can get no service on your own. And so, listen to me as though I were speaking in your own person, and for the sake of a little money, do not resist the temptation to have an impression made of those *Trionfi*, of the body of which I should like to see at least a member, as I have told you. Let me be your messenger in the matter, if you love me as I love you, and as I shall love you so long as I am able to love myself.

From Venice, the 7th of July, 1537.

To Messer Agostino Ricchi   LVI
   Winter and Summer.

If science and learning were dearer than life, I, my son, should exhort you to the accustomed tasks; but since living is of the greater moment, I beseech you to come here with us where, without disturbing your memory with the deviltries of Aristotle, you may study to be healthy while the dog days[1] are on, which are very trying on the person and the patience. I, for my part, take more pleasure in seeing the snow falling from heaven than I do in feeling myself wounded by the gentle breezes. Winter impresses me as an abbot who, floating at his ease in the heavens, likes to eat, sleep and to do, with a little too much relish, that other thing. His case is like that of a rich and noble prostitute who, disgusted, throws herself down and, sprinkled with foul smells, does nothing but drink and drink some more. And all the fresh wines and gaily bedecked rooms, all the artificial fans and foods of June and July, are not worth a mouthful of that greasy bread which is eaten before the fire in December or January, while one drinks with it a few musty cups and, in stooping to turn the roast, detaches for himself a bit of salt fried pork, without any thought of mouth or fingers, though the latter are cooked in the course

[1] *rabbia del caldo.*

{ 142 }

of the theft. At night, you enter where the warming pan has done advance service for you, and you take your companion in your arms, all cozily under the covers, and she warms you with her own temperamental heat; while the rain, the thunder and the fury of the north wind merely assure you an unbroken sleep till morning. But who could endure the bestial entertainment of the fleas, bedbugs, gnats and flies and all the other annoyances of the summer season? You lie on the sheets, naked as a new born babe, dependent for a fan upon the mocking services of a treacherous family servant, who leaves you planted[1] there as soon as he thinks your eyes are closed; and you wake in the middle of the finest sleep and turn over on your other side to sweat some more; you take a drink, sigh and, turning over again, you long to flee from yourself and, if possible, to disappear from your own sight, so great is the importunity of the heat, which annihilates you in a universal perspiration. And if it were not that the memory of watermelons, those pimps of the palate, assailed you, which is the only thing that makes their summer temple desirable, you would flee the heat as knaves do the cold. There are those who like the season on account of the abundance of its fruits, lauding the cherries, the figs, the fishes and the eggs; as if the truffles and the olives of winter were not worth more than all those things. And there is quite a different sort of conversation around a fire than there is in the shadow of a beech tree,[2] for in the latter place a thousand harlot appetities attack one. In such a case, there is a call for the song of birds, the murmur of waters, the sighing of zephyrs, the freshness of a lawn and similar conceits; but four dry logs have in them all the circumstance necessary to a conversation of four or five hours, with chestnuts on the plate and a jug of wine between the legs. Yes, let us love winter, for it is the spring of genius. But to come back to ourselves, I tell you, you ought to come

[1]*Che ti pianto*, etc.
[2]Cf. Virgil [*Eclogues* I]: "*sub tegmine fagi.*"

straight off, for our Messer Nicolò Franco, a most learned and the best of youths, has found a little room outside in which he can sleep. I have nothing more to say to you, unless you choose to remember me to Signor Sperone and to Ferraguto.

From Venice, the 10th of July, 1537.

To MESSER TARLATO VITALI   LVII
  On Seeing One's Native Land Again.

If, my brother, a man of some merit, desiring to rid himself of all cares and to taste an interior contentment, were to go back to see his native land once every ten years, there is no doubt that, in the brief space of fifteen days, he would experience all that beatitude which souls feel when they return to heaven. For the love of relatives and the charity of friends takes you into the arms of good will with so much gentleness and joy that the spirit, drunk with such affections, sees nothing and tastes nothing except the well-being and the welcome which it receives from one and the other; and, finding nothing but courtesy and honor, a day seems to him an hour, as he delights in the streets which he has not seen for so long a time; it appears to him that he receives a heart-felt greeting from every citizen, and that every one, from the lowest to the highest, receives him as a companion or superior. For a smile which shows you the face of your own fatherland elevates you more than the ranks which others confer on you, and a "good-day" from an old neighbor is worth more than a reward from this prince, or from that, and the soul senses more joy in glimpsing the smoke from the paternal hearth than it takes in the flames kindled by the glory of its own virtues. But he who would not lose an iota of this felicity, does not burden others with his presence overmuch, giving them a chance to take his measure; but rather, by making a famine of himself upon his return, creates in those of quality and benignity, who hold him so dearly and who look upon him with so much good will, the desire of seeing more of him. Your gentleness would always find a kind and reverent reception from the *aretini*, and when you had stayed a century, it would seem, upon your departure, that you had been with us but a month. And if my people cannot be consoled with your presence, since you are not always able to put yourself out on account of us, may we at least see the proofs of your affection in those fresh wines and precious fruits, for I cannot compete with you in the delights in which that province of yours abounds. It is true, Messer Francesco Bacci was recently here, and we were able, in embracing him, to show the sort of brotherly love there is between us, a love which, it may be said, beginning in the cradle, has reached the height of perfection, nor is there any possibility of its ever being broken, even by death. And you said as much to him of me. To Eugenia, your daughter, I say the same, although I am sure she has forgotten me, as has her husband, although Madonna Tita, her mother, will swear that I am wrong in thinking such a thing. I would have you, then, remember me to them, as would the one who is more than a daughter to me and her sister, Lucrezia, and Girolamo, their brother, who has promised to supply me with watermelons night and morning. I hope you keep well; as for me, I have had three most dangerous attacks of fever, from which I only escaped by the grace of God and not thanks to my having observed the doctor's orders.

From Venice, the 13th of July, 1537.

To Signor Mario Bandini   LVIII
   *He Prophesies to Cardinal Piccolomini That He Will
      Become Pope*

I, Captain, would not excuse my not having replied at once to your letter, which was not less gracious than it was gentle, by the fact that I have been very busy or the fact that I have been ill, for I ought to put work aside and forget the fever in order to return the kindness of such a cavalier as you, showing you by my good faith that you are as near my heart as those who do not imitate you in virtue and gentleness are far from mind. If it were permitted to advise God and to give laws to heaven, I should say that God and heaven, for the common welfare, as soon as the pontiff's seat is vacant by death, ought to take your uncle for the place, so that Rome once more might adorn itself with that joy, those pomps and that spirit of which ugliness of mind on the part of others has deprived it. Certain it is, fortune may make a prince of a plebeian, but over nature it has no jurisdiction. And so it is, he who is born without a generous zeal, the greater the altitude to which he is raised, the more he is abased; for blood that thinks it is made illustrious through the favor of fate, becomes obscure; becoming villainous, it is interred with its titles and cognomens. But are you reading what I write to you without taking from it an augury for your future felicity? I have said so many true things in my day, that I will say one more; and that is, that, by the virtue which he inherits from the two Pii, if Cardinal Piccolomini were to succeed them, it would be no miracle but something which had to happen. I was with the great Giovanni de' Medici at Fano, when he swore to me that if Jesus ever did him a favor, it was in blessing him with me; and yet, I believe I was soon out of his fancy, for such a one as he does not remember even himself. But, on the other hand, I, who am become so much yours that I no longer appear to have a part in myself, after thanking you for the courtesy you have shown in writing me, would pray you not to disdain my services, which shall be prompt in pleasing you. And in case you write to the valorous Archbishop of Siena, your brother, not because I deserve it, but because you are kindness itself, remember me to him. But look you, even as I close this page, my dear and rare Varchi appears and, upon glimpsing the superscription, restrains the reproofs he was about to address to me, for he believed, as you yourself must have done, that I had forgotten my duty in not replying to your courteous Lordship.

From Venice, the 15th of July, 1537.

To Messer Antonio Gallo   LIX
    In Which He Exhorts Him to Cultivate Poetry with Originality.

With that good face, my delicate youth, with which one plucks and tastes the first fruits of the year, I took and read your words, pleasing and savorous as the most pleasing and savorous apples that ever were tasted. And I have taken no less pleasure in your own writing than in the wonderment which you express at mine, according to what you tell me; for the deep and gentle love I bear you in my heart, the rare virtue of poetry that is in you, and your manners, which are so richly adorned, are the causes which impel me to praise you and to exhort you to continue your studies, since to tire himself in studies is the duty of him who, with glory, has begun to climb the ladder of fame. And so, flee laziness, which, while it produces an immediate delight, ends in the sorrow of repentance. And know that nature without exercise is a seed shut up in the pod, and art without practice is nothing. Be, then, assiduous in composition, if you would be the best of poëts, and above all, see to it that you steal the fine strokes and the spiritual acuteness from your own genius, for he is certainly mad who thinks he can make a name for himself through the labors of others. Strive to draw your conceits from your own thoughts, which are born in you out of memory, while you are engaged in raising yourself to the heights, with the fury of Apollo. Doing this, your judgment will find satisfaction in its own works, and you will be baptized as a son of the muses, and not as the offspring of literary thefts.

And now, speaking of something else, I will say that the

signor Guidobaldo would not be the son of so great a father, if he were not constantly mindful of the services and the virtue of others, as he is mindful of myself and of Lione: of me, on account of the desire I always had to obey his wishes; of Lione, on account of the life-like medallion which the latter made of him, and which is one of my own possessions. Wherefore, I pray God that our gratitude may be equal to his Excellency's goodness. And when we can do no more, we will consecrate to him our good intentions, beseeching your gentle breeding to keep us in your honored graces, trusting that you will take comfort in regarding the person, aside from those accidents and disorders which are the pleasurable food of youth. Adieu.

From Venice, the 6th of August, 1537.

To THE MAGNANIMOUS ISABELLA, EMPRESS   LX
    Praises.

Although Your Majesty, being the handmaid of Christ as well as the wife of Caesar, needs no praise, having received your gift from the hands of the perfect Don Lope, in order not to publish myself as an ingrate, I will say that he is wrong who does not believe, and he errs who does not assert, that you were conceived through the centuries and reserved in the mind of God to be joined by His will with Augustus; for surely it is not permissible that to him, who is more than mortal man, should be given a wife who is less than superhuman. And so, it is no marvel that you are the most excellent in virtue, the most deserving of glory, the most pure in mind, the most tender in heart and the most chaste in body of all women, of whatever age they may be. Adorned, then, with grace and beauty, with that simplicity which shines from your forehead, bring serenity to minds that are clouded with affliction. That tranquillity which quiets the tempest of hearts gladdens your brows, which are a miniature of honesty's self. Your eyes, turning in modest movements, console the soul of the one who wonders at them, and in their gentleness, filled with love and grace, it is as if green and marvelous emerald vistas were recreated. Your cheeks are the flowers of our hope. With your glance, you entice the good, and with a sign, you admonish kings. Your actions are a lesson in holy customs, and in your countenance, true beatitude is to be discerned. Charity opens your hands, and mercy moves your feet. Constancy, humility and concord are your companions and ministers. In your step and in your presence, you reveal the favor of heaven. Faith and religion point you to your own good sense and your own valor. And with the pomp of those virtues which adorn you, you make no fewer conquests with your courtesy than the emperor does with his arms. Hence, the world is half yours and half his. And while you employ the solemn office of liberality, he is astonished at you, as he is at himself; and he has reason to be astonished, for Charles and Isabella, looked upon by God and adored by men, live and reign for the honor of Jesus and the welfare of the peoples. I thank you, therefore, for this divine favor, since by sending me this collar, you who are the first lady of the universe,[1] you are paying tribute not to my merits, but to the most chaste and venerable qualities of your own Serene Highness, and all the ladies of Italy bend the knee at the sound of the name of your Illustrious Highness, whose sacred hands I kiss, with those of your most holy and Christian consort. And it is befitting that every one say as much, for his goodness and religion have drawn upon Catholic shoulders the burden of one title and the other.

From Venice, the 20th of August, 1537.

To Signor Girolamo Montaguto   LXI
   In Which He Exhorts Him to Give No Heed to Delusions,
        but to Live to Himself.

Since, signor, I always give every one his dues, no matter

‾‾‾‾‾‾‾‾
[1]Going one better than "the first lady of the land."

from where he comes as whence he goes, I will say, in response to your request and commission, that I did not blush upon receiving your letter as I should have blushed if I had not done so; for certainly I should be the first to remind you that, at a time when I barely knew what such an acquaintance meant, I knew you with genuine intimacy, and from that day to this, the love I have for your good and illustrious person has ever grown. And I swear to you, by the power which God has given to His Majesty, and which His Majesty has given to me, that if, with the exception of yourself, all the others of the court have been forgotten by me, it is for no other reason than that you are so far removed from envy, slander and the greed of enriching yourself by the death of others. And if, under the harsh Clement, the conqueror of three papacies, your firm faith, with twenty-five years of service behind it, appears to have grown old in vain, congratulate yourself on the fact, for it would not be possible to produce a testimonial which would better enlighten every one as to your own sovereign goodness. I, for my part, not only pride myself on being a good man, seeing I have received nothing from two pontiffs, but I am inclined to exalt myself with the title of perfect, when I see that prelatures are given to plebeians and the worst of men, rather than to gentlemen and the just, like you. Learn to poison, to betray, to gossip, to be a drunkard and a pimp, adulating always, if you do not wish, after your youth has been consumed in robbing and robing a pope, to return to your own house a beggar. The memory of His Holiness ought to be ashamed, since his life knew no shame, at not having made you at least a bishop of your fatherland, not merely a decurion of his chamberlains, for you have all the gentleness, nobility and patience in the world; but the benefices and the abbeys go to the vituperators, in whom never was and never will be religion or good custom. But who is happier than I, who have been able to publish the nature of the priestly nature, to the shame of which the world honors me with its tributes? Let your heart be at peace, dear and gentle brother, and rest content with what you have, though it is little enough for your mind and merit; let your joy be in Arezzo. And let the plain citizens among whom you were born take the place of the great personages who used to entertain you at Rome. Rejoice and feast and take your pleasure with them, for in them is the greater security, and they show you the mind on the tongue without fraud. Look at our Francesco Bacci, who wears his mind on his forehead; look at all the other grateful companions; grow young again in their company, and have no longer a desire to wander among strange nations, since you know how many heart-breaks there are in the desire of rank and honors. He who does not die with an aversion to bending the knee to a cavalry stripling and a Trojan is an ass in human form, while he who never has revered them is the victor over fortune and entitled to sit at the right hand of the blessed. And so, live cheerfully, and be to me as you have always been. With this, I kiss your reverend Lordship with all the affection that I bear you.

From Venice, the 22nd of August, 1537.

To Messer Giovanni Pollastra   LXII
    *In Which He Defends Himself Against the Accusation
        of Slander.*

Our circumspect Messer Tarlato, revered friend, has placed in my hands the book you gave him, as he told me, with your own hand. I have had it now three or four days, and I have run over almost all of it, both the prose and the verse. And then, backed by your letter, he asked me for it back, and I restored it to him. As to its merits, I will say that I, who am a man of no judgment, ought not to pass judgment, for a judge should be possessed of conscience, prudence and experience; otherwise, his ignorance brings public blame on others. Nor does it seem to me a thing quite worthy, after confessing that I am not fitted to do so, to go ahead, for the sake of displaying my wisdom, and defame others by the act of judging. Hence, I shall not endeavor to pass sentence upon your work, but shall merely discuss it. You say that you are sending it to me as you would your own daughter to a very harsh uncle, and your sincerity moves me to say that the style out of which you have woven so impressive a fabric is supported by heroic fibres and breathes an heroic spirit; if you continue to write verse so great as this, you will end by being second to none. There are, in your *Trionfi*, certain tercets which are high and clear and fine; then come uneven and poorly conceived passages. To me, the Dantesque vocabulary is not annoying, as you employ it, as would be, ordinarily, for example, the use of "*perplesso*," which those well versed in the Latin tongue do not use. It strikes me as too much of an innovation when Pollio, a learned man, fails to distinguish a noun from a verb and, for the sake of the rhyme, writes "*l'erra*" for "*gli errori*," and "*sono*" for "*sonno*," making "*relligion*" a trisyllabic word, which is harsh to the ears and difficult to pronounce. And I wonder even more at the mere stuff which I often find, along with harsh constructions. I love you and, because I love you, I would sooner have you hate me for telling you the truth than adore me for telling you lies. It seems to me that so profound a subject should depend for decoration only on its own dignity and should not make poetic license out of whatever comes to the mouth. Root out from your compositions all the terms of Petrarch; and since you are not pleased to stroll in such streets, do not harbor in your house his "*unquanchi*," his "*soventi*" and his "*ancide*," the costive superstitions of our language; and in dealing with stories and names employed by him, get as far away from him as you can, for these things are too trite. Enter, with the scythe of your own novel judgment, that meadow which I have glimpsed in your book and mow down the disgressional hay I have come upon. When one is dealing with faith, hope and charity, it is not fitting to hand out idle chatter. Pure and candid are those three virtues; and so, seek for them pure and candid ornaments. Do not think that I am advising you in this manner because, in your discourse, you have blamed me for slander; for if you did it to praise me, I thank you; and if you did it to blame me, I pardon you; and since my name occurs to you in this connection, do with it what seems good to you, for it is known to all the world, and the world knows that I repress the vices of others and do not speak evil of my fellow men. And at the sound of the name, "Pietro Aretino," as many princes as there are reigning over the face of the earth lend their ears. It shall be the glory of your book to have mentioned my own sacred[1] and veracious compositions, and I would remind you that it is necessary in the treatise, *De la caritade*. I laugh at you when you boast that you have not wished to acquire fame by biting this one or that one; and all the while, you are even outraging the sisters, reprehending the brothels which they make of their cloisters, pardoning neither the flock nor the pastors. And now may you take every word I say as it ought to be taken; for I swear to you on my soul that when you shall have purged your book of this sorry stuff, you will add so much splendor to your own name and that of your native land that whoever looks upon Arezzo will behold another sun. And by God, I tell you that all it needs is to be properly clothed. In it are all the qualities which are asked of a writer; you do not pass over any fact ancient or modern in silence. You are admirable in cosmography; to it add grace and elevation of diction. Finally, I would make it clear to you that this depends upon your will alone and your patience in better thinking over your things; on this hangs the glory of Pollio, whose choice has given me for niece that daughter whom I have chastised as you perceive. And if you were not as a brother to me, I should not

[1]The *prose sacre*.

{ 153 }

have spoken so freely what I have said in all affection.
From Venice, the 28th of August, 1537.

To CARDINAL DI RAVENNA   LXIII
     The Woes of Pedantry.
Even as to Cosimo de' Medici it has been a good augury,
his having taken, at the beginning of his reign, his most
important adversaries, so to you it should be a harbinger of
happiness that I, before the end of your journey, moved by a
better spirit, come back to pay you the reverence which the
world pays you, when envy, with the tyrannical eye of
avarice, does not turn the mind to those riches which the
virtue of your kinsmen has procured for you. I am ashamed
that my ears and my tongue, which are accustomed to hear
and speak the truth, with a notable injury to their nature,
have allowed themselves to be corrupted by a lie. I confess
that, in return for one of the minor offices you performed for
me, which was the marrying off of a sister (a good turn never
done me by either of two pontiffs whom I served), I believed
and, believing, blamed you for what the dogs barked against
your rank and your merits. And the cause of this has not
been my own defection, but the malignity of the fate that
hung over you, which forced those of good integrity to put
faith in the falsity of wretches. Surely calumny with you
has exhausted all her poison, without perceiving that the
true gold which is in you has been merely refined by the
torments you have undergone. All the evil comes from your
not being of a hypocritical humor and the fact that you were
not one of the pedants who reigned about you. How much
better would it be for a *gran maestro* to have in his house a
few faithful fellows, free folk and persons of good will,
than to attempt to adorn himself with the vulpine modesty
of the asinine pedants who write books; who, when they
have assassinated and, with their labors, have succeeded
in croaking the dead, do not rest until they have crucified

the living. To tell the truth, it was pedantry that poisoned the Medici; it was pedantry that cut the throat of Duke Alessandro; and what is worse, it has provoked a heresy against our faith through the mouth of Luther, the arch-pedant of them all. Certain it is, all the *literati* are not virtu-ous; and when letters are not at home in the gentle mind of a noble or a good man, they may be said to be nothing but bits of torn parchment. There is, indeed, a difference between a virtuous man and a literary hack, for virtue is founded in pure goodness of intention, and literature in the captious malignity of thievery. A man like Molza may be said to be "virtuous" and "literate," for he, through his own high nature, and not through thefts, is glorious; and he has forced himself to honor you. A man like Ubaldino is not virtuous, though literate, and by a continuous and splitting effort appears to be learned; and from this come his attempts to abase your reputation. But is there any wickedness, pride or worthlessness which is not hatched in the felonious minds of pedagogues, while they, in their poltroonery, seek to cover their dishonest vices with the venerable name of science? Cherish, then, you gentlemen, lovers of the useful and of your honor, and bind to you with courtesy your solicitous servants, knowing there is more virtue in a fellow of the stalls or in a lackey, who is only alive when his master is looking at him, than there is in all the lettered ones that ever were. For learning is the property of those who fear to do disagreeable things; and woe to your welfare, if it lay in the hands of one of those untamed Ciceros instead of Messer Giambattista Pontano! His, indeed, may rightly be called "virtue," seeing he left country, wife, friends and estates to guard your innocence. You may, then, thank God that you not only have learned to know the sincere from the wicked, but that, in the perversity of circumstance, you have always submitted to the judgment of your own intrepid mind the perfidy and the deceit of enemies, which accounts for the state in which you find yourself today, more honored than ever. For it is well known that Fortune, by way of demonstrating the sovereign power she exercises over princes, sometimes incarcerates them, as she incarcerated Pope Clement and King Francis, though for different reasons; since for the imprisonment of His Holiness, misery was to blame; for that of His Majesty neglect; but your own came from the perverseness of envy. And envy, in this case as I see it, should be praised, since your rights were defended by the emperor, our true lord, whose religion is as powerful in heaven as his dominion is on earth; and so, I hold your state a blessed one, since you have been condemned by others and absolved by Caesar. Divine is the judgment of Charles, and his mind is just. And if any one requires proof that your deeds were not what others would have made them out to be, let him find an argument in the love which Augustus bears you and in the respect in which the good Ercole di Ferrara holds you, to whose Excellency I am indebted for the major part of anything I may in the future accomplish in the way of writing, such has been his courtesy towards me. And so, I, with the affection of an unpretending man, kiss the hands of His Most Illustrious Lordship and those of Your Reverence.

From Venice, the 29th of August, 1537.

To MADONNA PIERINA RICCIA[1]   LXIV
  *In Which He Urges Her to Return from Her Country
    Place.*

There is a proverb of the wenches, my daughter, which says that "Every agreement is not a swindle." You and Messer Polo and Caterina,[1] with the groom and the maid, asked permission to stay in the country, if you pleased, eight days; and since ten have passed, it seems to me it is about time you were coming home. I am glad your mother, to her own great satisfaction, has shown those rude folk

[1]See *Introduction.*

what sort of son-in-law she has. I am glad, too, that you have been praised for taking such a husband on your own initiative. Every one has seen the abundance of clothes you have, which shows that you are deserving of the splendor I have conferred upon you. You will come, then, unless you find the Gambarare gives you more reputation than this city, and that the Brenta is of a more jocund aspect than the Grand Canal. As I told you, you were to stay a week in the country, no more; for in a short time like that, the freshness of the air, the wildness of the place and the rusticity of the people with the general novelty of the thing, provide pleasant food for conversation. But beyond that period, the roughness of the site, with the strangeness of the inhabitants, converts every recreation into an annoyance, until you are forced to reduce, at once, your store of convenience and your stock of civility. And so, as I wait for you, it seems to me that, with five mouths less to feed, I suffer as much pain as a cardinal would if he saw one more. It seems to me, too, when I do not see you at table with me, that I have a premonition of misery. To such a degree that, I confess, the sight of you at meat is to me the triumph of a generous nature, and not merely of a sumptuous pride. Moreover, your pleasant ways, to which I am so used, my daughter, are a sweet nutriment to the years which are beginning to fall upon me. That prudent honesty with which you are endowed is to me an entertaining recompense for the pains I am at to provide those hundred *scudi* a month; and by the grace of God, we shall go on eating, giving and spending with the permission of those who hate me, though I wish evil to none.

From Venice, the 30th of August, 1537.

To FRIAR VITRUVIO DEI ROSSI   LXV
    In Which He Thanks Him for a Gift of Things to Eat
    And Speaks of His Own Frugality.
If the princes that rule us, father, showed as great haste

in keeping their promises as you do, what a fine life and what a fine age ours would be! The sacristan of San Salvatore, who is very gentle and very courteous, has given me the mush-rooms which you sent, and I have enjoyed them out of love for your Reverence; for I love you no less now that you are a religious than I did when you were a secular. And since truffles, oysters and fruits are not foods but pricks to the appetite, forcing us to eat until we are overstuffed, I hope the pleasure which I had in eating them will not lead you to believe that I take an unduly vicious delight in my palate and for that reason am in danger of slipping into the devil's claws, all for the sake of four fungi. My mind, I am sure, if it had the means would feed on real grandeur, but my mouth, which exercises some little sway over my taste, finds its nourishment in rustic victuals. If it is a sin to devour a whole salad, along with an entire onion, then I am branded, for I find in them a sharpness of flavor which those kitchen-falcons who flock about the table of Leo never enjoyed. I am aware that there are times when the church forbids lettuce to those priests who blame the herbs, but I feel like declaring two more days of jubilee on account of it. But do not think that similar gewgaws must, of necessity, fill the mind of one who takes such pleasure as this. For according to the opinion of Nero, *antipasti* are of the gods, and his good memory went to heaven by that means; and the same witness is borne by Sire Claudius, who was more gluttonous of them than he was of empire. However that may be, I give you more thanks than you gave me gifts, and while your gifts lasted, I abandoned all other ragoûts. If there is anything here that smells good to your nose, let me know, and it shall be sent you at once. *Non altro*. Remember to commend me in the prayers of your continuous offices.

From Venice, the 6th of September, 1537.

Concerning the Successes of Cosimo de' Medici.

I had thought, signora, that it was enough to adorn you with the virtues of your husband, which are of more splendor and of greater price than gold, without speaking of those with which you yourself shine, as is apparent, and those which are due to the fortune of that most excellent son of yours. But what cannot the heavens do? What reward do not the good deserve? It is very evident, since Leo, beginning to fear the young military power of the signor Giovanni, seeks to crush him. Look at Clement, who did everything in his power, since his own works could not exalt him. And then, upon his death, Alexander turns his attention to the great Cosimo and, inheriting the suspicion of his two papal for- bears, does a dishonest wrong to his own right and honest reason by abandoning all thought of Cosimo's greatness. But God, who never opposes what he has willed to be, has seen to it that he was placed in that seat which was his from the day he was born, so that he might establish peace and union everywhere, reigning in justice and in continence. And the glorious beginning which Christ has given to his reign is a testimony of the favor which the stars show him. Surely, if Fate had said to you: "What will you have?" your desire would have been in doubt, in order not to appear bold by asking the half of what the success of the enterprise has placed in your hands, since that enterprise was guided so foolishly by wise men that excuse finds no tongue to defend it. But everything goes as the planets will, and our designs never take form without their consent; deeds are vain, and thought builds up its edifices in vain, if God does not look approvingly upon them. And so, we throw away time, money and fame because the celestial influences show us a bad face. For this reason, their prudence is divine who, yielding to one who makes us yield by love and force, act in obedience to the supernal will and are not stubborn, as are those who stand in contrast to the emperor, whose Majesty reduces itself to a miracle; even while he appears to have been cast down, we hear the cries of his victories, so that no one is safe who provokes him. I, then, who, from the antiquity of my service, share in that felicity with which, from day to day, you enlarge your own mind and the confines of the State, congratulate myself, not on the miseries of others (for I am a man and not a beast), but on the honors and prosperity which are yours. And if I have delayed doing so up to now, it has been to give full play to the consolation of your justice and your clemency, praying God that He would make hard hearts tender and harsh minds gentle, so that concord may embrace all with an equal will. In the meanwhile, the dagger of deceit and the sword of treason shall be far from you, for neither the one nor the other has power over His Legitimate Lordship nor over Your Excellency.

From Venice, the Day of Our Lady, September, 1537.

To MONSIGNOR ZICOTTO   LXVII

> *Of Pierina Riccia,*[1] *Whom He Keeps and Loves as a Daughter.*

Who would have thought, Messer Francesco, that our distant friendship would have brought us together in so close a relationship? Look you: God, by sending to my house Pierina Riccia, your kinswoman, has overcome the influence of Verona, for whose sake you had let the intimacy contracted between us many years ago grow cold; and so, I congratulate myself beyond measure. Your virtues and the consideration I have for your gentle way of life give me so much true joy that they drive away the melancholy which comes from plans frustrated by chance. And I will tell you, you might lump together all the loving tenderness which four fathers have for their sons, and you would not arrive

[1]See *Introduction.*

[160]

at the minor part of that which I feel for so light and lively a girl as this, whose own innate goodness keeps her beauty locked in the fortress of her modesty in so obvious and pleasing a manner that I weep for joy even to think of it. How is it possible she, in less than fourteen years, should have acquired the wisdom to pick a husband who holds her dearer than his life? I spend whole days thinking of it, while she is busy with her sewing, her reading, her embroidery or in arranging her wardrobe in that neat fashion which she brings with her from the cradle; and I am prepared to swear to you that I have never seen such habits as those which are the fruit of her gentle nature. And I would to Christ that the gratitude she shows for the benefits she receives from me might be an example to others whose wants I have relieved! She calls me "father and mother," and I am, in truth, the one and the other to her; and when I am asked how many daughters I have, I reply, "Two," putting first the one who, by coming to comfort me in those infirmities to which I am subject, takes precedence over the one produced by my own blood. Her courteous kindness is so dear to my heart that I do not know what pain is; and I so rejoice when I see her sporting with Polo, the most discreet of consorts and my own dear creature. And it seems to me beyond all feminine custom that she shows no haughtiness at seeing herself mistress of all that I have and all that I am. It is nothing less than a miracle to me to see her and Caterina with their arms always about each other's neck, and my life knows a peace that it never before experienced. And my contentment attains the summit of joy, when I see that you and Messer Ognibene, good fellow that he is, appreciate the charity with which I have provided, at once, for the honor of the young man and of the young woman; a thing which is the astonishment of her—I will not say stepmother, since the conscience and reason she shows rather entitle her to be called mother. I hope, with all the hope there may be, that I shall soon be able to assure the future of our bride and bridegroom, so that they may share in whatever I may have. And so, put aside forever any thought that may disturb you, thinking only of the welfare of your niece and my daughter.

From Venice, the 15th of September, 1537.

To THE DIVINE MICHELANGELO   LXVIII
    Of His "Last Judgment"

As, venerable man, it is a shame and a sin on the part of the soul not to remember God, so it is a reflection on the virtue and a dishonor to the judgment of every one who possesses virtue and judgment not to revere you, for you are the target[1] of wonderment, at whom the stars in rivalry shoot all the arrows of their grace. For in your hands lives the occult idea of a new nature, whence it is, the difficulty of line (which is the highest science, so far as the subtlety of a picture is concerned) with you is so easily overcome that, in your handling of line, you appear to attain the extremity of art; things which art itself confesses it is impossible to bring to perfection—for the line, as you know, must encompass itself—you accomplish in such a manner that you seem to be demonstrating the undemonstrable, giving us such promise as do the figures of the *Capella*, which you are fitted to judge, rather than to marvel at. And so I, who, with praise and infamy, have given the last touch to the merits or de-merits of others, in order not to convert into nothing the little that I am, salute you. Nor should I hasten to do so, if my name, which is acceptable to the ears of every prince, had not been sufficiently robbed of any indignity attaching to it. It is fitting that I should treat you with such reverence, since the world has many kings but only one Michelangelo. It is a great miracle that nature is not able to place a thing so high that you, with your industry, are not able to attain it, and to use it in your works, the majesty of which shows the immense power of your style and your chisel; hence, he

[1]The "bull's eye": *bersaglio*.

who has seen you need have no concern about not having seen Phidias, Apelles or Vitruvius, since their spirits were but the shadow of your own. I consider it a good fortune on the part of Parrhasius and other ancient painters that time has not preserved their works to be viewed today; for we, giving credit to history which trumpets their merits, put off awarding you that palm which they themselves, if they were to sit in judgment with our eyes, would give to you, calling you the one sculptor, the one painter and the one architect. Since this is so, why not be content with the glory which you have achieved? It seems to me, it should be enough for you to have overcome the others by other methods. But I know that, with the *End of the World*, which you are at present engaged in painting, you think to surpass the *Creation*, which you have already painted, so that your paintings, conquered by paintings, may give you a triumph over yourself. But who would not be terrified at the thought of putting his brush to so terrible a subject? I see, in the middle of the crowd, the Antichrist, with a countenance which could only be conceived by you. I see the fear on the faces of the living. I see the signs of extinction which the sun, moon and stars give. I see the spirit leaping up, as it were, from fire, air, earth and water. I see Nature horrified and sterilely recoiling in her decrepitude. I see Time, emaciated and trembling, who, having come to the end of his reign, is seated on a withered throne. And while the trumpets of the angels shake all hearts and breasts, I see Life and Death thrown into a frightful confusion, the one tired of raising up the dead, the other preparing to cast down the living. I see Hope and Despair guiding the hosts of the good and the throngs of the damned. I see the theatre of the clouds colored with the rays that come from the pure fires of heaven, on which, among his soldiery, Christ is seated, cinctured with splendor and with terror. I see the refulgence of His face and the scintillation of those flames of light, joy-ful and tender, which fill the good with gladness and the evil with fear. And in the mean time I behold the ministers of the abyss who, to the glory of the martyrs and the saints, deride the Caesars and the Alexanders, since to have conquered one's self is something different from having conquered the world. I see Fame with her crowns and her palms under foot, cast there under the wheels of her own chariots. And finally, I see coming out of the mouth of the great Son of God the last great sentence. I see it in the form of two arrows, one bringing salvation, the other damnation; and as I watch them come down, I hear fury crashing through the mechanism of the elements, with tremendous thunderbolts undoing and dissolving all. I see the lights of paradise and the furnaces of the abyss, which cut the shadows that fall upon the face of the windy universe. I am so moved by the thought which the image of the ruin of that last day inspires in me that I find myself saying: "If you fear and tremble so at the sight of Buonnaroti, how will you fear and tremble when you come to be judged by Him who is your judge?" But does not Your Lordship believe that I shall have to break the vow I have made never again to set eyes on Rome, in order to view such a history as this? I had rather make myself a liar than offend your virtue, which I hope will cherish the desire I have to publish it abroad.

From Venice, the 16th of September, 1537.

To KING FRANCIS I.[1]   LXIX

Upon the Reasons for His Majesty's Abandoning the Turks and Entering the League.

Your Majesty knows the good, religious and magnanimous deliberation which, from duty and from custom, the good, religious and magnanimous Venetians make use of. You know how they have scattered their riches in the Levant and the treasure which they have brought back, the blood that was shed and the unheard-of offers of the Turk, and how

[1]The letter which, as Hutton remarks, "reverberated throughout Europe."

these things, through Peter and Caesar, have moved the forces of land and sea in the service of Christ. For this reason, the world is bent upon asking you, which weighs the more in your most lofty breast, the hatred you bear to others, or the love that you owe to God? If hatred is the stronger, look to your title of "most Christian," for if it is not becoming to oppose one of your rank, neither is it permissible to assail him with names favorable to his dignity. But if love is the stronger, look at the most holy league, which is willing not merely to make a place for you, but to receive you with open arms to the place of greatest eminence. Collect yourself, and reflect that God, who has given you the finest kingdom there is, the most generous nature that breathes, the greatest knowledge that was ever heard of and the most affable grace that was ever seen, does not deserve that you should betray Him by becoming the despair of your followers and uniting them with their adversaries; in which case it would appear to the peoples that the virtue of the royal goodness had been conquered by the perfidy of stubbornness. Fortune breaks the glass in all the facets that gleam in your diamond. And from this it follows that, by bending your every thought and every effort in a contrary direction, she is in a position to laugh at the two millions in gold which France has spent against the three-hundred-fifty Ottoman sails, when they were pressing Castro. I tell you, Sire, these are the facts: that if, yielding, you seize the occasion to be reconciled with your great kinsman, you are putting yourself directly in God's favor, by being able to participate in the recovery of His sepulchre. Let yourself be moved by the example of Pipino and of Charles, and those who came before and after, by the might of whose arms, the fourth and Fifth Stephen, the third Leo, Urban, Pasquale and Gelasio the Second, Eugene the Third, with the fourth Innocent and other pontiffs, overcome by the fury of pride, were placed back on their thrones. But is not your heart perturbed at the thought of the confidence you would have to have in the

[165]

suspicions of the infidels? Do you think that two diverse creeds, mingled by the madness of revenge, can make one good end? Do you think you can domesticate Turkish barbarism with Gallic humanity? If you reflect on the temerity of Selim, vituperated in Hungary and outdone in Persia, tell me: what price can he pay for the concord of forty years, demonstrated to you by this omnipotent city? And then, one must not forget his being at Rhodes, one might say, a prisoner. Alas! Look, illustrious king, to your own rank and the office that you hold, and do not put your soul in peril, for with it, fame goes. Displeasing to true ears is the cry of irreligion, which will be the sound of your name, in case you remain allied with him who stands apart in the insolence of the pride he takes in the magnitude of his empire and the infinite number of his hounds, and whose arms are deprived of all art, all reason and all counsel, the principal spiritual supports of any army. And so, lay all your disdain in the firm hands of our faith, joining your mind with the minds of those who follow Jesus; for the glory of losing life and kingdom for His baptism is greater than the vituperation which follows one who lives and rules forever by any other circumcision. Disembarrass yourself, then, of this great monster, an alliance even more frightful than it is offensive; for he who trusts in such a thing shows his lack of trust in God, and an alliance of that sort might be called a "separation," rather than a "confederation," since it is one better fitting rebels against heaven than the princes of the universe. Beyond this, his arrogance will make a slave of your friendship, and he will boast of you as of a conquered thing; and he may well do so, since you teach him to do it, when you, who so many times have caused the Orient to fear and tremble, are found bowing to the banners of Mahommet. Ah, that worst of all passions, the passion to rule! Ah, the cruel desire of revenge! You—should you confiscate the mind of the most candid and the noblest king that ever was? Where, Francis, is that prudence of yours which, being born between victories, has won you so many triumphs? It is with you still. And so, listen to the supplications of the church and the vows of your people. Behold Paul who calls you, behold Charles who receives you, behold Mark who exhorts you, so that you should be glad of haste, rather than of delay, knowing that every reason which you appear to have on the human side is a wrong done to Christ.

From Venice, the 18th of September, 1537.

To The Duke d'Urbino   LXX
   *In Which He Congratulates Him on His Nomination
   to the Post of Generalissimo of the League.*

I do not congratulate myself, signor, on the act of His Holiness, His Majesty[1] and His Serene Highness[2] in choosing you, because whenever the Pope, the Emperor and the Venetians have thought of uniting their power to crush the Turk, you have been the general of the most Christian League. Every thought would be in vain, if it were not put into execution through your knowledge; and so, the rank which appears to us a new one is really very old. I take comfort in the reflection that the good qualities of my signor, which in the past have wrought good works, will now work miracles; and to this, God is witness, whose kindness, despite the fact it was provoked with the Church, has permitted his vicar to commit the hopes of his arms and his honors to the capacious counsel of Francesco Maria, who is a manifest example of religion, of merit and of experience. But if Fortune who, not to lose her reputation, has learned discretion from your enterprises, treats us too kindly to make us unhappy, how will she treat you, who have already placed your foot on the ladder of blessedness? It is a great thing that what you say and what you do is the very soul of what can be said and can be done. And it is astonishing to

[1]Charles.
[2]The Doge.

imagine how it is possible for you to think and foresee with a firm judgment what is not thought or foreseen, bringing peace to all the princes and putting an end to all wars, as if peace and war had consulted with your own admirable genius, whose prudence has a seat in the tribunal of memory, the three being rectors of virtue, as it were, in the form of a republic. So true is this that not only are they who fight by your side audacious against the enemy, benevolent with their soldiers and wise in grasping opportunity; but even those who merely hear you speak are learned in these matters; and so, we are proud of the victory even before you move against the monstrous adversary, sure of the truth that is in the laws of Christ, which, thanks to Your Excellency, shall have absolute authority throughout the Orient.

From Venice, the 18th of September, 1537.

To MADONNA ISABELLA MARCOLINA   LXXI
A Generous Lady Cannot Be an Immodest One.

I, godmother, take more satisfaction in the fact that you have given away the turquoise set in gold than if you had kept it as a remembrance of me, for the young girl whose finger it adorns will always remember your courtesy. However, I have no need of a noble act like this to certify to me the kinship which exists between generosity and your mind, for I have seen it too often in greater things; and Messer Francesco, your husband, well may boast of the liberality of a nature such as yours, for it is a sign of the chastity in which you are rich. Moreover, it is not possible for an unavaricious woman not to be modest. Need and avarice are the pimps for the virtue of other women, but she who is beyond need and avarice, as you are, is not known by blame; and yet, it would be easier to find a thousand close-fisted than two magnanimous women, thanks to the cheapness of the sex. And for no other reason do they violate their good and solemn duties, except for gain. And every time, through the fault of this woman or that, goodness and faith fall in ruins, it is the fault of misery, the mind of princes, a life of luxury or the desire to provide for old age. See, then, that, without ever departing from or becoming tired of it, you follow the old saying: It is better to give than to receive; for, giving, you are bartering things for benevolence and, receiving, you are selling benevolence for things; and since love is something more than utility, he who gives, receives, and he who receives, loses. I greatly praise your native disposition; in attempting to change it, you would become nothing.

From Venice, the 18th of September, 1537.

To DON LOPE SORIA   LXXII

Of the League Against the Turks.

The holiest procedure and the most approved practice are assured, signor, of a proper conclusion by that grave sufficiency of yours, which has been heard of ever since the idleness of princes, who burned with the usual desire for immortality, gave it birth, as a pleasure to the mind and a delight to the ambition for glory, the happiness which the mind finds in fixing its thoughts on high things. And so it became a business to find for emperors and trafficking kings a way of putting into effect their wills, from which come wars, peace and laws. Truly, you are deserving of the greatest reward and the highest honor a man ever had, since it is you who have brought to a conclusion the will, let us say, of God; as it is for the interest of his faith that the incredibly good and religious Venetians have come to act, bringing into the field a power of will and not an excuse for a lack of power. There is no doubt that, though no reason were just which did not aid our credit, yours would be most just, since the ancient commerce between Venice and Constantinople is well known. But where Christ is not, their hearts are not. Wherefore, let the great emperor congratulate himself that he has such friends; and following it up with arms which represent the Christian intention, the eagle and the lion will soon be beating their wings through the air of all the Orient, to the supreme happiness of yourself, who are an astonishment to every one who considers the apt manner in which, serving His Majesty, you satisfy the will of this most serene republic. Beyond this, how can it be that, on top of all these occurrences, you should be as mindful of the needs of the virtuous as you are of the servants of Caesar? Is there a person who cannot boast of the pleasure he has taken in the graceful courtesy of your nature? And among others, I am one of those who, with tongue and with pen, always shall speak well of Your Lordship, whose hands I kiss and to whose gentleness I am indebted for the state, praise God, in which I find myself.

From Venice, the 19th of September, 1537.

To The Marchese Del Vasto   LXXIII
    On the Same Subject.

In the greatest necessity, signor, which Christianity ever had, in the extremity of the religion of Christ, on the most worthy occasion of honor, Your Excellency, by taking from the nest the cocks[1] of Italy, has done a work of such a sort and so suited to the public good that even Envy, which would have no one merit praise, reproves Fame for not crying through the world the reward which should be yours, a reward for beating back the other kings from the place whence His Majesty thought to hunt down your emperor. But if you, with the breast of valor's self, do not turn back the French fury, how can the chain of our faith be made to bind together the ecclesiastic mind, the Caesarean heart and the Venetian soul? Certainly, your conduct, past and present, is not merely a model to the one who would be victorious in enterprises and rule republics, or to the prince who gives ranks and rewards, but it is the key, also, which opens the

[1] *I galli d'Italia.*

[171]

gates of Constantinople to the ships and horses of the people of God, who would fear for His own safety if France, escaping your arms, were to succeed in effecting an alliance with the Turks, who, sunk in their own bestiality[1] and maddened by others, with flesh and blood would make Corfu more eternal than Rome. Exercise, then, that care, governed in military fashion by your accurate foresight; for one wiser or more courageous could not be hoped for in any part of an army. And so you, returning to clear the Alps, which you passed with Augustus, will complete the work which he began. In the meanwhile, your name flies with the wings of a new fame; new, I say, because it is not a poetic adulation, not an historic lie, but the public voice which exalts you, and no praise is so clear as yours, since even the striplings are singing it. Nor should I refrain from telling you of Messer Angelo Contarino, who is no less learned than he is good, and who said, in a circle of senators: "The Marchese del Vasto is the wood of India which will cure Italy of the French plague."[2] It is no wonder, then, if I, with the pen and tongue of a pure and true man, find food in writing of the operations of the most excellent Alfonso d'Avolos, my lord.

From Venice, the 20th of September, 1537.

To Messer Girolamo Molino   LXXIV
    On the Same Subject.

Any one, brother, who would like to see the love which I, without desire of favor or reward, bear this city of God should have been able to lay his hand on my breast when your advice made me a party to the deliberations of the most serene senate against the Turks. I am sure my heart, at this news, indulged in such movements as it never shall know again, from any joy whatsoever. If it had not been that my judgment in the eleven years of Venetian liberty which I

[1]Cf. *Schrecklichkeit!*
[2]*mal francese*: the syphilis.

have enjoyed had taught me to know the goodness of the Venetian nature, I should have been transported at such tidings. Any one who knows how much I love the religion to which we are born, how I desire the glory of the divine place which I, by my own choice, inhabit and how I long for the greatness of the emperor, whose Majesty holds my virtue as his handmaiden—any one who knows this, will believe me. What a fine boast will be Venice's, throughout the world and in every century, that for Jesus she spilled blood and riches! But if I, merely by living here, feed on such a reputation, what should you do who, thanks to your learn-ing, your wide experience and your all-sufficient worth, are established with us as a gentleman? May God never let the thought enter my mind of moving foot out of these secure and sacred waters; and so may my mind always be bent to consider the excellences of such a republic, which, holding its right direct from God, commands and forbids dishonest things, by custom and not by code, and so has created most chaste laws, which restrain the audacious and assure the innocence of the good, the dominion of which shall be con-current with the eternity of the universe. It could not be otherwise, for these people rule their magistrates, not their magistrates them. And from this, it follows that the dignity of Christ is placed before the interest of individuals, and established law has placed the heart of St. Mark in the palm of the Christian faith, so that princes may see its pure inten-tion. Then, get your pen and paper ready, for the fortunate outcome of the holy and ordained enterprise will provide you with plenty of material, and such a subject is proper food for your intellect.

From Venice, the 22nd of September, 1537.

To Messer Lorenzo Veniero   LXXV
    Against the Pedants.
    I, magnificent son, had thought it impossible, even though

fate smiled upon my virtues, ever to disentangle myself from the hands of necessity; and now, thank God, I find myself in the arms of want, which to my judgment is a thing more tolerable than the beggary of utter poverty. But I swear to you that the claws of envy, which have so plucked my feathers, are a thing I never hope to escape, living or dead. Would you believe that the inventors of envy were the pedants? I assure you, I think it came from their swinish attempts to prove that two negatives made an affirmative. But I am really much obliged to the malignity of my cruci-fiers, for the thought of them leads me to smite their horse's buttocks continuously, giving them a hundred blows for their own faults and a hundred for the virtues of others. But how insolent that herd which devours me with its envy would be, if God, in his goodness, were to show them the grace he shows to me, such grace that no prince appears to be a prince, if he does not witness the fact by paying constant tribute to my virtue? By my faith, in all the happiness which my virtue brings me, I have always shown an extreme modesty; for this, I have fled neither the light of day nor the occult arrogance of the worst of men. Since it is not true that he who hates a virtuous man is good, it is not seemly to offend the academy of all the virtuous and all the good! And if it were not that I know envy always trails glory, I should lose patience, as you have with the advocates, for advocates are the night of the day of justice. In refusing such a title, you display the mind of a gentleman; and so, leaving the quarrels over the rights and wrongs of the widow and the orphan[1] to those who have at heart gain rather than conscience, seek to procure rank for yourself in other offices, spending the hours, which with you are coming along, in poetry, for as you well know, you and your brothers owe this to your own reputations. The learned look with great expectation to the *Rime* of Messer Domenico, and the work of Messer Fran-cesco is beyond expectation, since he is not of the profession.

[1] *queste vedova e . . . quel pupillo.*

I believe that the seed of the magnificent Messer Gian-nandrea which is in you comes from Parnassus; and so, all his sons should be Apollos and Mercuries. Virtue is a fine thing in any one, but it is of the finest when joined to nobility, in which case it grows by its own grace and the graces of the one who adorns himself with it. May you have, then, no other concern; for a little glory is worth a vast deal of wordly goods.

From Venice, the 24th of September, 1537.

To MESSER BERNARDO TASSO   LXXVI
    On the Death of a Friend.

Just as I was reflecting, illustrious spirit, on the praise which the voice of public acclaim gives your facile and felici-tous labors—such praises as those judges give who, by their knowledge, are worthy of passing judgment on you—just as I was thinking this, I was told: "The good Ferier Beltramo is dead! And then, with such an accident upon my mind, the joy that I had in thinking of your honors changed to grief in thinking of his death, and I was sad for the loss of a friend. But since I know that you know that he loved me as I am aware[1] he loved you, I am sure you will mourn the immeasurable lovableness and the courteous manners of such a nature, even as I mourn for them. Truly, man is a bundle of weaknesses, devoured by misery and by time; and so, when, fortune scorning him, he draws up a balance of envy, he ought to reflect on the danger to his soul in confid-ing in life; for life is a toy made of glass; it appears to be of inestimable price, but in reality it is very cheap. And I, for my part, would compare it to the sun in winter, the cloud in summer, the flower in spring and the leaf in autumn. But what displeasure have I given Death that she must every day so fiercely outrage me? She meets revenge in you, who dwell beyond her jurisdiction; let her turn to Sperone or

[1]An example of Aretino's occasional perverted word-play.

Grazia or Molino, who are immortal, but not to me, whose eyes are always fixed on her eternal sleep. How cruel she is, since, without looking, she, with one stroke almost, has taken away from me Luigi Gritti, Anton da Leva, Francesco Sforza, and Ippolito and Alessandro de' Medici, without having also to rob me of the signor Giovanni and of Bonifazio, marchese di Monferrato; for all these deaths have left me without hope, and if the goodness of Charles were to cease, I should be as little a thing as he is great. And for a final blow, she has taken from me as much tenderness, as much gentleness and as much lovableness as could be desired in the rite of friendship. There will never be a more courteous, a more loving or a more cordial companion. He was affection itself; and it is for this reason that I have been unable to express to you my astonishment at the manner in which you, by your works, have put an end to slander; nor can any one tire of reading those works or of exalting their vivacious, novel, sweet and candid spirit. They are such as to cause Fame, when she thinks of them, to marvel, to the great honor of your name.

From Venice, the 26th of September, 1537.

To Messer Matteo Durastante da San Giusto   LXXVII
   Fungi, Quail and Thrushes.
By grace of being a good fellow, which is a title I must accord you, you sent me not merely the fungi, which I expected, but a mess of quails and thrushes, which I did not expect; and so, I really ought to thank you for ten gifts; for these are a safer diet than those perilous mushrooms and are cooked in two turns of the skillet, sandwiched with lettuce and sausages in careless fashion. But you cannot do that with the fungi, which must be boiled with two slices of bread and then fried in oil. And moreover, one likes to eat them in the morning but not so well at night, from fear of being poisoned, when it is not so easy to wake up their

excellencies, the doctors. The churchmen do well who confess themselves and go to communion before they put them
in their mouths. I take great pleasure in watching a cowardly
glutton who likes to fill his belly with them, and in laughing
at him when he bends double as the odor assails his nose
and fear his mind. But he who does not know how cheaply
life holds itself may get some idea by putting in his mouth
such victuals as these, which are no less poisonous than they
are vile. And yet, don't fail to send us some! But may God
guard you from these and other accidents.

From Venice, the 20th of October, 1537.

To MESSER BERNARDO TASSO   LXXVIII
    Of His Own Loves.

How often, honorable brother, have I smiled to myself at
the venereal intrigues of our Molza. I have laughed as I
thought of all of them and of the miracles which his sacred
genius works for its own pleasure. I never have seen the
snow falling from heaven without remarking: "Molza's
amours are more numerous than all those flakes," being prepared to swear that Cupid had spent all his arrows on my
friend's account and so had been forced to beat into submission with his bow and quiver the hearts he would conquer.
And I was stupefied to think how so generous-minded a man,
coming from the holy temples and the grand *palazzi*, should
turn to the synagogues and permit himself to be ensnared by
a Jewess, known to all the world as such. But now that I
begin to have some knowledge of myself, I laugh at myself
and wonder; for running from one madness to another, I
doubt if my own love-escapades are not eternal. Look you,
the second follows the first and the fourth the third, crowd-
ing as thickly on one another as do my prodigal debts. Surely,
there must be in my eyes so tender a fury that, attracting to
itself every bit of loveliness, it still can never get enough of
beauty. And I often have been inclined to think that in this

[177]

I was avenged for the blasphemies of the priests, resolved to thank God that nature more often shows me objects of love than objects of hate, thanking fate who has made me a lover and not a tradesman. And except that I ought not to be practicing such a trade at my age, I would look upon myself as blessed, for amorous desire is a delightful torment, and the teeth of concupiscence bite sweetly and gently; for in such vexation as this, you look for good things to come and take no less pleasure in future than in present joys, delighting yourself even with those that are past. If I, by some necromancy, were able to rid myself of the weight of eight or ten years, I should be wise and triumph by making a change from month to amorous month, like a sharp and stingy courtezan who, by changing her servant every fifteen days, finds herself well served and with no salary to pay. But it is the very devil to try to make such changes as this in your old age, for age has a good mind and sorry shanks. And it is a sin that the poor old lady cannot close her eyes, at midnight or dawn, from suffering all the passions and jealousies of youth, fixing her thoughts, which ought to be on death that holds her by the hair, on some *diva* who makes sport of her solicitudes and her cares. Any one is surely crazy who thinks that all the gifts of old men and the trouble to which they put themselves do them any good. The insults and vituperations, the outrages and infamies of beardless youths are more grateful to the women than all the fame and all the glory which he who has fame and glory can possibly give them. And I ought to know, who have made the heavens ring with the name of the one I loved with the holiest and most chaste affection,[1] and who have had for my reward my own disgrace. And with this, I commend myself to you.[2]

[1]Pierina Riccia.
[2]Without date.

In Which He Remembers the Friend Who Has Never Abandoned Him in Adversity.

You can see, brother, God has willed that I should conquer, with patience and with virtue, the perversity of the times, the avarice of princes and the envy of men. Despite the sorrows that banished my virtue from Rome, those virtues have remained unchanged. And I, satisfied with my own honors, flying with the wings of the very best reputation, am known to all the world, just as you have heard of me even in Leo's temple. And so, joining yourself to me in that true friendship which never belies the name, you have always suffered, in my persecutions, the same pains that I suffered. Nor did I ever sigh or grieve at the wrongs done me that you also did not sigh and grieve. I have seen you, in the course of the treasons that have befallen me, preferring, for my sake, to leave the service of Cornaro and Rangone, your most revered patrons, showing to him who had robbed my seven years[1] of service of the hope that was theirs that fate was not thereby able to rob me of your friendship, of which I never have despaired in the most tempestuous or the most calm and tranquil fortune. All this you do for the reason that your own joy stands in no need of comfort nor the upright man of support. Truly, I prefer my own good fortune to the victories of the emperor, because I have been able to acquire and to keep such a friend as you. And there is more glory for you in being such a friend than if you were the repository of all wisdom. The zeal of one who knows how to exercise charity and benevolence is of more merit than are the works which the soul performs out of pity. It is proper that the terms, holy and wonderful, be applied to the best of friends, whose tender offices produce such holy and miraculous fruits. That those fruits are holy is shown by the good that follows them; and as to how miraculous they are,

[1]The *sette anni traditori*. See the sonnet.

I who, through them, feel myself transformed into you, am a demonstration. I am grateful to you for having always, with all your faculties, watched over and succoured my happiness, which draws tears of joy from your eyes, as my adversities have drawn tears of compassion.

From Venice, the 25th of October, 1537.

To MESSER DOMENICO BOLANI   LXXX
   Description of the House Which He Had Rented of Him.[1]

It would appear to me, honored gentleman, a sin of ingratitude, if I did not pay in praises the debt I owe to the divinity of the place in which your house is situated, where I dwell with all the pleasure that there is in life, for its site is the most proper, being neither too high up nor too low down. I am as timorous about entering upon its merits as one is about speaking of those of the emperor. Certainly, he who built it picked out the best spot on the Grand Canal. And since it is the patriarch of streams and Venice the popess of cities, I can say with truth that I enjoy the finest street and the pleasantest view in the world. I never go to the window that I do not see a thousand persons and as many gondolas at the hour of market. The *piazze* to my right are the *Beccarie* and the *Pescaria;*[2] as well as the *Campo del Mancino,* the *Ponte* and the *Fondaco dei Tedeschi;* and where these meet, there is the *Rialto,* crowded with men of business. Here, we have the grapes in barges, the game and pheasants in shops, the vegetables on the pavement. Nor do I long for meadow streams, when at dawn I wonder at the waters covered with every kind of thing in its season. It is good sport to watch those who bring in the great stores of fruit and vegetables passing them out to those who carry them to their appointed places! All is bustle, except the spectacle of the twenty or

[1]See Hutton's chapter.
[2]The meat and fish markets.

{ 180 }

twenty-five sail boats, filled with melons which, huddled together, make, as it were, an island in the middle of the multitude; but then comes the business of counting, sniffing and weighing them, to judge their perfection. Of the beautiful housewives, shining in silk and superbly resplendent in gold and jewels, not to appear to be indulging in an anticlimax, I refrain from speaking. But of one thing I shall speak, and that is of how I nearly cracked my jaws with laughter when the cries, hoots and uproar from the boats was drowned in that of grooms at seeing a bark-load of Germans, who had just come out of the tavern, capsized in the cold waters of the canal, a sight that the famous Giulio Camillo and I saw one day. He, by the way, used to take a delight in remarking to me that the entrance to my house from the land-side, being a dark one and with a beastly stair, was like the terrible name I had acquired by revealing the truth. And then, he would add that any one who came to know me would find in my pure, plain and natural friendship the same tranquil contentment that was felt on reaching the portico and coming out on the balconies above. But that nothing might be lacking to my visual delights, behold, on one side, I have the oranges that gild the base of the *Palazzo dei Camerlinghi* and, on the other side, the *rio* and the *Ponte di San Giovan Grisostomo*. Nor does the winter sun ever rise without entering my bed, my study, my kitchen, my other apartments and my drawingroom. But what I prize most is the nobility of my neighbors. I have opposite me the eloquent, magnificent and honored Maffio Lioni, whose supreme virtues have taught learning, science and good manners to the sublime intellect of Girolamo, Piero and Luigi, his wonderful sons. I have also His Serene Highness, my sacramental and loving godfather, and his son. I have the magnanimous Francesco Moccinico, who provides a constant and splendid board for cavaliers and gentlemen. At the corner, I see the good Messer Giambattista Spinelli, under whose paternal roof dwell my friends, the Cavorlini (may God pardon fortune for the wrong done them by fate). Nor do I regard as the least of my good fortune the fact that I have the dear Signora Iacopa, to whom I am so used, for a neighbor. In short, if I could feed the touch and the other senses as I feed the sight, this house which I am praising would be to me a paradise; for I content my vision with all the amusement which the objects it loves can give. Nor am I at all put out by the great foreign masters of the earth who frequently enter my door, nor by the respect which elevates me to the skies, nor by the coming and going of the bucentaur,[1] nor by the regattas and the feast days, which give the Canal a continuously triumphal appearance, all of which the view from my windows commands. And what of the lights, which at night are like twinkling stars, on the boats that bring us the necessities for our luncheons and our dinners? What of the music which by night ravishes my ears? It would be easier to express the profound judgment which you show in letters and in public office than to make an end of enumerating all the delights my eyes enjoy. And so, if there is any breath of genius in my written chatterings, it comes from the favor you have done me—not the air, not the shade, not the violets and the greenery, but the airy happiness I take in this mansion of yours, in which God grant I may spend, in health and vigor, the remainder of those years which a good man ought to live.

From Venice, the 27th of October, 1537.

To Tribolo, the Sculptor   LXXXI
    On the "St. Peter, Martyr" of Titian.
Messer Sebastiano, the architect, knowing the great delight I take and the small judgment I possess in sculpture, pleased me much by making me see, through his description, the facile manner in which the folds of the Virgin's robe fall[2]

───────────────

[1]The state barge.

[2]It is interesting here to compare the things which the early Cubists [see Salmon] found, or thought they found, in El Greco. See also what Roger Fry says of El Greco ["Vision and Design"].

in the work of genius which you dedicated to me. He described to me also how languidly the members of Christ droop, the dead Christ whom you, with a fine stroke of art, have placed in her lap; and he did it so vividly that I beheld the affliction of the mother and the misery of the son before I really saw them. As he told me of the wonderful work you had done, I thought of the author of that *San Pietro Martire*. You remember how astonished you and Benvenuto[1] were upon looking at it. Closing, in the presence of such a work, your physical and mental eyes, you felt all the living terrors of death and all the true griefs of life in the forehead and the flesh of the one who had fallen to the ground, and you wondered at the cold and livid appearance of the nose and the bodily extremities; nor could you restrain an exclamation when, upon beholding the fleeing multitude, you perceived in their countenances a balance of vileness and fear. Truly, you pronounced a right judgment upon my great table when you told me it was not the most beautiful thing in Italy. What a marvelous group of cherubs in the air, amid the trees which shelter them with their trunks and leaves! What a wonderfully simple and natural landscape! What mossy stones that water bathes which issues here from the brush of the divine Titian! Who, in his benign modesty, salutes you most warmly, proffering himself and anything he has, swearing there is no equal to the affectionate interest he takes in your fame. Nor can I tell you how eagerly he awaits seeing the two figures which, by your own choice, you have decided to send me: a gift which, I assure you, shall not be passed over in silence nor with ingratitude.

From Venice, the 29th of October, 1537.

To Messer Bernardo Navaiero   LXXXII
    In Praise of Venice.
Your literate and laudable testimonial, excellent youth,

[1]Cellini.

together with that of the honored Messer Girolamo Quirini, is well adapted to make clear to others how, in the breasts of the chieftains who have been elected to admonish and to punish, there is no benevolent affection, either new or old, with which I have not been tenderly received and sheltered, as an act worthy of the deeds of the magnanimous Venetian nature. I, while the high favor of the most illustrious Pietro Zeno and the most excellent Marcantonio Veniero was lift- ing me from the earth, took occasion to look up and saw, at the top of the tribunal, all the sincere modesty which goes to enrich the gravity of justice; I saw also honor, glory, praise, power, presidency, reputation, eloquence, magistracy, clemency and felicity. Whereupon I, bowing my mind to such virtues, blessed in my heart the instant and the hour in which fate brought me here, that fate which, in return for my piety, removed me from the malignity of courts. For popes, emperors and kings, to those who serve them, are the source of calumnies and adulations, as well as of poverty and misery, whence it is, hope, when it grows a little larger, becomes at once the object of an envy grown more bitter, a hatred more perilous and an emulation more acute; a thing which has no place in the service of a republic, in which, while particular interests may puff the minds of a few, the eye of duty, which looks always to the public good, sees to it that, in whatever happens, malevolence is converted into love. But those peoples who trail out their years in the wake of princes become mad and devour, with a constant rancor, both themselves and others. And so, my situation here, in the bed of this lagoon, is my consolation. I am looked upon gently by the most esteemed and the wisest. I obtain the benignity of all pleasures and graces. And I enjoy, above all my other noble customs, your conversation, which to me is dearer than the intimacy of any lord whatsoever, since from your spirit come not only examples, judgments and doctrines, but honesty, good manners and gentility. And it seems to me, as I look upon you, that I am beholding the image of the

[184]

Greek and Latin tongues and the very statue of goodness. And so, I pay you my respects and celebrate you.

From Venice, the 3rd of November, 1537.

To MESSER GIROLAMO SARRA   LXXXIII
  Of Various Kinds of Salad.

As soon, my brother, as the tributes of salad begin to fall off, giving rein to my fancy for divination, I set about astrologizing the reasons why you are withholding payment in foods from my appetite and my taste. But if I had carried my thoughts on to the olive-oil press, I never would have suspected that you would deprive me of such provision, replacing it with citronella, which is as pleasing to your throat as it is displeasing to mine. And so it is, man says: "Whence come enmities?" They come from that herb, which you could not refrain from sending me nor I from throwing away. What the devil should be done with one of those who neither drink wine nor eat melons, when they take away from a good companion his drink-money,[1] at the request of Monna Ranciata, whose overbearingness is to be seen in all the gardens? Surely, she must have bewitched you and left you with a sibyl in your arms, from whom you are taking orders. Alas! I suppose I shall have to accustom myself to doing without, and I hope to be able to do so, since I am used to being without a farthing, which is quite different from opening the mouth and sending down a good swig. And so, change your mind and send me the tribute which your own courtesy lays upon you, so that I may enjoy those fruits which you plant in the soft March earth for the pleasure of the merchant-porters. Ask the good Fortunio what pleasure I take, what praises I give and what a welcome I extend upon the receipt of a gift of salads, as well as to the servant who fetches them. I perceive in what manner you have tempered the bitterness of some herbs with the sweetness of

[1]*regaglie:* cf. the French *pourboire.*

[185]

others. It takes little learning to know how to mitigate the sharp and biting taste of certain leaves with the flavor, neither sharp nor bitter, of certain others, making of the whole a compound that is satisfying to the point of satiety. The blossoms scattered among the little greens of such fine appetizers tempt my nose to whiff them and my hand to pluck them. In short, if my servants knew how to make spices in the Genoese manner, I should leave for them the breast of wild chicken which, very often, for lunch and for dinner, to the glory of Cadoro, the unique Titian sends me; although, not without blame to me, who am a Tuscan, for not remembering it, I leave the preparation of it to the one who killed it. I do not know what pedant it was, making a face at one you sent me the other day, entered upon a eulogy of the lettuce and the endives, which were quite without odor; until Priapus, the god of gardeners, becoming angry with himself, debated whether he should not hunt them all down from behind, most bestially. For I prefer a handful, not of home-made salad, but of wild succory and a little catmint, to all the lettuces and endives that ever were. I am astonished that the poets do not become drunken in singing the virtues of the salad. It is a great wrong to the friars and nuns not to praise it, for they steal whole hours from their orisons, to spend it in cleaning the leaves of little stones, and they throw much time away as they sweat in gathering and curing those leaves. I believe the inventor must have been a Florentine—he could not have been any-body else—for the laying of the table, decorating it with roses, the washing of beakers, the putting of plums in rag-oûts, the garnishing of cooked livers, the making of blood-puddings and the serving of fruit after meals all come from Florence. Their pigs' brains, thirst-inciters and *diligentini*, with their other thoughtful subtleties, cover all the points by means of which cookery may appeal to the jaded appetite. In conclusion, I will say that the citronella is only remem-bered by me with annoyance. And so, tomorrow will be as good a time as any to put me back in the good graces of your garden. And avoid the deadly rue; for when I come upon a salad that has been well rolled in a vinegar fit to grind stones, I rebel at the very smell of it.

From Venice, the 4th of November, 1537.

To The Marchesa di Pescara   LXXXIV
    Praises.

This century of ours, signora, which has nothing left to wonder at, such are the works it has produced through its genius, may still be astonished at those it has given birth to through the spirit. But in avoiding all comparisons which are better suited to the soul than to the intellect, it is difficult to make a beginning, when one opens his mouth or raises his eyebrows. Two things the world has not seen the like of: one, the invincible spirit of your consort; the other, your own high and invincible mind, whose kindness gives you the palm; for as he, with his force, won the battles of the people, so you, with such valor as that you possess, win the wars of the senses. And while the purity of those flames with which the angels glow lights your heart, you are vaunted by the true voice of a holy fame, for which reason heaven reserves for you other palms and other crowns than mortal ones. What an augury of happiness it was the day you were christened "Vittoria." What fatality was in the name, since, conquering, as with arms, all the wordly vanities, you adorn yourself with the spoils and trophies acquired in the confiscations of a firm well-doing and a constant faith in the face of earthly deceits. You, not to lessen the rank of your great husband, have discovered the spiritual militia, whose cohorts come into camp under the ensigns of reason, which, for the honor of Jesus and in the service of the soul, triumphs over its adversaries in every campaign. As a demonstration, while he, in order to dominate the inexpugnable, was putting into operation what the school of Mars never knew, so you,

to subjugate the abyss, employ all that you have learned from the studies of Christ, holding at low rate those who are more interested in acquiring earthly than heavenly glory, and who display more heart in making themselves lords of the cities of the earth than of the kingdom of paradise, shedding with greater lealty their blood for men than they do their tears for God, repudiating, in their hope of praise and gain, the life that is in death, being afraid of the shadow which surrounds the service of our Redeemer. For the conquerors of any clime never wore a diadem as resplendent as that which gleams in the cap of the man who has learned to subdue himself, for all the difficulties of bravery and prudence lie in this, and not in the overthrow of empires. This being so, what chariot and what garland should your just goodness have, since it, always being conscious of the public good, never fleeing the assaults of error, but maintaining constantly a war with vice and peace with virtue, has made itself its own prisoner? O elected lady, you alone know how to live at the celestial board, making your food of those viands which are cooked with the fervent fires of charity, which in your firm breast finds the inn of all delights, chaste, sweet, gentle, clear, sacred and holy. And since your desire is none other than to hear the word of God, as enclosed in the bosom of the Scriptures, you make merely a change of lesson and, transforming the poetic books into prophetic volumes, you study Christ, Paul, Agostino, Girolano and the other pens of religion. Happy, then, in the memory which you leave with us here below, and which you store up for yourself in your eternal fatherland above, have compassion, being such as you are, on those who are otherwise; for you know (you who are so restrained with the manners of your father and adored with the graces of your mother) that all our little brief mortality is a thing we hold in common with the animals; whence it is, avoiding all gifts that depend on time and fortune, you procure for your constant soul eternal things, thus satisfying God, who always was, and yourself, who will be always. But terrestrial magnificences would yet be excellent, if only the princes who are monarchs of them would set before themselves a standard of high living such as that you have set yourself.

From Venice, the 5th of November, 1537.

To MESSER ANTONIO BRUCCIOLI   LXXXV
   Against the Ignorant Friars.

Why, my good fellow, do you pay any attention to the idle chatterings of the friars, since hatred is an essential of their nature, and all they know how to do is to bark and bite? You ought to know well enough that love never goes un-accompanied by jealousy or glory by envy. I do not deny that, in a few monasteries, there are fathers worthy of praise and rank; I believe in this, just as I believe in miracles; but by Christ, take away the few truly good, and you will see what sort it is who put on the habits, so called, of your saints. Scarcely does their arrogance scent accomplishment or learn-ing on the part of others than, being ashamed that others should do what they by profession and by sacrament are obligated to do, they at once attempt to take vengeance for their own natural ignorance by taxing the life, name and works of the chaste interpreters of the Old and New Testa-ments. Growing old, in the footsteps of the *maestri* and the wiseacres, they lose all hope of being able, through their own industry or genius, to walk with new feet in the true paths of God's Scriptures, and so, they annoy with a Lutheran calumny those who are most just and most Christian. Our defense is the credit which they have lost, in fact and as a result. The wrongful sway which they formerly exercised over our rightful merits has become the handmaid of him, who, with deeds and not with fictions, speaks well and writes better. Go on, then, driving them to despair with the volumes which your profound and sincere wisdom gives the world; for the *Bibbia*, the *Salmi* and the other immortal

{ 190 }

labors of Bruccioli are not food to the taste of such as they. What a benefit it would be to our souls and their lives, if, changing their nature and their literary style, they would only mount their pulpits as preachers and not as cavillers! For the good and simple know that the coming of the Son of God will make manifest to us that which is hidden in each and every prophecy. Hence, whoever believes in Jesus finds that such a belief has infused into his intellect the Virgin birth, the immortality of the soul and the resurrection of the dead. Every impossible effect may easily be demonstrated by one who is not doubtful of his birth. For this reason, the reverend fathers have no business going about vociferating in their pulpits about the manner in which the divine Word was incarnated in Mary, nor how it is the spirit leaves our members cold, nor how the dust of flesh and bone, tossed to the winds or scattered on the sea, must be brought together again in order that we may be resurrected alive. Surely, such brazen arguments are a reproach to the silence of Christ, who simply gives us a sign, in order not to take away the premium which he puts on faith, which is a blessing to those who, believing, seek neither testimony nor pledge. We go to church clean of those scruples which the perverse find in religion, and, thinking we are going to hear a sermon, we hear a strident dispute, which has nothing whatever to do with the gospels or with our sins. As a result, even the barbarians look upon the whole thing as a fantasy. The root of the evil lies in the desire for transcendental knowledge on the part of those who would do themselves more honor by commending and bowing to you than in offending and injuring you; for you are a man without an equal in your knowledge of the Hebraic, Greek, Latin and Chaldean tongues, and so good at heart that you would rather teach those who reprehend your writings than revenge yourself on them. And so, you are bound to live happy and honored.

From Venice, the 7th of November, 1537.

The "Annunciation."[1]

That was wise foresight on your part, my dear fellow, in deciding to send your picture of the Queen of Heaven to the empress of the earth. Nor could that high judgment from which you draw the marvels of your painting have found a loftier lodging place for the canvas in which you depict such an Annunciation. It is dazzling in the rays of gleaming light which issue from the rays of paradise, from whence come angels, gently wafted down in diverse attitudes over the gleaming, light and lively-hued clouds. The Holy Spirit, surrounded by the lamps of its own glory, makes us hear the beating of its wings, so life-like is the dove whose form it has taken. The heavenly arch which spans the air over the country revealed by the glow of dawn is truer than that which we actually see of an evening after a rain.[2] But what am I to say of Gabriel, the divine messenger? He, filling everything with light and more refulgent than ever in the inn, is bowing so gently, with such a gesture of reverence, that he forces us to believe he is actually appearing in the sight of Mary. He has a celestial majesty in his countenance, and his cheeks are trembling with the tender hue of milk and blood, which your coloring has very naturally counterfeited. His head is haloed with modesty, while gravity gently abases his eyes; his hair falls in tremulous ringlets. The fine robe of yellow cloth is not incompatible with the simplicity of his attire and conceals without hiding his nudity. Nor were wings ever to be seen before with such a fine variety of plumage. And the fragrant lily in his left hand shines with an unwonted candor. Above, his mouth is forming a saluta-tion, expressed in the angelic notes, "Ave." The Virgin is first adored and then consoled by the courier of God, and you have painted her so marvelously and in such a manner that all other lights are dazzled by the luminous reflections

[1] A description, the only one we have, of the famous painting now lost to us.
[2] Aretino, as has been said (see Introduction) was a realist in his art criticism.

of her peace and piety. So that now, in the light of this new miracle, we are no longer able to praise as before that history which you painted in the *Palazzo di San Marco*, as an honor to our lords and an annoyance to those who, not being able to deny your genius, gave you the first place in painting and to me the first in evil-speaking, as if your works and mine were not visible throughout the world.

From Venice, the 9th of November, 1537.

To Messer Fortunio LXXXVII
  In Which He Exhorts His Friend to Free Himself of the Snares of Love.

Why, honored brother, do you seek to flee love by going to the country? Do you not know that what you need is a change of mind, and not of place? Desire, the image of the loved object, like a mirror of the heart, always stands before you with an image of the one for whom you sigh, burn and weep; and so, putting distance between you and her is merely making a martyr of yourself for her sake. The bird whose wing has caught fire cannot put out the flame, but only kindles it the more, by flying; and when the mind, with an arrow in its side, takes flight, it is simply speeding its own end. Hence, betaking yourself here and there will only be the death of you. Moreover, think how shameful it is to commit one's self to such an experiment when one knows, one can with difficulty stay away. In case you wish to forget the affection you bear another, the best thing is to root it out with love of the soul, which is a subject worthy of the dignity it lends us.[1] In loving the body, you have forgotten how praiseworthy is constancy, the principal virtue in a lover. The lady knows that you repent loving her; and so, resolve to break the yoke of servitude with the free hand of prudence, being unwilling to permit the gifts of friendship, conferred upon you by the stars, to be rendered sterile by

[1]"Sublimation"!

[193]

venereal pains. What more can the skies give you than they have given you already? You have a majestic presence, gentle manners, ability in action, a graceful bearing, good nature, a happy genius, praise for your works and a glorious name. So true is this, that many persons often blame the planets for the poverty of their intellects and envy your wealth of spirit. Therefore, compose your reason, which has been upset through the wrong done your vanity by the gentle love god. Turn your thoughts to the exercises of science, so that our own times and centuries to come may not have cause to curse the inactivity which, with idle flattery, keeps you marking time, to the delight of death, who always tries to put fancy to sleep because those who give praise do not place the seat of immortality in her dominion. Of what use to us is that familiarity which you have with the learning of all tongues, if your industry stands idle and time is wronged by the silence of your pen? Although I am the greatest loser of all, since I learn from you what I do not know and what no other can teach me. But if you are not moved by considerations of your own honor and the common profit, then I trust you will be moved by the debt you have always felt you owed to Your Lordship's rank, being not unmindful of the fact that we are of the same native land; as a sign of which, witness the bonds of benevolence which of old have bound *aretine* minds and the hearts of Viterbum. For you in Arezzo and I in Viterbum are in a position to enjoy those magisterial privileges which the statutes in either city give us. But this is little in comparison with the place which friendship holds with you, for your kindness joins me to you in an affection which can never be broken. Finally, I would conjure you, by the dear gentleness and the charity that is in you, to make your peace with your books, which, now that you have cast them aside, you seem to hate; for Italy well knows that you not only write books worth reading but speak, always, things worth writing.

From Venice, the 15th of November, 1537.

In Which He Dissuades His Friend from Going to War.

I do not know what well known man it was who swore to
me recently that some whim had seized you again for some
business or other. Stay at Coreggio, my sire; stay with us;
or, *al corpo di me*, you'll be hunting me up to write your
epitaph. I had thought that the *cacaruola* of Montemurlo
would have made you wise, but you are worse than ever.
And the reason for this is the Ciceronian judgment in the
treatise, *Del tiranno*, which is the a-b-c of your propositions.
I tell you, you would do better to make it your business to
confabulate with your lyre at the fireside of our patroness,
Signora Veronica, improvising a couple of stanzas in heroic
fashion and leaving weather-veering to the weather-cocks.
I think of how I found you at Prato, buried in that vat of
straw (from which you cried out to the cavalryman, who, not
knowing you were with us, wished to take a couple of
mouthfuls: "I surrender"); and I wonder that you did not
make a vow to all the Virgins in the world to say nothing
more about liberty or pay. But alas! madness and the devil
tempt you and drag you away; go, then, but take it easy
behind the baggage trains, for in a "*Salvum me fac*" lies the
safety of *nos otros*, and not in getting into the rout, receiving
half a dozen wounds and, in addition, being looked upon as a
beast. You know that in the house of the Count Guido
Rangone I counseled you not to be stubborn in the matter,
endeavoring to make you feel that killing or crippling others
would not be to your credit, since you are not *armorum;* follow my advice, and you will not have to give an account to
the mourners; for if Your Lordship is killed, every one will
say: "Served him right!" And so, when you return to the
danger-zone, using a couple of nails as a spur to your steed,
imitate the fellow who, on account of the movement of his
body, kept his heels tied with a pair of shoe-strings. Thus,
staying with the rear-guard and hurling defiance, you will

make the crowd believe that it is woe to the enemy if your pony does not shed its shoes! In case the battle is won, spur forward and mingle with the victors and, cocking your ears to the cries of "Viva! Viva!" enter the conquered land with the first, and with the face, not merely of a captain, but of a very giant. If worst comes to worst, lose no time in getting out, take to your legs, fly away, for it is better for your hide that they should say: "What coward is fleeing there?" than "What corpse is lying here?"[1] Glory is good enough in its place; but when we are dead, old lady Fame can sound the bagpipes and play the Pavan all she chooses, but we will not be there to hear them; we shall be crowned with laurel and mingling with the dust of Cyprus. And if you do not take my word for it, take the assurance of Messer Lionardo Bartolino, that war is something more than talk. He leaves it to those who are masters of the art, laughing at the ones who are willing to lose their hair in hot lye. I, for my part, never heard of a brain that was more apt at sifting brains than his; nor do I know a more liberal or a more discreet friend or a person less envious of the good of others; for which reason, I love him, holding it a very graceful thing, his having borne witness to my goodness in the same manner in which I shall testify to your wisdom, when you become content to bring up the military rear and are satisfied with the name of poet, leaving the title of *Rodomonte* to the bolt-eaters and pike-swallowers. And with this advice, *bene valete.*

From Venice, the 16th of November, 1537.

To MESSER LACOPO SANSOVINO   LXXXIX
In Which He Dissuades His Friend from Leaving Venice.

There is no doubt that the execution of those works which come from your high genius provide a complement to the pomp of this city, which we, thanks to its goodness and liberality, have chosen for a fatherland; and it has proved to

---

[1]"Better be a live coward than a dead hero."

be our great good fortune, since here the desirable foreigner is not merely the equal of the ordinary citizen; he is looked upon also as a gentleman. Look what good has come out of the sack of Rome,[1] since out of it, by God's favor, we have your sculpture and your architecture. It is no news to me that the magnanimous Giovanni Gaddi, an apostolic church-man, together with the cardinals and the popes, are tor-menting you with requests in their letters to return to the court, that they may again have you for ornament. To me your judgment would appear very strange, if you were to seek to flee the nest of safety for the perch of danger, leaving the Venetian senators for the courtezan-prelates. But they must be forgiven their eagerness in this matter, for you are, indeed, very apt at restoring temples, statues and palaces. And in former times, they never had seen the church of the Florentines, which you erected upon the Tiber to the astonishment of Raffaello da Urbino, of Antonio da Sangallo and of Baldassare da Siena; nor do they ever turn to your work at San Marcello or to your marble figures or the sepul-chres of *Aragona*, *Santa Croce* and *Aginense* (the very incep-tion of which would be beyond most) without sighing for the absence of Sansovino; and in the meanwhile, Florence grieves even as she revels in the spirit of Bacchus which you have given to the gardens of Bartolini, as in all the other marvels which you have sculptured and erected. But if they must do without you, it is because your wise virtues have found a good place in which to set up their tabernacle. A salute from these noble sleeves is worth more than a present from those ignoble mitres. If any one who wishes to see in what respect this republic holds the virtuous, let him look upon the house in which you dwell, as in the worthy prison of your art, and where you every day produce marvels from your hands and from your intellect. Who would not praise the per-petual defenses with which you have sustained the church of St. Mark? Who is not astonished at the Corinthian work-

[1]Described in the *Ragionamenti*.

[197]

manship of the *Misericordia?* Who does not stand lost in thought before the rustic and Doric architecture of the *Zecca?* Who is not dumbfounded upon viewing the Doric carving, which has been begun opposite the signorial palace, with, above it, the Ionic composition with the needed orna- ments? What a fine sight the edifice will be, with its marble and precious stones, rich in great columns, which must be erected to go with the other! It will have, in composite form, the beauties of all architectures and will be a fitting *loggia* for the promenades of such nobles as these. What shall I say of the foundations on which should arise the superb roofs of the *Cornari?* or *la Vigna?* or *la Nostra Donna de l'arsenale?* or that wonderful *Mother of Christ,* extending the protect- ing crown to this unique fatherland? A history which you have made us see in bronze, with wonderful figures, in the *pergolo* of your dwelling; for which you merit the rewards and the honors conferred upon you by the magnificence of the most serene-minded ones who devotedly look upon your work. And so, may God grant our days be many, that you may keep on serving them and I praising you.

From Venice, the 21st of November, 1537.

To The Magnificent Messer Girolamo Quirini   XC
   In Which He Excuses Himself for an Outburst of Wrath.
   Sudden wrath, magnificent one, is very familiar to the *aretine* tribe; nor does this appear to me a blameworthy thing in such natures as these, for anger represents a certain power, when a great mind, prevented from executing its own generous desires, is moved by it. For this reason, I, the other evening, as you know, being a prey to the impetuosity of the moment, spoke disagreeably, my face being kindled with flames to the disdain of just cause; in which I was like a lamp which, from an abundance of oil, shoots forth sparks without giving light. Truly, angry men are blind and foolish, for reason at such a time takes flight and, in her absence,

wrath plunders all the riches of the intellect, while the judgment remains the prisoner of its own pride. However, do not believe that, merely because I was so possessed of bile, there was in me any evil desire of revenge. For the case which wrath made out in my heart appeared to me so infamous a one that I should have looked upon it as a disgrace not to have become angry. But the ability to defend one's self against the assaults of lust and anger is one which few or none of us possess; and so, either of these two passions is deserving of pardon.

From Venice, the 21st of November, 1537.

To THE MAGNIFICENT MESSER GIOVANNI BOLANI   XCI
    A Caricature.

I hear, signor, that Messer Pietro Piccardo is at Padua and with a paucity of thoughts in his head that would be a disgrace to a young wind-hover. It is a good thing the surcharge of years gives him not a pain in the world! And yet Fabrizio da Parma and the Pope, who are the two oldest whores[1] in Rome, swear that they knew him when he had a beard two fingers long. This, however, does not keep him from putting on the armor of love and neighing for the fray. I nearly burst my jaws with laughing when I saw him with a crowd of women behind a shop. He, every chance he had, would come out with an "I kiss your hand" or "Your ladyships" in a manner that would have outdone a Spaniard. Of his bowings and scrapings I do not speak, for it is impossible to find words spicy enough to express them. He would lay out before his friends certain little enameled rings, certain little baskets of silver-thread and certain collars and trifles, accompanied by certain crude jests of his own and very solemn ceremonies. And when he had done displaying these modern relics, he would make a shovel of some kind of old cornucopia he had; whereupon Monsignor Lippomano

[1] *i piu vecchi cortigiani di Roma.*

would remark to him: "Put them away, for you, *domine*, are the finest antique I ever saw." . . . Certainly, our signor ought to put him up in marble or bronze over the door of all the wine-vats, with a Bible at his feet which should contain the names of all the pontiffs and cardinals he has known. I could spend whole days in hearing him tell how San Giorgio won sixty-thousand ducats from the Signor France shetto, the brother of Innocent, and how with these winnings was built the *palazzo* in the *Campo di Fiori*, coming then to the flasks with which Valentino poisoned himself and his father, thinking he was brewing it for their reverences. He remembers the blow which Julius on the bridge gave to Alessandro *in minoribus*. One night, he was routed from his bed at five o'clock in the morning by an uproar in the corridor outside, and going out, he ran after some one who was going up and down singing "Oh, my hard, blind fate" and thinking the fellow was burlesquing the bad news which His Holiness had just received from the field, and not listening to Accorsio,[1] who kept saying to him all the while "Holy father, go to bed," he broke the head of the steward, an old man of sixty years, who had heard the noise and come running, in the belief that the steward was the musician. He has been present at all the schisms, all the jubilees and all the councils. He knew all the whorishness. He saw Iacobaccio da Melia go mad. He knows where the mange comes from and all the other ribaldries of the court. And so, I judge, he would as soon sell himself for a chronicle as for a statue. In short, he is virtue, friendship and pleasure itself to all men. Nor did I change my opinion when I heard him in conclave with my friend, Ferraguto, who nearly split as he heard how, when the old fool threw a pail of water on Ziotto, the latter tore away one whole side of his face, leaving the skin hanging in a thousand pieces; but his anger was gone a month before his hair had grown back. The conclusion of the whole matter is, I should like to be living with him and with your own

[1]The papal favorite.

magnificent and gentle self, so that we might topple backward in the laughter we should have in conversation.[1] But
since, on account of the public business which occupies you,
I cannot always have you with me, why not come here sometimes, knowing that honorable recreations merely serve to
hearten the leisure of the good? But whether you come or
not, I am indebted to that affection which, by nature, by
custom and your own nobility, you entertain for me and for
my writings.

From Venice, the 22nd of November, 1537.

To MESSER LUIGI ANICHINI   XCII

    Against Love.

    I thought yesterday, when I saw you running like a
courier, that you must be bringing some great news to the
Rialto. But I found you merely had accompanied the
Signora Viena to church for the christening of a baby.
O my brother, this Love is an evil beast, and the one who
tags its behind can neither compose verses nor carve gems.
The little thief, in my opinion, is nothing more than un-
tempered desire, nourished by our own fanciful thoughts,
and when the pleasure it produces lays hold upon the heart,
the spirit, the soul and the senses are all converted into one
affection. And for this reason, the man who is in love is
like one of those frantic bulls, goaded by the "gadfly," which
in my country is the name given to the bites of ticks, flies
and wasps on the flanks of horses and she-asses. That is
what Love does to sculptors and poets. The chisel cannot
carve nor the pen write when we are eaten up by a cancer.
But you are young and fitted to endure any evil. Sansovino
and I, on the other hand—old men, halleluiah—deny the
"*Omnia vincit*" when we see the deadly swindles it perpe-
trates upon us, by swearing to us that the hoe and spade
will relieve our heat. And so, knowing you have a good

---

[1]Cf. the manner of Aretino's death. See *Introduction.*

recipe for dyeing beards black, *me vobis commendo;* but see to it you don't make mine turquoise, for then, by God, I should be like those two gentlemen who, in such a case, had to stay shut up in the house for a whole year.

From Venice, the 23rd of November, 1537.

To Messer Giovanbattista Dragonzino   XCIII
    Poetry Gives Nothing but Immortality.

The sonnet, good man, which, with your accustomed candor and charity of mind, you have drawn from your genius in praise of me has been read by me with the greatest pleasure and laid away with care, for my heart appreciates the good will you showed in desiring to honor me, as well as the good quality of the verses with which you have honored me. I am very sorry that I am not a master of physical force, instead of being merely a man of rank, for this prevents me from rendering you payment in anything but hopeful words. The Muses have need of money, and not of lean thanks and fat offers. Surely, if the poor dames had crucified Christ, they would not be more persecuted by poverty. My friend, Messer Ambrogio da Milano, when he saw a fellow with a worn-out hood, pointed his finger at him and said: "He ought to be a poet." But we are here, thank God, and we ought not let the cruelty of fate drive us to despair, since it is a fine thing to put one's name on sale at all the fairs, along with hearing one's self sung in the bank, causing Death to give up hope by confessing that poets are not flesh for her teeth; though they make a good meal, hot or cold. By God, that murderous necessity they feel is like the nature of princes, since it takes a pleasure in seeing them suffer in the frying-pan of discomfort, giving them for sustenance the excrements of glory, when a "Here lies so and so" makes the crowd come running to their sepulchre. Our only hope is to make merry in the other world, being content in this one with a *quantum currit.* And so, whoever likes to go barefoot and bare of back, let him transform himself from a man into a chameleon and become a maker of rhymes. But to stop gossiping, I am at your service, as I always have been and shall be always.

From Venice, the 24th of November, 1537.

To Messer Gianfrancesco Pocopanno   XCIV
    On the Virtues and Vices of His Century.

Your dear and courteous nephew, together with your letter, gave me the shears, which were so brand-new that they made even me leap for joy, although I am but a man and shall not have to use them, to say nothing of Pierina, who is a woman and needs them in her business. Finally, Brescia produced *goffi* and arabesques and other works, armor and gilded artifices and damaskins, perfected in design and with various arrangements of leaves, such as only come from overseas. I cannot help believing that the blood of the brave ancients would curdle in beholding our Master Arque-buse and Don Cannon, for these would seem to them too bestial in aspect when compared with the bows and arrows with which Mars used to embroider his cuirasses. Surely, if our age were as good as it is fine to look at, we would not regard with such envy the excellences of the past nor be so doubtful as to future inventions. We see all the arts brought to a miraculous climax and everything made great. For example, these scissors you sent me are a great trophy. Another commenced to change his tune, as soon as he saw the clothes of Leo and Capella, worked in silk and gold after the designs and colors of Raphael. They no longer use little flowers in damasks or ray-work; the verdure of the espaliers is visible from afar. Habits are long and wide. One no longer suffers the torment which shoes used to give. Everything is richly cut. Even to handwriting, as a sample of which, take that of Messer Francesco Alunno, which makes print look as though it had been done by hand and work done with the

〖 203 〗

pen as if it were print. Look where Michelangelo has placed
the art of painting with his astounding figures, depicted
with a majesty of judgment and not with the mechanics of
art. And you, too, make of man a natural prodigy, adding
tone and sound to sound and tone in poetry, resuscitating
style, which had died, with the spiritedness of your subjects. For there is no food more satiating than milk and
honey; and just as such foods produce disgust for the palate,
so perfumed and gallant words make our ears belch. But let
this be said with the permission of him who thinks otherwise. And to Your Lordship I commend me.

From Venice, the 24th of November, 1537.

To Messer Francesco Bacci   XCV
  Of Rome and Venice.
     If I, brother, with regard to your coming had believed
what your letters promised and what the words of Messer
Tarlato confirmed to me, I should have been angry with
myself for my own simple-mindedness and with you for
not coming; but knowing as I do what an effort it is for you
to put foot out of Arezzo, when I received your last, I
believed it, but as one does who, when his sleep is disturbed,
gives denial or consent with a nod of his head. I wish, for
the sake of friendship and for love of me, you would come
here just once, in fact as you have so often in intent. You
may believe me that those who have not seen Rome and
Venice have missed the objects of all wonderment, although
in a different manner in the two cases; for in one you will
find the insolence of fortune, and in the other the gravity of
a monarchy. It is a strange thing to view the confusion of
that court, and a beautiful spectacle to contemplate the
union of this republic. You may even, in a manner of speaking, let your imagination go as far as paradise, but you would
never be able to picture in your mind the evasions of the
one nor the calm ways of the other, for the two are one im-

〖 204 〗

mense structure of labor and of quiet. I do not know what Mantuan it was, wishing to demonstrate how this city stands in the sea, filled a basin of water with half-shells of walnuts and said: "There it is!" While, on the other hand, a preacher, not caring to tire himself in describing the court, showed his flock a picture of the inferno. You certainly should hesitate about visiting it, then, if you wish other lands to give you hospital. I had to laugh at a Florentine who, seeing in a richly fitted gondola a most beautiful house-wife, was astonished at the crimson, jewels and gold with which she was bedecked and exclaimed, "Why, we are a mountain of rags!" Nor was he so far wrong, for here, the wives of bakers and tailors go dressed in more pomp than do gentlewomen in other lands. And what sights we have here and what food to eat! Great ignorance was that which first located Venus and Cupid in the island of Cyprus; she reigns here with all her troop of little sons. And I know I am only speaking the truth when I say that God here is in a good humor eleven months of the year; for here, there is never a headache nor a suspicion of death, and liberty goes with flying colors, without ever meeting any one who says to her, "Get down where you belong!" And so, when you come, make up your mind to come here, for I should like to make you confess that Pope Clement, who with us was of minor rank, was wrong when he refused to pardon some one who had stolen something there to spend here. Think, moreover, what standing you will have in being a friend of mine, who in less than eleven years have received and thrown away ten thousand *scudi*, acquired through my own virtue.

From Venice, the 25th of November, 1537.

To THE CAPTAIN VINCENZIO BOVETTO   XCVI
    *In Which He Congratulates Him on His Progress in the
        Army.*
    I, who have followed from time to time the achievements

of your youth in Africa, in France and wherever there has been a war, have praised and thanked the choice and military judgment of the great Giovanni de' Medici, when, with a true insight into your character, he decided to make you a soldier; which pleases me as much now as it displeased me then. You well know with how much care and how much affection I have reared you, making no difference between a father's love and that I showed you, recognizing you as my own son; and the affection of my heart grew with your own virtues. Surely it was from me you learned kindness, generosity and animosity; and for this reason it is, you are loved, praised and feared. I weep when I remember the gentle Signora Lucrezia da Correggio and the courteous Signor Manfredo, her consort, whose natural modesty and good manner you are heir to. But I cannot quite comprehend it, when I hear of your deeds of arms and the high reputation they have brought you; I hope to see you one day in the rank which I desire for you. Go on, then, serving our magnanimous Signor Ippolito, who wisely proceeds outside the common path; for he who follows the trail of others leaves on the earth no footprints that may be called his own; and he who would amount to something in such a profession has the right even to do evil.[1] All princes are creatures of violence, and without that violence on their part, the ferocity of soldiers would become brotherly love. For no virtue does the army have a higher regard, nor is there one more convenient in serving its dignity, since by maturing the hatreds that motivate it, it achieves glory. And so, may His Lordship, to whom I pray you to remember me, imitate the tremendous example of him of terrible memory,[2] so that fortune, who is the principal support in all enterprises, may favor his valor and discover your own.

From Venice, the 25th of November, 1537.

[1]How new is Nietzsche?
[2]Giovanni.

In Praise of Medical Science and His Charity.

When I heard, my brother, that you had journeyed all the way to Rome, I was beside myself with thinking that the devil had tempted you from your quiet state. And then, when I was told that you had decided to remain there, I lost all the respect I had had for your counsels and your experience and said: "Can it be that when the senate of his own country has placed a man, on account of his merits, in the catalogue of its illustrious citizens—can it be that a person of so much worth, and who is so necessary to his countrymen, should place himself and his faculties in constant peril, a peril that we always knew, and you always will know, thanks to the malice of all concerned? But now that I know from your own hand, that you are back in Bologna and anxious to return, my mind is revived at the thought of seeing once again the man to whom God gave my own life and that of Lionardo, and also at the thought of the welfare of this illustrious city, which embraces no less the kindness with which you are filled than the virtue of which you are the summit. Putting aside incantated water, the canonical procedure, what do you not do in the case of a mortal wound! Safe and gentle is your surgery, which you practice out of charity and not out of avarice. The world is quite right in exalting you, since you alone, in attempting to save the lives of others, transform yourself, through affection, science and your artful practice, into the remedy which you place upon their wounds; and thus, curing others, do you procure health for yourself. For which reason, God gives you a green old age, consoles your mind and multiplies your riches; by which means you are enabled to ennoble with honored gifts your many nephews, whom, with paternal love, in place of the sons that you have not, and to the great delight of your good and valorous wife, you are every day marrying off; for which act of piety, Christ shall double your years and your contentment of mind and body.

From Venice, the 25th of November, 1537.

To Messer Pietro Piccardo   XCVIII
　　Bantering.

I had thought, you old gossip! that you were still babbling away at Rome, and here you are sanctifying the benefice of my friend, the Monsignor Zicotto, arch-pope of Coranto; and what upsets me still more is to hear that you are con-ducting yourself like a brace of pontiffs, giving jubilees, intimidating councils and canonizing saints. They tell me that you are crucifying bandits, absolving vows and hurling excommunications right bestially; and I congratulate myself on the fact that you are bringing the clergy under a new monarchy, castrating and uprooting the sects of the hypo-crites and consoling with regressions, reservations and hopes the vagabond herd: hence, it cannot be that the priest, Ianni, has not already unloosed upon you a pack of ambassadors; and perhaps even the Turk, in whose dominion the aforesaid diocese is situated, will come to terms with you. And so, keep your bridle well in hand, and see to it that the "sol, fa, me, re" of the *quondam* Armellino pulverizes your tympa-num. In the meanwhile, Your Most Reverend Lordship, who is a trifle asthmatic, might do well to barter his goods at some of the fairs, confirming, blessing eggs and confessing the countrymen, in which there is no danger. But are you not ashamed to make sport of Verona, Chieti and all the abstinence there is in the world? I have a high regard for your thoughts, which surge up like a piece of camel's hair cloth. The man who does not envy you is the town idiot,[1] for you have a kindness that is so attractive and a grace that is so penetrating that it is all the good folk can do to keep from running after you. All houses are open to you,

[1] *pazzo publico.*

[208]

and from all the *piazze* you are called; it is "Zicotto" on this side and "Piccardo" on that. And so, move your bowels with the full moon and not merely every ten days, putting a stop to the "Spain will urinate and France will defecate" contests. You need not give a pistachio either to know why summer has long days and winter short ones, making a bid for the enmity of neither hot nor cold, holding as bestialities all syllogisms and all aphorisms, so that it is of no difference to you whether it is cloudy or fair, as you rejoice in snow and rain alike, with your breeches down. And do not break your head in endeavoring to ascertain whether the fire which lightning-bugs carry on their tails is an elemental substance or not, or whether the cicadae sing with their bodies or with their wings. You are thus in a position to laugh at the big blockheads who affirm that a certain river is a foot wider than Ptolomy estimated it and that the Nile has not so many horns, making sport of certain astrologers who would like to make out that the spot on the face of the moon is a ringworm and not the edge of a yellow boil, giving as much faith to prognosticians as Guarico does, now that he has no need of such quackeries. Saying nothing and doing nothing which you ought not to do and ought not to say, you render immortal graces to the one who put the tail on the breviary; and so, go on saying your offices from horseback and away with melancholy.

From Venice, the 26th of November, 1537.

To Messer Giovanni Agnello   XCIX
   Against the Life of Courts, in Praise of Venice.
   The signor Benedetto, the ducal orator and your brother, asked me yesterday how I was and what I was doing, saying he wished to advise you, since, from love of me, you desired to know. And so, I will tell you that I am fine and am doing very well. And not only I, who am likely to be well off where another would not be and to do well when another

would not; but any poltroon would be well and do well away from the pope and the emperor, in this city and removed from courts. I was never in paradise, that I know; for I am not able to imagine how its beatitudes are composed. I know that to die of hunger is to cheat the world by evading its little hells. Courts, ah? Courts, eh? It seems to me better to be a boatman here than a chamberlain there. Hopes there, favors here, greatness afterward. Behold yourself there, a poor servant, on foot; see yourself martyred by the cold and devoured by the heat: where is the fire to warm yourself by? Where is the water with which to refresh yourself? and if you fall ill, what room, what stable, what hospital will take you in? Behold there the rain, the snow, the mud which kill you when you ride with your patron or in his train. Where are your fresh clothes to put on? Where a good face to put on for all this? What a cruel sight it is to see mere children growing a bear before their time and the white hairs of youth consumed at the tables, the portieres and the privies. "Take the rest of it," said a good and learned man, who had been hunted to the gallows because he would not commit a piece of pimpery. Courts, eh? Courts, ah? It is better for us to live on bread and capers than on the smoke from fine viands on plates of silver. Nor is there anything to compare with the pleasure which you get from a walnut or a chestnut, either before or after a meal. And just as there is no suffering like that of the courtier who is tired and has no place to sit down, who is hungry and has nothing to eat, and who is sleepy and yet must keep awake; so there is no consolation equal to my own, who sit down whenever I am fatigued, eat when I am hungry and sleep when I am sleepy, and all the hours are the hours of my own will. What shall we say of the craven state of those who think that being able to stumble into a bit of straw is ample compensation for any servitude or any fidelity? For my part, I am satisfied with my want, since I am not obliged to take off my hat to Duranti nor to Ambrogio.[1] Think it over, and see if you do not agree that I am well off and doing well. But my pleasure would be immensely increased, if Your Lordship would make constant use of this house, for I cannot think of a habit that would content me more; and, when we are talking or dining together with Titian, I would not say "your reverence" to the whole college, much less to Chieti. The days seem to me years since Your Excellency has been keeping himself with Caesar's Majesty in Spain. I like lordly philosophers and those of a nobler manner, such as you are and such as was the good Gianiacopo Bardellone, and not those who, like ragamuffins, are all the time busy concealing their rags. And so, I commend me to you with the reverence of a younger brother.

From Venice, the 26th of November, 1537.

To THE LITTLE MONSIGNOR POMPONIO   C
    In Which He Exhorts Him to Return to Venice.

Titian, your father, has conveyed the salutations you sent me, and I was scarcely less delighted with them than with two wild chickens, which I took the liberty of presenting to myself, being commissioned by him to present them in his name to a lord. And, since you perceive my liberality, I pay you back "*mille millanta, che tutta notte canta*"; requesting that you give the leanest ones to your good little brother, Orazio, since he has forgotten to tell me what his fancy is about spending, as soon as he can, this world and the other; for your thrift is enough for one who gets the goods,[2] since, being a priest, we must believe that you cannot depart from the custom of Melchisedek. Health, then, shall be the gift I wish you. It is time now to get back to work, for the villa, it seems to me, is not keeping school; after it, the city is a winter cloak. Come, then, straightaway, so that, with your thirteen years and your Hebrew, Greek and Latin

[1]Papal favorites.
[2]*guadagna la robba.*

we can drive all the doctors on the map to despair, just as the fine things your father does routs all the painters of Italy. I am telling you the truth. Keep warm and a good appetite.

From Venice, the 26th of November, 1537.

To Messer Francesco Alunno[1]   CI

Of the Crowd of People Surrounding Him.

To the prayers, my brother, with which others work upon me I add my own and, binding them all together, send them to you for your inspection, begging that you will let me have a sample of anything you may produce in the way of lettering. While you may reply that I, in my request, am looking for the fair of Ricanati, I know that you have a sufficient store to draw upon, and the tongues of the Tower of Babel were not so numerous as are the various manners in which, with your diligent and patient genius, you compose and draw your characters, your pen all the while painting the small details and sculpturing the great ones. The great Emperor, in Bologna, spent an entire day in contemplating the greatness of your art, marveling at seeing written, without abbreviation, the *Credo* and the "*In principio*" in the space of a denary, laughing at Sire Pliny, who speaks of a certain Iliad of Homer as being contained in a nutshell. Pope Clement also was astonished when you unfolded for him your cartoons, whereupon Iacopo Salviati, eyeing some of your majescules, ornamented with leaf-work, exclaimed: "Holy father, look at those crests!" I prefer above all others, that style of letter which is round and antique, of which the honor of the world, His Caesarean Majesty, is so fond; and I am seeking an example of this sort for one of those lords who give me a constant headache with their visits, until my stairs are worn out with the tramping of their feet, even as the pavement of the Campidoglio is with the wheels of

[1]The calligrapher.

triumphal chariots. Nor do I believe that Rome, in a manner of speaking, ever saw so great an admixture of nations as is to be met with in my house. To me come Turks, Jews, Indians, French, Germans and Spaniards: and then, think of what our own Italians do to me. Of the smaller fry I do not speak, but I tell you, it would be an easier thing to break your devotion to the emperor than to find me for a moment alone, and without a throng of soldiers, scholars, friars and priests about me. From which, it would appear, I have become the oracle of truth, since every one comes to tell me the wrong that has been done to him by this prince and that prelate; and so I am the secretary to the world, and it is as such that they address me in superscriptions. And now, I am still waiting for the dial-plates, as well as the pearls, which I have asked of you, but which I fear I am not to have, not because you are not courtesy itself, but because, in addition to the fame which comes with the profession in which you stand unique, you wish also, while making yourself honored with your design, the glory of poetry, laying down new rules for locutions and giving no heed to the throngs who storm your imagination merely for a glimpse of your handi-work, while those who would like to imitate you rob you with their eyes. So please lay aside one of the two virtues given you from above and serve me, who am always at your service.

From Venice, the 27th of November, 1537.

To His Messer Ambrogio Eusebio   CII
In Which He Advises Him Against the Army.

I, you big madman, was forced the other day to put out of your head, with threats of excommunication, the fancy of taking a wife; and now, I have to set to work to disabuse you of the whim of going to camp. It is gospel truth that bread and soldiers are not worth much in the end; although you might reply, "What are you going to do in time of famine or time of war?" It seems to me you are mad even to think of going, and madder still to adhere to the purpose; for the art of war is like the art of the courtezan—indeed, they might be called sisters, since both are the slaves of desperation and the step-daughters of that swinish fortune which never tires of crucifying us at every turn. Certainly, the court and the field may be embraced together, since in the one you will find want, envy, old age and the hospital, while in the other you have only to gain wounds, prison and fame. I am aware of all that fine talk which goes on about the table, when they begin to lay plans for going to Rome. Some one of an ambitious turn of mind leans back at the end of the meal and remarks: "I'd like to put on the habit, take horse and service and go with the Pope, or with the Reverend So-and-So. I am a good musician, I am not unlettered and I delight in— and he goes on talking. I like such crazy dreaming, because a man in such thoughts appears to himself a very Trojan; but I very much disapprove of putting those thoughts into action, for if you do, in two months you will be eating your own clothes, your servant and your pony, having made an enemy of your patron and of paradise, in case you go there. That martial and fulminating manner you should regard as a bizarre and bestial gesture, that bragging of what you did and said to the French, as, giving yourself a thousand followers and two hundred helmets, you proceed to take castles, burn villages, plunder peoples and seize treasures; and if you merely wish to cut a couple of capers on your charger in front of your lady love, with your head all decked out in feathers, stay at home; you can do it just as well here! For a *gaudeamus* in front of a hen-roost, you go without bread for supper for a week, and for a bundle of rags, which is your booty, and a prison, which is yours whenever God wills it, you have as recompense the right to come home with a staff in your hand and to sell everything you have, even to your vineyard, in order to keep out of the *domo Petri.* When you tell me of the aglets, the medallions and the collars of those whom you have seen return, for example, from the Piedmont, I reply that if you had seen those who have come here and stayed with us without a *picciolo*, you would feel compassion for them, as one feels pity for those poor wretches who are subject to the knaveries of courts. And so, changing the argument, since you are better fitted to making a sonnet than to raising a levy, you would do well to go on having a good time at my expense; for those who get a nibble at the big tickets in a lottery are very few. Finally, the pay which a soldier gets goes as it comes,[1] as with gamblers and churchmen. I have seen the nephews of cardinals reduce to nothing the benefices left to them and die of their necessities; and I, whom you see, have held the pay of fellow soldiers, and woe to them if I had not done so! Buckle this to you, and then go dress yourself in armor. The signor Giovanni de' Medici said on one such occasion: "They prattle about my being a valiant man, and yet, I have never been able to achieve fame."

From Venice, the 28th of November, 1537.

To MESSER LODOVICO FOGLIANO   CIII
    In Which He Praises a Plain Style.

I would to God, dear brother, that the masticated prose which many employ were as pure and common as are the words which, when you speak, you draw from familiar usage. For the ruggedness of the compositions of others does not induce, at first glance, any desire to read them. I am aware that my judgment has nothing to do with the good will I feel for you; and so, believe me when I swear to you, on the sacrament of friendship, that, if you were to commence to translate into our vulgate the Greek of Aristotle, you would be the means of humanizing a sufficient number of persons who, not understanding any other tongue, are unable to exhibit the benefits conferred upon them by nature. Certain it is, you are fitted to enlighten their darkness with the plain-

---

[1]"Come easy, go easy."

ness of your diction, making gently apparent the sense of things confused in the clouds of matter. It is a good thing, in the formation of a vocabulary, to pay some attention to the sound, and not to fall into the use of *"altresi"* and *"chenti,"* when *"ancora "*and *"quanti"* are quite as pleasing. What have we to do with words which have been used in the past, but which are no longer in use? Surely, any one now who saw a cavalier in armor would think that he was either mad or masquerading. It seems to me, I see Sire Apollo with his *stockings* in the belfry when I come upon *"uopo"* at the top of some *canzone* or other. To those pedagogues who assert that all the better writers never lift their pens from the Latin of Cicero, I reply that every man of good genius, writing familiarly, almost never employs the Tuscan of Boccaccio. Go on, then, with that honorable translation, for it will be an enrichment to pleasant intellects. In the meanwhile, you behold me the prey to your bounty, with all respect to that science of which you are the repository.

From Venice, the 30th of November, 1537.

To Messer Lionardo Parpaglioni   CIV
    Definitions.

I, generous son, have looked at the verses which the gracious Messer Giuffre Cinami personally fetched me, and they appear to me of too great a style and invention to have come from a youth like you; I have for them more respect than you yourself profess. And since, in the letter which accompanied them, you say you have been requested to ask me what fame and ambition are, I, my son, will reply that I am not the dragoman of philosophy nor Aristotle's secretary; and so, I will simply say that, to me, fame is the stepmother of death and ambition the excrement of glory. I hope you are well.

From Venice, the 2nd of December, 1537.

Against the Game of Lotto.

Feeling, my good fellow, the blasphemies of sixty-thousand on my shoulders—sixty-thousand persons with their bowels beaten out, crucified and chopped to mince-meat by the expectations of the game of lotto, I put up in your behalf a strong talk[1] to quiet those stubborn-headed ones who would have made you out to be the author of the game. I assure you, I put up a better defense for you against the storming of these swine[2] than you would have had from a basket of scimitars. For this novelty, in truth, is the invention of ill-fated asses and hopeful cows;[3] they take pleasure in providing a thousand forks for a man to hang himself on. Those ribald sisters, Fate and Hope, are like a pair of gypsy wenches who, at the fair of Foligno or that of Lanciano,[4] make a fool of this knave or that. Hope takes the clowns by the hand, while Fate, pretending to be a party to the joke, keeps them at bay. In the meanwhile, the purse remains as empty as a pricked bladder. Hope, eh? Fate, ah? If in the house of Satan one did not have to associate with such bitches as these, one would not mind going there. The false and lying ones, when they have assassinated a good man, go into ecstasies, like villagers in eating oiled bread. To tell you the truth, I should like to know: is this lotto male or female? For my part, I believe it is an hermaphrodite, since it has the names, "*lotto*" and "*ventura*."[5] And it must be the best stuff in Italy[6], since it gives a knockout[7] to a world

[1]*sciorinai . . . una strenua diceria.* This letter, giving so vivid a picture of manners, is extremely colloquial—so colloquial that translation is alsmot impossible at times, and a literal translation frequently is out of the question—and I have, accordingly, endeavored to preserve this colloquial quality by seeking, where such search would not be far-fetched, the contemporary Americanism.

[2]*cancari.*

[3]*de la sorte asina e de la speranza vacca.*

[4]Popular fairs of the *cinquecento.*

[5]One masculine, the other feminine in grammatic gender.

[6]*la miglior robba d'Italia.*

[7]*da martello.*

of people at one blow, mixing even with the whores, drag-
ging along at its tail the populace and the arts. As soon as
"he" appears in the *piazza*, behold, all the twelve thousand
chosen ones come trotting: Noah's ark, the temple of Solo-
mon, the synagogues, the mosques, the cohorts of the priests,
the hierarchies of friars, with all the sinners and half-
desperate wretches. And then, the big fox stands there like
one who has taken a basket of snails into the light and is
beside himself with astonishment at seeing them put out
their horns. I tell you, the niggard will bring forth his cups,
his rings, his collars and his *denarii*; and then, the fellow
kids the crowd[1] of aimless ones who have gathered to see the
show. He bursts into a guffaw when this one or that, giving
him the eye, fetches a couple of sighs and says to himself:
"Who knows? And why not?" Some other stretches out
his hand and takes the jewel or chain which he happens to
fancy and places it on his finger or at his throat; others paw
over the beakers and basins. This one displays a contempt
for his ducats, this one for his possessions, and this other for
his houses; and in all this madness, swarms of persons are to
be seen, trampling and suffocating one another in the crush
to place their bets. And such language! The ugliest, most
traitorous, silliest, spiciest, dirtiest and most diabolic of any
in the world.[2] Words from the Psalms, the Gospels, the
Epistles and the Calendar, half verses and whole verses.
But these are merely gallantries to such as these. The cruel
thing is to see the poor wretches so drunken with them.
Here is one taking the bed from under him and selling it for
a couple of policies. A widow is saying to a little priest, all
wrapped up in his hospital blouse: "Take this chaplet, and
say for me the masses of Saint Gregory for the good of my
soul." "Masses, eh?" responds the sire. "There won't be
any too many of them, for I'll soon be defecating on the red

[1] *soia le turbe.*
[2] This was the milieu which Aretino loved to depict and the language he loved to
employ, e. g., in his *Ragionamenti.*

candles." And taking two strides toward the church with the step of a canon, he explains to the good lady that the three *lire* which he has on the lotto will be enough to take care of him. A countryman coming upon the scene and learning that six *marcelli* are enough to win the lottery, sells his winter's coat and buys a ticket as though he had won it already. He's not going to touch the spade any more, if Christ himself turns gardener.[1] One of them who stood by my side for some time, all puffed up because he had won three tickets, upon hearing me curse because I did not have the means, said to me: "Don't worry, boss; I'll stand by you."[2] How many house-wives throw away their allowances here? How many concubines all they have gained from the tread-mill of their trade? How many grooms pledge their feast-day socks for this?[3] Every one who is trying to get rich here would be happy, if no one ever won anything; for the winnings are every one's when they go to no one. The air at such a time is finer than that of *Arabia Felice*, so many gardens are planted here by hope and fate. It would be a comedy that would make a weeping man burst into laughter, if one could make a book of the thoughts that are fixed on those six thousand sequins in the lottery. This one is dreaming of houses, this one of embroidered clothes, this one of buying horses, this one of putting money in the bank, this one of marrying off his sisters, this one of investing in farms. The servant I have spoken of writes to his father of a palace with a garden which he is sure of getting with his winnings and tells the old man he need not speak of a hundred more or less. But it is all a joke. See how they do away with the good chances and keep the bad ones. "Go hang yourself!"[4] exclaims one who had sold the winning ticket, retaining the

---

[1]Exceedingly idiomatic: *non averia tocco la zappa, che tenne in man Cristo, transform-ato in ortolano.*

[2]"*Non vi disperate, padrone, che non son per mancarvi.*"

[3]*impegnano le calze dal di de le feste per cio:* cf. our "bet your Sunday socks."

[4]Literally: *Va' e non t'impicca.*

"*alba ligustra cadunt,*"[1] as the pedant says. But how do they feel when it is all over? Watch them throng about the box, which is upon high and so well fitted out that it would seem Messer Lotto had taken a wife or Mistress Chance had married. Now the lad has his hand in the urn filled with tickets, and hearts are beating and everybody stops breathing while eyes and ears are fixed on the fellow who, in a gross and laughing voice, first reads and then sings out: "White!" And a gift is not so soon gone as fall the babble and the faces of those thousands, and when the big hope-killer takes his departure with a "*leva eius,*" he leaves the crowd as a coward who has surrendered on the field is left. Whoever has witnessed the breaking up of these disappointed mobs, knows what the household of Pope Leo is like, when, after the exequies, they return weeping to consume their forty-days handout.[2] Certainly, he is wise who, amid all these madnesses, can say that he has played, locked up and consumed his last ticket in this fine device. But those who blame fortune for their ruin in this path, as if their very lives had been stolen, so breathe maledictions upon Your Lordship's head that, if it were not for your friends' defending you from their fury, as I have done, you would be worse off than those who, when the votes are counted, fall into despair because their name is not among the lucky ones.

From Venice, the 3rd of December, 1537.

To The Captain Faloppia   CVI

Of a Stable-Boy Who Plays the Poet.

Since all the poets of the Round Table[3] take advantage of you, teasing your brains with their cobbler's chatterings, I shall take refuge in that same patience of yours by sending you one in praise of that strenuous man, Lord Malatesta, a mortal philosopher, although one ought to be happy to

[1]"The white privets fall": Virgil, *Eclogues*, II., 18.
[2]*le regaglie dei quaranta giorni.*
[3]*la Tavola ritonda.*

escape his verses, which have neither feet to run with nor a behind to sit on. He makes them of half syllables or of fifteen and a third, employing the rules of Fra Giannino, who measures his with a pair of compasses. And now, surely, we have seen everything there is to be seen, when even the *maestri* of the stables begin poetizing; and Petrarch is but a graceless wretch, since he could not make such lined and relined verses, in the manner of the stable-boys. What kind of expression is "*rumica e buffa cornacchia*," which he uses under the beard of the Tuscan tongue? I never thought to laugh so much as I did yesterday. I said to him: "How goes it with Your Highness, *arcifanfana*[1] of Immortality?" "Fine," he replied, "since, thanks to God, I've been able to fart twice on Parnassus, as well as any other." A saying worthy of Cino da Pistoia, not to say of Dante. And so, you may show my sonnet to the most illustrious Signor, Count Guido, and may His Excellency provide the chains for it, as it is certainly unshackled enough.

From Venice, the 15th of December, 1537.

The Sonnet[2]

I'm astonished, Malatesta, the laurel tree
Isn't crazy about[3] giving you a crown;
All the old blades and old loves in the town
Should split their breeches[4] over your poetry.
A million wrongs men do you, I can see,
By not hymning your fair name, and doing it brown;[5]
Apollo himself isn't worthy to let down
Your socks, nor all his tribe to wipe your lee.
By God! I cannot think how you can write
Such verses as you do out of your head,
And dress them up till they're so brave and bright.

[1] great swaggerer, great boaster.
[2] Doggerel, of course. I have preserved the doggerel character.
[3] *faccin le pazzie per coronarvi.*
[4] *sbraghino.*
[5] *frastagliare.*

Monsieur the cook, you may be comforted,
Is your very slave, and I doubt not but he might
Even urinate upon you, when you're dead.

To Monsignor Biagio Iuleo CVII

Caricature.

I more than congratulate myself, Sire Pecora,[1] that you
have been published as the chaplain of the muses. But
watch out for your tail, for Sire Apollo is a hard lad, and
when he gets jealous, is just as likely to give you a good
wallop on the behind with the bow to his lyre as he is to
spit on the ground. For this reason, it would be a good thing
to get yourself castrated, and I beg you to do so; and then,
Sire Phoebus, old hatchet-face, will give you a present on
Easter and Christmas and, more than likely, all the old
blades, worn-out currycombs and other asses of their kind.
But that's enough: I know what they say about that bald
head of yours, "*quoniam frigent in veste camoenae,*" and in
memory of it I kiss your hand with the following sonnet:

> Iuelo, immaculate and strenuous sire,
> My detonating, titubating friend,
> May Apollo bind you to his chariot-end
> And Orpheus teach you to cook nuts in the fire.
> Of hearing the *Te Deum* we may tire,
> But not of your majestic verse; you bend
> The sword of poetry and straightway send
> Old Petrarch back to polish up his—lyre.
> This asinine and silly century
> Should carve you up in wood and caviare,
> To the praise and glory of high poesy.
> If marble weren't so dear, I should take care
> To embalm you with a perfumed eulogy
> In a temple fit for Heaven's only Heir.

[1]*pecora:* ewe-sheep.

To Signor Domenico Gaztelu CVIII
In Which He Bemoans His Friend's Absence.

I recall how, when you were here, you used to knock at my door, and I was like a baby who knows its father is bringing apples and comfits. I had grown so used to seeing you constantly at the door that, now I know you are gone, I am sad whenever any one else comes to the house. Your virtue and courtesy have so made me yours that I am no longer myself, except when you give me a sight of you. Nor shall my heart ever forget the contentment of soul I felt that evening when you brought me word of Caesar's gift; the happiness which you felt upon that occasion equaled and even surpassed my own joy. That is the way good friends ought to be. But rest assured, I shall pay this debt in eternal coin. Do not forget to remember me to Messer Aniballe Palmegiani da Forli, to Messer Marcantonio Patanella and to all the other gentlemen of the court:

From Venice, the 5th of December, 1537.

To Signor Gianiacopo Lionardi CIX
A Dream.

Although the ambassador of a Duke d'Urbino, who is always wide awake, has nothing to do with dreams, I am going to give you one which is so enormous it would prove too much even for a Daniel.

Tonight, not from superfluity of food or melancholy, but simply from my accustomed thoughtlessness, I was sleeping the best sleep ever, when there suddenly appeared to me a gentle dream-creature. I said to him: "What is it, Sire Girandolone?"[1] "The mountain of Parnassus, which you see there," he replied. And then, I found myself at its foot, and looking up, I was like one of those who contemplate the difficulties of San Leo. But it was a devil of a story getting over it; the easy thing was to go down it. From the sides of the mountain, where St. Francis had his stigmata, rose

[1]*girandolone:* roamer.

〚 223 〛

masses of earth and stone, intermingled with uprooted trees; but from above were falling heaps of men, so horrible that it was a cruel and inhuman sport to see them grasping at this or that trunk, sweating blood all the while. Some, who appeared to be like those who scale a garden wall to write their names with carbon on the top, would fall to the ground with a sickening thud;[1] others, half way up, would stop without being able to go further. Some would seize the leg of the one above; others would go mad and bite those who drew near them. Still others, when they perceived they were but a little way from the top, would come tumbling down, like one of those who, when they reach out their hand for the capon, seeing the rope under their feet, slide down the greased pole,[2] at which sport the populace fills the air with hoots and shouts. Still others, on striking their heads against the buttocks of the pharisees above, would experience the same madness that moves those who kill cats. And the cause of all this was a garland, similar to the hoop of a hostelry. These madmen with the slackening arms were breaking their necks in a lake of ink blacker than a printer's river; and there was no sport that equaled such a spectacle as this. He who did not know how to swim drowned; and he who swam came to the other bank with a more horrifying aspect than any Dante ever saw, even in the intercourse of little souls, which he places in the pitch of the inferno.

I fixed my eyes on all the faces; but the masks of various colors did not permit me to recognize any of them; the disgraceful cries they made, yes. Some were lamenting the criticism which their translations, some that which their romances and other works had encountered. I, who could not help laughing, said to them: "You, who are learned, ought to note and follow the example of Caesar, when he saved his *Commentaries;* you ought to thank fate for bringing you out alive; for it is certain that commentators and

[1]Exactly: *matte piattonate.*
[2]*legno insaponato:* the sport appears to be an old one.

translators are less than those who plaster walls, chalk tables, or grind colors for a Giulio Romano or some other famous painter." This was the way I spoke to them. And, even as I perceived that my own clothes had been soiled by contact with such as these, I discerned my fine Franco[1] coming up the very path which I myself had made over the back of the mountain, and it was not without pleasure and wonderment that I beheld him in this by-way. And it appeared to me also that Ambrogio,[2] my own creation, was clinging close to my heels, hastening his steps.

And then, behold me in an inn, set down by the wayside to ensnare the assassins of poetry. As I entered, I could not resist exclaiming: "He who has not been in a tavern does not know what a paradise it is," as Cappa says. Repressing my appetite in my stomach, I thought of turning tail and running.[3] At this, behold, there appeared to me one Marfisa,[4] clad in helmet, breastplate and sword. To discern this sight, to say to myself, "Be brave," and to feel myself snatched upward was but the work of a moment. I, who was in a bad way and could only console myself with repeating, "I'm dreaming," became discouraged when I reflected, "I was dreaming, at least!" But all this, I assure you, my brother, happened of itself.

Maestro Apollo, before whom I was brought, I cannot tell you how, had one of my heads on a medallion; and suddenly, espying me, he opened his arms and gave me a kiss on the middle of the lips, so sweet that some one, I do not know who, cried out: "Sassata!" Oh, he was the fine lad![5] Oh, he was fine! Surely, if Rome had been lying there asleep instead of me, she would have wished never to awake. And would you believe there was a pan of ox-herbs there, long and tender? He had two smiling eyes, a happy face, an airy

[1]Nicolo, his secretary and, later, betrayer: see *Introduction*.
[2]His secretary: see *Introduction*.
[3]*alzare il fianco per una volta*.
[4]Aretino's epic: sée *Introduction*.
[5]*Oh, egli e il bel fanciullone!* Cf. the stage Hibernianism, "broth of a boy."

forehead, a wide chest, two fine legs, and two of the finest pairs of feet and hands you ever saw; on the whole (to speak a little flowerily), he looked like a composition of breathing ivory, over which nature had scattered all the roses from Aurora's cheeks. The short of it is, this acme of loveliness made me take my place among the muses. And as I sat there among them, it seemed to me I was in my own house, as I looked upon a certain figure of Time and another mask of Comedy. As I contemplated the cymbals, the bagpipes and the other instruments with which they passed the time, look you, the good Febo divulged, to the tune of *Salamone*, two stanzas of the *Sirena*, the sound of which made me weep not from the sweetness of the rhyme, but for the ignorant nature of the subject. Fame, moreover, kept up a constant chatter, and this spoiled the song. She, as soon as she knew me, began to deck herself in my honors, in a manner which I recommend to the ears of all the poor ladies who, when they hear it, will burst with envy. And then her prattle, which was of the *sine fine dicentes* order, changed, and she recited the praises of God as composed by the divine Pescara, with a few things of the learned Gambara, which, I would have you know, made the ladies leap for joy, for, being women, they took pleasure in such things as these.

After this, my lady Minerva, perceiving that I was a man of merit, took my hand and said, blushing and wise: "Let us walk a little way alone."—And so, we came to the stall of Pegasus, who was being curried by Quinto Gruaro, while Father Biagio was filling his hay trough. He was a fine animal and one suited to bearing on his crupper the reverend testicles of those who, to leave a name for themselves, per-form a thousand madnesses. And while I was wondering at the manners and wings of the beast, he consumed as much bewitched water as two Frenchmen with a cold chill would have drunk, if it had been wine. In color and in taste, it was like that of the *Tre Fontane*.

After we had soaked our beaks a while, we came to a little study, filled with pens, inkstands and paper; and without my asking, the armed lady said to me: "This is the place in which shall be written the deeds which your Duke d'Urbino must do against the enemies of Christ." And I to her: "It could not be for anything else." Having seen the writing room, I beheld a secret garden, full of palms and of laurels as green as possible; and divining that they were reserved for crowns of triumph, I, as she opened her mouth to speak, said: "I know what you wish to say." And then, I perceived marbles, which I knew were being worked for the arches and statues of Francesco Mario and his son.

And then, I was with him in the church of Eternity, made, it seemed to me, of a Doric composition, signifying by its solidity his own eternal nature. I scarcely had entered, when I met my two brothers, Sansovino and Titian. The one was working over the bronze door of the temple, where were carved the four thousand followers and eight hundred horse with which His Excellency traversed Italy when he brought the plague to Leo. And when I asked him why he was leaving a certain space vacant, his reply was: "So that I can carve there what Paolo is going to do." The other was placing over the great altar a tablet which depicted in most vivid form the victories of our emperor.

Having seen everything, they permitted me to go to the gate of the principal garden, and there I saw, approaching me, a number of youths, Lorenzo Veniero[1] and Domenico, Girolamo Lioni, Francesco Badovaro and Federico, who, with fingers on their mouths, made me a sign that I should walk gently; and among them was the gentle Francesco Querino. Meanwhile, the scent of lilies, hyacinths and roses filled my nostrils with comfort;[2] whereupon I, drawing near my friends, beheld upon a throne of myrtles the great Bembo.[3]

[1]His secretary: see the story of the *Puttana errante, Introduction.*
[2]Aretino like Baudelaire, appears to have been particularly sensitive to odors
[3]The pedant: see *Introduction.*

His face shown with a light not seen any more.[1] Seated on high, with a diadem of glory on his head, he had about him a coronal of sacred spirits. There was Iovio, Trifon, Gabriello, Molza, Nicolò Tiepolo, Girolamo Querino, Alemanno, Tasso, Sperone, Fortunio, Guidiccione, Varchi, Vittor Fausto, Contarin Pier Francesco, Trissino, Capello, Molino, Fracastoro, Bevazzano, Navaier Bernardo, Dolce, Fausto da Longiano and Maffio. And I saw there, also, Your Lordship, with every other person of name, without giving heed to the manner in which I seat my guests, as I mention them in this case. I might tell you that this chorus of excelling genius stood attentive to the *Istoria Veneziana*, the words of which fell from the tongue of the man above with the same gravity with which a cloud climbs the sky. But since one had here to hold even his breathing in leash, and since I was not used to remaining quiet for so long, giving one glance at the resplendent clouds, which distilled a sugared blush on the open mouths of the listeners, wondering at the atten-tion which birds, winds, air and foliage gave, none of them moving a bit, while even the odor of the violets was a respectful one and the flowers neglected to rain down for fear of breaking the spell of ears—with all this, I said to myself, very softly: "*Valete et plaudite.*"

But then I came to a kitchen, and near it I beheld I cannot tell you what skeleton throng, with the faces one sees in visions; and as I looked upon them, I perceived that their prosopopoeia lay in the fact that I was still very much in the flesh. Being more interested in looking upon the victuals than in contemplating these, I, with a fraternal presumption, saluted the cook, who was on the verge of despair because I had interrupted a *capitolo* of Sbernia or of Sire Mauro, whichever it was, which he was singing to the tune of a turning skillet. The fellow was roasting a phoenix over a fire of incense and aloes. You may be assured, I did not invite myself to a mouthful. As I stood there considering with my

[1] *luce non piu veduta*: cf. the "light that never was."

palate's best judgment the sweetness, sustenance and savour of it, I was like my knave drinking a julep, standing there with arms extended and spread out like a priest whose privates itch. At this, I perceived Apollo, who said to me: "Eat, so that those carrion there, who have consumed all my cabbages, herbs and salads, may know a greater hunger." I, who was not able to say him nay, thanks to a beaker of the wine of God which I had just swilled down, thanked him with a nod. But as I changed place, I found myself in a prison paced by a folk clad in worse harness than the he-courtezans[1] of today; and hearing that they had stolen, upon every occasion, pearls, gold, rubies, purple cloth, sapphires, amber and coral, I remarked: "These are poorly clothed, indeed, seeing they have committed such great thefts." I saw also certain others who, upon making restitution to one another, were going out with slates as white[2] as if they had just come from the Maker.

The conclusion of the dream was, I found myself in a market-place, as it seemed to me, where starlings, magpies, crows and parrots were imitating the geese on the eve of All Saints. With these birds, which I am telling you of, were certain togaed, wise-bearded and hopeless pedagogues, whose only occupation was to teach them to chatter by the points of the moon. Oh, what sport you would have had with one jackdaw, who was specifying "*unquanco*," "*uopo*," "*scaltro*," "*snello*," "*sovente*," "*quinci e quindi*" and "*restio*."[3] You would have burst your jaws at seeing Apollo, flaming with anger, make a blockhead leap who could not succeed in making a nightingale say "*gnaffe!*"[4] whereupon, he broke the bottom of his cithara over the fellow's hole, while Fame broke the handles of her trumpet. I know you will understand the reason for their penitence. It is the truth I am telling you, that it ended with my being given a basket

[1] Or courtiers: *cortegiani*.
[2] *carete bianche*: cf. *carte blanche*.
[3] Aretino's pet aversions in diction, which he lists over and over again.
[4] In truth, by my troth.

of laurel with which to wreathe myself. Whereupon, I said to them: "If I had the head of an elephant, I should not have the heart to wear it." "Why not?" said my friend. "This bit of rue is given you for your acute and whorish dialogues, this nettle for your pungent priestly sonnets, this bouquet of a thousand devices for your pleasing comedies; this one of thorns for your Christian books, this cypress for the immortality that is your's from your laudatory works,[1] this olive for the peace you have made with princes, this laurel for your military and amorous stanzas, and this oak for the bestiality of your mind, which has vanquished avarice." And I to him: "Look you, I take them and give them back to you; for if tomorrow I were to be seen with such fripperies in my cap, I should be canonized as a madman. The laurels of poets and the spurs of cavalrymen have played the devil with Reputation's purse. And so, I beg you, rather, to give me a *privilegio*, by means of which I shall be able to sell or pawn those virtues which the heavens have given me in passing; for thereby I not only shall have quite a few *denarii* without labor, but I shall not have to listen to my name being taken in vain in all the libraries, by the pedants with their fine points. Reserve for me, therefore, enough genius to excuse you for being a stable boy to these dames—" At least, I was about to say this. But the noise which was made, thanks to Monna Thalia, when, she, in a manner to make you split, had so tangled up the wings of Fate that the latter looked like a thrush in the birdlime—the uproar woke me up.

From Venice, the 6th of December, 1537.

To MADONNA MADDALENA BARTOLINA   CX
  Olives.

If the olives which you sent me had not been good, you would not have had two vases from me to fill with more. I

_____
[1] Which Aretino himself would seem to have fancied above all.

swear to you, I never have tasted better or finer. Even Tuscany, mistress of the gentle art, has to bow to the manner in which yours are dressed. Those of Spain are haughty and large; those of Bologna, like those of Spain, not being split, retain something of the bitter flavor they get from the tree; those of Apulia might be called "spit-breads," from being so dwarfed. Hence, the balance of praise must remain on your side. And so, I am going to ask you if we may have a few more, since the two baskets we had barely touched the palates of my friends.

Messer Polo, your son and mine, is playing the gentleman and only lives when he is with Madonna Pierina,[1] his wife and your daughter-in-law. Nor would you recognize the latter, so greatly has she grown in beauty and manners, which makes her much esteemed. You should be glad that, thanks to God, she is a vessel of gold, holding all the virtues which are to be desired in a young girl. If you could see the timorous prudence she exhibits in her relations to her husband, you would love her. And what touches my heart is the mother, who is beside herself with contentment. I, as you have asked me, have not consented that she should quarrel with her son-in-law; instead, the good lad has shared his own with her; and when her days are ended, all shall be theirs. Finally, greet in my name my daughter's kinswomen, and tell them I shall soon see to it that their brother comes to visit them. Remember me to Messer Vincenzio.

From Venice, the 10th of December, 1537.

To Don Ambrogio, Monk   CXI
   In Which He Praises the Benedictines.

If the valiant man, father, to whom you consigned the letter which was brought to me had not delivered it through another, I should have been able to offer him my assistance whenever it was needed. But since I did not see him, I will

[1]Pierina Riccia: see *Introduction* and preceding letters.

tell you that any labor will be sport to me, if I can only give pleasure to you and to your friends. To those persons who love me I am bound, and these may dispose of me as they will, as may always Your Reverence, whose kind breast was opened to me the first day you saw me; and the reason of this was, there reigned in your mind no trace of the friar, so well did you have it under control. For in the religion which you follow and observe, there is no niggardliness; Saint Benedict was a personage different from all the others in the calendar; and as he foresaw the scandal which would arise in the thoughts of others who were consumed by want, he threw open the door of commerce to his sons, in order that they might, with nothing to hinder, turn back to their offices and their orisons. I know with what a brave fantasy I set myself to write when the manna of liberality is raining down upon me! I know also in what a devil of a whirl my brain is when I lack *omnia bona*. At this point, I want to tell you of a wooden-shoe father, who was standing on the bank of a deep river that would have come above his cincture, waiting for some one, for the love of God, to take him across. And he would have stood there the rest of his days, had he not fallen in with a pair of religious of your order, whose rumps were most mundanely fortified with a brace of stallions. No sooner did the poor wretch catch sight of them than he began twisting his neck in a gesture of hypocrisy and begged from them, in the name of charity, the crupper of one of those bays. Leaping into the torrent and tucking up the ends of his monk's cloak, he held on to the saddle for dear life; but he was scarcely across before the demon tempted him. He thought of his wooden shoes, and then the devil put the fancy into his head, and he thought how fine it would be to be carried always; he had a vision of himself never getting off, and when they said to him, "Come down now" and urged him with words and elbow-digs to do so, he replied: "This beast is as much mine as any body's else, for I have decided to become a member of your order."

Nor were they able to make him dismount. And when they came to the monastery, he put on a black habit, saying: "Take your gray, St. Francis, for those, too, who are rich, and who do not bore holes through their hands, go to heaven." It is foolish to believe that nature does not resent the injuries which she receives from heat and cold. It is suicidal not to take water for one's thirst and bread for one's hunger; shivering or perspiring limbs must be refreshed with fire and wind; otherwise, one falls and is no longer able to keep his heart fixed on God. Any one who would bear so unbearable a thing is nothing more than an "*anima mea Dominum.*" But after all this gossip, when you write to the learned, best and most reverend Don Onorato Fassitello, that *luminare maius*, do not forget to commend me to his most egregious person.

From Venice, the 11th of December, 1537.

To Sister Girolama Tiepola   CXII
   In Which He Praises the Life of the Cloister.

It was sweet and dear, reverend mother, to hear from Madonna Francesca Serlia, my godmother and sister, of the desire you, in your goodness, have to hear my words, since it is not permitted you to see me. A thing which at once pleases and displeases me. It pleases me, because imagination cannot take away what absence deprives me of; and I am displeased because I am not permitted a sight of that venerable lady who has learned how to despise the world and to overcome fortune. The loss of husband, son and title have been recompensed to you, thanks to the manner in which you bear so great a loss—a recompense which no emperor would be able to give you; for that circle with which you enclose your sacred person is more spacious than the fields of the moon. If it appears little at times, it is still the model of that paradise which you have learned to achieve, the walls of which are not to be assaulted by peoples or by arms.

In it, there is nothing that has to do with poison or with treason; in it, tyranny gives no commands, for the reason that old age and death do not discommode or grieve you, nor deprive you of your strength; here, indeed, time and death mean nothing. Happy you, who have learned at once to procure quiet of body, and well-being of soul! With us rule those who have learned how to bear suspicions, cares, wars and cruelty; but the one who would rejoice in security, liberty, peace and piety takes himself from us. The drawingroom of the wordly is an image of the abyss, and while you feel not the least pain, we never know an hour's repose. Far removed from your cell are all deceits, envy does not lacerate you, sins do not tempt you, desires do not inflame you and avarice does not torment you. The hours which you steal from sleep, the food which you deny your hunger and the pleasures of which you deprive your will, being of your own choice, adorn, feed and comfort you. Nature is satisfied with very little; herbs and water are enough to sustain it. She is not to blame for the desires of the throat; pheasants and peacocks are the pomps of the palate. He is better off who is content with homely foods than the one who fills himself with varied viands, for sumptu-ous lunches and magnificent dinners are the parents of dis-ease. And so, do you remain in your nun's robes, and a single habit shall cover you, who once went clad in purple and fine gold. The brides of Christ have no need of pearls or rings. They find with their eternal Lover neither sighs nor jealousy nor infamy. The songs of the offices are their only delight, and the sound of the psalm-raising organ. To your ears comes no report of the doings of others nor the cries which they send up in their ruin. You see nothing of blood, fire, rape and adultery; and so, do you pray God that he may not correct us with his wrath nor chastise us in his fury. Woe to us, if your tears and your prayers did not possess that efficacy conferred upon them by Jesus! Look you, infidel flights and Christian concords come,

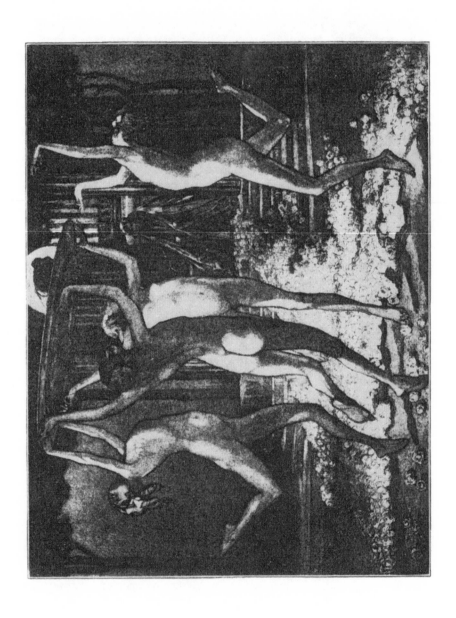

alike, from the merits of your sincere mind; and heaven shall deny you none of those graces which your heart knows so well how to say. I never enter the churches conducted through the diligence of the godmothers of the Virgin Mary that I am not aware of the sweetness and fragrance which breathes from their chaste sanctity. Regard yourself, then, as in the number of the blessed, since, satiated with the miseries which, in the guise of rank and honor, are presented to us, you have elected a secure mansion and a laudable life. And so, by that faith and hope which I have in the fervor of your vows and the merit of those works with which you please and serve God, I beseech you to obtain for holiness and length of days for that life which Jesus has given me.

From Venice, the 13th of December, 1537.

To THE SIGNORA ANGELA ZAFFETTA   CXIII
   In Which He Lauds His Courtezan.

Since Fame, putting on her armor, has gone trumpeting throughout Italy the report that Love, in the person of you, has done me wrong, I may say, I have always regarded it as a great favor that your manners were so far removed from any kind of fraud. Indeed, I give you the palm, among all those that ever were, for knowing how to put upon the face of lasciviousness the mask of decency; and hence it is, by your wisdom and discretion, you have procured money and praise. You do not exercise the quality of astuteness, which is the very soul of a courtezan, in order to work treason, but rather with such a dexterity that he who spends with you swears he is the gainer. The manner in which you establish new friendships is indescribable, as is the manner in which you draw into the house those who are doubtful, hesitating between a yes and a no. It is difficult to imagine the care you employ in retaining those who have become yours. You dispense so well your kisses, hand-squeezes, smiles and bed-

fellowships that a quarrel or brawl or any complaint whatsoever was never heard of. Your outbursts of anger are
suited to the occasion nor are you anxious to be called "the
mistress of all praise," having a contempt for those who
study the artifices of Nanna and of Pippa.[1] You are not suspicious where there is no cause for it, converting every
thought into a jealous one. You do not draw from your bag
woes and consolations, nor, feigning love, do you die and
come to life again when it pleases you. You do not hold to
the flanks of the credulous the spurs of a servant-maid,
swearing to them that you do not drink, eat or sleep on
account of them, affirming that you came near hanging yourself because your lover had visited another. You are not of
those who always keep their tears on tap and, while they
weep, mingle with their tears certain sighs and a few sobs,
a little too nimbly drawn from their hearts, furtively scratch-
ing their heads and biting their fingers with an "*Ei si sia,*"
in a hoarse and mincing voice; nor are you industrious about
retaining the one who would leave, forcing him to go who
wants to stay. There are, in your mind, no such deceits.
Your womanly intuition[2] clings to reality, nor are feminine
gossipings to your taste, nor do you collect about you a
throng of vain wenches and idle boasters. Your decent habits
rejoice in a genteel beauty, which makes you shine most
rarely; firm are the hopes of that way of life in which you
triumph over the things you must do. Lying, envy and
slander, the fifth part of a courtezan, do not keep your mind
and tongue in constant motion. You caress virtue and honor
the virtuous; and in this, you are far from the nature and
custom of those you are pleasing. And while I am, of a truth,
devoted to Your Ladyship, it seems to me Your Ladyship
is worthy of such devotion.

From Venice, the 15th of December, 1537.

[1]Of the *Ragionamenti.*
[2]*saper donnesco.*

Against the Doctors.

Give yourself no worry, most excellent genius, over the persecutions of the doctors, who would have you walk in line with their canonical procedure; for the benefit of him who would know what you are, let it be said that you employ syrups in place of medicines (may God forgive the man who invented the latter). I would compare medicines to the fury of a violent river, which takes with it in its course fields, stones and trunks of trees. I will tell you, their ribald mixtures take whole months and years from our viscera, leaving us a dried-up life. If it were not for the respect I have for Their Excellencies, I should baptize the doctors as the "alchemists of the human body," since the presumption with which they are drunken brings an ounce of health for every two lives they take; and the laws support them in it, and they are not punished but paid for their homicides. In great travail, the valiant fellows enter and question the patient as to whether he is doing well. "Yes, sir." For the whole art of Galeno lies in an injection of mallows. What a pity it is to see a poor wretch stretched out there and emaciated from the diet which they have given him, understanding, as they do, neither the nature of the malady nor the strength of the patient's constitution; for which reason, the big blockheads go on prescribing distillations, sedatives, the candle and the grave. How cruel are the colleges, disputing at the expense of the one who puts faith in them! Wise peasants who, without resorting to such treacherous measures, treat one another in an honest fashion! How many, while they are dying, are reassured with a *coram vobis;* and how many, given up for dead, leap out of bed the very next evening! And all this comes from the doctors' having no judgment whatever as to inequalities of condition among the infirm. Do they not, in their avarice, prolong a little fever for a whole month? They probably would have gone more than once to take the pulse of St. Francis, if the latter, who never had a *denarius*, had paid them. All this is said, saving the peace of the truly expert, learned and good Iacopo Buonacosa of Ferrara, a splendid physicist, and others like him. And now, turning to you, I exhort Your Lordship to persevere in those incorruptible distillations with which Your Lordship's great father resuscitated the peoples, to the highest glory of the city of Castello.

From Venice, the 15th of December, 1537.

To MESSER GIANFRANCESCO POCOPANNO   CXV

   Verses and Pears.

The fruits of your genius and of your garden have been such sweet food to my intellect and to my palate that I never have experienced the like before. Surely, the sonnet is sweet, but the pears (saving the grace of the bergamots) excell all others in sweetness and juice. It has been some days since I received a gift so gracious or one that gave me more delight; and so, in memory of the tree that grew them and of you who sent them to me, I will say that if the rich Brescia had nothing else that was fine or gentle, these would still give it a famous name.

From Venice, the 15th of December, 1537.

To FAUSTO LONGIANO   CXVI

   Against Pedantry.

I have learned, my brother, from the letter which you sent me, what criticism is and what I have been able to accomplish in the works I have produced. How is it possible your intellect, inspecting so minutely the labors of others, knows and sees so much? Any ancient or modern author that I know would go to heaven from pride or to the abyss from shame at hearing himself praised or blamed by your insight, which is so much sharper than that of science. Nothing, it appears to me, is of greater value in a man than the power of judgment; and the man who has it may be compared to a chest filled with books, for he is the son of nature and the father of art. Not by any fault of it, but by the presumption of others are they led astray who trust in it, for we are often vituperated by the opinion which stubornness passes on our work. Happy is he who considers the merits of a writer with the wisdom of a friend! But I laugh at those pedants who believe that learning consists of Greek and Latin, affirming that he who does not understand these languages has no business to open his mouth, making all reputation rest upon the "in *bus*" and "in *bas*" of the grammar. It is judgment I am speaking of; for other things are good for seeing the genius of others, by which your own may be awakened and corrected. Take the case of one who knows as much as it is desirable to know in sculpture and in painting; nevertheless, the marble Nostra Donna de la Febbre is sufficiently younger than her son, and the figures in their flight do not give the impression of flying. We must take into consideration what the *maestro* who made the *Laocoon*[1] did, if we wish to know what judgment is. Behold those two serpents which, in assailing three persons, have in their likeness all there is of fear, grief and death. The young lad, girdled round his bust and extremities, is filled with terror; the old man, bitten by their teeth, wails; and the infant, poisoned by their fangs, dies. The artist deserves more praise for having been able to express the effects of such passions as these, making fear the first motive, suffering the second and death the third, than those who would have occupied themselves with the style in which they would have depicted the bodily members. How many volumes do we see without any organization and without any decorative effect,[2] and yet, their authors are supposed to be learned men? The short of it is, he who does not possess judgment, has none too much authority with Fame, but he whose capacity renders him

[1]The Laocoon appears to tempt the critic: e. g., Lessing.
[2]*senza disposizione e senza decoro*: sounds like the terms of modern painting criticism.

worthy shares all her honors. This is seen in the case of the great Duke d'Urbino, who by administering with discretion and counsel all the circumstances of his own life, has been made administration-secretary of the army; and for this reason is conceded to him, not otherwise than to you, all due respect for whatever he may think or write, and his poems are acknowledged to be neither greater nor less than those which are the product of your care and labor. For which reason I, when I hear him exalting my own works, congratulate myself in the manner of a man who, beholding the riches of his inheritance, finds them so much more than he had thought. It is not out of ignorance that I have declined to follow in the footsteps of Petrarch and Boccaccio, for I know what they are, but I have not wished to lose time, patience and good name in the effort to transform myself into them, since this is not possible. Better is bread eaten in one's own house than that accompanied by fine viands at the table of another. I walk with tranquil step the garden of the muses, nor does there ever fall from me any word that I have learned from any stinkpot of old. I wear the face of genius unveiled, and, not knowing an h, I still can give lessons to those who know their l's and m's; and so, they ought now to keep still who do not believe there is a better school under heaven than the *Dottrinale novellis*. Imitate here, imitate there; all is trifling, it might be said, including the compositions of the majority of writers; and hence it is, readers have become like the enemies of abstinence who tack on a *vigilia* to the skirts of Venus and the Sabath.—"Bring us something besides salad," cry those who have achieved fame. What do you think of those who believe they can come down *per omnia saecula* with their *capitoli* of the *Cardi*, the *Orinali* and the *Primiere*, not perceiving the fact that such babblings as these give birth to a name that dies the day it is born? In another fashion, after the *Lodi de la mosca*, did Luciano compose. Georgio of Vicenza, who reduced the clock to the size of the great Turk's ring, need not sweat so industriously over the ship which sails above the table or the figure which dances through the room, for these are good only to move the laughter of foolish young women. The thing to do is, as I have done, to reduce to half a folio the extent of history and the tedium of orations, the effect of which may be viewed in my letters, and I shall keep on doing this in all the things that come from my pen. I hope also to be able to let you see comedies relieved of the expense of scene and the tedium of interlocutors; as it is, one needs only to divide the five acts in the manner of a sermon. In conclusion, I, who know so little, offer myself to you, who know everything.

From Venice, the 17th of December, 1537.

To THE MAGNIFICENT MESSER PIETRO TRIVISANO DAI CROCICCHIERI   CXVII

The Pessimist.

As soon as I saw you at the bedside of the Signor Don Lope Soria, whence her Excellency, the Duchess d'Urbino, had just departed, having paid a visit to the sick man, I felt overcome by the remembrance of Messer Ferrier Beltrami, and it seemed to me that, without his presence, the day was without sunlight. How many times, seeing you together in church, at confession, on the river and at home, I have said to myself: "Behold the witness of perfect friendship and the example of honest pleasures!" But since God, who gave him to you, has taken him away, I counsel you, you seek to console yourself. Moreover, we ought not to be sad, if others precede us in the path which all must tread. The world is a room, rented to us at the good pleasure of Christ and nature; and he who stays the shorter time here lives the longer there; for death is but life, issuing with a freed spirit from that prison in which all the pains that could be imagined have kept it locked. Look at the scene: In the city, envy, injustice and ambition traffic; in the country, civil customs are transformed into those of wild beasts; sons give us the care of enriching and the fear of losing them; seeing our-selves without them, we long to have them; peace gives birth to lust, and wars sow blood; the ruler is the prey to suspicions, and the servant is the subject of despair; poverty is fled, and riches are stolen by every one; youth is given to impetuosity and to fury and old age to ills and procrastina-tions. And so the best thing for a man to do is to be born and, being born, to die at once.

From Venice, the 18th of December, 1537.

THE SONNETS

THE SPORTIVE
SONNETS

⟦*I Sonnetti Lussuriosi*⟧

"*I must teach her the whole book of verse; line by
line, the . . . . sonnets of Pietro Aretino.*"

from

The Very Pleasant Memoirs
of the
Marquis de Bradomin

To Ben Hecht, Rabelais and Others

To render Aretino's Sonetti lussuriosi into English (or, for that matter, into almost any other language) with anything approaching literalness would be to achieve a work of unredeemed pornography; and while pornography undoubtedly has its value in this republic, it is not the end sought here, which is to give as accurate as possible an idea of Aretino's work. Such a procedure on the part of the translator would, accordingly, be an unfaithfulness to his author; it would be, as translators too often do, to betray the latter by a false faithfulness. For the Italian, in portraying the nuances and delicate shadings of debauchery, possesses certain advantages which are not to be found outside the Latin dialects. Take the Seven Freudian Sins and set them to music, and the effect is rather different from that attained by our harsh nordic gutturals. Even the Germans, whom we may sometimes take to have been the inventors of sensual expression in paint and words, have found this to be true. Upon reading over my own version, I am convinced it is nearer the spirit of the original than any of the alleged literal renderings I have seen. In view of the invincible pruderies ("reticences" is the college professor's word) of our English speech, it is as faithful as it feasibly could be. Incidentally, it is better poetry.

S. P.

Prefatory Garland

Reader, I bring you here a perfumed song,
  And yet, you'll find, no sentimental ditties;
  The songs I sing are of the little pretties,
And not for saints—if you think that, you're wrong!
Sunrises are all right—where they belong!
  I sing the ones that rise in hardened cities,
  Of facades front and rear and—a thousand pities!
If we mix metaphors where truth's too strong.

Our city, you'll perceive, is all aflame;
  But, strange to say, the elevations stand:
  What's architecture in a case like this?
And, street or alley, what is in a name?
  Look at this pillar rising with a grand
  And overawing gesture: let us kiss!

Of Sylvan Tourneys

At sylvan tourneys let us joust, dear one,
   As Adam did, and Eve, in Eden's shade;
   And if I break a lance, don't be afraid:
That is the sequel to our rustic fun.
Speaking of Adam, it is sad that he has run
   His last brave course and no more bends a blade;
   Sad, too, that in that dull and heavenly glade
One cannot do as one on earth has done!

I know, they blame the apple: that's not true;
   Look at the birds and beasts, and you will see
   That we on earth do merely what we must.
But this is not a time for jest; do you
   Not feel the wave that's swelling up in me?
   Then, come! Take arms! against a sea of—Lust!

Of Fireside Sports

And now, of feasts and fireside sports we'll sing,
  And I will teach you a new game to play;
  But you must come around the other way,
Though not too fast!—tap gently: that's the thing.
Oh, it's a very merry prank to bring
  A guest 'round by the rear! Then, let him stay—
  From deepest midnight till the dawn's first ray—
Let's hurl a spear and stop this chattering!

And now, we enter a moist woodland dell,
  Whose scenery would leave me breathless quite,
  If I had any breath from that last kiss!
Is this not better than the tales they tell
  Around the fire upon a winter night?
  My tale, too, has a point you cannot miss.

He Struts the Field

A knight, it seems to me, may be right proud
   That kings and emperors do not possess
   A pike or shaft of greater comeliness,
Or one with greater deadliness endowed.
I know that, till they wrap me in my shroud,
   I'll tourney with my lady and her dress;
   I cast no puny dart, as you may guess,
For darts like those are by decorum cowed.

And you, my lady, like them quite as little —
   Indeed, I know the counter-move you'd make,
   If I were such a craven cannoneer.
But the arms I wield are neither small nor brittle;
   And so, they may assail the front, or take
   —Let's say, their choice, though that's too mild, I fear.

IV

Light Arms Practice

Then, light arms practice, dear! Yet not so light!
   You must learn to hold a broadsword in your hand—
   I need not tell you more; you'll understand:
We'll leave the rest to instinct and the night.
But there's one lesson which you must not slight,
   To be a member of our valiant band:
   A lesson that is known throughout the land,
And one that even horses can recite.

I'll help you learn it, though I know it's hard,
   And, dear, you must not let it slip away,
   For you're a backward pupil if you do!
To lances, then! For I would not retard
   Your progress or the pleasure of the fray:
   The Queen of France tonight might envy you!

Military Excavations

And next come breast-works; I must teach you how
   To dig a trench—I'll dig one for you, see?
   Now, don't you think that's very kind of me?
That rampart, look! A beauty, you'll allow.
But there are other tactics wait you now:
   Tactics, dear one, you might learn from the bee;
   The queen of the hive might teach you a strategy
That you will master very soon, I vow!

Oh, why does Nature love variety?
   Why am I not all this, and you all that?
   Then, this and that—well, that would be good sense.
But, viewing Nature's contrariety,
   We must make the very best of it—have at!
   And this must be a swordsman's recompense.

Ground Arms!

The weary warrior now grounds his arms,
   And if his method is not orthodox,
   Call him a lunatic or cunning fox:
My helmet's found where there are most alarms.
In this bombardment, you will encounter charms
   Which will remind you of the barnyard cocks
   And other beasts; and if you find it shocks
Your modesty, learn rapture from the farms!

Do you not feel my gentle gunnery,
   Which peppers from the rear with such fine aim
   A duchess might be proud to be the mark?
Then, come my dear; this is no nunnery.
   Let's play our pleasant little soldier's game:
   With weapons such as these, war's but a lark.

Stragglers

My fingers are but stragglers at the rear,
  Who go a-foraging for what they find;
  And they are not ashamed to lag behind,
Since there's no foe in front they need to fear.
They've wandered through a tufted valley near,
  And you yourself have said they were most kind,
  And so, I know, my lady will not mind
If they seek other booty, nor think it queer.

And yet, it may be, you prefer the Lance;
  Then, let *your* stragglers reconnoiter, sweet,
  And guide him like a blind man to safe cover.
He is no coward, since he takes a chance,
  Though he, my dear, has neither eyes nor feet;
  For a soldier always makes a perfect lover!

VIII

The Poacher

The subject is a full one I would broach,
   And very delicate, as you will see;
   For I must reprimand your cruelty
In holding that there is but one approach.
Why do you never let me, then, encroach
   Upon those fair preserves, that greenery
   Which lies behind the hill; this scenery
Grows too well known: then, dearest, let me poach!

The poacher, after all, 's a pleasant fellow,
   And when you've seen him draw his bow and quiver,
   You'll know that he 's right clever with the dart.
His manners, it is true, are old and mellow,
   But still, they needn't make our morals shiver,
   Since archery's a very ancient art.

Fortune of War

Quarter, my dear! You have me on my back,
   And if there must be slaughter, let me slay;
   You'll like it just as well, I think, that way.
You are a prisoner, but you shall not lack
The amenities of war, though I hew and thwack
   Right valiantly. Some men there are who may
   Prefer to feast and drink, but I must say
That I prefer the battle and the snack.

To the field, then! I'm neighing for the fray,
   My monstrous dart, my polished lance in place,
   With my two henchmen bringing up the rear.
Then, do your duty on this glorious day,
   And win your spurs, for you shall have to face
   Quite soon again this doughty cavalier.

X

The Secret Sin

There is, they say, a certain occult sin
   That dwells in monasteries, where one brother
   Doth sometimes turn for comfort to another:
 Tis a peccadillo that they revel in.
Then, pardon me, if my excuse is thin.
   My lance is not—indeed, there is no other
   Can cut so wide a swath and so can smother
An enemy in carnage. If you would win

The day with me—but I must not forget,
   You are the victor, and the spoils are yours:
   Do with me as you will, and with my sword,
That gallant shaft which even now I whet—
   But what is this? You've stolen all my stores!
   What matter? Drop compunction by the board.

Narcissus

Narcissus was a very silly boy:
   He looked into a pool and fell in love
   With his own image; I am not above
Narcissus' folly, as my glances toy
With what my lips would like well to enjoy:
   Before the lancers come, with thrust and shove
   Of amorous war, I, like a billing dove,
Survey the scene of bellicose employ.

For this is what I live for, if you'd know—
   Dearest, the mystery is solved at last;
   I'll whisper it, before I turn to dust.
Lie still and listen till your blood runs slow,
   Till flowers are withered, ecstasy is past;
   And then, too late! you'll know the answer: Lust.

The Last Feast

They tell a sorry tale of old man Mars—
　　You know the chap, the blusterer of battle—
　　And lady Venus, comeliest of cattle,
And a certain night they spent beneath the stars.
But there are gods, it seems, have better spars,
　　Like Hercules, of whom the poets prattle:
　　Hand me my club, and stop this tittle-tattle;
Leave goddesses to those old Grecians jars!

Though you're a goddess in my sight, dear one;
　　A marble goddess, too, in certain parts.
　　Bring music, then! We will be gay tonight.
God give me this one feast; when it is done,
　　Death, I am yours! Meanwhile, young Cupid's darts
　　Flash home in an unmythologic light.

Stage Directions

Must I, then, be specific? Dear, I blush!
    This is a theatre where every cue
    Must be observed. I'll teach them all to you.
Now, when you see me enter thus—but hush!
My role's a rigid one; you see me flush—
    And must I tell you what you are to do?
    How you should turn your back when I pursue?
The part I play, you'll see, is very lush,

While you may play the Queen, but play it well:
    A queen, you know, has certain royal duties,
    And must be generous when closely pressed.
When you, my Queen, feel insurrections swell,
    Marshal to meet them all your regal beauties,
    And clutch at anything till you're redressed!

To Beatrice From Hell

'Tis an old torture that you put me to
   Tonight, beloved, though, I know, they say
   That in the fashions of an elder day
Lies, sometimes, novelty—or seeming-new.
I'm sure, my dear, I don't know what to do.
   The fires of an inferno lap and play
   About me; I cannot forget, this way,
A sweeter torture I have taught to you!

Thus, Beatrice, I can but kneel and pray
   That you'll forgive me for my lack of ease;
   My eyes and thoughts are on forbidden fruit.
But, in my punishment, I *will* be gay
   And, even in hell's fires, seek to please,
   While dreaming of another, fairer loot!

Plain Song

I am a glutton for the thing called love,
   A bigger glutton than the ones who sit
   All day at table, as the full hours flit,
And hold they're happier than the gods above.
They swill down wine, while I, my turtle-dove,
   Choose milk and find I am content with it—
   Turn on the spigot! let us draw a bit:
Yes, I'm a very glutton, dear, for love.

And what, in truth, is more divine than—Lust?
   To Lust and Love we'll raise a litany
   And do a little genuflection, too;
Since when all's said, we do but what we must,
   Like any abbess in her priory,
   For an abbess, dear, is just like me and you.

SERIOUS SONNETS

In Questa Chiara Sacrosanta Notte

On that clear, calm and more than holy night,
  Followed by Friday, Venus' own day,
  On which all faithful, pious creatures pray,
With broken tears, Nature, for boon or blight,
Brought spirit and my members to the light,
  From the dark maternal grotto where they lay;
  And the fates that watched were good to me, I'll say,
Since I've willed to endure them, bad or bright.

As Jesus suffered for the good of men,
  So I, on coming from my mother's womb,
Being liberated from my prison pen,
  Came forth into the world, wailing His doom.
Christ died for me upon the cross again,
  And I was born in Christ as from a tomb.

Mentre Voi Titian, Voi Sansovino

While you, my Titian, Sansovino, you
   On canvas and in marble immortalize
   An art resplendent as the splendid skies,
The goal of pilgrim spirits, I, with true
And heart-felt zeal, reverently pursue
   The task of one who upon paper tries
   To paint and carve Lucretia's grace and size,
The native and divine gifts are her due.

And yet, I know my style's not able quite
   To capture form and color that lie within,
As yours gives color, form to the things of sight;
   But if, from my own ink, I could but win
Your mind and valor, then, indeed, I might
   Erect a shrine for the world to worship in.

Togli il Lauro Per Te Cesare e Omero

Caesar and Homer, I have stolen your bays!
   Though not a poet or an emperor;
   My style has been my star, in a manner, for
I speak the truth, don't deal in lying praise.
I am Aretino, censor of the ways
   Of the lofty world, prophet-ambassador
   Of truth and smiling virtue—if you'd hear more,
Here's Titian's masterpiece; you've but to gaze.

And if you find the face he's made strikes fear,
   Then close your eyes, and they'll not be offended;
For though I'm but in paint, I see and hear.
   My worship, Lord Gonzaga, is extended
To Signor Giovanni, whom I hold dear,
   The three of us being by our merits blended.

L'Eterno Sonno in un Bel Marmo Puro

Sleep, Ariosto! in a fine marble pure
    The eternal sleep, and may your great name wake
    At burst of day in that fair clime and take
Its ease there as you watch, glad and secure.
But for the gifts of the sky, he would assure
    Us, he does not care; he stands with wonder-ache
    Beneath the stars, when a sad and solemn quake
Of sound assails him with its tender lure,

As Phoebus' sisters, in their sorrow, add
    Words to their tears: "O blessed spirit bright,
With a brightness sun at midday never had,
    We bring you our widowed wonder; you see us clad
In robes of grief, while flowers shed their light
    Above your tomb, and song is bowed and sad."

Sett' Anni Traditori Ho Via Gettati

Seven traitor years I now have thrown away,
   With Leo four, and three more with my sire,
   Pope Clement; I have won the people's ire,
More through their sins than through my own; my pay
Has not been two whole ducats; one might say,
   Gian Manente's the better; if you but fire
   Your mind with filthy things, look in the mire,
Then you have every hope of the papal bay.

And if there were no other wounds to feel,
   Warding the honor of some patron friend,
Five or six times a day I'd take the steel;
   For benefits, offices and pensions tend
But to make the holy fathers a pleasant meal
   Of bastard scoundrels—two mouthfuls—that's their end,
     While the good, faithful servitors who bend
     Their energies to serve are left to die
     Of hunger, for their sin against the Most High.

APPENDIX

APPENDIX I

CRITICAL AND BIOGRAPHICAL NOTES

Eugenio Camerini, mid-nineteenth century Italian critic, published in 1869, in the *Rivista critica*, of which he was then editor at Milan, an article on "The Correspondents of Aretino" (*I corrispondenti dell' Aretino*). Part of this material is reproduced in the *Prefazione* to his edition of the *Commedie* (*Casa Editrice Sonzogno, Milan*). His preface to the comedies begins with a section on the "Life and Customs" (*Vita e Costumi*) of Aretino:

> Pietro Aretino, the bastard son of one Luigi Bacci of Arezzo and one Tita, was, as it were, consecrated to impure loves from his mother's womb, and to this consecration he was faithful all his life. Born in 1492, he died at about the age of sixty-five, in 1557.
>
> Margutte died from laughter at seeing a female monkey trying the tricks which Morgante had endeavored to conceal from her. Of Aretino, it is said that he died in a fit of laughter at hearing his sisters tell of the experiments in lust which they had made in a bordello of Arezzo, experiments of which Giulio Romano had not dreamed in those designs which Aretino illustrated with his pen and Marco Aurelio Raimondi with his burin.
>
> I do not know, I am sure, how Catholic writers feel when they recall Aretino's words after he had received extreme unction:
>
> *Be sure the rats don't get me, now that I'm all greased up.*
>
> I am not certain about this. What I am certain of is that his procuress, Monna Alvigia, represented well enough his double character, when she inserted into the versicles of the *pater noster* lustful references. It was common in the *Risorgimento*, this mingling of devotion and carnality, of scepticism and superstition, but in none other was it carried to such a degree as in Aretino; and in his letters, if we turn the pages, we find the solution of a number of theological doubts . . .
>
> Diogenes told Alexander to get out of his light; Aretino abandoned a position at the right hand of Charles V. because he did not want to go to Germany. Venice was his rock, and from there he spread his nets for the great ones of the earth.

He visited the poor and the studios of great artists; through his generosity, he had his roots in the hovel, as he likewise sunk them, through his importunacies, deep into courts.

Berni compared him to dogs,—

Which, if you beat them, as you may know,
Jump better than ever where their masters go.

He was as rich in blows and dagger thrusts as he was in gifts. His body, said Boccalini, looked like a ship's chart . . . and I once knew the editor of a theatrical journal who would show the marks of blows he had received from his beloved choristers with the same pride with which a Roman legionary would have displayed his wounds.

On all sides . . . he felt the gnawings of appetite; he rejoiced in it, with his friends and mistresses; he praised gifts and givers, but if the present was not to his taste, he would speed back a letter of reproof.

With one hand he took, and with the other he gave; he was a born philanthropist. But he was a man, not a chest of gold; and so, he sometimes found himself in straits. When he wished to make a dot for his loved Adria, he had to appeal to the princes and their secretaries to make up the sum needed. We have a number of letters of his in which he replies sharply to those who counsel him to be a better manager. He was the vase of the Danaids.

He knew that he was ignorant and willingly admitted it, but he was unable to stand by when others called him an idiot, maintaining that the fruits of his genius, which had the savor of certain wild plants, were worth more than all those which others had transplanted, with great sweat, from the Greek and Latin gardens.

Hyperbole, a simple rhetorical figure, made his fortune. But just as, even in the most hyperbolical praise, there is always some substance, so in the one who employs such praise there is always a rock-bottom of truth. And so he, with the strangest metaphors in the world, goes on exaggerating his ideas and the merits of others, and with the newness of his verbal coin, he makes an effect which a soft and simple speaker never could hope to obtain.

It is notable that the influence of Aretino carried over into the sixteenth century. When the other great writers of the *cinquecento* were being forgotten, his works were being travestied, disguised and read, *sotto mano*, on account of the attraction exercised by their obscenity, as well as because of their vivacious and original force.

Here, we find again the persistence of the Aretino legend, traced by the pseudo-Berni. Pietro is the bastard of Luigi

Bacci and Tita. The latter, it is true, is not here referred to as a prostitute, but it is the same Tita. The "consigned from his mother's womb to impure loves" is like the "because he was vile and a poltroon" of De Sanctis; it is another mark of that moralistic claw of which Aretino, for four centuries, has been the victim. The story, in the second paragraph, of Aretino's death is to be noted. That, of course, and the son-of-a-prostitute angle constitute the punch of the tale. Nor is the "mixture of devotion and carnality," one fancies, limited to the "*Risorgimento*;" the Messers. Krafft-Ebing, Havelock Ellis and others have observed it since. Berni crops out in the bit of doggerel about the dogs. As to the "gnawings of appetite," that, as De Sanctis saw, admits of a slightly larger interpretation: "What they (Machiavelli and Guicciardini) thought, Pietro was." There is something spiritual in Aretino's disdain of money; as Hutton and others have pointed out, he preyed on the powerful. "Ignorance," in Aretino's mouth, is merely a word used to confuse the pedants; it is a boast.

As to "Hyperbole," Hutton (*op. cit.*, pp. 265ff.) lifts a number of allusions from Gabriel Harvey's *Marginalia* (Edited by G. C. Moore Smith, Shakespeare Head Press, Stratford-upon-Avon, 1913). Harvey refers to the Italian as "Unico Aretino:"

> Unico Aretino in Italian, singular for rare and hyperbolical amplifications. He is a simple Orator, that cannot mount as high as the quality or quantity of his matter requireth. Vaine and phantasticale Amplifications argue an idle or mad-conceited brain: but when the very Majesty or dignity of the matter itself will indeed bare out a stately and haughty style; there is no such trial of a gallant Discourse and no right Orator.

Notating "I would . . . find some supernatural cause whereby my pen might walk in the superlative degree," Harvey writes:

> In hoc gener Lucianus excellebat: et post eum plerique Itali: maxime Poetae Aretinus voluit albis equis praecurrere et esse Unicus in suo quodam hyperbolico genere . . .

Unicus Aretinus erat scriptoris hyperbole, et actoris paradoxum. Illius affectatissima foelicitas fuit, omnia scriptitare hyperbolice, singula actitare ex inopinato. Qui velit Unicum vincere, eum oportet esse miraculum eloquentiae, oraculum prudentiae, Solem Industriae.

Yet, Harvey admits that "Aretino's glory" was "to be himself."

Camerini then goes on to present extracts from the Aretine correspondence. These extracts are particularly valuable for the light they throw on the relations between Aretino and Giovanni delle bande nere. They may be taken as refuting De Sanctis' implication, which I have previously annotated: "What grieved him (Giovanni) was the sight of a poltroon."

"The affection," writes Camerini, "which Aretino bore toward the great Giovanni de' Medici, the creator, under the name of the Bande Nere, of the only effective military force at the time of our national shame, is well known. Giovanni de' Medici, on the other hand, loved him well enough."

A letter of Giovanni's is then quoted, in which the great captain says: "I will give you this praise, that while all others may bore me at times, you never have done so as yet." In another letter, written from Pavia, Giovanni says, there is "no living without Aretino."

A letter of the widow, Maria de' Medici, is given, in which she writes to Aretino with the warmest and most intimate affection of her late husband and their young son. Cosimo de' Medici, the son, when he becomes Duke of Florence, also writes to Pietro concerning the friendship between Aretino and Giovanni.

"I could never bear," he says, "that you should live in misery."

There is also a correspondence between Cosimo and Aretino over the dowry to be paid to Adria, the latter's daughter, or rather, to her husband. The Duke is frank but friendly:

> "It is not because we doubted your daughter was to be married that we deferred the payment of what we had promised for her dot; but in order that the money may reach its proper destination, we would suggest that you send her consort with the license to get it. It will be paid at once, and you will be better off; since it is better for him to use it to pay his debts than for it to fall into your hands, which through their natural liberality, which is not a vice, might convert it to some other use."

Camerini himself, speaking of the relations between the writer and the captain, remarks that "It is impossible not to sense here the accents of a true affection." All this, it seems to me, should tend to dispose rather effectually of at least one of the numerous back-thrusts which Pietro has received at the hands of the moralists.

Aretino's boast (See De Sanctis' essay) about the ponies, the vases, the women and the street named after him is borne out, in almost the identical words that Pietro employs, by Doni in one of the latter's letters to the "Scourge."

> I am at Mantua, and here I have seen a kind of pony out of your very fine nag, and upon asking what it was, I was told it was the Aretine. I go to Murano, and there they show me some very fine crystal vases, a new sort of glass work, and they are called Aretini. The street where you have lived for twenty-two years has acquired you for patron, to such an extent that one says to those who live there—Where do you live? In Aretino's house, in Aretino's lane, on Aretino's bank .... Many beautiful women, who inspire much jealousy, bear your mark: this one is your procuress, this one something else, and many of them are known simply as Aretino's sweeties. And then, there's a third class, your housekeepers, and I am now the master. By my faith, if one night I didn't come on one of them who, when I asked her what her name was, replied, "I have no other name than 'the Aretina.'" I laughed then, and I'm laughing yet. I told her, "Since you're an Aretina and I'm an Aretino, we must be one and the same thing . . ."
> I must also give you a list, which I have compiled (as a remembrance), of the different manners in which I have seen you portrayed: in marble, in natural bas-relief; in cameo; in miniature;

and in medallions of gold, silver, copper, brass, lead and wax. As well as a picture from the hand of the admirable Titian, one by Fra Bastiano dal Piombo, and portraits by other valiant painters in more than thirty different places. Finally, I have seen you stamped on combs, in brass . . .

If Aretino exercised a considerable influence over the French literature that was to come after him—Rabelais, Moliere and others—it is not surprising; for he was known all over the world of his day, which was the world of the Emperor Charles V. From Giuseppe Horologgi, writing from Rouen, we learn that Aretino was a household author in France:

> I swear to your lordship that I do not go into a place where I do not find some of your works on the table, and I do not speak with a man who knows that I am an Italian without his asking after the divine Aretino; and if your lordship does not believe me, I can show you the life of the Virgin Mary, that of Saint Catherine, the Humanity of Christ and the Psalms and Genesis translated into this language, and they are read with more satisfaction than I could tell you.

The Prior of Montrottier also writes to him, flatteringly, from Lyons.

As for his influence in Germany, we may hear Johannes Herold, writing from Basle, September 1, 1548:

> A short time ago, I read your letters, printed by Marcolino in the year XXXVIII., and in swallowing the Genesis of Messer Pietro Aretino, I became a beggar, thanks to the altitude of your genius, which fitted my wings to fly upward, and the weight of my own ignorance, which held me down . . . You are, then, an imitator of Circe in that, while rendering me a man with your presents, you make me a monster through the beverage of your sweet writings. Following out the comparison, I shall make of my German country-men, through the subtlety of your works, semi-Italians out of bar-barians, even as Pietro Aretino, with his immortal glory, has made a semi-barbarian of me, speaking the vision of Noah in the German language.

Aretino's boast about being known in Persia and the Indies (see the letter quoted in De Sanctis' study) also was true. One of his secretaries, whom he had discharged for theft and unfaithfulness, Ambrogio degli Eusebii, had carried his master's name to the Rio de la Plata. And the celebrated *casa Aretina* on the Grand Canal, as De Sanctis remarks, was thronged with artists, beautiful women and others. Alessandro Andrea of Naples tell us this, in a letter which he wrote seeking audience with Aretino:

> From you come continually, in addition to our own Italians, Turks, Jews, Indians, French, Germans and Spaniards; nor are you ever to be seen an instant without a throng of soldiers, scholars, priests and friars, who recount to you the wrong done by this prince and that prelate; so that you really ought to be addressed by the title of secretary to the world.

"Secretary to the world." It was far from being a bad title for Aretino!

De Sanctis refers in passing to the friendship between Aretino and the corsair, Barbarossa. This is a highly picturesque sidelight on the man. Barbarossa's letter is worth quoting:

> To the first of Christian writers, Pietro Aretino . . . Ariadin Bassa Barbarossa, general on the seas and of the armies of their Imperial Lordships, the Sultan Salim and the King of England, salutes you, Aretino Pietro, the Magnificent and circumspect. I would tell you that I have received your head in silver, along with the letter which you wrote me. Surely, you have the head of a captain, rather than of a writer. I have heard the fame of your name throughout the world and have asked after you a number of times of some of my Genoan and Roman slaves, who know you by sight; and I have been pleased with the report of your virtue, to which I feel indebted for the praise you have given me, as well as for the faith you have put in my valor, which makes me dear to the Turks as to the French. I should like to see one of those images which are in the likeness of my face, and which are common throughout Italy. I have instructed Bailo of Venice to tell you that you should excuse me if I have not yet rewarded you, for the great Signore commands me to be about his business in distant parts, but when I come back, I shall not be found lacking in courtesy, I promise you. Written at Constantinople in the middle of the month of Ramesan in the year 949 of our great prophet Maumeth. (Translated from the Turkish into the Italian language.)

Aretino, evidently, was animated by the desire of getting something out of Barbarossa, but the latter was quite as wily as he. It took, though, some little courage to praise a man like Barbarossa, publicly. The latter's remark about the character of Pietro's head is to be noted. It is a point, possibly, which has not been sufficiently stressed in Aretino's case: he was really a pirate of the high seas of literature, and there was no little of the soldier in his makeup; it may be this, as has been remarked elsewhere, that accounts for his friendship with the leader of the *Bande nere*: he may have been vile, upon more than one occasion, but he was not a poltroon.

Speaking of this aspect of Aretino, Camerini says:

> From the life of the camp, then, Aretino drew in part that verbal license which he displayed in the matter of religion and the religious, and also with regard to men of state, a license which was as great in those days as civil oppression was intense; and this attitude of the cut-throat, if it failed to inspire fear, resolved itself into fear.

Personally, however, I should be inclined to doubt if Aretino ever really knew fear; it would not appear to have been a part of his nature.

If Aretino has been the object of almost universal detraction on the part of posterity, he was, only too frequently, overpraised by contemporaries, who feared him, sought his favor or who, in some cases, did, quite sincerely, overestimate him. His religious writings, in particular, drew a saccharine praise, which is the only kind of praise most religious writings deserve. Coriolano, bearing the formidable titles of cavalier di San Pietro and Hierosolomitano di Roma, on January 6, 1551, gives Aretino the title of "light of the most holy and omnipotent scriptures" and adds that "You have always been known to be as a trumpet of faith against the heretics." But probably, Bartolamio Egnatio da Fossambrone gets the medal for adulation: "I should call you the little son of God . . . since God is the highest truth in heaven, and you are truth on earth."

It was, always, Pietro's highest boast that "I speak the truth." He endeavored to speak the truth in art, as he did in life, and on this side of his character, the side that has to do with his artistic importance, his contemporaries, some of them, really began to lay hold of the man. Pietro Spino da Bergamo called him "the little son of truth and the disciple of nature," and Antonio Cerruti of Milan, writing on the seventh of June, 1550, addresses him as "Your Lordship, in whom intellect is married to nature."

Nowhere does this tendency to a modern realism come out more clearly, perhaps, than in the *Ragionamenti*, but it also shows in the letters.

The truth is, there was in Aretino, as a writer, what Camerini calls "a double aspect." Perhaps, we had better say, there were two men, two writers: one, the "literary mendicant;" the other, "the independent writer," who anticipated modern frankness, "a frankness that was slow in coming, even in a free country like England." And so, Aretino, for the most part, was content to go on with his game of literary brigand. His success here is indicated by Ariosto's tribute, for Ariosto was the big man of his day. This is borne out by Battista Tornielli, who writes to Aretino:

> Your pen may truly say that it has triumphed over practically all the princes of the world, since practically all of them are your tributaries and, as it were, your feudal subjects. You ought . . . to take to yourself all those titles which the ancient Roman emperors were in the habit of assuming according to the geographic situation of their subjects.

Gianiacopo, the ambassador of Urbino, remarked that "Aretino is more necessary to human life than all the preachings;" and Jacopo Gaddi, commentating Pietro's title of "*il divino*," wrote:

Cum vero sibi arrogaverit aliorum consensu divinitatem, nescio, si forte Dei munus exercuisse dicendus sit, cum summa capita velut celsissimos montes fulminaverit, lingua corrigens et mulctans quae ab aliis castigari nequeunt.

Aretino himself was conscious of all this. He writes to Ersilia del Monte, parent of Pope Julius III.:

All this is shown by the fact that I am known to the Persians, to the Indians and to the world . . . what more? The princes of the tributary peoples, constantly and everywhere, look upon me as their slave and their scourge.

All this hardly could fail to attract Charles V., the tactical superman of the age. It was not merely Charles' munificence; Aretino really was, personally, more drawn to Charles than to Francis I., who was not only stingy, but appears to have been lacking in imagination. On this point, Camerini says:

By his very prophetic quality, he was bound to please Charles V., the renovator of Europe, as much by his resistances as by his concessions in the matter of religion, as well as by his revolutionary spirit in the matter of ancient adjustments and political equilibrium. And Aretino felt himself attracted to Charles, rather than to Francis, not so much because the former was potent and great (and it does Aretino no little honor to have perceived . . . the capacity of Charles), as because in the one he saw movement, in the other historic reminiscence. Charles V. was also pleased to perceive in the letters of Aretino something of the color of Titian, and the effulgence of the former's phrases did not appear morbid to a Spanish flamingo.

We have seen that Aretino was almost a library-table author in the France of his day, and well known also in Germany. Montaigne, however, and, later, Bayle found fault with his style. The former referred to it as "*Une façon de parler bouffie et bouillonnée de poinctes ingenieuses à la verité, mais recherchées de loing et fantastiques.*" He conceded Aretino, nevertheless, a certain eloquence. Bayle had this to say:

Ce poète si satirique prodiguait les louanges avec les derniers excès. Nous trouvons les hyperboles les plus pompeuses et les flatteries les plus rampantes dans les lettres qu'il écrivait aux rois et aux princes, aux généraux d'armée, aux cardinaux, et aux autres grands du monde. Tant s'en faut que l'on voie là les airs d'un auteur qui se fait craindre ou qui exige des rançons, que l'on y voit toute la bassesse d'un auteur qui demande très-humblement un morceau de pain. Il se sert d'expressions touchantes pour représenter sa pauvreté; il recourt même au langage de Canaan, je veux dire aux phrases dévotes, qui peuvent le mieux exciter la compassion, et animer à la charité les personnes qui attendent de Dieu la récompense de leur bonnes oeuvres.

In any event, Camerini finds, Aretino was "the precursor of the sixteenth century" and had "a just conception of art" (De Sanctis, Hutton and others agree on this). "In a century of imitation," writes Camerini, "he aspired to be original." Surely, that is something! Sometimes, it is true, in his effort to be new, he merely fell into the bizarre:

But more than in his semi-official style, the genius of Aretino is to be recognized in those places in which passion enters the picture, as the flamingoes of his domestic life do in certain paintings; and then, we have a mixture of lasciviousness and virtue, of the insolences of lust and the niceties of good taste.

The Aretino that we have here—the Aretino who wrote that marvelously sensuous and marvelously plastic letter to Titian—together with the Aretino who wrote his Nanna into the dialect of his people and his age, and whose desire it was, always, to be true to nature—this is the Aretino who is to be rescued from the obloquy and oblivion of a moralistic world and given the place that is his due, as the first great realist of the Renaissance and the first modern critic of art.

APPENDIX II

An Anonymous Estimate of Aretino

In the Giulio Bertoni edition of the *Ragionamenti* (Parma, 1923, *"Classici dell' Amore"*), there is an anonymous *Introduzione* that impresses me as worth reproducing. I give it below:

Of Pietro Aretino, it has been said that he was the representative of the most visible side of Italian life in the *cinquecento*. In truth, he was the most significant type, and one endowed with a degree of genius, of the moral baseness of that age. The son of a cobbler of Arezzo, he succeeded, with his native impudence, in rising, if not to the pedestal of glory, at least to that of fame. Scholastically, Aretino is to be classified among those versatile writers who are occupied with diverse literary forms, from letter writing to comedy, and so are called polygraphists. A personality purely artistic these writers never possess.

They treat of everything, but, principally, of what has reference to private life, mediocre and little things, in opposition to which the Aristotelians rear the classic concept. The fame of Aretino comes, indubitably, not so much from the spirit of the time as from the fact that he had forged from his pen a tremendous weapon of derision and satire and so struck all with admiration. Especially against the powerful and the high prelates did Aretino direct his injurious, and often merited, darts. But it is not for this reason to be believed that his cutting vivacity as a flaying polemic had any noble end, animated, as it was, by an expressive exuberance that frequently became vulgarity. Aretino was bent upon lucre, which he—euphemistically—called "the moving power of my ink." He adulated the powerful, making them pay profusely, and at times he would not keep still about their faults, even when he had received the highest sums. An inspired letter writer has said that Aretino had for successors in the art of blackmail "certain journalists." And indeed, the system by which Aretino organized those speculations which procured him the money to live surrounded by a court of vicious men and women does anticipate that of certain libellists of our time. Typical and to the point were the *Giudizii*, which were no more than an almanac, in which, with the contempt of the most immaculate moral paladin, Aretino denudates the vices and the obscenities of the patrician world. And then, there were gifts, sums and favors which were made to the impudent writer because his "company" had ceased. Aretino knew profoundly the vices of the society of his time and the cowardice of others, and so, he drew down a profit for his own audacity.

The phenomenon of the predominance of this uncultivated man over his powerful contemporaries is not otherwise to be explained. The fluent ability of his pen—Aretino had a style puffed, awkward but sufficiently expressive—and the audacity of the man in his character of filibuster permitted him to live as a prince on the tribute which his vassals paid him as his right. The power of Aretino was so great, so great the terror which was felt of him, that he could even dream of obtaining a cardinal's hat, and, to the end, he wrote religious works. Changeful by temperament, Aretino was, some would tell us, always sincere, as much so in his invectives as in his eulogies, in his hates as in his amends. This hypothesis, which sees men as the offspring of their age and of the society in which they live, from which they have inherited in the most visible manner their vices and their virtues, strikes us as being excessively benevolent. Otherwise, those biographers of Aretino are rare who do not constantly speak of their subject in the language of reprobation.

Among the typical works of Aretino are the Pasquinades on the occasion of the election to the papacy of Adrian VI., the pontiff who reacted against the licentious and worldly life of the court of Leo X. Through some of his attacks, Pietro Aretino ran more than one risk, and one time he even received a dagger thrust. At Venice, whither he had repaired, he lived surrounded with the halo of "scourge of princes."

We have already said that, in literature, he belongs to the rebels against the Aristotelian rules. Aretino had, in fact, much genius and little culture. But of these qualities he was fully conscious, to such a degree that he defended rigorously the law of pure genius and set up against classicism the imitation of nature.

And yet, his writings, in a style that is often awkward, give the effect of great haste, and it cannot be denied that there is lacking in them the free and true effect of life. From his pen are known his letters, which are superabundant, his comedies and also a tragedy, the *Orazia*, which draws its motive from the episode, known in Roman history, of the Orazi and the Curiazi. His best things, those which truly attain a perfected artistic form, are represented by the *Ragionamenti* and by those celebrated *Sonnetti lussuriosi*, commentating certain precious designs by Romano.

APPENDIX III

Aretino and Michelangelo

In his book on Michelangelo, quoted in the *Introduction* to this edition, Merejkowski has the following account of the relations between Buonarrotti and Aretino:

At this epoch, there lived in Venice Pietro Aretino, the celebrated writer. He was the son of a prostitute of Arezzo, whom he had quitted in his childhood after having robbed her. Monk, vagabond, and valet by turn, he had known misery, cold, and the blows of innumerable misfortunes, but, thanks to his pen and, according to his own expression, "the sweat of his ink," he had acquired fame and riches.

By means of calumnies and flatteries, by the threat of Pasquinades and the promise of panegyrics, he obtained from the powerful money and honors. Many Italian princes and even the Emperor himself paid Aretino an annual tribute. The Most Christian King of France had sent him a golden chain with an exergue in the form of serpents' tongues, emblem of his satiric and venomous traits. In his honor, a medal had been struck, bearing on the obverse side the effigy of the poet crowned with laurel, with this inscription: Divus petrus aretinus, flagellum principum. *("The divine Pietro Aretino, the scourge of princes.") And on the opposite side, one read:* Veritas odium parit. *("The truth engenders hatred.")*

His libels, the most perfidious and the most insolent, directed against those monarchs who were slow in sending him gifts, were signed: "Divina gratia homo liber." ("By the grace of God a free man.")

He composed, readily and promptly, whatever was com-
manded of him on whatever subject. He had been charged by
Vittoria Colonna to write pious meditations and a Life of the
Saints; on the order of Marcantonio, the pupil of Raphael, he
wrote sonnets for the engravers' designs which were so licen-
tious that the Pope, despite the intervention of numerous
cardinals, had the painter thrown into prison. In his superb
palace on the Grand Canal—the celebrated Casa Bolani—
Aretino lived in a royal fastness, surrounded by objects of art
and by a harem of pretty women which was constantly renewed.

Titian flattered him, painted his portrait, and presented him
with his works. From all corners of Italy, pictures, designs,
bas-reliefs, medallions, bronzes, antique marbles, majolica
plates, cameos and precious vases flowed to him in a constant
stream. When his palace became crowded to the point where
there was no room for more, he would share his artistic loot
with the lords and princes who had merited his good graces.
As he himself said, "The poet distributed to kings the crumbs
of his table."

From vanity as much as from love of the beautiful, Aretino
for some time had deplored the fact that he had in his museum
not a single work of Michelangelo. Employing as intermediaries
his friends, Benvenuto Cellini and Biogo Vasari, he, on a
number of occasions, had given Michelangelo to understand
that his turn had come, but the latter did not deign to respond.
Then the writer resolved to hurl the gauntlet himself. In 1537,
he addressed to Buonarrotti one of his celebrated letters, thou-
sands of copies of which were spread over Italy.

He began by praising the great artist; then he explained to
him what were the qualities in his talent which he, Aretino,
prized the most. The essential passage of the letter commenced
with this apostrophe:

"And so I, whose praise or criticism is so powerful that the
glory or dishonor of men depends on me alone, but who am,
nevertheless, of little worth and in myself nothing, I salute

Your Grace, a thing which I should not have dared to do if my name had not acquired some renown, due to the respect which it inspires in the greatest princes of our century. But in the presence of Michelangelo, there is nothing to do but to admire. There are in the world many kings; there is but a single Michelangelo; and he by his glory has eclipsed Phidias, Appele, and Vitruvius."

The letter continued in this tone until it came to the question of the Last Judgment. Here Aretino gave advice to the artist and attempted to teach him how he ought to paint. He concluded by making renewed offers of service, proposing to glorify Michelangelo's name.

Buonarrotti replied to him with a word that was polished and laconic, in which irony could be perceived, hidden under excessive compliments.

Aretino preferred not to remark the irony, and, in a new letter, solicited a souvenir, even if it was but a little drawing, one of those which the artist was in the habit of tossing into the fire.

Michelangelo did not reply, and for five years Aretino left him in peace.

In 1544, Aretino let Buonarrotti know that the Emperor Charles V had just accorded him—an unheard of honor—permission to ride on horseback by his side. Cellini had written him that Michelangelo felt kindly towards him, which was, above all things, precious to the poet. He loved and admired Michelangelo. He had wept from emotion at contemplating a copy of the Last Judgment. His friend, Titian, also admired Buonarrotti, and praised him with enthusiasm.

Michelangelo persisted in his silence. Two months later the poet, through friends at Rome, reminded him that he was still waiting for a design. No response. He waited another year and then addressed a new reminder. Finally he received from Rome, in the guise of drawings, a few miserable scraps of paper in which was to be seen a mockery rather than a picture.

He wrote to Michelangelo that he was not satisfied and that he was waiting for something better. Again the silence endured for a number of months.

By this time, the patience of Aretino was at an end. He sent to Cellini a threatening letter. Had Buonarrotti no shame? He must declare openly u nether or not he had any intention of keeping his promise. Aretino demanded explanations, without which his love was to be transformed into hate.

Menace had as little effect as flattery. At this moment, Titian, who happened to be in Rome, profited by the circumstance to slander Michelangelo to Aretino, Titian's protector, and this resulted in a definite break.

In November, 1545, Buonarrotti received from Venice the following letter: "Messer, now that I have seen copies of the Last Judgment, I recognize in the conception and execution the celebrated charm of Raphael. But, inasmuch as I am a Christian who has received holy baptism, I am ashamed of the unbridled liberty which you have taken with what ought to be the supreme end of virtue and the Christian faith. This Michelangelo, so great in his glory, this Michelangelo who astonishes all the world, has shown to men that he is as far removed from piety as he is near to perfection in his art. How can it be that an artist, who considers himself as a god and who, for that reason, has broken almost all bonds between himself and common mortals, should have profaned by such a work the temple of the All-Powerful God, the first altar of the world, the first chapel of the universe, where the greatest cardinals and the Vicar of Christ himself communicate in the divine and terrible mysteries of the Body and Blood of Our Lord?

"If it were not that it seems almost criminal to compare such things, I should permit myself to remind you that, in my frivolous dialogues on the life of courtezans, I have endeavored to veil with delicate and noble words the indecency of the subject. You, on the contrary, treating of things so high, deprive the angels of their celestial glory and the saints of their terrestrial modesty. But pagans themselves covered Diana with veils, and when they represented *Venus* nude, they were careful that the chaste gesture of her hand should replace her vestment. And yet you, a Christian, have arrived at such a degree of impiety that you dare, in the chapel of the Pope, to offend the modesty of martyrs and of virgins. Of a truth, it would have been better for you to deny Christ altogether than, believing in him, to turn into derision the faith of your brothers. Be assured that Heaven will not permit the criminal audacity of your art to remain unpunished. The more astonishing this picture is, the more surely will it be the tomb of your glory!"

Then Aretino passed to his personal griefs, reminded the artist that he had not kept his promise and that he had not sent the design:

"However, if the mountains of gold which you have received from Julius II have not been able to incite you to fulfill your duty by completing the promised mausoleum, what may a man like me hope? In putting into your own pocket the money of another and in being false to your word, you have done what you should not have done, and that is called theft!"

In conclusion, he counselled the Pope to destroy the Last Judgment, displaying the same pious fervor that Pope Gregory did when he caused the pagan statues to be destroyed no matter how beautiful they were.

"If you had followed my advice," he added, addressing Buonarrotti, "if you had listened to the directions which I gave you in that letter which today is known by all the universe, and in which I explain in detail and according to science the ordering of Heaven, earth, and hell, nature would not now have to blush at having given so much genius to a man like you. On the other hand, my letter would have been a defense of your work against all the hatreds and all the jealousies throughout eternity. Your servant, ARETINO."

This epistle was recopied by a strange hand, in order that Michelangelo might not doubt that it had been made public and scattered throughout the entire world. But at the end there were these lines from the hand of Aretino himself:

"Now that I have in part recovered from the fury I felt at the grossness of your conduct in responding to my kind advances, and now that you, I am led to hope, know well enough that, if you are divine—divino—I, on my side, am not made of water—this being so, destroy this missive, as I am ready to do myself, and realize that, in any case, my letters deserve a reply, even if you were an Emperor or a King."

APPENDIX IV

Bibliography of the Aretino Literature

The Aretino bibliography is an extensive one, particularly in Italian, and there is also a growing Aretine literature in German. Works in French and English are, it will be noted, few. The following list makes no pretence to exhaustiveness. It does not, for one thing, include the periodical literature, which is especially extensive in German. At present, it would be impossible to compile a bibliography that would be absolutely exhaustive.

Opere

Opere di Pietro Aretino; ordinate ed annotate per Massimo Fabi, precedute da un discorso intorno alla vita dell' autore ed al suo secolo. 2. ed. Milano, C. Brigola, 1881. 381 pages.

I Ragionamenti

Ragionamento della Nanna e della Antonia, fatto in Roma sotto una ficaia, composto dal divino Aretino per suo Capricio a correttione de i tre stati delle donne. Egli si e datto alle stampe di queste mese di aprile MDXXXIII nella inclyta citta di Parigi (Venezia).

Dialogo di Messer Pietro Aretino nel quale la Nanna, il primo giorno, insegna a la Pippa, sua figliola a esser puttana; nel secondo gli conta i tradimenti che fanno gli huomini a le meschine che gli credono: nel terzo la Nanna et la Pippa, sedendo nel orto, ascoltano la Comare et la Balia che ragionano de la ruffianaria. (Turin (Venezia), 1536.)

La Prima (Seconda) parte de Ragionamenti cognominato il Flagello de
Prencipi, il Veritiere e il Diuino, Divisa in tre Giornate; Doppo lequali
habbiamo aggiunte il piaceuol ragionamento del Zoppino, composto da
questo medesimo autore per suo piacere.—Commento di Ser Agresto
da Ficarvolo, sopra la prima Ficata del Padre Siceo. Con la diceria de
Nasi. Bengodi, 1584. (This was printed by John Wolfe in London.)

Ragionamento nel quale P. Aretino figura quattro suoi amici che favellano
de le corti del mondo e di quella del cielo. (Nova [Venezia], 1538).

Dialogo nel quale si parla del gioco, con moralità piacevole. (Vinegia per
Giovanni, 1534.)

Capricciosi et piacevoli ragionamenti. Nuova ed. Cosmopoli, Elzevir.,
1660. S.

...I ragionamenti...Firenze Libreria Dante, 1892-93. 2v in 1. "Edizione
di soli cento esemplari per ordine numerati. n. 93" (pt. 2. n. 30). "Per
la presente edizione seguiamo fedelmente l'edizione senza luogo, dell
anno MDLXXXIV."

I ragionamenti di M. Pietro Aretino. Roma, Frank & Cia,. 1911. (1914).

I ragionamenti di Pietro Aretino. Lanciano, Carabba (1914). 2v. (Half-
title: Scrittori italiani e stranieri novelle). "Introduzione" signed: D.
Carraroli.

Ragionamento de la corti, di Pietro Aretino. Lanciano, Carabba (1914).
138 p. (Half-title: Scrittori italiani e stranieri, Belle lettere). "Introduzione" signed: Guido Battelli.

COMMEDIE

Il Marescalco (Venice, Vitali, 1533) (F. Marcolini, 1536).

Il Filosofo (Venice Vitali, 1533).

La Cortigiana (Venice, Marcolini, 1534).

Lo Ipocrito (Venice, Bendoni, 1540) (F. Marcolini, 1542).

La Talanta (Venice, Marcolini, 1542).

Quattro Commedie (Il Marescalco, La Cortigiana, La Talanta and Lo Ipocrito: Venice, Marcolini, 1542).

L'Horatia di M. Pietro Aretino. Con Priuilegio. In Vinegia Appresso
Gabriel Giolito de Ferrarri, 1546, 1549.

Quattro commedie del divino Pietro Aretino. Cioe Il marescalco; La cortigiana; La talanta; l'hipocrito, novellamente ritornate per mezzo della stampa, a luce, a richiesta de conoscitori del lor valore. (Venezia?) 1588.

Commedie di Pietro Aretino, nuovamente riv. e cor., aggiuntavi l'Orazia, tragedia del medesimo autore. 3. ed. stereotipa. Milano, E. Gonzongno, 1888, 431 p. Contents.—Il marescalco—La cortigiana—Lo ipocrito—La Talanta—Il filosofo—La Orazia.

Teatro. Lanciano (1914) 2 v. (Scrittori italiani e stranieri) Introd. signed Nunzio Maccarrone. Contents: v.1. Il Marescalco. La cortigiana. Lo ipocrito. v.2. La Talanta. Il filosofo. La Orazia.

Il Marescalco. (In Fleischer, E. G., ed. Teatro classico italiano antico e moderno, no. 8, pp. 171-195.)

La Ninnetta, comedia & inuentione del Sig. Cesare Caporali. Novemente data in Ivec da Francesco Bvonafede . . . Venetia, Appresso G. B. Collosini, 1604.

LETTERE

Del primo (-sesto) libro de le lettere. Parigi, appresso Matteo il Maestro, 1609, 1608-09. 6 vol. Vigns.

L'Aretino; ovvero, Dialogo della pittura di Lodovico Dolce con l'aggiunta delle lettere del Tiziano a vari e dell' Arentino a lui. Milano, G. Daelli e comp., 1863. 117 p.

Il primo libro delle lettere di Pietro Aretino, Milano, G. Daelli e c., 1864. 430 p. (Biblioteca rara, pub. da G. Daelli, vol LI.)

Lettere scelte di Pietro Aretino, a cura di Guido Battelli. Lanciano, R. Carabba, 1913. 136 p. Scrittori nostri (36).

Il primo libro delle lettere, a cura di Fausto Nicolini, G. Laterza e figli, Bari, 1913.

Il secondo libro delle lettere, a cura di Fausto Nicolini, Bari, 1916. (This "splendid new edition," as Hutton calls it, is as yet incomplete.)

PROSE SACRE

Gli Sette Salmi di penitentia (Venice, 1534) (Marcolini, 1536).

Il Genesi (Marcolini, 1538).

La Vita di Maria Vergine (Venice, 1539) (ristampata, 1545) (Aldus 1552).

La Vita di Catherina Vergine (Venice, 1539) (Marcolini, 1540).

La Vita di San Tomaso Signor d'Aquino (Gio. de Furri, 1543).

Prose sacre. Lanciano (1914) 175 pp. (Scrittori italiani e stranieri). Introd. di E. Allodoli. Contents: Da il Genesi. Da L'umanita del Figliuol di Dio. Dalla Vita di Maria Vergine. Dalla Vita di santa Caterina. Dalla Vita di s. Tomaso d'Aquino. Dai sette Salmi.

Miscellaneous

Rimi diversi di molti Eccellentiss. Autori (Venice, 1545, et seq.).

Opusculi, Florence, 1642.

Le Carte parlanti, Venice, 1650.

Opere burlesche, Florence, 1723.

L'Orlandino; canti due. (Edited by Gaetano Romagnoli. Bologna, 1868. pp. 31. (Scelta di curiosita letterarie, 95.)

Novella di M. Pietro Aretino. (In Papanti, Giovanni. G. B. Passano e i suoi novellieri italiani. Livorno, 1878.)

Un pronostico satirico (MDXXXIII); edito ed illustrado da Alessandro Luzio. Bergamo, 1900. xli, 163 p. (Biblioteca storica delle letteratura italiana; ed. by Francesco Novati. v. 6).

Le carte parlanti di Pietro Aretino. Lanciano, Carabba (1914). 208 p. (Added t.'p.: Scrittori italiani e stranieri. Belle lettere). Preface signed: F. Campi, Introduction by E. A Allodoli.

V. Rossi: Pasquinate di P. A. ed anonime (Palermo, Turin, 1891).

Works on Aretino

Mazzuchelli: Vita di Pietro Aretino (Padua), 1741; second edition, Brescia, 1763.

Vita di Pietro Aretino, formerly attributed to Berni, Ed. Milano, Daelli, in Bib. Rara (1864) (the "pseudo-Berni").

A. Luzio: Pietro Aretino nei primi suoi anni a Venezia, Torino, 1888.

Rime di Nicolo Franco contro Pietro Aretino, Lanciano, Carabba (1916).

Diodoro Grasso: L'Aretino e le sue commedie. Una pagina della vita morale del cinquecento. (Palmero, A. Reber, 1900).

Schultheiss, A. Pietro Aretino als stammvater des modernne litteratenthums. Eine charakterstudie aus der italienischen renaissance. 1890. (Sammlung gemeinverständlicher wissenschaftlicher vorträge, neue folge. 5te. serie. hft. 114.)

Gerber, Adolf

Pietro Aretino faksimiles, von Adolf Gerber seinem früheren kollegen Hans Schmidt-Wartenberg ... gewidmet. (Gotha, Druck von F. A. Perthes) 1915. front., plates, ports. facsim.

Chasles, Philaréte i. e. Victor Euphémion Philaréte, 1798-1873.

Etudes sur W. Shakspeare, Marie Stuart et l'Aretin; le drame, les moeurs et la religion au XVIc siecle ... Paris, Amyot (1852). 523 p.

Gauthiez: L'Aretin, Paris, 1895.

Kinck, Hans Ernst, 1865:

... En penneknegt. Kristiania, H. Aschehoug & Co. (W. Nygaard) 1911. 94 p.

Pietro Aretino, the Scourge of Princes, by Edward Hutton, with a portrait after Titian, Constable and Company, London, 1922 (American edition by Houghton Mifflin and Company, 1923).

WORKS CONTAINING EXTENDED REFERENCES TO ARETINO

Girolamo Muzio: Lettere Catholice, Venice, 1571.

G. Rossi: Vita di Giovanni de' Medici, Milan, 1833.

A. Luzio: Pietro Aretino e Pasquino, in Nuova Antologia, Ser. III., Vol. XXVII., 1890.

Vasari: Vite, ed. Milanesi, Florence, 1906.

Trucchi: Poesie Italiane, Prato, 1847.

A. Luzio: La Famiglia di Pietro Aretino, in Giornale Storia della Lett. Ital., IV., 1884.

D'Ancona: La Poesia pop. it., Livorno, 1906.

F. De Sanctis: Storia della Lett. Ital., Milan, Treves.

Baschet: Doc, inediti su Pietro Aretino, in Arch. Stor. Ital., Ser. III., Vol. III., pt. 2, p. 110.

V. Rossi: Un Elefante famoso, in Intermezzo I., pp. 28-30.

A. Graf: Un processo a Pietro Aretino, in Attraverso il cinquecento, pp. 89-167.

Schultheiss, Albert:

Pietro Aretino eine literar-historiche studie pp. 660-671 of Illustrierte Deutsche Monatshefte. (The copy of this which I find in the University of Chicago library has been torn from the magazine; so I am unable to fix the date.)

Renascence portraits, by Paul Van Dyke. N. Y., C. Scribner's Sons, 1905.

Euvres choisies de P. Aretin, tr. de l'italien, pour la premiere fois, avec des notes par P. L. Jacob, bibliophile (*pseud.*) et precedees de la vie abregee de l'auteur, par Dujardin, d'apres Mazzuchelli. Paris, C. Gosselin, 1845. (Contents: Vie de Pierre Aretin. Le philosophe. La courtisane. La Talanta.)

Oeuvres choisies, Paris, 1845.

L'Oeuvre, ed. Guillaume Apollinaire, Paris, 1909-10.

(The *Ragionamenti* have been done into French under the title of *L'Academie des Dames*. There is also a French translation of the *Sonetti lussuriosi*, which I have been unable to run down.)

Coloquio de las damas; en el cual se descubren las falsedades, etc., de que usan las mujeres enamoradas para enganar a los hombres que de ellas se enamoran. Agora nuevamente traducido de la lengua toscana en castellano. por Fernan Xvarez. (Seville?) 1607. (Reprinted Madrid, 1900.) (Colleccion de libros picarescos. 2.)

La cortesana; original comedia en cinco actos. Escrita en Venecia el ano 1534, traducida por primera vez al castellano por J. M. Llanas Aguilaniedo. (Madrid, 1900) (Coleccion de libros picarescos, 2, ii.)

Italienischer Hurenspiegel (*Ragionemanti*), Verlag Die Schmiede, Berlin, 1925. (In the same volume with Ferrante Pallavicino's *Der Gepluenderte Postreuter.*)

The Ragionamenti or Dialogues of the Divine Pietro Aretino literally translated into English, 6 volumes, with Introduction and Portrait, Isodore Liseux, Paris (?), 1889.

(In addition, there is the booklegged and filthy translation of the *Sonetti lussuriosi*, referred to in my introduction.)

I am indebted, for valuable assistance in the compilation of this bibliography, to Mr. Theodore Wesley Koch, librarian of Northwestern University, to James Thayer Gerould, librarian of Princeton University, and to the University of Chicago library.

S. P.

CPSIA information can be obtained at www.ICGtesting.com
Printed in the USA
BVOW07s0204290814

364794BV00001B/22/P